I0779063

JOURNAL OF THE SUPERNOVA

Also by Robert Brace

Floreat Lux

Andromeda Graphika

Ash Wednesday

Lysander Dalton series

Black Tiger

Iron Butterfly

Speed Graphic

JOURNAL

OF THE

SUPERNOVA

Robert Brace

JOURNAL OF THE SUPERNOVA. Copyright © 2025 by Robert Brace. All rights reserved.

Front cover photograph: The Crab Nebula, the result of a supernova observed in 1054 A.D., taken from the Hubble Space Telescope
Photo Credit: NASA, ESA, J. Hester, A. Loll (ASU)
Acknowledgment: Davide De Martin (Skyfactory)
Front cover photograph: Venus Arising from the Celestial Void © Robert Brace

Cover design by the author.

First Edition: October 2025

Library of Congress Control Number: 2025904984

ISBN 978-1-968103-00-2

Privately published, October 2025, New York.

www.robertbraceauthor.com

If I held all truth in my hands, I would be careful not to open
them.

—Fontenelle

JOURNAL OF THE SUPERNOVA

I

BETELGEUSE IS ABOUT TO EXPLODE. ALL THE FUEL AT the core has been consumed in its thermonuclear furnace, we are told, and the fires are going out—the star, once tenth brightest in the night sky, has already dimmed to just a third of normal, and it no longer possesses sufficient energy to counteract its own gravity. The star will collapse and the shock wave will be on an apocalyptic scale, hurling material the size of planets through interstellar space.

This is not without consequence for us.

Betelgeuse is a red supergiant, a thousand times the size of the Sun. If placed in our puny solar system it would encompass the orbit of Jupiter—not just Jupiter itself but the entire breadth of that planet's long twelve-year circumnavigation of the Sun. When something that big blows up, it does so with a bang.

Actually, Betelgeuse blew up long ago but, since the star is 724 light-years distant from Earth, its cataclysmic demise is only now becoming visible to us.

What will happen to humanity? Speculation—even informed scientific speculation—varies wildly from nothing much to complete extinction.

For sure there will be a supernova and for several months Betelgeuse will be by far the brightest object in the night sky. But then it will again dim, and the remnants will form a black hole with a voracious appetite that will begin engorging itself like some galactic Gargantua. It will consume everything in its path: asteroids; nebulae; whole stars.

But it will be something invisible that most threatens us on Earth. The supernova will produce a burst of cosmic radiation, that is, atomic nuclei accelerated to near light speed. The atmosphere protects us from the Sun's meager output of cosmic radiation, but the energies of these particles will be orders of magnitude greater, and nothing will stop them. This barrage, being slightly slower than light speed, will arrive shortly after Betelgeuse blows up. The result, at minimum, will be spectacular light shows—auroras everywhere, not just the Arctic—but most modern semiconductor-based electronics will likely be destroyed.

Whether life, human and otherwise, can withstand this onslaught is an open question. The radiation will rip apart the ozone layer, exposing us to a shower of secondary particles that will boost rates of genetic mutation—monsters will be born. One theory has it that the resulting increase in lightning strikes will engulf the planet in a conflagration of wildfires whose smoke, shielding Earth from solar energy, will induce a new ice age. Some say that the particles themselves will simply kill anything above ground.

Complicating the issue is the question of proximity. It turns out that the 724-light-year calculation might be wrong—a joint air force/navy research satellite took a closer look at Betelgeuse back in 2020, and analysis of the resulting data has led to a reappraisal: much of the scientific community now believes that Betelgeuse is only 548 light-years away. It does nothing to inspire confidence in their other assertions that they managed to get such a basic measurement wrong by twenty-five percent. It also means that assurances based on the premise "it's too far away to affect us" are now necessarily one-quarter less convincing.

It is an irony of history that five hundred years ago, just as Europe was emerging victorious from the millennium-long struggle against barbarian invasion, and in that expansive mood Columbus was about to sail the ocean blue, Betelgeuse was blowing up. Right when Western civilization was hitting stride on the long road that was to lead through the Age of Reason, the Enlightenment, the Industrial Revolution, the rise of the great democracies, and culminating in our own triumphant and terrible Reign of Technology, in all that time the instrument of our oblivion had been relentlessly hurtling toward us at 186,000 miles per second.

Five centuries of remarkable human progress, but mankind's fate had been sealed before it even began.

Everything is changing. Canned goods are in short supply; lead shielding is unobtainable. In a reversal of the usual practice, basements now command a premium in real estate, and in New York the penthouse apartments atop tall towers, once billionaires' trophy homes, have become unmarketable—the billionaires have moved on to lavishly equipped caves or abandoned mine shafts. Electronic vacuum tubes, impervious to radiation but last manufactured in bulk in the 1960s, are suddenly worth more by weight than gold bullion. The suicide rate has doubled. Even the word *supernova*, whose role was once restricted to that of a noun, now does steady duty as a verb—*Betelgeuse is to Supernova* one tabloid headline read.

But for all that, most people, like me, have done nothing other than carry on as normal and wonder what will happen. The one change I have made is to commence this journal, something to chronicle such events as are worth recording. In the interests of preservation, I am writing it the old-fashioned way, ink on paper, composed in laborious longhand and already bearing the cross-outs and corrections of someone long-used to keyboards. The book itself is a fine Italian volume bound in soft black leather and further secured with an elasticized band to help withstand the rigors of whatever is to come.

There is a second and more personal reason that I chose to begin this missive to an uncertain future, and which is why I am starting it today: an invitation arrived in the morning mail, a strange and unanticipated one. A double invitation, to be precise, and into these pages I paste the original of the first and transcribe the text of the second.

Mr. Rothesay Ambrose Urquhart

Cordially requests the pleasure of the company of

Dr. Hugo Evans

*On a summer cruise with him & his guests
aboard the*

Motor Yacht Mulvane

*Departing from the harbour at Monaco on the
First of July
And thence exploring the Eastern & Western
basins of the Mediterranean Sea while observing
the coming Apocalypse
before terminating at the Piraeus, on or about
the Twenty-sixth of September.*

No RSVP, but its absence was explained by the second invitation, this one handwritten with nib and ink on a sheet of notepaper slipped inside the envelope with the first.

I am sure that this invitation must come as something of a bolt from the blue, but I have been asked to explain the circumstances and fill in the details, after which perhaps it will seem less peculiar. I wonder if afternoon tea at my club might be convenient? Would 4:00 P.M. suit?

O. Welles

O? Orson? It made me wonder if I had become the butt of a practical joke. Someone at the gallery, perhaps, although I knew of no one likely to be behind such a thing.

Attached to the note with a paperclip was a business card, quite striking, the front rendered in a textured gold covering as if embossed with genuine gold leaf, like a Byzantine icon. It had a large black CC in the center and four small symbols at each corner. The back was plain stock bearing the name Cato Club and below that an address on Pall Mall in St. James's.

I had never heard of the place, although it was within walking distance of where I work on Portman Square. I looked it up. There was a website but it required a login to access anything other than the landing page. The only information on that first screen was an explanation of the club's name.

Cato the Elder (234-149 B.C.)
Roman senator who rejected all novelty that debased citizenry

Absolutely no electronic devices of any kind
are permitted on the club premises

There was no telephone number or email address, either on the note or the business card, perhaps unsurprising given the warning on the website. Their presumptuous absence tempted me to walk over and leave word at the front desk that it would not be convenient for me to call this afternoon. But I was going to do no such thing, and maybe this O. Welles already knew there was nothing that would have kept me away, given the role that Rothesay Ambrose Urquhart has played in my professional life.

II

I JUST NOW REALIZE THAT I HAVE FAILED IN THE FUNDAMENTAL requirement of any first-person narrative: to explain who it is doing the narrating.

My name, as will have already been noted by the observant reader from the invitation, is Hugo Evans. Do not ask why my parents chose to burden their only child with *Hugo*—it is a mystery to me. There is a middle name too, even worse.

My parents are otherwise sensible people. Both are academics, both English, but early in his career my father was offered a position at Harvard, too prestigious to decline, so my parents moved to Cambridge, Massachusetts, and never left. I was born during a blizzard at Mass General (a favorite story of theirs: the struggle to make it to the hospital before I emerged—my father has only owned four-wheel-drives ever since). And so, with the characteristic generosity of Americans, I acquired U.S. citizenship from the geographical accident of my birth in addition to the U.K. citizenship inherited as part of my patrimony. This transatlantic dipole has been a defining framework of my life ever since.

My early education took place in the local elementary and middle schools, but when high school approached my parents, perhaps feeling that it was time I acquired a modicum of Englishness, packed me off to the U.K.

I became a boarder at Harrow.

Harrow is a "public" school, which in Britain, with the deceptive circumlocution of the English, actually means a private school. Every day as school uniform I wore a shirt and tie, navy blazer, gray trousers, polished Oxfords, and a varnished straw boater—an outfit that was unamusing to a thirteen-year-old used to jeans and sneakers.

The food was a shock to an American kid—about as gray as my pants and as flavorful, too. Worst were the sandwiches: miserable little things composed of two thin pieces of over-processed bread containing just a single slice of filling. The "ham" in a ham sandwich came from a gelatinous block extracted from a tin can. No mayo or mustard but instead butter, the only ingredient provided in abundance, and something that gave an already strange foodstuff a highly unpleasant mouthfeel. We were assured that, despite appearances, the food provided nourishment, and it is true that no student died of malnutrition during my time at the school, but there was no such thing as a fat kid.

At Harrow, I learned rugby, dead languages, how to behave like a gentleman, and to spell color with a *u*: "colour"—something that still looks strange to me on the printed page, all this time later. And so passed the next four years, digesting the indigestible by way of food, but the standard of instruction was high, and intellectually we boys feasted like princes.

It had always been assumed that I would follow my parents into university life, but then I unexpectedly found myself heading down a different path.

I cannot say what got me interested in art. Like a thousand others before me, I fell first for the Impressionists—the only worthwhile subject of art was light. Then, with the transitory passions of youth, it was on to the post-Impressionists, and nothing painted before Cézanne would do. Next came the early Florentines, above all Botticelli, plus the contemporaneous Venetians: those multiple Bellinis and the impenetrable Giorgione.

But in general I was indiscriminate, and with London so near I soon devoured the capital's art institutions. By my junior year—Harrow's "fifth form"—I was spending term breaks on the Continent combing through the great museums, although not Saint Petersburg's Hermitage: the House Master resolutely denied that request, refusing to allow one of his charges to step foot onto soil controlled by that nasty little troll in the Kremlin.

Despite this fascination with art, I never had the urge to myself be an artist. Instead, I wanted to be an art historian, to unravel that mysterious creation of meaning from a few simple brushstrokes or blows of the chisel's blade—cracking the code, so to speak. I suppose I wanted to be a detective of sorts, a skill which I was soon to use in a more practical sense.

So I immersed myself in Ruskin and Berenson and studied with envious wonder the career of Kenneth Clark. But when I graduated from Harrow with helpful references from the beaks—intended to ease my way into Oxbridge—I confounded both them and my parents: I returned to Massachusetts.

But not Boston; instead, I enrolled at Williams, a liberal arts college nestled among the distant Berkshire Mountains. Williams had two attractions: an excellent art history program and the Clark Art Institute, which is both a first-rate museum and an advanced research institute—an amazing thing to find in the remote pastoral countryside.

At Williams, I gradually acquired the fundamentals of my chosen trade, but there was to be a fateful interruption: during my junior year, traditionally spent abroad, I again crossed the Atlantic: I went to Oxford University.

This was not without reservations, especially about the food.

It was one of those decisions, seemingly unimportant at the time, which in retrospect illustrates the profound role that chance plays in life. Williams maintains an exchange program with Oxford's Exeter College, and so it was to Exeter I went, especially welcome as that institution counts among its alumni William Morris and Edward Burne-Jones, twin pillars of the first organized rebellion against the Old Masters, the Pre-

Raphaelite Brotherhood, antedating as it did the Impressionists' revolt by a generation.

At Exeter, I was to discover something that would change my life. Two things, in fact, both of them encountered on the same day and at precisely the same moment.

I remember the day exactly: it was Thanksgiving. Because of its American associations, Exeter celebrates this essentially U.S. holiday: turkey, cranberry, cornbread, the whole shebang. Before the feast the Rector invited us American students to drinks in his quarters. I should explain that to the English, I sound American; to Americans, I sound English—it is my curse to always have to account for my accent. The college's prize paintings are usually hung in the Dining Hall, but in the Rector's Lodge I found a portrait that eclipsed them all.

It hung above the fireplace in the drawing room where we were gathered, and I was standing there staring at the thing, sherry in hand, when the Rector joined me.

"I wanted to ask you about this painting," he said. "It was donated to the college by an alumnus during my predecessor's time. He had it hung here and then promptly forgot about it—the old boy was about to retire and was too distracted to have the matter seen to properly. I was going to ask a friend from the Slade to come up and take a look, but since you're here..."

It was not a large work, less than two feet a side, depicting a young woman. She was standing side-on but looking back over her left shoulder, gazing at the viewer in mild surprise. She was dressed in what might have been medieval finery, richly embroidered robes, a wreath-strewn headscarf with long tails reaching down her back and which completely concealed her hair, rendering the face in vivid relief: a girl portrayed playing dress-up, or perhaps on her way to her first costume ball.

"It's after Vermeer, I think."

"Vermeer?"

"The *Girl with a Pearl Earring*," I explained. "In the Mauritshuis."

"You mean it's a copy?"

"No, Rector, not at all. But I do think that the composition is based on that painting. A deliberate quotation: the posing of the figure; the exotic clothing; the rich coloration, particularly the Prussian blue; the expression on the girl's face."

But even as I said it, I knew that this last was not strictly accurate. In Vermeer's painting, the girl's expression radiates a fresh and unencumbered alertness, someone taking quiet pleasure in discovering life, but you knew that, for all her present charm, in twenty years she would have devolved into a sturdy Dutch matron. In the painting before me there was something different, a more formed inner life and a sense of underlying intelligence that would have shunned anything bourgeois. Whatever the girl in this painting was destined for, it would not be matronhood.

"Do you think it has any artistic merit?"

"Yes, very much so."

"Fine enough to be hung in Hall?"

"Yes, Rector," I replied. "Fine enough to be hung in Hall. Who painted it?"

Given the college's associations, I assumed that it would be a Pre-Raphaelite, particularly with the sitter's medieval dress harking back to chivalric times, a traditional trope of the Brotherhood. Not one of the big names, since I was already familiar with their works, but a painter belonging to the same period and sharing their sensibility, someone yearning to break from the patriarchy of Mannerism and revert to something more fundamental.

"Can't remember the name," the rector replied, "but I'll look it up in the alumni records."

"The artist was an alumnus?"

"Yes, it's one of the fellow's own paintings, you see, hence my predecessor ignoring it, assuming that it was a conceit on his part to have burdened us with the thing."

"You mean it's contemporary?"

"Certainly, if three years ago counts as contemporary."

I was left more-or-less speechless and gazed anew at this artifact from a previous age that had apparently time-traveled to the present. The artist was living, and I sensed without consciously thinking it that I had suddenly found the subject for a doctoral dissertation.

And the sitter: she existed, too. A girl at the time—fifteen or sixteen, say—but if the painting was three years old then currently at least eighteen, and assuming that it had not been given to the college before the artist had lived with the work a while, then in her early twenties by now.

"Are you alright, Mr. Evans?"

The Rector's wife had joined us, and I realized that apart from the porters clearing up everyone else had left, and we three were alone. The other students had already made their way to Hall, their departure unnoticed by me in the thrall of this amazing find.

"I wonder if I could take some measurements?"

I meant if I could come back at some convenient time and take measurements, but the Rector's wife immediately slipped from the room, returning a moment later with a tape measure. I took the two basic dimensions, height and width—17.5 by 15 inches—thanked my hosts, and left the Rectory.

I must have walked around the Front Quad and over to Hall that day, but I have no recollection of doing so because by then I was enraptured—doubly enraptured: by the painting, and by the girl that it depicted.

III

ON THE MORNING AFTER THANKSGIVING, I FOUND IN MY pidge a note from the Rector with the name of the alumnus who had painted the portrait: Rothesay Ambrose Urquhart. Always referred to by all three names; unlike me, he does not detest his middle name. The surname is pronounced ˈ**erk**-et; he once walked out of a television show when the host—a BBC interviewer who had not done his homework—introduced him with the second syllable dominant and voiced the silent *h*: erk-ˈ**heart**.

I immediately began doing research. This turned out to be easier than expected, as he came from a prominent family. His paternal grandfather, David Urquhart, was from the Victorian era—a Scotsman born in 1873 who early in life made his way to London and founded a newspaper, the *Daily Courier*, more restrained than the scandalous tabloids but less reserved than the stodgy broadsheets, instead exploiting an untapped middle ground, and so it prospered—David Urquhart soon became a rich and influential man.

It is the habit of the English establishment to recruit such men to their cause with honors, especially when they own newspapers that might engage in criticism of the government. In 1916, at the height of WWI, David Urquhart was made the first Viscount Rosewell. Urquhart got the message: the casualty figures, on an appalling scale even for that appalling war, were suppressed in the *Daily Courier*.

His eldest boy, Harold, was killed the following year at Ypres, and so the second son—the Evelyn Curzon Urquhart who was to become Rothesay Ambrose Urquhart's father—suddenly became heir to the title. Evelyn served as an eighteen-year-old artillery officer late in the war and, having survived, came home with a determination that from now on he would live life to the full.

He became a leading figure in the fast set of his time—literally fast: he raced Bentleys at Brooklands. He nominally worked at the newspaper under his father's tutelage, but long evenings spent carousing in Soho nightclubs typically restricted his time in the office to just a short few hours, most of them spent recovering. On weekends, he could usually be found at the country estates of his friends, often having flown there in his Gipsy Moth, which he would leave sitting out in whatever field he happened to set it down in. He moved in the circles of the Mitfords and the Astors, and counted among his friends such diverse characters as Charlie Chaplin, Lawrence of Arabia, and Oswald Mosley.

In 1933, he married Lady Eleanor Parker. The ceremony took place in Rome; Mussolini was the guest of honor. She was soon installed in the family estate on the Sussex Downs, giving birth to a brood, while Evelyn continued his carousing up in town. In '37 his father died, leaving Evelyn, now the second Viscount Rosewell, in charge of the newspaper. By this stage he was firmly in the fascist camp, opposed to war, and supportive of Hitler's claims that the shackles of Versailles should be cast aside. The *Daily Courier* began to concern the authorities.

All that changed with the invasion of Poland, and overnight the editorial slant of the newspaper became fervently patriotic.

His mercurial ways continued after the war. He toyed briefly with becoming the King of Bohemia. His mistress at the time was a Czech princess, and the *Daily Courier* became a vocal supporter of the party proposing to break up the restored Czechoslovakia. They invited him to become a reestablished Bohemia's first monarch—the communist coup of 1948 put an end to this plan. His dalliances with women and intrigue continued apace—he was a minor figure in the Profumo affair—and in

1964 he married his third and final wife, Julie Beresford, whom he had met at Cliveden, a friend of Christine Keeler and forty years his junior. The only issue of this union was a son, Rothesay Ambrose Urquhart.

After a long life of ardent dissipation, Evelyn Urquhart died at the age of one hundred and one, and Rothesay Ambrose Urquhart, the only surviving son, inherited both the viscountcy and the newspaper. He had no interest in either, renouncing the former and putting the latter under the control of a trust over whose editorial concerns he exercised no oversight.

Instead, he pursued art. After coming down from Oxford—having read Greats—Urquhart enrolled for a time at the Royal College of Arts in Kensington, but left after two years without taking a graduate degree. Like many budding artists before him, he moved to Paris, but unlike a young Picasso or Modigliani he was not constrained by poverty. His version of the artist's garret was a luxurious penthouse apartment on the fashionable rue du Faubourg Saint-Honoré whose sunny conservatory he turned into a light-filled studio.

I assumed, given the excellent rail system radiating out from Paris, that during this period he would have taken excursions to nearby cities and his acquaintance with the Vermeer which was to be the inspiration for the Exeter portrait had resulted from one such visit to the Hague.

Or, rather, half the inspiration: I discovered no clue as to who the model might have been.

Paris was a period of sampling styles and testing techniques, but it was not until he moved to New York that Urquhart found a vocabulary of his own. Suddenly, the coloration was gone, replaced by shades of gray with vague color washes. The brown sauce of the Old Masters became in Urquhart a nebulous mist, the industrial outpouring of America perhaps, or maybe just the steam that belches from the streets of Manhattan, as if a separate steampunk civilization lived underground, hidden beneath the city's surface.

Urquhart was never wholly abstract, but the imagery became fractured, shard-like glimpses of things, or many glimpses of the same thing, depicted at different angles, as if in an explosion of broken slivers of a mirror—representation by reflection only, never the thing itself.

Reviews were rare—Urquhart was slow in making a name for himself, but he was wealthy enough not to care. One article in a New York paper described his work, exhibited at the Bellingham Gallery in Chelsea, as "surrealist smoke and mirrors." It sounded clever but I thought it missed the point: smoke and mirrors suggest deception, but there was no attempt to deceive in Urquhart's work. Just the opposite, he sought to elucidate, and the function of those many steam-shrouded shards was not to conceal but concentrate focus.

Although still an undergraduate I already had a title for my projected doctoral dissertation: *Revelation in the Catoptrographic Art of Rothesay Ambrose Urquhart*, "catoptrographic" being a word I coined, derived from the Greek *katoptron*, mirror, and *graphikos*, picture—an etymology that I imagined the artist himself might appreciate, given that he had read Greats. Like Urquhart thirty years before me, I was finding my professional vocabulary. I returned to Williams for my senior year and spent the breaks in New York, where Jeremy Bellingham—only too happy to help me add academic luster and thus commercial value to his unsold Urquharts—acted as a go-between with those of his clients who had purchased the paintings, allowing me to compose if not quite a *catalogue raisonné*, then at least an adequate accounting of the paintings Urquhart had produced while living in America.

Urquhart himself had long since left New York, and the only address Bellingham had for him was that of his London dealer, Sylvester Sykes, who was to prove far less forthcoming than his American counterpart. Sykes did not respond to my letter explaining why I was asking to be put in contact with Urquhart, but soon I would be back at Oxford and in the same small country as the subject of my dissertation—when I returned to England I could track down my elusive quarry at leisure.

It was not to be. After having settled back into Exeter I went down to London and called on the Sykes Gallery. After Sylvester Sykes' epistolary snub, I fared no better in person: I never met the man and was dealt with by an assistant.

"I'm sorry that we can't help you," she told me, "but Mr. Urquhart's instructions are very clear: short of a court order or criminal inquiry, we are simply not permitted to divulge any contact information. In fact, there's an NDA."

"NDA?"

"Non-disclosure agreement—his lawyers insisted on adding it as a rider to our usual contract of representation."

"Can you give me a general location? London? Britain, even?"

"Nothing at all, I'm afraid."

I took from my pocket the envelope with which I had come prepared.

"Would you at least be willing to forward this letter? I'm sure that once he understands my interest is purely academic he would be happy to be in contact."

She looked at the envelope without taking it.

"Well, of course, we forwarded the first one that Mr. Bellingham sent, and if you received no reply..."

"Perhaps it was lost." I offered the envelope. "After all, what artist would not wish to be the subject of a doctoral dissertation?"

"Mr. Urquhart isn't like most artists. I understand that even his own newspaper is not allowed to report on his work."

"Still, one has to try." I held the envelope a little further forward.

"Very well," she said, in the hopeless tone of someone called upon to do something that cannot possibly succeed. "But please don't expect a reply." She was asking not to be pestered, and an idea suddenly occurred to me—someone else might have been pestering them on the same subject.

"I'm not the first person to have tried to get in contact with him, am I?" This flustered her even further, and I could tell that my guess was correct.

"Well, I'm really not in a position to—"

"Man or woman?"

"I cannot help you, Mr. Evans. We'll undertake to forward your letter—*again*—but beyond that we simply cannot get involved. Now, if you'll excuse me."

I left the gallery, wondering who this other person was trying to track down Rothesay Ambrose Urquhart.

IV

THERE HAD TO BE A WAY TO UNEARTH URQUHART IN THIS so-called Information Age. The obvious thing was to use the internet, but no matter how many variations I tried, the hundreds of returned hits usually concerned the *Daily Courier*. When I emailed the contact address for that newspaper I received no response.

Trying relatives was no more successful. His mother had died of a drug overdose in 1999—sleeping tablets, ruled accidental, but perhaps this was just polite window dressing and, having found the prospect of entering a new millennium with the old man intolerable, the overdose had been deliberate. The family seat in Sussex was sold off long ago. Since he was such a late child, his siblings were much older and by now had all died. Urquhart never married and had no children. The one cousin I contacted said she had not seen Urquhart "since he stopped wearing shorts," and that he had cut off all contact with the family following the death of his father—I gathered from our conversation that the renunciation of the viscountcy had been a sore point for the relatives, severing as it did their connection with the peerage.

As for Urquhart himself, I never got the least hint of where he now lived. It was as if Rothesay Ambrose Urquhart had slipped off the edge of the world.

For the next two years, I immersed myself in the imagined mind of Rothesay Ambrose Urquhart. Despite the differences in technique and subject matter between the painting in the Rector's Lodge—an example of the Pre-Raphaelite phase, as I was calling it—and the middle-period Catoptrographics, I saw, or thought I saw, a commonality between them, a single sensibility that sought to get at the fundamentals not through the artistic manipulation of image (which is the history of art to the mid-Nineteenth Century) nor in the outright abuse of image (art thereafter) but by the careful and critical examination of image, a concentrated focus that bordered on the profound.

This fanciful nonsense formed the core of my dissertation—indeed, in expanded form, it was to become a monograph. I suppose the thing was no worse than many a thesis, especially in my field, and in due course I was awarded my DPhil.

FOLLOWING THIS LONG COCOONING IN ACADEMIA, REAL LIFE came as a shock. It turned out that there was little demand in the outside world for people trained in art history. I applied to a select grouping at first—the publication-of-record broadsheets, the arts programming division at the BBC, and the influential East Coast magazines: *Time*; *New Yorker*; *The Atlantic*. As the rejections piled up I became less discriminating: regional dailies; the art-centric presses; even commercial television. After four months of otherwise fruitless searching, in which it seemed increasingly likely that dry academia would be my fate after all, I eventually landed a job as an arts reporter for a weekly Washington newspaper. I was already wary of the location—D.C. has first-rate art museums but little in the way of creative juice; at bottom, it is a company town—but the interview was even less encouraging.

"Where did you go to school?" the jowly creature on the other side of the desk demanded, someone who despite being the "lifestyle" editor of a newspaper was not enough of a word guy to have read my resume.

"Oxford."

"You went to Oxford?"

"Exeter College."

This response seemed to puzzle him, and he stared at me for a long time, as if unsure whether he was being made fun of.

"So which was it?" he eventually asked, "Oxford or Exeter?"

I became the newspaper's assistant reporter for the arts (*arts*, not *art*—I had to cover the other arts, too, like television sitcoms). I was paid not by salary but by word count. No benefits, which has serious consequences in the U.S.—it means that you dare not get sick. I lived in a tenement in a seedy part of town, again sharing a bathroom as I had as an undergraduate, but now surrounded not by pupils and professors but pimps and prostitutes. Basically, I just tried to not get murdered.

Newspapers were dying, and this one deserved to go. Soon the print version ceased to be, and the organization reverted to something called an "online portal," although what it was a portal to was never made clear. Certainly not the arts: I was shown the door after less than a year.

So ended my brief career in art journalism.

I WAS NOT ESPECIALLY DISPLEASED BY THIS: IT HAD BEEN clear from the beginning that neither the paper nor the city was for me. I resumed searching job postings, struggling to staunch the evaporation of my meager savings. I was determined not to ask my parents for help, to the point of near starvation. Rejections were few now; most people did not bother replying. Then, one day, a miracle occurred. A gallery wanted to interview me, a real gallery in a real city: the Wentworth in London.

The Wentworth Collection is located on Portman Square, housed in what had once been the London townhouse of the Higham family, Marquesses of Wentworth. The core was the family's own collection, mostly Baroque and Rococo works bought on the cheap from *ancien régime* exiles fleeing the French Revolution.

Thankfully, the interview was conducted by video; I would not have had the funds to make it there and back had I been required to show up in person. The Wentworth's director, Dr. Gibbons—Sir Richard Gibbons, KBE, but his preferred form of address was the academic title—was the polar opposite of my editor at the newspaper: Oxbridge; Received Pronunciation; stunningly peculiar visage with lips that seemed too big for his mouth and which looked uncharmingly moist; a stutterer as so many of them are; obviously intelligent but too shy to show it; and almost embarrassed by the necessary but ill-mannered impertinence of asking me questions.

I had been wondering why an institution famed for its collection of Eighteenth-Century art would have shown any interest in me, but after a long series of *ah—ah—ah*s that I thought would never end, the reason for the interview was revealed.

"You see the thing is," he said, "I've gone and bought a pair of Urquharts. Saw them in a Sotheby's catalog. Pretty little things—the paintings, not the catalogs—although somewhat puzzling. But I got 'em cheap." This last comment caused him to gurgle somewhere deep in his digestive tract, something that I would later come to understand was laughter.

He described the paintings, clearly and succinctly, at last revealing the incisive mind that underlay the superficial oddness. I had never seen them but recognized the style at once, and immediately began adding context, essentially retelling my doctoral dissertation. The conversation soon transitioned from a job interview to a professional discussion.

"Well, then," he said, "perhaps you'd better come over and take care of them for me."

"Certainly," I said. "Would a week from now suit?"

"Oh, yes, yes—just take your time and show up when you're ready to start. I'll let the people in front know that you're on the way, and when you arrive they'll take care of you: introduce you to your colleagues, show you to your office—all that sort of thing. Once you've had a chance to settle in and get acquainted with the place we'll have lunch at my club."

So ended the interview. There had been no discussion of salary—far more than I had hoped for, it turned out. I did not know my job title, nor what duties I would be expected to perform—"Curator, Contemporary Collection," I was to learn. But I was wildly elated: an office, and two Urquharts of my very own!

I packed my bags and my *u* and headed back across the Atlantic once more.

It has now been three years since I joined the Wentworth. The contemporary collection for which I am responsible was just twelve paintings, now fourteen—I managed two acquisitions, including a third Urquhart, bought privately from an American investment banker who had lost his job but did not want the world to be made aware of this by the painting going to public auction. It was a bargain: by then Urquhart was no longer an unknown and his major works were fetching six figures. The two "pretty little things" turned out to be enormous, each eight feet by twelve, and obviously a pair. They were Catoptrographics, the much-repeated image in the first being a woman's wrist, and in the second what is probably the angle of the jaw just below the earlobe, presumably the same woman. They are superb paintings, intimacy on a grand scale, something difficult to pull off—Sir Dickie, as he is affectionately known behind his back, has a good eye.

The monograph was duly written and edited, essentially a rehash of my dissertation but now focusing on these two artworks to which I had been granted unfettered access. It was published by the Wentworth's favored press.

I give gallery tours from time to time, show the paintings to occasional VIPs, and regularly field requests for the Wentworth Urquharts and other works to be reproduced in art publications. I have given guest lectures at various art schools, including the Ruskin and the Slade, and authored several articles in the usual art journals. In short, I am about where you would expect a mid-career art historian to be: comfortably cocooned with an appropriate position in a suitable institution and occasionally dabbling in scholarship—although woefully behind Kenneth Clark who at the same age as me, twenty-nine, had already authored *The Gothic Revival* and was the director of a major museum, the Ashmolean.

So there you have your narrator. I suppose I could paste in a photo, but that seems an immodest thing to do, and so instead I will do as I was trained to: use words to describe pictures.

The picture is this: a man steps down from Higham House onto the sidewalk of stately Portman Square. His clothes—Savile Row suit and Jermyn Street shirt—hint at pride, although in fact he is just a man of modest means having donned his Sunday best. Navy Burberry, worn as a topcoat. The weather is winter cold; the air moist; the sky leaden (a little too obvious, this artist: he might as well have included storm clouds to convey *ominous*).

As the streetlights slowly blink into life in the early dusk of this far northern city, we follow the man on his short stroll to Pall Mall. He approaches the pillared and pedimented entrance to one of the clubs, those bastions of entitlement that congregate in St. James's, as if in mutual self-defense, and our impressions seem confirmed: he is a person of privilege, someone without the doubts and struggles that afflict the average Joe, and we find ourselves gradually taking the side of the Fates, for who can now doubt that this is an allegorical work, depicting the opening act of a Greek tragedy perhaps, one in which our protagonist is presented as someone ripe for being taken down a notch or two.

So as I unsuspectingly stepped up onto the portico of the Cato Club that day, my life was indeed about to undergo a profound change, and due to much more than just an exploding red supergiant.

V

T HE LOBBY OF THE CATO CLUB WAS DARK-PANELED, PLUSHLY
carpeted, and manned by three unsmiling people: the doorman, a
footman, and behind the front desk a registrar who looked at me with a
single raised eyebrow, wordlessly inquiring if I was sure I had the right
address.

The porters at Exeter had the same look.

"My name's Evans," I told him. "I'm here at the invitation of a
member whom I've never actually met, O. Welles."

I was hoping this might prompt an offer of some background about
Welles or at least a first name, but the registrar was having none of that.
He wordlessly checked not a computer but a physical ledger mounted on
a wooden lectern, folio-sized, ruled, and with thick blue-tinted pages that
made a fine full sound as they were turned—a guest register, I assumed,
and the sort of impressive document that were it ever to be presented as
evidence in a courtroom would leave the jury in no doubt whatsoever.
He must have found my name: following an almost imperceptible nod,
the footman was suddenly behind me.

"May I take your coat, sir?"

It was removed and deposited in a closet whose door was concealed
in the paneling.

The registrar reached under the counter and withdrew a long metal box, lockable, like a safe-deposit box.

"If sir would be so kind as to place his mobile telephone and all other electronic devices in here."

I took out my cell phone and put it in the box, but the registrar made no move to close it.

"All such devices, sir."

"That's it."

In response, he cleared his throat and gazed meaningfully at my left wrist. I followed his look and saw what it was that had caused this alarm: my watch, not a real watch but one of those devices that monitors physical metrics and relays the data via a wireless connection.

I unstrapped the thing and placed it in the box with the phone.

"What do you do if someone has a pacemaker?"

"We tear it from their chest cavity and return it when they leave." For the first time, the registrar smiled. "Mr. Welles is in the library, sir. Beatson will escort you."

I followed the footman through to the club.

The entrance vestibule had been subdued, but when we passed through that second set of doors into the club itself—no longer visible from the street—the need for discretion was gone, and the interior space opened up into a grand marble-and-gilt palace.

I glimpsed a dining room set for dinner, all glistening crystal and gleaming silverware, and a large salon furnished with big Chesterfields, a rack of newspapers mounted on bamboo spines, and several gentlemen of advanced years who ignored me and each other.

We entered the library. Three walls were lined with bookcases, stuffed full. The fourth was mounted with woodcuts—one might have been a work by the younger Holbein, long thought lost—and included a fireplace, alight on a chilly day like this. Sitting by the fire was the room's sole occupant.

The footman announced me and left. Welles was not what I expected. For a start, I had imagined someone of the same vintage as the members I had seen in the salon, but Welles was near my age. Moreover, Welles was a woman.

She stood and we shook hands.

"You look rather startled, Dr. Evans."

"At the front desk, you were referred to as *Mr.* Welles."

"And so I am. Women are not permitted in the Cato Club."

"Yet here you undeniably are."

"Because I have been made an honorary man—it was the only way the rules committee could allow me membership. While within these walls I am expected to behave accordingly, with calm logic and judicious prudence, just like a real man. Were I to become all weak and womanly or, worse still, gigglingly girlish, they would no doubt blackball me. Shall we sit?"

We sat.

"Would you care for tea?"

"Yes, please."

A tea service had been laid out on the small table separating us: porcelain cups bearing the club's logo; a silver teapot; a hot-water pitcher. As she reached for the strainer I noticed on her wrist a real watch, one that must be wound, and from whose distinctive bezel I could tell was an expensive brand.

"Cato distrusted females," Welles said as she poured. "*Suffer women once to arrive at an equality with you*, he famously said, *and they will from that moment become your superiors*. What do you think, Dr. Evans?"

"I think that Cato needed to loosen up."

As she served, I took the opportunity to inspect this faux-hermaphroditic O. Welles. She wore a simple black dress with a collar high enough to disguise any hint of décolletage, which no doubt would have disturbed the club's denizens, but whose knee-length hemline and three-quarter sleeves revealed slender, well-shaped limbs—I wondered if the rules committee had required much persuasion. No rings or other jewelry; perhaps they would have been too womanly. The shoes, however, were unapologetically feminine: high-heeled and sharp-toed, black patent leather, not the sturdy lace-ups that one associates with the sort of English woman often referred to as *sensible*. She was handsome rather than pretty, an effect aided by her hair, pulled back in a neat bun.

I was thinking that with glasses she would pass for a librarian, or at least a fantasy version of one, when I noticed that she had faint impressions on either side of her nose: she did wear glasses but had removed them for meeting me.

"What should I call you?"

"Mr. Welles while in here. Ms. Welles, should we happen to meet outside." So much for my attempt at a first name. She made no reciprocal inquiry as to how I might like to be addressed and instead passed me a cup and saucer. "Would you care for a scone?" She pronounced *scone* in the English manner, rhyming with *gone*.

"No, thank you."

"And so, as to the invitation. I'm sure that it must have come as a surprise, but the gist is plain enough: Mr. Urquhart is intending to cruise the Mediterranean this summer and has included you among those invited to join him."

"I should say from the start that I've never met him."

"Nor indeed have any of his guests. Mr. Urquhart wanted to do something different this summer, given that we may all be about to be extinguished by the supernova. He feels that the most should be made of the remaining time. His idea is to gather a group of people with whom he is unfamiliar and who are themselves unfamiliar with each other, so as to maximize the newness, the sense of discovery, if you will, the pleasure in new people and new things that makes us all human. Plus, being at sea and away from light pollution on land, passengers will have the opportunity to appreciate those colorful auroras that we are assured are to come."

"Although I have never met Urquhart, I am professionally familiar with him. I am an art historian by trade, and he was the subject of my doctoral dissertation. I tried to get in contact with him at the time that I was writing it but never received a reply."

"Then this would present an ideal opportunity."

"A little late now."

"Perhaps you weren't ready before."

It was clear from her tone that she was already acquainted with this history, and that I was to expect no explanation for Urquhart's apparent about-face now.

"Who are the other guests?"

"The details are still being finalized. Everyone will be provided with a guest list before the cruise commences, so you wouldn't be going in blind: there'll be an opportunity to familiarize yourself with who your fellow passengers are before sailing."

"The itinerary?"

"Open. Apart from the start and end points, it will be determined by the desires of those on board. Weather will no doubt dictate part of it, and availability of dock space might limit some choices, but in general the idea is to allow whimsy to be the guide. Carthage, I hope."

"You hope?"

"Yes. Cato ended every speech to the Roman Senate, no matter what the subject, with the same phrase: *Ceterum, Carthago delenda est*— 'Besides, Carthage must be destroyed.' So it was, but I would like to see whatever might have been spared."

"You mean that you will be joining us, Mr. Welles?"

"Yes."

"So not everyone is a stranger to Urquhart?"

"In fact, I too have never met him—our communications have been entirely by mail. Mr. Urquhart lives abroad and has not visited England for many years, since before I represented him."

"You represent him? Sylvester Sykes is no longer his dealer?"

"I am a lawyer, Dr. Evans. I represent him legally."

"Oh, I see. And are there many other guests?"

"Twelve in total; that's as many as the *Mulvane* accommodates."

"She's small then?"

"No, just the opposite. But she's a prewar vessel, built back when motor yachts were laid out not with charters in mind, and so for economic reasons designed to maximize capacity, but solely for the comfort and pleasure of the owner and his guests. The accommodations are quite splendid, as is the entire vessel. She has been meticulously restored by the same yard that built her—Camper & Nicholsons—and I can imagine no finer way to cruise the Mediterranean. By the way, that brings me to clothing. You are of course welcome to wear whatever you wish, but I should tell you that Mr. Urquhart will be equipping each cabin with a full wardrobe in 1930s fashions so that we can fully immerse ourselves in the prewar world, when the most threatening thing was not an exploding star but a Stuka dive-bomber. I do hope you'll enter into the spirit of the thing and give them a try."

"Sounds like the setup for a whodunnit."

She inspected me with an appraising eye, as if I might be a candidate for the corpse. "I would say that you're a size thirty-eight?" I nodded in agreement, and she withdrew from her bag a little silver case that opened to reveal a pad with a thin pencil beside it. She put on a pair of spectacles and made a note. "And hat size?"

"Hat size?"

"The wardrobe will be period-correct, Dr. Evans, and in the 1930s gentlemen customarily wore hats."

Luckily, I knew my hat size, having worn one every day at Harrow.

"Six and seven-eighths."

"And lastly shoes."

"Nine and a half in U.S. terms, which is size nines in the U.K."

She jotted that down, too, and then put away the notecase and glasses. The removal of the latter had nothing to do with vanity, I realized; she only wore them for reading.

"You can see her this May if you like."

"Her?"

"The *Mulvane*. She's a veteran of the Dunkirk evacuation and will be taking part in this year's celebrations marking the anniversary. She will be docked in Dover."

"I hope that she's able to make it down to the Mediterranean in time."

"Oh, with ease. The *Mulvane* will outlive us all, Dr. Evans—cosmic radiation will do no more harm to her than did those German dive-bombers."

A steward in a stiffly starched white linen jacket came to her side and offered a printed card. After a moment's inspection, she passed it back. "The turbot, Carruthers, plus a half-bottle of the hock." He acknowledged her order and retired.

There was no offer for me to join her, although she was obviously dining alone—along with the continued absence of a first name and misjudgment about the spectacles, I had been put in my place.

"And so, Dr. Evans, I do hope that after due consideration you will choose to accept Mr. Urquhart's invitation."

"No consideration necessary: I accept it now, with much pleasure— nothing could keep me away."

"Very good. Let me give you my card."

She passed it to me, a plain business card that I briefly inspected. *Oriana* Welles. No firm, no address, not even an email, just a telephone number. "Should you have further questions, please feel free to call me. I should also tell you that on the night before sailing there will be a room arranged for you at the Hôtel de Paris in Monte Carlo—you might find it convenient to avoid any possibility of missing the boat."

"Thank you."

We stood and shook hands.

"Don't overpack," she warned. "Everything you need will be on board. Which reminds me: the Cato Club rules will also apply on the *Mulvane*: no electronics are allowed."

"And what about women?"

"That particular regulation has been suspended for the cruise."

"Perhaps when we're aboard you'll permit me to address you by your first name."

"No gentleman would suggest such an impertinent familiarity in the 1930s, Dr. Evans. I do hope you'll remember to stay in character." She was smiling as she said it, an impenetrable bastion laughing at those who might besiege it.

The footman Beatson was suddenly at my side, although how she had summoned him I could not tell.

"So nice to have met you, Dr. Evans. I do look forward to your company again this summer."

"The pleasure was all mine, Mr. Welles. See you in Monaco."

And with that, I was escorted from the premises.

VI

I WAS BACK AT THE CATO CLUB THE FOLLOWING MORNING. More precisely, I was by the Crimea monument in Waterloo Place, keeping watch on the Cato Club from across the street.

Welles' assertion that she was a lawyer was a mistake. Legal qualifications are a matter of public record, and after arriving home the previous evening I had gone online to the Barristers' Registrar. There was no Oriana Welles. I checked all of the *Welles* and *Wells* listed, seven in total, in case of a surname misspelling or if Oriana was a diminutive or nickname. None of them was her; all of them were male, genuinely male.

I had pulled out a sheet of my best Smythson-blue paper and composed a short thank-you note. A thank-you note is a little extravagant for afternoon tea, but not absurdly so. However, what I did the next morning was definitely over the top.

I went to a florist located close enough to the Cato Club that they would likely deliver on foot and selected a bouquet to accompany the note. Flowers were necessary: a note could be forwarded by mail, but flowers are perishable and so they would need to be sent around to wherever Welles worked directly. I would follow and discover who she really was.

I had borrowed a small motor scooter from one of the Wentworth's front desk staff and now sat astride it, helmet on, ready to follow if a vehicle got involved.

The flowers arrived on foot. I had selected a large bouquet to ensure that it would be conspicuous, and the flowers were in a tall vase with a big cellophane covering to protect the blooms (anemones, primroses, narcissi, and mimosas—a spring posy). The delivery man entered the club and emerged a few minutes later, still holding the flowers but now with a cell phone in hand, probably mapping his route.

He walked up to Piccadilly and over to Mayfair; I followed him with ease. He came to a halt at an address in Half Moon Street, a bow-fronted townhouse that had once been a residence but which judging from the brass plaque by the front door was now a business of some kind. The woman who opened the door and signed for the bouquet wore a suit and heels: a secretary or receptionist rather than a housekeeper or maid.

The messenger departed and I crossed the street to read the plaque: *Saunders Walker Investigations*.

When I returned to my office I looked them up. It seemed that their core business was background checks, and I could see how that would be a promising trade in prosperous Mayfair—people wanting to know exactly who it was proposing an investment, or perhaps to a daughter— but the firm also provided services in "surveillance, tracking, tracing, due diligence, corporate intelligence, and information technology forensics," the last of which I supposed meant bugs. The principals, Messrs. Saunders and Walker, were profiled—one ex-Metropolitan Police, the other ex-MI5—but there were no further staff listings other than a statement that they were usually recruited from law enforcement or the intelligence community, with the unspoken implication that they still had contacts in those services.

So Oriana Welles was a private investigator. The prospect of the summer cruise had just become more interesting.

VII

I DID GO DOWN TO DOVER THAT MAY, AS WELLES HAD suggested. The Dunkirk celebration began with a parade of ships at sea, and I stood with binoculars atop the blustery white cliffs watching as they approached. The line of vessels appeared to have been ordered by reducing size: the aircraft carrier *Queen Elizabeth* was in front, fighters arrayed in a file on her flight deck; behind her were two destroyers that the program identified as the British *Dauntless* and the French *Normandie*; a Canadian frigate, *Ville de Québec*, and then a dozen or more much smaller vessels that were veterans of the Dunkirk evacuation, the so-called "little ships" whose owners back in 1940 had put to sea without having to be asked, crossed the treacherous Channel, and helped rescue the army.

Two tall plumes of water suddenly emerged ahead of the *Queen Elizabeth*, higher even than her flight deck. The naked eye might not have noticed that the aircraft carrier was not the lead ship after all, but now the *Mulvane* had announced her presence with what I saw through the binoculars were firehoses mounted on swivels with their nozzles pointing skyward, one a little to the left, the other a little to the right. The program revealed that the *Mulvane* had been given this position of honor due to her intrepid service at Dunkirk and further asked that as she passed we observe that from her stern she flew a white ensign, normally reserved for warships alone, instead of the traditional red—a right rarely granted to a non-naval vessel.

Soon the *Mulvane* was close enough to be made out, far smaller than the mass of the aircraft carrier looming behind her. She had a navy blue hull and white superstructure, but even through all the spray from those firehoses I could see that unlike a modern motor yacht she was well furnished with woodwork and brass, sparkling in the spring sunshine. There were varnished handrails and doorways, plus teak decking that had no doubt been freshly sanded for this important day. The portholes were ringed with bright brass frames and the lanterns on her bridge wings gleamed.

Dover Castle fired a canon salute as they sailed past, and in response I could see clouds of black cordite emerge from *Dauntless*'s big 4.5-inch gun as she acknowledged, far deeper, the sound of those rhythmic discharges echoing along the cliffs, twenty-one rounds in total (a number reserved for heads of state: the British monarch, himself a former naval officer, was embarked for the day).

The people ashore burst into spontaneous applause.

After it was over, I decided against going down to the harbor to see the *Mulvane* up close. The day had been too enjoyable to risk spoiling it with crowds, and I would soon be aboard her myself for three months, so instead I strolled back to the station and returned to London.

As I considered the day during that railroad journey north across the rolling downs, I could not help thinking how much bigger people had been in 1940, how much more capable of great things. Churchill, of course, and Roosevelt, too, but it was not the top brass I had in mind— quite the opposite: it was the men who had manned those little ships that I was thinking of, otherwise ordinary folk who, perceiving the stakes, had risen to the occasion and put to sea unbidden, facing the rigors of the Channel and the strafing of the Luftwaffe to bring the stranded soldiers back to England.

Such a thing today seemed unimaginable. People were too soft now, always expecting someone else to pick up the slack. Perhaps we deserved no better than whatever Betelgeuse had in store for us.

VIII

Having received the necessary permission from Sir Dickie—who, given my host, was never going to say no to my taking three months away from the Wentworth—I arrived at the Hôtel de Paris in Monte Carlo on the appointed day.

The cab dropped me amid a sea of expensive machinery parked out front: Rolls-Royces; Bentleys; Ferraris—mostly convertibles with their tops down, icons of the Riviera. The building itself, an elaborate Beaux Arts confection, faced onto a cafe-strewn square across which stood the casino, its exterior more fanciful than even the hotel, something to distract from its true purpose, which was to operate as the chief source of revenue for the principality's treasury—there is a reason Monaco has no income tax, and that building is it.

I entered the Hôtel de Paris.

The lobby was palatial, a blaze of marble tile and mirrored glass, the capitals and spandrels carved in rich relief. The only thing larger than the floral arrangement dominating the scene at center stage was the crystal chandelier hanging above it. The space was topped by a stained-glass dome. Check-in was conducted not at a public registration desk, which would have been too déclassé, but in a private chamber where the details were discreetly dealt with in a manner that patrons would be familiar with from dealing with their private bankers.

I was shown to my suite, a cool expanse of Art Deco contrasting with the extravagance in the lobby below.

There was an ice bucket with champagne on the sideboard and by it a leather portfolio that I first thought was the hotel's service directory, but the gilt-etched emblem embossed on the cover turned out to be the *Mulvane*'s crest.

There were three items inside.

The first was a cover letter from Oriana Welles, handwritten, and I wondered if she had copied the same thing out twelve times, one for each guest.

The second item was printed on stiff card stock, a guest list not just naming the passengers but also attributing occupation, birthplace, and current place of residence.

The last item was a fold-out deck plan, a series of them, going from top to bottom, starting with the "sun deck" which was the roof of the superstructure, then the "boat deck," which was the upper level of the deckhouse with the bridge right forward and in back the yacht's two boats, depicted in a pair of superimposed positions: stowed inboard and swung outboard. Below that was the "main deck," the first that ran the entire length of the vessel and whose deckhouse portion contained the primary public rooms. Last was the "lower deck": crew quarters in front, passenger quarters in back, and the two separated by the engine room. The deck plan was printed but an item had been added by hand, an arrow pointing out which cabin was mine.

I put it aside for now and read the letter.

Dear Dr. Evans,

A brief note to welcome you to Monte Carlo—I hope that you had a pleasant flight.

You will be pleased to know that the Mulvane *has arrived as expected and is secured alongside in Port Hercule. The street leading down to the harbour is part of the Monaco Grand Prix racing circuit, so when you're ready to come aboard just follow the red-and-white track markers. The* Mulvane *will be easy to identify: glossy dark blue hull, white superstructure, and she's the only one with a proper buff funnel—she's berthed port-side-to at the end of the Quai l'Hirondelle and her name is painted on the stern. We'll be expecting you tomorrow morning in time to settle in and meet your fellow passengers. We'll put to sea at 5:00 P.M.*

Please leave your luggage in your room; a porter will collect it and bring it aboard before we sail.

I look forward to seeing you again tomorrow.

Regards,
O. Welles

She had not kept tabs on me as a good private investigator should: I had traveled by train rather than air, and so the remark about a pleasant flight told me that whoever the target of her inquiry was, it was not me. I was suspicious about the arrangement with the luggage, though: it seemed designed to provide an opportunity for the bags to be surreptitiously searched before coming on board.

I poured a glass of champagne and, guest list in hand, went out onto the balcony. Initially, I had been disappointed that my room gave onto place du Casino rather than the harbor, thus offering no view of the *Mulvane*, but when I stepped onto the little wrought-iron-railed terrace I realized that I had been fortunate. Garnier's magnificent Belle Époque casino was just across the plaza, the architectural detail much more accessible than from down in the square, and so a vista given to very few: mosaic roundels below the cupolas rendered in burgundy red and cerulean blue; bronze angels flanking the clock; and the verdigris-covered crown of the atrium, wonderfully ornate but invisible from street level.

I sipped the champagne and sat back to read about my fellow guests.

MY Mulvane—Passenger List

MR. ROTHESAY AMBROSE URQUHART — ARTIST; BORN HILL GROVE HOUSE, SUSSEX; RESIDES ISLAND OF LEDOS, GREECE

LADY ISABELLA DANIELLA LUCIANA PALLAVICINI–GIUSTINIANI — MARCHESA DELLA BRIANZA; BORN COMO, ITALY; RESIDES BELLAGIO, ITALY

LADY ADELINA CHIARA PALLAVICINI–GIUSTINIANI — GRAND-NIECE OF THE MARCHESA; BORN MILAN, ITALY; RESIDES MONTREUX, SWITZERLAND

MR. KIRILL VERKHOVSKY — INDUSTRIALIST; BORN NOVOSIBIRSK, RUSSIA; RESIDES VILLEFRANCHE-SUR-MER, FRANCE

MS. MALGORZATA (MARTA) DOMARADZKA — NIECE OF MR. VERKHOVSKY, BORN GRODNO, POLAND; RESIDES VILLEFRANCHE-SUR-MER, FRANCE

MS. BABILINA (BÉBÉ) NIKOLAISHVILI — NIECE OF MR. VERKHOVSKY, BORN TSKHINVALI, GEORGIA; RESIDES VILLEFRANCHE-SUR-MER, FRANCE

MR. FRANKLIN GILBERT — MEDIA MOGUL; BORN CHICAGO, ILLINOIS; RESIDES NEW YORK, NEW YORK

MS. RASPUTINA QUANTRILL — DAUGHTER OF THE ACTRESS AMELIA QUANTRILL; BORN LOS ANGELES, CALIFORNIA; RESIDES BEVERLY HILLS, CALIFORNIA

DR. HUGO EVANS — ART HISTORIAN; BORN BOSTON, MASSACHUSETTS; RESIDES LONDON, ENGLAND

MR. JACK SHOTTER — PHOTOGRAPHER; BORN KANSAS CITY, MISSOURI; RESIDES MILAN, ITALY

MS. TESS LYSETT—OXFORD UNIVERSITY STUDENT (SOMERVILLE); BORN SALISBURY, ENGLAND; RESIDES OXFORD, ENGLAND

DR. WU HOI–ON — PHYSICIAN; BORN VICTORIA, BRITISH CROWN COLONY OF HONG KONG; RESIDES VICTORIA, BRITISH COLUMBIA

MS. ORIANA WELLES — ASSISTANT TO MR. URQUHART; BORN JOHANNESBURG, SOUTH AFRICA; RESIDES LONDON, ENGLAND

Thirteen in total: Urquhart plus twelve guests—at least that much Oriana Welles had told me was true. But it was not true that they were all strangers to one another: three were listed as nieces of another two, although in the case of Verkhovsky I think *niece* was assumed to be a euphemism—perhaps Welles had meant only that all the parties were unknown to each other.

I spent a long time studying this list. The fiction that Welles was a lawyer had been dropped, or at least not emphasized, and instead she was characterized as the much more malleable *assistant*—something easier to disguise her true occupation. The only name I recognized was Amelia Quantrill, the screen actress. When looking her up I discovered that the daughter was the result of a brief affair between Quantrill and her costar in the movie *The Potsdam Directive*, Broderick Duckworth. Perhaps I should also have recognized the name Franklin Gilbert: he was indeed a media mogul, being the head of a company that controlled newspapers across the U.S. There was nothing about Tess Lysett or Dr. Wu Hoi-on that I could find, but Shotter turned out to be a well-known photographer working mostly in fashion—the reason that he lived in Milan, no doubt—and he had had several books of his work published, both fashion-specific and in general art photography.

Verkhovsky was a Russian oligarch, having long ago snapped up some oil and gas concessions on the cheap that had soon turned him into a rich man. He was now in his late fifties and, according to the biography I read, lived not in Villefranche-sur-Mer but in Moscow, Russia. The one photo I found was not flattering: square head atop a squat body, and with a face bearing a broad grin of immense self-satisfaction.

The Marchesa was an interesting figure. While she was still an infant her father had been a fighter with the partisans late in the Second World War, hiding out in the hills above Lake Como and carrying out clandestine raids against the Germans. After the war, the Pallavicini family rose to prominence as shipbuilders and flourished in the European economic rebirth. Titled or not, as a young woman Lady Isabella had been sent to the shipyards to work and became an expert welder in aluminum, a difficult skill. Perhaps it was this ground-up beginning that had allowed her to manage the business after her father's death, something she continued to do until the late 1980s when the shipbuilder was acquired by an industrial conglomerate. There was no mention of the grand-niece.

But the person who most interested me was, of course, Urquhart himself. Now at last I had found him, or at least discovered why I had been unable to find him. Ledos turned out to be an island in the Cyclades, just a rocky outcrop less than a square mile in size and completely barren. There were no streams or springs and hence it was previously uninhabited, although the ancients had once quarried it for marble, and there were still the ruins of a small temple and amphitheater on the island. In the Greek financial crisis, when the country had been gripped by austerity and the government was selling everything it could to raise funds, the island had been leased for ninety-nine years to an undisclosed private entity, someone who it was assumed intended to use it as a tax haven. There had been a minor outcry at the time—the terms of the lease included provisions under which there would not only be no tax but no application of Greek law in general: it effectively became a private sanctuary. The only stipulated governance was in matters of foreign policy, national defense, and whatever might become necessary in the event of force majeure—I wondered if the supernova counted as such a case.

This was why I had been unable to track down Rothesay Ambrose Urquhart—he lived as a recluse on his own sovereign isle.

That evening I went over to the casino, primarily to view the interior, but one cannot go there without playing the tables. I failed miserably—four consecutive turns of the roulette wheel, all losses, and my puny collection of chips had vanished—but I did come across three of my new shipmates. Kirill Verkhovsky arrived in the ornately frescoed Salle Europe, flanked by his nieces, both looking like runway models straight from a fashion show. They were much younger and taller than Verkhovsky, and made taller still by high heels—he looked like a building awaiting demolition between a pair of sparkling new skyscrapers. Verkhovsky wore a strange outfit: an open-necked polo shirt with a green blazer, as if he had just come from Augusta after winning the Masters; white trousers that failed to reach his ankles; tasseled loafers with no socks, revealing between his pants and shoes a repelling expanse of pudgy flesh mottled with bulging and broken veins. His wristwatch was oversized and had no face under the hands, something that allowed the complex movement beneath, presumably tourbillon, to be viewed—it must have weighed as much as a small gold ingot and been as expensive, too: a device whose primary purpose was not to tell time but display wealth. The overall effect of his entrance, no doubt intended to impress, was something between comical and stomach-churning.

He spotted a door marked *Salle Privée* and barged on through. The private rooms are for serious gamblers, with larger limits than the ordinary tables. Too high-stakes for me, but there was something compelling in Verkhovsky's charmlessness, like a hideous amphibian in a zoological vitrine that one cannot take one's eyes off—I followed him into the chamber.

He sat at a blackjack table and demanded champagne. When asked which brand, his answer was "the most expensive!" The skyscrapers stood towering behind him, bored but trying not to look it.

The seats on either side of Verkhovsky were taken but the one right at the end was free and feeling the eyes of the security people on me—no gawkers in the *salles privées*—I took it. It was not until I was seated that I saw the little sign with the table minimum: 500€. I emptied my wallet, took my single chip in return, and placed it humbly before me. Miraculously, I won—the dealer busted against my lousy sixteen. Verkhovsky had already busted, losing, I think, 10,000€ in that single hand. He continued to lose—even I could see that he played blackjack badly, and the dealer once paused to double-check that he genuinely wanted another card with a soft nineteen showing against the dealer's seven: Verkhovsky did not understand that in blackjack an ace can represent eleven as well as one, as the player so chooses.

I won and lost, not much one way or the other, but never again reduced to a single chip.

Soon Verkhovsky had had enough and left the table while loudly declaring to anyone within earshot that, "It means nothing to me," and it probably did not, but I could see that he was annoyed just the same. He flounced from the room, attendant skyscrapers obediently following, and demanded to be taken to caviar. In those few minutes at the table, he had lost a sum approximately equal to my annual salary. I gratefully took my chips and left the casino up 1,000€, which elated me whether or not the supernova would soon render all currency worthless.

It was clear that as a fellow passenger Verkhovsky was going to be a bore, but I nevertheless left the casino that night delighted that he had intruded on my evening.

IX

TWO GUESTS WERE ALREADY EMBARKED WHEN I ARRIVED on board the *Mulvane* the next morning. I saw the first as I clambered up the brow, a young woman on deck talking with Oriana Welles.

Welles introduced us; she was Tess Lysett.

"Did you just walk down from the hotel, too?" I asked her.

"No, I was picked up at the airport and brought directly on board. It seems that I'm considered too young to be allowed to stay on my own or have any fun."

Tess attempted an accompanying pout of displeasure but did not quite pull it off, being too amenable by nature to manage it. She was instantly identifiable as one of those guileless English girls for whom simply to be is to be happy.

"Tess is not yet eighteen," Welles explained, "which is the minimum age for entry to the casino."

"My birthday is in two weeks. I'm going to ask Mr. Urquhart if we can come back then, and I shall break the bank."

"Do you know him?"

"No, but my father does. They were in the same Divinity class when they were up."

This casual revelation crackled down my academic antennae.

"Urquhart read Divinity?"

"No, he only took some courses for a lark. Heaven knows why: my father says he's the most frightful atheist."

Given how little I had previously learned, this young woman was turning into a biographical cornucopia.

"Does your father know him well?"

"He did, but Papa hasn't seen him in years, since he became a hermit on that island of his. They were great chums as students, I gather, even though Papa says that Urquhart is the Devil incarnate, and my father should know."

"How come?"

"He's the Bishop of Chichester."

"And which is why I had Tess picked up from the airport," Oriana added. "We're under strict instructions from the Right Reverend to not lead her into temptation."

"Yet here you are, delivered unto evil, according to your father."

"Oh, Papa has no fears on that front. He's quite certain that Mr. Urquhart would defend me to the death if need be."

"To the death?"

"I think it's rather wonderful that there's a man who would defend oneself to the death, especially a man one has never actually met, although of course I do hope that it doesn't become necessary."

These remarks made me reappraise this woman before me, someone whom I had too easily dismissed. I briefly wondered if she might be the subject of the Exeter portrait. She possessed the same long slender body type—how could anyone be other than slender on an Oxford college diet?—and the unconscious grace in her bearing was right, but Tess was too young: the Exeter girl would be a woman well into her twenties by now. Moreover, Tess was open and engaged; the girl in the Exeter portrait would be more reserved and composed, it seemed to me. And I could tell by the shape of her jaw that neither was she the subject of my two monumental Catoptrographics at the Wentworth.

I turned to Welles.

"Speaking of Urquhart, is our host about?"

"Not yet, but the harbormaster won't be giving us permission to sail until he's on board. Now, may I show you to your cabin?"

ORIANA LEFT ME OUTSIDE MY CABIN, BUT WHEN I OPENED the door I found it already occupied. A man was standing surrounded by baggage, mostly black hard-sided cases with sturdy metal edging and big secure latches. He looked up from his unpacking.

"So she didn't tell you either," he said. "We're apparently sharing the cabin—hope you don't mind."

"Not at all. I shared at Harrow for a time, and then again at Oxford."

"And I was in the navy, so I'm used to it."

He extended an arm.

"Jack Shotter. Everyone calls me Shotter."

"Hugo Evans." We shook hands. "I hate the name Hugo, so please just call me Evans."

"Evans it is. Upper or lower?"

The lower bunk was already strewn with artifacts of his profession: a tripod; bottles of chemicals; an open case revealing a long lens surrounded by protective foam.

"Upper's fine. They let you bring photographic gear? Welles confiscated my phone from me just now, and I was told that no electronics were allowed."

"I shoot on film. I have nothing against electronics; I just think film looks better than digital. Plus it forces you to focus more, to pay attention to composition and framing; digital makes you lazy."

"So we'll all be relying on you for our vacation shots?"

"Nope. Check out the stowage—yours is on the forward bulkhead."

The cabin was arranged with the bunks on the left, built-in cabinetry on the far side, a porthole beside that, then a door to a bathroom, and finally another set of built-ins on the right. I pointed to this last.

"Is that the 'forward bulkhead?'"

Shotter laughed. "Sorry, I should have said 'front wall.'"

"No, since we're going to be at sea for the next three months I might as well get the terminology right. Tell me what things are called."

"Well, front is *forward*."

"And so back is *rear*?"

"*Aft*."

"Ah, of course: *aft*."

"Or sometimes *after*, as an adjective: *after* davit, *after* brow."

"What else?"

"Floor's the *deck*, ceiling's the *deckhead*."

"And window's a *porthole*."

"Yep."

"I pointed to the bathroom door.

"*Head*, right?"

"You're practically an old salt now, Evans."

At that point, my baggage from the hotel arrived, brought down by a crewman. Shotter shoved his gear into a closet.

"I'm done," he said. "Catch you later." And with that, Shotter left, a man of few words and many of them nautical, but I could tell that we would get along fine—he was not done, he was just leaving me alone to settle in unmolested.

I stood still, taking in what was to be my home for the summer. The cabin was, notwithstanding the sharing, luxurious. The deck was covered in plush wall-to-wall or perhaps bulkhead-to-bulkhead carpeting. There were four seats: two desk chairs and a pair of comfortable armchairs in the corners. The cabinetry was made of burled walnut finished in high gloss. The light fixtures were milk glass panels in flowing nickel frames whose design matched the door handles and drawer pulls, a style that would have been fashionably modern when the ship was built. The switches were solid metal fittings whose levers went up and down with a satisfying thunk, something that has all but disappeared in this age of touchscreens. By the door were two bell pushes, one labeled *Steward* and the other labeled *Maid*, plus a black Bakelite handset cradled in a chrome bracket, marked *Bridge*.

The head was equally impressive. The deck was covered in small hexagonal white tiles, like an old-style steam room. A shower stall with a big round showerhead was fitted on one side; opposite was a porcelain sink three feet broad with a mirrored cabinet mounted above. The head itself was a mighty affair, flushed using a foot pedal that sent a torrent of seawater gushing down the bowl.

I imagined that this was how a first-class cabin on the original *Queen Mary* must have looked.

My stowage was already mostly full: plain cotton pants; collared safari shirts; tennis whites; navy blue swimming trunks embroidered with the *Mulvane*'s crest; there were even underwear and socks, the boxers a blazing bright-red tartan with a tag bearing my name sewn into the waistband. Among the linen suits and formal shirts hanging in the closet was a tuxedo, and on the shelf above two hats: a panama and a fedora. In a drawer at the bottom were shoes: two-tone wingtips to wear during the day; black patent leathers to go with the dinner suit; white canvas deck shoes; a pair of sturdy brown brogues.

I discovered why Shotter had said that we would not be relying on him for photographs: inside one drawer was a camera, an old Leica in a leather case shaped to accommodate it. There were several rolls of film beside it.

In another drawer was a box filled with cuff links, shirt studs, collar stays, and the like. A third contained two leather cases: one with a shaving kit—chrome safety razor; spare blades wrapped in waxed paper; shaving brush; lather bowl; a tin of soap—in the other was a traveling set of toiletries. Everything was from, or made to look like they were from, the prewar era—even the brushes had genuine bristles: badger for the shaving brush; boar for the hairbrush.

Part of the cabinetry opened into a fold-down desk with racks designed for correspondence. One slot was occupied by notepaper bearing the ship's crest on top and the agent's address at the bottom. Another held envelopes, similarly embossed. There were lots of little drawers containing the various things that might be expected in a well-stocked desk from the 1930s: bottles of ink, a porcelain inkwell cleverly embedded into a recess and further protected with a silver cap to prevent spillage, plus, if these precautions failed, blotting paper to clean up the mess.

Inside one of the drawers I found a wristwatch, obviously antique, a satin-face Bulova that had to be wound but which was already ticking and set to the correct time. There was no safe but the top drawer was lockable. Inside it, I found the key and an envelope with my name. It was a letter from the ship's captain.

Welcome aboard, Dr. Evans,

Here are a few notes to help you settle in and enjoy your time on board the Mulvane.

Firstly, the crew is at your entire service, twenty-four hours a day. A steward (for food & drink) or a maid (for housekeeping) can be summoned at any time using the labeled bellpushes in your cabin. Additionally, you can speak directly with the duty officer on any matter by using the telephone—just lift the handset to call.

In keeping with the theme of the voyage—harking back to a simpler age—we ask that if you have not already done so you surrender all electronics to Miss Welles, who will be acting as the purser for the voyage. The bridge is equipped with both a satellite phone and ship-to-shore radio, should any emergency arise, but otherwise we hope to remain cut off from the world and thus able to enjoy the voyage in uninterrupted repose—a rare luxury in this era of mobile devices. For photography, each guest has been provided with a vintage camera—Miss Welles will have completed rolls developed and prints provided (black-and-white only).

You will find your cabin stocked with the clothing and accouterments appropriate to the 1930s—please enter into the spirit of the cruise by using them: think of it as an opportunity to play dress-up. The more formal manners and modes of address from that era are also encouraged—it is hoped that this will be regarded as a welcome relief from the abrasions of our own less civil times.

In the absence of electronic communications, you may wish to write letters. Cabin desks have been stocked with writing paper and envelopes. Please put any correspondence into the slot marked "Letters" in the main salon—these will have correct postage affixed and be mailed by the staff at the earliest opportunity. Return mail should be addressed to M.Y. Mulvane, *care of the ship's agents in Southampton, whose address is printed at the foot of each sheet of notepaper. The agents will arrange for the correspondence to get to us at our next port of call.*

The time zone on board will remain that of Monaco (GMT + 2) no matter where in the Mediterranean we might be. A full breakfast will be available 8:00-10:00. There will normally be no lunch at table, but platters of sandwiches and such will be laid out in the dining room for guests to take from as they choose. Afternoon tea will be served at 16:00. Dinner will be at 20:00, always black tie. A steward will serve behind the bar in the evenings, but passengers are welcome to mix their own drinks whenever they choose: the bar is never closed. There is a small pantry adjacent to the dining room that is always stocked: feel free to indulge at any time.

Should any medical matter arise, your fellow passenger, Dr. Wu, has kindly consented to act as the ship's surgeon—your steward or maid can be dispatched to request his services.

It is a tradition that the first night at sea is informal, so please do not dress for dinner this evening: just come as you are to a casual buffet where you can meet your host and fellow passengers.

Lastly, I am available at any time. I can usually be found on the bridge. My cabin—clearly signed—is directly abaft.

On behalf of the officers and crew, it is again my pleasure to welcome you on board the vessel that I have the honour to command, the Motor Yacht Mulvane,

James P. Trevelyan

I noted the use of *abaft*—not *aft* or *after*—how many variations did these nautical types have for *behind*? I wondered if the camera arrangements were entirely an aversion to modern electronics, or perhaps also an excuse to maintain control over what gets photographed, with Oriana Welles in the position of censor.

I put my journal—this journal—into the top drawer, locked it, and headed back up on deck.

Two more guests had arrived during my time below. One was a tall man in a gray suit and tie, fiftyish, somewhat gaunt and granite-faced, the sort of no-nonsense fellow you instantly feel can be relied upon. He spied me and came over.

"Franklin Gilbert. You must be Hugo Evans."

We shook hands.

"Yes, that's me, but please just call me Evans."

"Last name for me, too—fits with this whole 1930s gig we've got going. I thought you were American?"

Once again I had to explain that I was indeed American-born but with English parents, that I was consequently a citizen of both the U.S. and the U.K., had spent my childhood split between the two, and was generally not wholly one thing or the other.

"Bet you get tired of accounting for your accent."

"I'm anticipating having to do it another eight times for the rest of the passengers I haven't yet met."

"Do you know our host?"

"No, but I'm an art historian by trade, and his work was the subject of my doctoral thesis—I'm assuming that's the reason for the invitation. What about you?"

"I've never met him, either. Never even communicated with him, except by proxy through his investment bankers. I'm trying to buy his newspaper, the *Daily Courier*, in which he holds a controlling interest. Apparently, this trip is to be an extended interview to see if I'm worthy of acquiring the family jewels."

"I thought newspapers were dying?" I described my brief foray into journalism.

"Yep, they're dying, but I'm guessing that with this Betelgeuse about to blow up people might start to pay attention to the outside world again. I mean the real objective outside world, not the solipsistic world of little screens with 'likes' to their favorite ranters. Being threatened with destruction should shake people up. In other words, I'm betting on a comeback for wanting to know what's actually going on."

"I believe that an American newspaper owner who uses words like *solipsistic* has every chance of success—the reason people don't buy papers anymore is because the stuff they print isn't worth reading."

"Then we're of a like mind—I can't abide sloppy journalism. I hope Urquhart feels the same way. I also hope he doesn't expect me to pay too much for his paper."

"By the way, I should tell you that it's ˈ**erk**-et," I said, correcting his mispronunciation. "He once walked out of a live television show when the interviewer pronounced it erk-ˈ**heart**."

"Thanks for the heads-up."

"You're welcome—we Americans have to stick together."

This remark amused him sufficiently for a smile, but not enough for an outright laugh. I got the sense that he was a man who was always just himself, incapable of pretense or affectation—another passenger with whom I would get along well.

The second newcomer joined us but I did not need an introduction to know that she must be Rasputina Quantrill, for she was the very image of her famous mother.

"Did someone say we fellow Americans should stick together?"

Gilbert performed introductions.

"Don't ask about his accent," Gilbert added. "English parents and English boarding school, but he's as American as you and me."

"I'm glad to hear it," Rasputina said. "Any idea why you were invited, Dr. Evans, or are you as in the dark as I am?"

I explained again about my tenuous connection. "What about you?"

"No idea. Maybe he's my father."

"Your father?"

"You never know with my mother—artistic temperament and all that. She's a romantic by nature and falls in love very easily. Out of it, too, equally fast."

The opportunity to follow up on this interesting line of conversation was cut short by the arrival on the wharf of two more passengers. They came in a Mercedes too old to be from a livery service: it was one of those squared ones with upright headlights from the previous century with an extended limousine body and little privacy curtains in the rear compartment.

The chauffeur got out and opened the rear door from which at first emerged a walking stick followed by an elderly lady, moving gingerly, and with a quick, "Excuse me, I'd better offer a hand," Gilbert had left us and was bounding down the brow to assist the woman aboard.

As the younger man that duty should have fallen to me, but I was frozen in place from having recognized the second passenger, emerging from the other side, although I had never before seen her in the flesh. She was unquestionably the mysterious and enigmatic subject of the Exeter portrait.

X

FRANKLIN GILBERT ESCORTED THE WOMAN WHO I assumed must be the Marchesa on board. Welles saw to it that she was comfortably settled into a bench seat built into the curve of the stern railing, all the way aft.

On the wharf below, her grand-niece supervised the unloading of the car. There was a lot of luggage and it needed two crewmen and twenty minutes of labor to get it all on deck. Meanwhile, I took the opportunity to observe unobserved this woman whose portrait had had such a profound influence on my life.

Mid-twenties, I guessed, which matched the assumption that she would have been sixteen or so at the time of the Exeter portrait. She wore a simple shift dress and a cardigan, unbuttoned, plus flat shoes that may have been for comfort or perhaps, already tall, she just preferred not to stand out. Her hair was bunched up in the back, but loosely, the way a woman does when she just wants it up and out of the way. No jewelry, no scarf, no fashionable sunglasses—she had not dressed to impress anyone; she had dressed for the practical business of organizing the passage of her great-aunt, herself, and a monumental amount of luggage from northern Italy to southern France.

How to explain the effect that her arrival had on me? It was more than just a jolt of recognition; I felt physically impacted by her presence, almost exhausted by it, as if having come at last to the end of a long quest: Raleigh finding El Dorado, say, or Galahad the Holy Grail. And coupled with this was an odd sense that she was somehow already known to me. I suppose the only explanation for this is that, in some individuals, inner character is subtly but clearly expressed in outer form. Perhaps it was partly her posture, perfectly straight but without any hint of stiffness, or the flow of a slender forearm and long-fingered hand as she gestured while explaining the disposition of some item of luggage, or the polite and measured tones with which she quietly but authoritatively directed operations, something accomplished without demonstration or fuss, or that one quick glance at the ship beside her, an eyebrow half-raised in idle curiosity, and then catching my eye, and piercing me like a butterfly being pinned in display.

Whatever the case, I felt that I already knew this woman whom I had never met.

I suddenly found Oriana Welles standing by my side.

"What do you think?" she said, following my gaze.

"Mercedes 600 Pullman, I believe—marvelous old car, isn't it?"

Welles just smiled in response. "Why don't you come and meet the Marchesa?"

I was introduced to Lady Isabella, the Marchesa della Brianza. It was clear that she was physically frail but I could tell right away that there had been no accompanying diminution of mind. She patted a place on the bench beside her in silent command. I dutifully took a seat and Welles went off to see to the transfer of luggage into the stateroom, leaving the Marchesa and myself momentarily alone, an opportunity that she was quick to pounce upon.

"I am informed that you are an art historian," she said, in slow and heavily accented English.

"And so I am, but not a very distinguished one. I am a minor curator at the Wentworth in London, and the total number of works for which I am responsible is barely a dozen." She ignored the self-deprecation and got down to business.

"I have brought with me some of my most treasured drawings from the villa—at my age one does so like to have some things of one's own when in strange surroundings, you understand?" A whole villa's worth, judging by her baggage. She lowered her voice and leaned closer, conspiratorially. "I wonder if you might care to take a look at them later?"

"I would be delighted, Lady Isabella."

"Shall we say at four? You may come to my stateroom."

"I shall be there promptly at four."

"Very good." Having gotten what she wanted, the Marchesa turned toward Welles, who had emerged back from baggage supervision to stand in readiness by the brow, and raised her voice more than I would have thought her capable to issue an imperious command.

"Now, my dear, perhaps it is time that I freshen up."

I had been dismissed. I took my leave, allowing Welles to take the Marchesa in hand.

Invitations to "take a look at" someone's old artworks are surprisingly common in my line. Professional appraisals are not cheap, or if done by the auction houses are often inflated and after which they will keep pestering you to put them on the block. No doubt the upkeep of the family villa was expensive and maintaining appearances would be a drain on dwindling resources—there was a reason the Mercedes was such an old one. The Marchesa presumably wished to turn a few of her choice works into cash and wanted some free guidance as to which ones were likely to fetch the best prices.

The Mercedes left and the Marchesa's grand-niece came on board. Welles and the crewmen were still away assisting the Marchesa and so we had the deck to ourselves.

I stood as she approached.

"I'm Adelina Pallavicini," she said. "Did you happen to see where my aunt went?"

We shook hands.

"Hugo Evans, and they just took her forward to her stateroom."

"You're the art historian?"

"Yes."

"Then beware my aunt."

"She's already cornered me. I am to come to her stateroom at four to inspect the goods."

"So I'm warning you too late," she said with a smile. "I'm afraid that my aunt is quite incorrigible."

"I don't mind at all, although I do find her accent a little difficult to follow. I thought you'd sound Italian, too."

"I boarded at Headington from the age of eleven."

"Ah—I was at Harrow, but that wasn't until I was thirteen."

The opportunity to further explore this common experience of English boarding schools was forestalled by the arrival of the next guest, announced by a loud exhaust note echoing down the dock.

We went over to the side. A Lamborghini came hurtling down the wharf and screeched to a stop, but the driver misjudged this spectacular entrance and ended up skidding twenty feet past the brow. The car was a convertible, top-down, and painted a strange lime-green color almost neon in its vibrancy. Although only a two-seater it contained three people: Kirill Verkhovsky in the driver's seat and on the passenger side the two skyscrapers, who began the difficult business of unfurling themselves from the cockpit like a pair of entwined stick insects emerging from a common cocoon.

"Excuse me," Adelina said, no longer smiling. "I must go find my aunt."

Oriana Welles emerged from the deckhouse, alerted by the noise. Verkhovsky revved the car loudly and pointlessly a few times before finally shutting down the engine and getting out of the vehicle. Today he wore a short-sleeved Hawaiian shirt open to the sternum—an arrangement that revealed an abundance of stomach, graying chest hair, and gold chains—plus white ducks and white loafers with little gold tassels and once again no socks. I hoped that the 1930s dress code would persuade him to wear some when we got underway.

He reached behind the seat and pulled out a naval officer's peaked cap, which he proudly put on. Judging by gold braid, it must have once belonged to an admiral.

By now Gilbert, Shotter, and Tess Lysett had arrived on deck, as well as two crewmen who stood by Welles.

The Russian lumbered aboard, skyscrapers in tow tottering atop their stilettos. No tourbillon timepiece today—it must have been an evening accessory—but instead three large jewel-encrusted rings that served only to emphasize rather than conceal the man's mottled hands and scab-crusted knuckles. After hitting the deck he announced in a loud voice to the impromptu assembly, "I am Verkhovsky."

I was tempted to applaud.

Welles welcomed him and made introductions—no handshakes; just a curt nod of the head. He turned toward a crewman and without warning tossed him the car key, adding a dismissive, "The bags are in front. Leave the key with the dock office: my people will pick up the Lambo." The crewman did well, catching the key despite having his attention distracted by the skyscrapers—one wore cutoffs and a silk blouse carelessly buttoned, the other a thin tank top tightly tucked into a micromini, and she was obviously wearing nothing beneath the tank top.

Verkhovsky looked about.

"Where is the pool?"

"We have no pool, Mr. Verkhovsky. The *Mulvane* was built in 1936, before yachts had such things."

"No pool?"

"No pool."

Verkhovsky made no attempt to disguise his displeasure.

"A bar?"

"Yes."

"Take me to the bar. You will all join me, yes?"

"A little early in the day for me," Gilbert said.

"I have to unpack," I offered.

"I'm not of legal age," was Tess's excuse. "For anything," she added.

Shotter just laughed and shook his head.

"This way," Welles said, leading Verkhovsky forward. He harrumphed and followed her, with the skyscrapers dutifully trailing behind.

The remainder of the party dispersed, no one willing to catch anyone else's eye. Suddenly, three months confined aboard a small vessel at sea seemed a very long time.

XI

A T 4:00 P.M. PRECISELY, I KNOCKED ON THE DOOR OF Lady Isabella's cabin. She had been assigned the owner's stateroom, located right forward in the deckhouse rather than below deck like the rest of us—Urquhart had apparently given up his accommodation for the convenience of the Marchesa, no doubt so that she would not have to negotiate stairs to access the public areas.

I had passed through the dining room on the way and found the table laid for afternoon tea—silver platters of finger sandwiches and scones with cream and jam—and saw with envy that my fellow passengers were already scoffing it down. The Marchesa had probably timed it this way: an excuse to get her grand-niece out of the stateroom and ensure that the staff were otherwise occupied so that we could have our consultation in private. I was not surprised when Lady Isabella answered the door herself.

"Do come in, Dr. Evans."

I entered the owner's stateroom and for a moment gazed about in astonishment. It was a magnificent suite, stretching right across not just the deckhouse but the entire width of the hull—*beam*, I think is the correct term—and since it was right forward but also projecting from the rest of the deckhouse all four bulkheads were pierced with windows, here not the little round portholes of below but big broad sheets of glass, and the room was awash with light. This effect was enhanced by mirrors, floor-to-ceiling ones fitted into the bulkheads on either side of the bed forward and the closet aft. An internal rear door led back to a second cabin with its own external access at the other end, probably originally intended for children or personal staff but having been refitted to a level of luxury commensurate with the stateroom and, judging by the cardigan on the bunk, apparently to be occupied on this voyage by the Marchesa's grand-niece. A second door, closed, presumably led to a bathroom. A large floral arrangement stood on a table in the middle of the room, and I wondered how it would remain upright at sea: perhaps the vase was screwed in place. Compared to this, my cabin, which I had lately thought luxurious, was more like steerage class.

The Marchesa escorted me to a desk built into the port side. A stiff cardboard portfolio, secured with a ribbon, lay conspicuously on top. The Marchesa bade me sit.

"Please take your time looking at them," she urged, "and do tell me if any among them strikes you as being worthy of note."

Worthy of note, I assumed, meant worthy of selling.

I sat at the desk, a superbly crafted piece of dignified Art Moderne, fit for a company director's office. I opened the portfolio and suppressed a sigh of disappointment. The first drawing and those that followed were unengaging: technically competent without being accomplished, attractive without being inspired, and the subjects predictably insipid rather than startlingly eye-catching. All of them were prominently signed, as bad art always is.

I tried not to flick through them too rapidly. The Marchesa sat in an armchair in the corner, situated where she could observe me but I could not observe her, and pretended to read while watching me unwaveringly.

The drawings even smelled ordinary: musty and lifeless, just like the art. Then, near the back, I found something different: a rider on a horse rendered in a series of swiftly executed swirls: circles and ellipses suggesting movement, done with no attempt at realism but wonderfully capturing the drama of the moment, and something else too: a whimsical dreamy sadness, I would have said—appropriate to the subject and the artist, for I instantly recognized both: it was a drawing of Don Quixote as imagined by Salvador Dalí. There were four of them, studies presumably, but all were unsigned.

I finished going through the remainder of the drawings, no better than the rest, and then retied the ribbon and laid the portfolio back on the desk. I turned to face the Marchesa.

"You understand that art history is highly specialized, Lady Isabella, and I have little competency in this area?"

"Nevertheless, I would appreciate your opinion."

"I believe that all but four of these drawings, while perfectly well-executed and pleasing works, are not of the type that would excite enthusiasm among those who make it their business to collect such things."

"And the other four?"

"The equestrian sketches. They are in a style that suggests the Twentieth-Century Spanish Surrealist, Salvador Dalí. They are perhaps copies or just works executed in his manner. They may even be genuine Salvador Dalís, but unfortunately they are unsigned. If they could be authenticated, then no doubt they would be of considerable monetary value, but I cannot say whether or not it would be possible to do so."

"Oh, of course they're Dalís. He did them for me."

"For you?"

"I was a young girl at the time. He did them to amuse me while he was visiting us. I think it was in 1949."

"You're sure it was Dalí?"

"Who could forget those magnificent mustaches? Such a charming man; he let me wax them."

"Then I believe that you possess four drawings of some value, despite the absence of Dalí's signature. There are other means of verification that, along with your knowledge of the provenance, would allow for a professional authentication—a prerequisite, should their sale ever be contemplated."

"How very kind of you to have helped me in this matter, Dr. Evans."

No one knows how to dismiss like a Marchesa. I stood.

"It has been my pleasure, Lady Isabella. If I can be of any further assistance, I hope that you won't hesitate to ask."

"I rather think I might," she said, with the hint of a smile, "but for now you have been extremely kind to have indulged a lady of advancing years."

"Not at all." And with that, I took my leave.

I EMERGED FROM LADY ISABELLA'S STATEROOM TO FIND myself face-to-face with a Chinaman.

"Wu," he said, holding out an arm.

"Evans," I replied, and we shook hands. "A pleasure to meet you, Dr. Wu."

He was tall for a Chinese man, middle-aged, and bore the beginnings of a Fu Manchu, as if an Oriental version of Dalí. He was dressed in a dark suit and sober tie, and carried a little leather bag such as doctors do in old black-and-white movies, but which I had never seen before in real life.

He noticed my eyes go to the bag.

"An affectation, yes, but a practical one: I may need to make cabin calls. Nevertheless, my colleagues back in Canada would laugh at me if they saw it. The mustaches too, but I am growing them in keeping with the 1930s theme. I believe they make me look inscrutable."

"Very inscrutable, Doctor. Are you making a call on the Marchesa now?"

"No, my cabin is here." He pointed to a door giving onto the passageway on the starboard side. "The remarkable Miss Welles tells me that it is nominally the owner's day cabin, a place of retirement when the stateroom is being serviced, but it has been assigned to me, no doubt so that I might be ready at hand should the Marchesa require my services."

"Then you're lucky. The rest of us are below deck by the engine room and with stairs to negotiate. Tell me, why do you call Miss Welles remarkable?"

"Were I to reveal that, Dr. Evans, I would no longer be inscrutable." This remark was accompanied by a smile of sly good humor—here was another passenger whose company would be a welcome counterbalance to Verkhovsky.

"Just plain Evans, please—you're the only real doctor on board."

"As you wish."

"I'm going to go see if any afternoon tea is left."

"Good luck, but I fear that you might be too late."

I WAS TOO LATE: THE STEWARD WAS CLEARING AWAY THE last of the platters when I passed by the dining room. I continued through the main salon and out onto the rear deck, where I found my cabinmate leaning on the rail and looking down at the dock. I joined him.

"Is this the *after* deck or the *abaft* deck?"

"Neither, it's the quarterdeck."

"Quarterdeck?"

"That's the traditional term, from back in the days of sail."

I followed his gaze and saw what it was that had caught his attention: a Rolls-Royce parked on the wharf, very large, obviously old but well-maintained, the black paint gleaming and the enormous upright chrome grille glistening in the sunlight.

"Holy cow," I said. "Whose is that?"

Shotter turned to me in puzzlement. "You weren't here with the rest of us when our host came aboard just now?"

"No, I missed it. Heck of a car he's got."

"Rolls-Royce Phantom V," my companion said, "but it's not his."

"How do you know?"

"Check out the front fenders."

I checked, sweeping expanses of polished black metal that seemed to suggest nothing but bulk. Then I saw that atop the right-hand side, attached to a miniature chrome staff, was a little flag, the red-and-white national flag of Monaco. There was a chrome staff on the left fender as well, equal in height but currently unoccupied. I suddenly understood what Shotter was getting at.

"You mean it's the prince's?"

"Yes."

"Is he here, too?"

"No. According to Welles, who seems to know everything, if the prince had been embarked then his personal standard—the Grimaldi coat-of-arms—would have been flying from the other side. The only passenger was Urquhart, although obviously the prince lent him his car and driver."

I had imagined that the Hôtel de Paris was the finest place to stay in Monaco but then I realized that there would be one place finer still: the monarch's palace. Over a quarter century had passed since Urquhart renounced his viscountcy but it seemed that he remained on friendly terms with the titled nobility of Europe, enough to be the prince's house guest when in town. I now understood Welles' earlier comment that there was no chance of the *Mulvane* being given permission to sail before Urquhart was aboard.

XII

A LITTLE BEFORE FIVE P.M., THE MAIN ENGINES WERE started, announced by a background rumble that echoed through the passageways and a faint vibration that could be felt by touching any bulkhead—two sensations that were to be our constant companions in the months to come. The yacht had suddenly sprung into exuberant and pulsing life.

At five o'clock, the lines were let go and the *Mulvane* proceeded to sea.

Everyone came on deck for the departure except the elusive Urquhart, still unseen by me. The Marchesa once again settled onto the little bench seat installed into the curve of the *Mulvane*'s elegant counter stern—it was set higher than the deckchairs and so was easier for her to rise from, and by unspoken agreement this perch became the Marchesa's for the duration of the voyage.

The rest of us stood, Verkhovsky a little unsteadily—he had been at the champagne since boarding—but the skyscrapers buttressed him on either side, not unacquainted with his drinking habits. Rasputina Quantrill and Tess Lysett bounded excitedly to and fro, wanting to miss nothing, full of delight at the passing scene—being of a similar age but a little younger than the rest of us, they had quickly become friends.

Shotter brought a camera up on deck, a complex technical-looking device, and proceeded to take photographs, professionally and without urgency, capturing the harbor against its backdrop of firstly the city and then behind it the dramatic enveloping amphitheater of the surrounding mountains. Gilbert took snaps, too, but with a little Box Brownie, evidently the vintage camera he had been assigned.

Adelina dutifully remained by the Marchesa to begin, but the elder lady shooed her away, not wanting to be fussed over or maybe just encouraging her reserved grand-niece to venture forth. Although much the same age as Rasputina Quantrill and Tess Lysett she was a world removed from them in temperament, and I could tell that she would unlikely join them in their eager running about. Instead, Adelina and Wu chatted quietly; perhaps he had sought her out to ascertain the Marchesa's state of health.

Oriana Welles was by the rail admiring the view but she remained vigilant, never distracted for long from what was occurring on deck, and I supposed that personal security must be part of her private investigator mandate.

I leaned against one of the firehose mounts from which the *Mulvane* had so forcefully announced her presence in Dover Strait and took in the panorama of the Riviera. There are few vistas more spectacular than the Alpes Maritimes as seen from the sea, still snowcapped despite the season and tumbling all the way down to the warm blue Mediterranean. The *villages perchés* stood like little white pinnacles adorning the great cathedral of the Corniche, and lower down the coast was clothed in a rich vestment of villas, columned and arcaded, and with formal gardens that flowed down to the water. Yachts under sail dotted the sea, and speedboats made of glossily varnished wood with sparkling chrome fittings, like the one the *Mulvane* carried, carved vees across the smooth sea.

There was another thrill beyond that of the view: the exhilaration of setting out on a long voyage with all the uncertainty that entails, especially on a vessel filled with people one has never met. I suppose that this is what has driven men to sea since time immemorial: the elation of leaving land far behind and casting forth into the unknown. I could sense that my fellow passengers were feeling it, too.

And there was, in my case at least, something more: the prospect of getting to know the man whose artwork was my field, and the woman whose portrait he had painted.

AFTER WE HAD LEFT LAND BEHIND THERE WAS A LIFEBOAT drill. Maritime law, it was explained, required that passengers gather at their designated assembly points in the event of an emergency, something signaled by an alarm that was rung so that we would recognize it, a sound we were to hear again in the future, this time for real.

The drill was conducted by Captain Trevelyan, who turned out to be a short, round, good-humored Welshman whose dignity was assured by the four gold stripes on his epaulets. He introduced the first officer, a Spaniard by the name of Xavier Zabala-Extarte, and the engineer, Tom Simmons, a taciturn Lancashireman. They and the captain comprised the *Mulvane*'s officers.

Trevelyan returned to the bridge and Zabala-Extarte took over the briefing. The remainder of the crew was assembled and introduced on a first-name basis only. The chief steward was Milosz (pronounced ˈ**mee**-losh), a Serbian who was a little older than the others, mid-thirties, and a professional crewman for private yachts. His mouth was set in a constant half-smile that suggested either cunning or stupidity, it was not clear which.

The other seven were all young and eager. There was an Italian chef, Ernesto, who had trained as a sous-chef at Villa d'Este. The three maids—the Italian Fabia, the Czech Aška (pronounced ˈ**ash**-car), and the Herzegovinian Džana (pronounced d-ˈ**yar**-na)—were in correct parlance combination deckhand-stewardesses and they certainly looked the deckhand part, wearing French *marinière* tops horizontally striped in the traditional blue and white, navy-colored capri pants, and white canvas deck shoes. There were two stewards—Jamys, a Manxman, and

Kustaa, a Finn—who like the maids would also perform the duties of a deckhand. Finally, there was another Lancashireman, George, a trainee mechanic who was deputy to and a relative of the engineer.

WHEN THE DRILL WAS COMPLETED THE PASSENGERS DISPERSED. I went up to the library, located on the boat deck above the main salon, intending to find something to read. But before searching the shelves I was halted by what faced me on the far wall: a painting. As with the Exeter portrait, Adelina Pallavicini was the subject and, again as with the Exeter portrait, it immediately brought to mind another famous painting, in this case, Klimt's *Portrait of Adele Bloch-Bauer* at the Neue Galerie in New York.

I knew instantly that I was looking at a masterpiece.

It was a large painting, as big as could be hung there, about four by six feet. I went to the middle of the room, the best distance from which to take it all in. As with the Klimt, the subject seemed to arise from a whirling metallic maelstrom, but here rendered in shades of silver rather than gold. Adelina was cast as a stately shimmering creature, at once both sensual and remote, someone still human but not unacquainted with gods—a high priestess of Apollo perhaps, or a prelapsarian Eve. The clothing helped suggest the first allusion: she wore the flowing classical robe of a Greek goddess whose swirling folds mimicked the surrounding tumult.

I stepped up to inspect it.

"I wouldn't get too close; I think it's poisonous."

I turned to find Urquhart standing in the doorway behind me. I had not heard him come up the stairs; he must have been forward on the bridge for the departure, perhaps conferring with the captain, and noticed me on his way back aft.

"Poisonous?"

"Yes. It contains mercury. That's how I was able to get that peculiar glister: I've figured out a way to size pure mercury into tiny globules in the oil, although whether it lasts or not remains to be seen, especially with all this shaking at sea. I'll give you the technical details later, if you like."

"I should tell you right away that my boss, Sir Richard Gibbons, would never forgive me if I didn't explore the possibility of acquiring this work."

"Sir Dickie? How is the old fellow?"

"You know him?"

"I did, many years ago—he used to lecture at the RCA. But as for the painting, I'm afraid that it's not for sale: it is to be a gift."

"For whom?"

"The subject. I'm giving a welcome-aboard present to each of the women passengers, and this is to be Adelina's. I remembered just now that I'd neglected to cover the thing and was hoping to do so before anyone happened upon it, but I see I'm too late."

"Welles thinks that you've never met any of the guests."

"Nor have I. Adelina I've seen, but not met."

"What are you going to call it?"

"Call it? *Portrait of Adelina Pallavicini-Giustiniani*, I suppose."

"Two Adeles?"

"Huh?"

I noted the similarities with the Klimt.

"You're right," he admitted after having considered the matter for a moment. "It frankly never occurred to me, but now that you point them out the parallels are obvious. And yes, two Adeles—that would never do. Any ideas?"

"For a title?"

"Yes."

"How about *Lustration*?"

"*Lustration*?"

"It's the word I thought of the moment I laid eyes on the painting. I don't know exactly what it means, but for me it conjures up an image of being awash in lush waves of light."

"The washing part is true enough, but a *lustratio* is actually an ancient Roman rite used as a purification ritual, like cleansing the scene of a murder—Livy describes it in a passage I had to translate when I was sitting for my Mods. Of course, the word is derived from *lux*, Latin for light, and I suppose that in a sense it represents what I was trying to achieve: to invoke otherworldliness with light, but light can never be captured, except by reflection, hence the mercury."

So the painting was another Catoptrographic, I realized, one in which the nebulous gray gauze of the earlier works was replaced by a glittering silver glaze. Perhaps it was the culmination of a curious one-person art movement—an end-point to which his purpose had always been directed, even if only subconsciously, steadily pursuing his own path and ignoring the rest of the art world. I could feel the stirrings of a new academic paper, one in which I would play the role of Ruskin to Urquhart's contentious, reclusive, and half-mad Turner.

"But in ancient Rome," Urquhart added, "the rite always included a propitiatory offering."

"You mean a sacrifice?"

"Yes. A pig, or a ram, or a bull: sometimes all three. Occasionally, in times of great peril, men."

"If Betelgeuse blows up, then I guess we all might qualify."

"Indeed, if ever there was a time to seek favor from the gods I suppose it's now. So, *Lustration* it will be. Excuse me, but I must join the other guests." And with that, he left.

I resumed looking for a book, though it was hard to concentrate under the gaze of that glorious presence above me. Meanwhile, I reviewed the conversation with Urquhart.

The story that the work was a gift was probably true, as far as it went. But gift alone does not account for the creation of a masterpiece, nor a new material technique with which to make it. And neither did it explain how many years previously he had painted this same woman whom he had supposedly never met.

XIII

THE CASUAL SUPPER THAT FIRST NIGHT AT SEA CONSISTED of typical Mediterranean fare: olives; salade niçoise; grilled artichokes; sardines; humus; marinated octopus; peppers; several cheeses; flatbread with olive oil in which to dip it; pitchers of wine to wash it all down. This satisfied everyone but Verkhovsky, who complained that, being "virile man," he required red meat. Aška dutifully went to the galley and returned with a platter of bresaola slices most of which Verkhovsky managed to consume before loudly declaring that they were too salty and pushing the plate contemptuously aside. I decided to finish them and Rasputina Quantrill joined me: she must have felt embarrassed for Aška, too. Then, having discovered that the wine he had been drinking all afternoon was prosecco, which he derided as "poor man's champagne," Verkhovsky switched to straight vodka, which he slurped loudly and liberally. He inspected the bottle's label. "Polish," he declared. "Russian is better, in vodka and all other things, too." Skyscraper number one, the Polish-born Marta, remained impassive in the face of this denigration of her homeland, and I suspected that it was not the first time she had heard it.

I felt like tossing the fellow overboard. Instead, I took myself and my plate into the main salon for some relief.

Everyone else was still out on deck to savor the sunset; I had the room to myself. Piano music came from a player hidden somewhere, so clear that it must have been modern equipment rather than the old gramophone that would have fitted with the 1930s theme—a necessary concession, I supposed. The salon was the largest compartment in the ship, handsomely appointed with comfortable armchairs and sofas, side tables to rest a glass or coffee cup, and in one corner a card table topped in green baize.

A navigation station was fitted to the after bulkhead, a place from which guests could follow the yacht's progress without disturbing the crew. Mounted on the wall above was a chronometer that was the official time on board, no matter what anyone's watch might claim. There was a thick paper chart depicting the western basin of the Mediterranean. Our passage from Monaco was marked in pencil: we were headed for the Balearic Islands.

The piano piece ended. I waited for it to go to the next track, but instead I heard the turning of a page.

I went forward. There was a screen, rendered in mirrored glass patterned in a rectilinear style recalling Frank Lloyd Wright, separating the main salon from the dining room. Behind this, I found two interesting things: an upright piano in glossy black lacquer ingeniously fitted into the space, located here so that it could be heard in either room, and sitting on the piano stool was Bébé Nikolaishvili, brows crossed while staring fiercely at the sheet music.

She looked up at me, no less fiercely.

"*Le Cochon*. Him makes me infurious. Poor Marta."

The accent was thick and the grammar creative, but the meaning was clear. I generally try not to get involved in other people's affairs, but if we were to be confined together aboard a 185-foot motor yacht for three months it seemed unavoidable.

"I must say that neither of you seems particularly happy."

"Happy? Ha! That is a word only you Westerners use. It is to us unmeaning. Happy? Pfft!" She clicked her fingers in the air dismissively, like a gypsy. Actually, she looked like a gypsy, and I was again brought back to the Pre-Raphaelites, or at least their French equivalents, for Bébé bore a remarkable resemblance to Maria Latini, the gypsy-like model who posed for Regnault's striking *Salomé* that hangs in the Met.

"Unmeaning?"

"We don't look for happy, we only want free."

"Aren't you free now?"

She rolled her eyes: I was exceptionally stupid.

"I tell you facts, yes? Marta and me are same, born under boots. Only hope we have for normal life is to get to West."

"Since Marta was born in Poland, can't she go anywhere in the E.U.?"

"Marta Polish but not born in Poland. Marta says born in Poland, but not true. She was born in Grodno. Grodno once Polish, city where a great Polish king lived, but that ended with Second World War. Grodno now in Belarus, just fifteen kilometers from Polish border, but could be fifteen thousand. Byelorussians are worse than Russians; they are Russian lapdogs. So, Marta is Pole forced to live under people who despises Poles. I am same."

"You're Polish, too?"

She rolled her eyes again. At least I did not get a dismissive finger snap this time.

"I am Georgian. I come from a town in South Ossetia. In 2008, Russians invade South Ossetia. So, Russians now on top, Georgians now under Russian boot."

"Yet here you both are."

"Temporary visa, with renewal depends on *Le Cochon*."

"I see."

"No, you *say* you see and you *think* you see. But is impossible because you are born in West. To really understand, you have to live..." She paused, searching for the word.

"Repressed?"

She shook her head.

"Intimidated?"

She shook her head again.

"Downtrodden?"

She shook her head a third time and then snapped her fingers in triumph, having arrived at the right word.

"Humiliated," she said. "In West, you do not understand what it is to live every day humiliated."

THAT EVENING, Betelgeuse exploded.

XIV

THE SUPERNOVA SHONE LIKE A HIGH-INTENSITY DISCHARGE beam, bright enough to cast shadow, despite the sunny day. It flickered a little, as if a hole was being burned through the canopy of sky by some cosmic welder. It was not especially large, just several times broader than normal star size—a finger held at arm's length could cover it—but the thing was unmissable, dazzlingly luminous, vivid enough to require sunglasses to stare at comfortably.

Breakfast was ignored, at least by those lately arrived on deck, until they first had their fill of this new celestial apparition.

The day was windless and the sea uncharacteristically calm, flat as a pond, as if the advent of the supernova had halted weather itself.

The sense of otherworldliness invoked by the altered appearance in the sky was reinforced by the altered appearance of the passengers— today was the first day for us to discard our modern clothes and dress in the apparel with which we had been provided. I wore twill trousers and a shirt with the sleeves rolled; Gilbert and Wu had opted for linen suits. The women were fetching in their outfits: Tess Lysett looked as fresh as a newly plucked flower in a floral print dress; Adelina had opted for the Katherine Hepburn look: high-waisted trousers and plain white shirt under a navy-blue jacket; Rasputina Quantrill topped off her attire with a jaunty broad-brimmed hat, something she wore with an appearance of practiced ease that would have made her actress mother proud.

Eventually even the remarkable becomes secondary, especially when the stomach is involved, and we soon forewent observation of Betelgeuse in order to eat. Breakfast was served at an outdoor table set up under an awning behind the deckhouse. There was a buffet of fruit and pastries laid out on the dining room table, but Džana offered to make me a cooked breakfast, saying that she had purchased the eggs fresh in the Cours Saleya yesterday morning, and since this might be the last day of guaranteed non-cosmic-irradiated produce I opted for a full English breakfast.

The Marchesa was the last on deck—apart from Verkhovsky, who had drunk so much the previous evening that I doubted we would see him before noon—and she looked particularly impressive, emerging from the deckhouse in a high-necked Edwardian-era day dress complete with lace gloves, parasol, and pearls. She glided along the deck to her usual spot right aft like a ship under full sail.

"No cane, madame," Urquhart remarked after having bid her good morning, although she had used the folded parasol for the same function. "I think the sea air is doing you good."

"You must remember that I was once a worker in my father's shipyard," she responded, pleased with the compliment. "Ships are a natural habitat for me." Fabia, the Italian stewardess, was soon by her side, quietly conversing in their native tongue before disappearing toward the galley to fetch the Marchesa's breakfast.

Conversation fell to the new appearance in the sky.

"How long will it last?

"They say several months."

"Did anyone see it happen?"

"The bridge crew must have and they would have logged it—I'll ask later."

"Is it dangerous to look at directly?"

"Apparently not, according to an article I read."

"But nevertheless," Wu interrupted, "please wear sunglasses, and even then do not stare at it for too long."

"Are you able to photograph it?" This last question was directed at my cabinmate, who had already brought his equipment up on deck.

"I'm going to give it a try," Shotter said, "but I frankly don't know how they'll turn out."

"What's the program for today, Mr. Urquhart?"

"We'll spend today and tomorrow at sea. I thought we'd start the voyage with a long first leg to give everyone time to settle into the routine of shipboard life before we make landfall."

"Where will that be?"

"The Balearic Islands."

"Where are they?"

"Off Spain. They're Spanish. The three big ones are Minorca, Mallorca, and Ibiza."

"Ibiza," Rasputina said. "I've heard of that one."

"And that's the one we're headed for. If all goes well, two mornings from now you will wake up to find that we have anchored off Es Vedrà, a small but spectacular island rising like a mountain from the sea off the southwestern tip of Ibiza. The island is currently uninhabited, but supposedly it was the home of the Sirens whose song Odysseus contrived to hear by having himself tied to the mast while his crew plugged their ears with beeswax."

"Oh, how marvelous to be tied to a mast," Tess blurted out, before realizing that the remark had not come out as she intended, after which she looked down at her plate and turned pink.

"What shall we do there?"

"The water is pristine, excellent for swimming and snorkeling. The island itself is a national park brimming with flora and fauna, so the speedboat will land those who wish to go and explore. And there are many deserted beaches, perfect for sunbathing."

"Picnics ashore?"

"Of course."

"Sounds perfect."

"Then that's the plan. Forty-eight hours from now, we will have made our first landfall."

It was not to be.

I HAD ALREADY NOTICED THE PASSAGE OF THE CHIEF STEWARD, Milosz, up to the boat deck and then forward toward the bridge, not in the relaxed manner of someone going about their routine duties but with the purposeful urgency of a person who has a problem to report.

A minute later Captain Trevelyan came down with Milosz trailing behind.

"Ladies and gentlemen," he began, "I'm sorry to interrupt your breakfast, but I must ask all of you an important question: has anyone seen Mr. Verkhovsky this morning?"

A few people said no; most simply shook their heads.

"Miss Domaradzka? Miss Nikolaishvili?"

But neither of the nieces had seen him since they retired last night, heading to bed while Verkhovsky remained at the bar.

Trevelyan turned to Urquhart.

"Milosz went to check on Mr. Verkhovsky just now. He is not in his cabin and the head was unoccupied." Milosz nodded in affirmation, as if to assure us that Trevelyan was not making it up. "I regret, sir, that it will be necessary for the passengers to muster at emergency stations while the crew conducts a thorough search—we may have to declare a man overboard."

"Yes, of course, captain—go ahead and do whatever you need to."

Trevelyan turned to Milosz. "Fetch the first officer, would you?"

Milosz nodded and went forward while the captain returned to the bridge. A moment later the emergency alarm sounded and we dutifully gathered at the muster point, not far from where we had all been sitting beforehand.

No one said a word.

The search was made; Verkhovsky was not on board.

The *Mulvane* immediately reversed course and increased speed to the maximum that she could sustain. What had until now been a gentle passage across a placid sea suddenly became a rivet-rattling race to find Verkhovsky. A lookout with binoculars climbed the mast to the crosstrees, the highest accessible point on the ship.

The first officer, Zabala-Extarte, came and questioned us, trying to determine the last time that Verkhovsky had been seen by anyone on board. Predictably, Marta and Bébé were the last two passengers to have done so. When they left there was only one other person present, Kustaa, the Finnish steward, who was serving behind the bar. Zabala said he had already been questioned: Kustaa had been released at about 11:15 P.M. by Verkhovsky, who intended to continue his assault on the vodka bottle alone.

The alarm was raised with the authorities and not long afterward a Marine nationale helicopter came swooping over us—the big French naval base at Toulon was not far away, and so they had been the first to respond.

But it was the *Mulvane* that found Verkhovsky, aided by the supernova. It was mid-afternoon by then, and Betelgeuse was low in the western sky. The shallow angle cast anything floating on the surface into shadowed relief.

Verkhovsky made no acknowledgment of our approach. Kustaa dived over the side with a lifeline. He briefly examined Verkhovsky and then turned to us and shook his head before securing the line for recovery. The accommodation ladder was lowered and the body was hauled on board.

XV

I WOULD COME TO KNOW KIRILL VERKHOVSKY BETTER IN death than in life.

After recovering his body, the *Mulvane* headed not for nearby Toulon but instead more distant Marseilles—the Marine nationale made clear by radio that it was now purely a civilian matter. Marseilles made sense: it is the major French port on the Mediterranean and capital of the Provence-Alpes-Côte d'Azur region, therefore where the administrative officials with whom we would deal would be located. Arrangements were made to be berthed alongside and met on arrival by the appropriate authorities, but meanwhile we had a five-hour passage into port.

The corpse was taken below to the first officer's cabin, away from the passengers' part of the ship, but the awareness that there was a body on board cast a pall over proceedings—even dead, Verkhovsky was an oppressive presence. Afternoon tea had been forgotten and the formal dinner was abandoned. We made do with sandwiches.

The passage was uncomfortable in more ways than one. The harsh offshore wind that in the northern Mediterranean often blows down from the mountains of a late afternoon suddenly picked up—known here as the mistral, since we were off France, but the tramontana if we had instead been in Spanish waters, or the bora if in the Adriatic. The captain explained that, given the circumstances, he could not slow the ship as he normally would, and so we drove on into the disturbed water at speed, pitching and bucking. There was little interest in even the sandwiches.

I went up to the library. The *Lustration* was now covered by a black cloth, a mournful coincidence—it seemed like a Victorian-era funereal gesture to acknowledge the fact of a death on board. I was alone at first, but then Dr. Wu and Oriana Welles came in. They were looking not for books but for me.

"Dr. Wu is going to perform a medical examination of the body," Welles stated without preamble.

"It's necessary in order to issue a death certificate," Wu added.

"Won't the French do that?"

I had directed the question to Wu, but it was Welles who answered.

"They will no doubt perform an autopsy, which is routine for any non-natural death. However, if a death certificate has already been issued then there will be no need for them to do so a second time, unless of course they choose to dispute the original."

I understood: she wanted to forestall any potential complications by presenting the authorities with a fait accompli. What I did not understand is what it had to do with me.

"I'll be acting as a witness," Welles continued, "but I don't speak French." I was starting to get it now. "There are two French speakers on board besides yourself, Lady Adelina and Tess Lysett, both young and female, and so neither should be present at the examination of a dead body."

"You'll be there. You're young and female."

"But older than they are, Evans, plus you forget that I'm a member of the Cato Club, and therefore by rule male."

Dr. Wu was puzzled by this last and no longer looked inscrutable.

"Sure, I'll do it," I said, although I doubted that an examination of a dead body would have distressed the imperturbable Adelina, and it probably would have delighted Tess Lysett. "But I should warn you that my French is schoolboy-level only."

"That's all we need," Welles said, and I realized that she wanted it that way: I could communicate competently at a low level only, and so lack of fluency in conversational French would discourage too deep a questioning in that language. I could not help but admire the smooth efficiency of this not-quite-so-young pseudo-male private investigator.

WELLES LED US FORWARD ALONG THE BOAT DECK AND THEN down into the crew's quarters, normally off-limits to guests. There, the trappings of luxury were stripped away to lay bare the bones of the ship: steel ribs, metal deck, and unconcealed ventilation ducting. It was very cramped, almost claustrophobic.

Most of the crew berthed in bunks located in common mess decks right forward; only the engineer and first officer had cabins of their own. The three of us barely fit into the latter's—I suppose I should say there were four of us, since the bunk was already occupied by the earthly remains of Kirill Verkhovsky, lying prone on a layer of black plastic garbage bags, still dressed, but whose huge white belly stretched the one remaining shirt button to breaking point. Perhaps the long immersion had bloated him beyond his already abundant volume.

Dr. Wu opened his black doctor's bag and pulled from it not a medical instrument but a cell phone.

"Miss Welles returned it to me for the examination," he said, answering my surprised look. "I will use it to record my impressions as I proceed."

He turned on the voice recording application and began by stating the time and date, location, the names of those in attendance, and then proceeded with the post-mortem examination.

"The deceased is Mr. Kirill Verkhovsky, a passenger aboard the Motor Yacht *Mulvane*, known to and positively identified by all present. He is a white male, fifty-seven years old, morbidly obese, approximately 160 centimeters in height and 110 kilograms in weight."[*]

He took a note from his pocket and referred to it for the next part of the commentary.

---

[*] 5' 3"/240 lbs [Ed.]

"The body was recovered from the sea at 15:20 Central European Summer Time in a position determined by GPS coordinates as being 42.54 degrees North and 6.46 degrees East. The Commanding Officer of the *Mulvane*, Captain James P. Trevelyan, has stated that this position corresponds to that of the *Mulvane* at approximately 5:10 this morning and, given the calm wind and sea conditions since then, plus the limited tidal range of the Mediterranean, it is his professional opinion that this position can be assumed to be at or close to where Verkhovsky went overboard. Verkhovsky was last seen alive at 23:15 the previous evening by the steward acting as bartender, Mr. Kustaa Hämäläinen. Verkhovsky had been drinking alcohol since late morning of that day, and he was considered by Hämäläinen to be intoxicated, a view shared by his fellow passengers, including those present." Wu gave a little interrogatory tilt of the head, to which Welles and I both nodded in assent. "The body is dressed in the same clothing that Verkhovsky was wearing when last seen alive and exhibits no obvious signs of damage. We will now undress the cadaver and bag the clothing."

Welles and I lent a hand, and we were soon done. If Verkhovsky without socks was an unpleasant sight, Verkhovsky without anything at all after ten hours floating in the sea was hideous. Wu took out a stethoscope and spent a few minutes listening through it while tapping Verkhovsky's chest.

"Auscultation and palpation reveal pleural fluid accumulation. Thoracic distention characteristic of emphysema aquosum. There is no evidence of plume, but this is consistent with the assumption of a long water immersion post-mortem."

Wu replaced his stethoscope and took a loupe from his bag. He used the instrument to examine Verkhovsky's eyes, lifting the lids one at a time and peering at what lay beneath.

"Considerable ocular subconjunctival hemorrhage. Evidence of mild predation and scavenging by aquatic organisms in the ocular cavities, otherwise unremarkable."

Wu delved again into his bag, this time emerging with an otoscope which he used to examine the ears. "Bilateral evidence of mastoid congestion. The tympanic membranes exhibit hemorrhage consistent with asphyxia."

He used the same instrument on the nose.

"Rhinoscopic examination reveals perforations in the vestibule and anterior septum of a type indicating the habitual use of powdered cocaine, otherwise unremarkable."

He next checked inside the mouth.

"Minor predation and scavenging by aquatic organisms in the oral cavity, which otherwise appears grossly unremarkable."

Wu then did a general external examination of the body, rolling it first one way and then the other. Verkhovsky's back had broad reddish bruising across it, not easy to see with all the body hair. The doctor spent a long time with Verkhovsky's hands, inspecting each of the fingers one by one and carefully checking under the fingernails. Finally, he let the body flop back to its original position and continued his dictation.

"There is no evidence of gross post-mortem artifacts. There is a moderate but broad dorsal contusion that would be consistent with the body having impacted the surface of the sea back-first. There is no evidence of recent defensive wounds. However, there is mild metacarpal ecchymosis and minor abrasion of the metacarpophalangeal joints on the right hand, but the color and degree of crustation indicate that the lesions were sustained at least twenty-four hours before Mr. Verkhovsky was last seen alive."

I remembered noticing the scabbed knuckles myself when he first came aboard: Verkhovsky had been punching someone or something recently.

Wu continued the examination for another ten minutes but added nothing new, other than to note that Verkhovsky had shown no sign of "suicidal ideation"—he had not deliberately thrown himself into the sea. Wu concluded the examination by taking two fluids: a vial of blood and a sample of gastric content, the former taken not from the arm in the usual way but from the leg—the femoral vein, Wu explained—and the latter was achieved with a stomach pump, an operation that left my own stomach feeling less than comfortable.

At last, Wu put aside his equipment and ended the recording with an unequivocal statement of medical adjudication: "I find that death occurred at or about 5:10 on the morning of July 2. The manner of death was accident—specifically, falling overboard while intoxicated—and the cause of death was asphyxia by drowning."

XVI

AFTER THE MEDICAL EXAMINATION WAS COMPLETED, we made our way to the captain's cabin where Wu would write up his results—the no-modern-electronics restriction did not apply to the *Mulvane*'s officers, and Trevelyan had made his computer and printer available to the doctor.

We found the captain inside, looking distracted while puzzling over a chart and a *Nautical Almanac*, a book of astronomical tables intended for use in navigation. Wu briefed him on the results of the medical examination.

"Thank you, doctor," Trevelyan said when Wu had finished, "and I think that I can contribute some evidence of my own: I know why Verkhovsky was by the rail." He tapped a printout sitting on his desk. "We received a Notice to Mariners. Normally, these concern matters of local interest only, marker buoys being worked on, dredging operations in channels, that sort of thing. But this was a general notice warning all mariners that Betelgeuse is no longer suitable for use in celestial navigation."

"Obvious, surely?"

"One would think so, and in any case in these days of satellites nobody uses the stars anymore. However, bureaucrats must earn their keep, and so they issued this notice. The interesting thing is that the supernova is reported to have occurred at 3:06 GMT. That's 5:06 ship time. I've been doing the astronomical calculations: Betelgeuse would have just risen, bearing about 083°, and with an altitude of approximately 4°. In other words, it had just become visible to us when it exploded."

"You think Verkhovsky saw it and then went to the rail for a better look?"

"I do. Our heading at the time was 255°, which is southwesterly, and so the stern rail would have been the natural place to go, facing the supernova directly."

"A position from which, having spent the day drinking, he presumably fell over the side?"

"That would be the obvious conclusion. Not uncommon on cruise ships, I understand, though it's never happened before on the *Mulvane*."

"Would you mind writing up the astronomical details in a statement that I can give the authorities?" Oriana asked.

"Not at all. I'll print out the GPS data, too—they'll likely want that. And here's the ship's log. I closed it out and began a new one."

I picked up this last, a cloth-bound hardcover volume, and glanced through it. A notebook, evidently, like my journal but much less verbose, and here every entry began with the time.

"What exactly is a ship's log?"

"A sort of running record of the ship's activities," Trevelyan explained. "Any vessel of decent size will have one. It's maintained on the bridge by the officer on watch. Usually, it just contains position, course, and speed, noted every hour, plus any changes in weather. But it's also used to register any unusual incidents, and so as soon as we discovered Verkhovsky missing I used it as the primary record."

"It's filled out in pencil?"

"Always," Trevelyan said. "A hangover from the days when we navigated with paper charts, which of course had to be used over and over, and therefore pens were strictly forbidden on the bridge."

VERKHOVSKY'S CABIN WAS NOT AS SPLENDID AS THE stateroom occupied by the Marchesa, but it was not far short. There was a bed broad enough to have accommodated himself and the two nieces, were they so inclined. The bulkheads were paneled in blond wood with darker Art Deco borders and stylized geometric inlays. There were bedstands with drawers, more drawers under the bed itself, a wardrobe and dresser built into the aft bulkhead, and a large desk fixed to the outboard side. It had two portholes, plus a third in the adjoining head.

The desk included a small safe with a traditional rotary dial rather than the electronic keypad of a modern hotel safe. Welles immediately went to it and began dialing.

"How do you know the combination?"

"It was set to zero-zero-zero, and I'm guessing Verkhovsky hadn't changed it yet."

"Where should I start?"

"Why don't you check the drawers while I do the desk?" she suggested. "Leave everything that's obviously his on the bed and we'll pack it all into his bags when we're done."

As with my stowage, most of it was filled with items that had been provided to fit the 1930s theme, but several drawers were occupied by his own gear, distinguishable by the bad taste. The clothing was strangely threadbare for a wealthy man; maybe it was difficult to find things that fit so he just wore everything to destruction. The footwear was all loafers or sandals: no grown-up shoes for Verkhovsky. The underwear was execrable.

I heard the click of the safe opening and stopped to see what it contained. Money, mostly: big stacks of it, not just euros but also British pounds and, abundantly, U.S. dollars. There was also a passport, and Welles leafed through it with interest.

"You've seen it before, I assume?" Welles had asked for a copy of my own passport some weeks before the voyage began, and she had checked it again as part of the registration procedure after boarding.

"No," she said. "The one he gave me was Russian."

She took a photograph of the details page and then tossed it over to me. It did indeed belong to Verkhovsky: the picture was his and the personal details seemed right. The issue date—*date de délivrance*—was just three weeks ago. I looked at the front cover, black with gold lettering and a shield. The country's name was rendered in French and Arabic, but not English.

"Where's the Union des Comores?"

"Comoros Islands, in the Indian Ocean off Madagascar. Quite poor, but they have developed a lucrative revenue stream by selling citizenship to those who might find it convenient to have a second passport in addition to the one issued by their own country."

Beyond the money and passport, the safe contained nothing but jewelry. Not the nieces' jewelry: these items were big and bulky, like the pieces Verkhovsky had worn when boarding.

Welles was frowning at the safe.

"What's wrong?"

"I thought there might be something more," she said. "Let's keep looking."

She continued with the desk. I moved to the bathroom.

I checked the cabinets for bottles of drugs, imagining that someone as unhealthy as Verkhovsky would likely have been loaded with prescriptions by his physicians, but there was nothing, not even common over-the-counter analgesics like Aspirin.

But there was an abundance of aftershaves and eau-de-colognes, expensive ones conspicuously branded. Other toiletries, too, including many hair products—although otherwise hirsute, Verkhovsky was balding and had maintained the pretense of hair on the top of his head by a ferocious combover, so perhaps these products were intended to paste it down. I removed the liner from the trash can, put everything inside, returned to the main cabin, and deposited the bundle on the bed.

"Nothing of note in the bathroom," I said.

"Nor in the rest of the desk." Welles sat back, considering what she had found. "No pictures, no correspondence."

"Perhaps they're all on his phone."

"No, I checked earlier."

"How?"

"It uses a thumbprint."

Welles took up a pen and notepaper. "Let's do an inventory. You name the item; I'll write it down."

It was a tedious business, made more so by Welles' insistence on specifics: color, size, brand, and so on.

Her demand for detail soon paid off. She stopped me at the talcum powder.

"Did you say 'Old Spice'?"

"Yes."

"That's a cheap brand. But all the rest are expensive." She read them aloud. "Bulgari, Gucci, Dior *pour homme*."

"Perhaps he just liked the smell."

"Given the state of his nasal passages, he probably couldn't tell the difference. He didn't care about scent; he cared about image. Show me."

I passed her the container.

"A tin," she said.

"Is that significant?"

"Smell penetrates plastic," she said. "It doesn't penetrate metal. As long as you're careful to keep the outside clean, even a trained dog won't detect what's inside."

I was starting to get it now. She soon had it open, not the little round cap at the top, which it turned out did access talcum powder, restricted to a small sealed section just below the lid, but Welles had prized apart the whole top, which had been tightly sealed, revealing an abundance of white powder beneath, too coarse to have been talcum powder.

"Bingo," she said. "Cocaine."

XVII

I HAD IMAGINED THAT WHEN WE ARRIVED ALONGSIDE IN Marseilles that night there would be waiting for us on the wharf a jumble of emergency vehicles with their lights flashing and a team of forensic investigators anxious to get aboard. Instead, there were just four people, and none of them was in a hurry.

Two were paramedics who accompanied the meat wagon, not a real ambulance but one of those Citroën vans that are ubiquitous in France, this one painted an incongruous white. The paramedics were in relatively good humor. Perhaps they were on overtime, or if a regular shift then the occasion would at least have provided relief from the usual boredom.

The same cannot be said for the other pair, who made no effort to disguise their displeasure in having been incommoded by our arrival at such an inconvenient hour. The woman, a surly creature who seemed to be taking charge, was Madame Dubois, from the Agence régionale de santé—the health department. The other was a slight dark man who introduced himself as Lieutenant Renard, Préfecture de police des Bouches-du-Rhône, Police nationale. *Renard of the Sûreté*, I thought of him.

The bureaucrat and the policeman were invited into the library. The paramedics were taken in hand by the chief steward and followed us, but they remained standing by the door instead of sitting inside. I began by introducing myself and explaining that I had been given the duty of interpreter. Dubois looked unimpressed and Renard of the Sûreté visibly winced, much as my French master used to at Harrow.

"We can make do in English," Dubois announced, at which point Welles immediately took charge. She introduced herself and Dr. Wu. After explaining that she was acting as the ship's purser, and therefore charged with responsibility for passenger affairs, Welles got down to business.

"As I believe you may already know, the deceased is Mr. Kirill Verkhovsky, who was a passenger aboard this vessel. Here is his passport."

It was the Russian one, bright red. We had leafed through it earlier to see where Verkhovsky traveled, but it had only recently been issued and was blank. The passport was valid for just one year: this was presumably the Russians' way of keeping their people abroad on a short leash. She handed the passport to Dubois, who briefly checked the details page before passing it to the detective.

"He was last seen alive at 23:15 last evening," Oriana continued, "deeply intoxicated but still drinking, and discovered missing at 10:45 this morning. The captain immediately reversed course and notified the search-and-rescue authorities. The *Mulvane* herself found the body, which was recovered at 15:20 in a position corresponding to the location of the yacht at 5:10, a little over ten hours previously. That would make it shortly after Betelgeuse exploded, and it is assumed that Verkhovsky had gone by the stern rail to better look at the supernova. Here is the timeline and GPS position data."

This time Dubois passed the document directly to Renard without looking at it. He took out a cell phone and began tapping the screen. Oriana put her hand on the book lying on the table beside her.

"The captain also provided the ship's log covering that period, should you need it. Since we have a physician embarked, I asked Dr. Wu to perform a medical examination of the body. I should mention that Dr. Wu has extensive experience in emergency medicine, including drowning victims, from having interned as an emergency physician at Vancouver General."

The officials looked a little brighter now: twenty-five percent of Canada speaks French—they almost qualified as civilized.

"Following the examination, and given the circumstances, Dr. Wu concluded that Verkhovsky drowned after having accidentally fallen overboard at about 5:10 this morning. Here is a transcript of the medical examination, and here is a copy of the death certificate."

Dubois accepted them both without comment.

"It is of course a *provisional* death certificate," Wu humbly offered, "of the type issued at sea when facilities don't allow for a more comprehensive investigation. Your medical examiner will naturally arrive at his or her own conclusions when the autopsy is performed."

Renard looked up at this last. "Autopsy?"

"I'm afraid that I don't know the French word." Wu looked at me for help.

"*Examen médical du cadavre,*" I offered.

"I know what an autopsy is," Renard said. "What I don't know is why you think that we would perform one."

"But isn't it standard for any non-natural death?"

"Certainly, but the matter is not in our jurisdiction." He held up the cell phone on which he had been tapping so that we could see the screen. It showed a map recognizable as the Mediterranean coast of France. There was a prominent red pin in the middle of the sea to the south. "I have entered the coordinates of the position where the body was recovered and where he is presumed to have gone overboard. The nearest point of French territory is forty-five kilometers away." Renard referred briefly to the screen. "Which according to this application is twenty-eight miles—well beyond the twelve-mile territorial limit." He looked up at us again. "Furthermore, the *Mulvane* has British registration. Not French, not even European Union. Nor, given that the yacht was last in Monaco, did it set sail from a French port."

He sat back with the self-satisfied demeanor of a petty official who has found an unimpeachable excuse for doing nothing.

"But Verkhovsky lived in France," I protested. "In Villefranche-sur-Mer."

"No, monsieur, I regret to inform you that you are incorrect. Kirill Verkhovsky was legally domiciled in Russia. His status in France was not that of a resident, which would have required a *carte de séjour*. His status in France was that of a visitor, which enables stays of up to one year only."

"Still, resident or visitor—you would perform an autopsy on a tourist who died unnaturally, wouldn't you?"

"*Bien sûr*, but Verkhovsky ceased to be a visitor to France from the moment that he crossed into international waters. From an administrative viewpoint, Kirill Verkhovsky is a *Russian* national who went overboard from a *British* vessel and drowned in *international* waters. The matter has nothing to do with France."

He looked pleased, having saved the French taxpayer the cost of an autopsy and himself the bother of an investigation.

"I quite understand," Welles said. "You're perfectly correct, Lieutenant, and we will happily leave the disposition of the matter entirely to your discretion."

She looked meaningfully at the two paramedics, silently inviting him to have them go fetch the body.

"I'm afraid it is not quite so simple," Madame Dubois said. "As the lieutenant has explained, Verkhovsky has the status of *étranger*. We will of course work with the Russian consular officials and make our best efforts to contact next-of-kin to determine their wishes, but I must make clear that the French government cannot be expected to accept the body of M. Verkhovsky without adequate provision for the means of disposal, should the requirement fall to the state."

"Ah, of course. And how much would the provision amount to?"

A sum was named, the size of which made me cringe, but Welles' expression remained impassive.

"It is not a fee but a bond," Dubois added. "Any balance remaining after the matter is concluded will be refunded, *naturellement*."

"Certainly," Welles said. "Would a check drawn against a Monégasque bank suffice?

"Perfectly."

The check was duly written. At the moment it passed into the grasping clutch of Madame Dubois, Renard nodded to the paramedics, who now went with Milosz to retrieve the body.

There was more paperwork, surprisingly little considering the French reputation for bureaucracy, but after their earlier bravura display this pair had no further point to prove.

We returned with them to the brow as the paramedics were closing the van's rear doors on the remains of Kirill Verkhovsky. The mood was much lighter now, at least on the French side. There were handshakes all round, and as he held mine Renard of the Sûreté took me aside and lowered his voice.

"You know, Verkhovsky did try to gain residency status in France."

"I didn't know."

"Yes, and he wanted it quite badly—enough to have offered a substantial *douceur* to the official with whom he was dealing at the Préfecture."

"What happened?"

"His request was denied. After that, he applied for political asylum—apparently, the Russian government was pressuring for the return of both him and his offshore wealth to Moscow."

"Would asylum have been granted?"

"There was no chance of that after the attempted bribery. On the contrary, deportation proceedings had already begun."

"Deportation?"

"Yes. And it is possible that a man faced with the prospect of being forced to return to Russia after having lived in France might choose another path, yes?"

"You mean suicide?"

But the detective just opened his hands and offered a Gallic shrug, indicating that I should draw the obvious conclusion for myself.

XVIII

THE TRADITIONAL DISH OF MARSEILLES, BOUILLABAISSE, is a fish stew cooked in a single pot but consumed as two separate courses. It was when the first of these—the bouillon, served as a soup—was brought to our table that Oriana Welles revealed why she had suggested that we dine ashore, away from the other passengers.

"There's a security camera above the front door of my offices in Mayfair," she said. "The coverage extends to the other side of Half Moon Street."

"So you saw me?"

"Nice trick with the flowers. I liked the primroses particularly."

"At least I don't have to pretend that you're a lawyer anymore."

"But I am a lawyer."

"I checked with the Bar Association. They don't know you."

"That's your American upbringing deceiving you. In Britain, not all lawyers are called to the Bar, only barristers, the advocates who argue cases in court. But the briefs they argue from are prepared by solicitors, which is what I am. The professional organization for solicitors is not the Bar but the Law Society, of which I am a fully paid-up and qualified member."

We were sitting outside by the waterfront in the Vieux-Port, cafe-lined and still bustling despite the late hour. Across the water, the great symbol of the city, la Bonne Mère, rose like a citadel atop la Garde. It was floodlit, something still effective because Betelgeuse had not yet risen. A gibbous moon hung low in the east. I could hear the sound of halyards tapping against masts as boats gently rocked at their moorings. A soft breeze wafted off the water and the broth, for some reason always served scalding hot, had now cooled sufficiently for consumption. I took a slice of toast and began rubbing it with a peeled garlic clove before slathering it with rouille, the bright saffron-flavored paste that is the traditional accompaniment to the first course.

"Saunders Walker Investigations doesn't sound like a legal firm."

"Nor is it, but I was not made for the dreary business of preparing legal briefs and of course an investigative agency frequently requires the services of a lawyer."

"Are you saying that you were hired by Urquhart to conduct an investigation?"

"Not exactly. My firm was initially engaged simply to track down names on a list—the passenger list. Following that, the assignment was to inquire into their present circumstances, arrange for them to be invited as guests, and then oversee the cruise itself."

"Nice work if you can get it."

"Until this morning."

"Accidents happen—you can't let it spoil the show."

"If it *was* an accident."

I put down my spoon. "I was wondering if anyone was going to bring up the other possibility. I have to tell you that Renard of the Sûreté took me aside before he left this evening. He told me that Verkhovsky wasn't going to have his French visitor's permit renewed. Just the opposite: they'd begun deportation proceedings against him, and he was going to end up being sent back to Russia. It seems that Verkhovsky was destined to go from a villa in Villefranche-sur-Mer with nieces on tap to a Soviet-style apartment block in some dreary Moscow suburb where no doubt his only female companionship would be the surly old babushka watching his every move."

Welles looked at me in the manner of an otherwise patient teacher confronted with a particularly dull child.

"Suicide? Verkhovsky? The last thing on Verkhovsky's mind was suicide."

"But he was going to be sent back to Russia."

"I am well aware of Verkhovsky's circumstances—I'm the one who did the background check, remember?"

"Having to go live in Russia would make me suicidal."

"Verkhovsky had no intention of returning to Russia. Think, Evans: does a man contemplating killing himself acquire a no doubt very expensive Comoros passport just three weeks beforehand?"

I had forgotten about the passport, but the need to reply was cut short by the arrival of the second course, the fish itself. You can tell the quality of a bouillabaisse by the ugliness of the fish: the really good ones are made with the most hideous of sea creatures: scorpion fish, conger, monkfish, all served cut into chunks but still bone-in, and sea urchins slit open and emasculated immediately before serving. Judging by the gruesome array on the platter before us, this was going to be a very fine bouillabaisse. I waited until the wine glasses were topped up before resuming our conversation.

"Okay, there was the new passport. But maybe he'd just come to the end of his tether. He'd been drinking all afternoon."

"Verkhovsky drank every afternoon."

"So what then?"

"Must I spell it out?"

"Huh?"

"Murder, Evans—are you normally this slow, or have you just been stupefied by all this food?"

"Murder? You were there when Wu did the medical examination: there wasn't a shred of evidence to suggest such a thing."

In response, Welles opened her bag and extracted a small round tin which she passed to me.

"Be careful," she warned.

I gently unscrewed the lid, but there was nothing inside.

"It's empty."

"No, it's not."

I looked more closely.

"Okay, there's a little grit or something."

"Or something. Specifically, wood fibers."

"So?"

"They came from underneath Verkhovsky's fingernails."

"What?"

"And if you examine the rail at the rear of the main deck you'll find several very faint scratches—faint, but fresh. Not something that someone committing suicide would leave."

"Wu said there was nothing under Verkhovsky's fingernails."

"Of course not."

"Wu lied?"

"Oh, you really are extraordinarily obtuse. I *removed* the matter from beneath Verkhovsky's fingernails before Wu conducted the examination—you can't imagine that I would have allowed him to inspect the body without having first inspected it myself."

"You tampered with evidence in an investigation?"

"What investigation? You heard Renard: there is no investigation with which to tamper."

"But Wu issued a certificate saying that death was accidental."

"Which is as I intended."

"Why?"

"Tell me, what would have happened if instead of 'accident' the finding for the manner of death had been 'could not be determined,' which is what they put down when foul play can't be ruled out?"

"I don't know."

"Would the French have investigated?"

"No. They told us they have no jurisdiction."

"Correct. But Captain Trevelyan would still have been obliged to have the matter officially followed up, would he not? So what would he have done?"

"I'm not sure."

"He would have consulted with the charter company—his bosses. They would have had three options: one, do nothing and continue the charter, but apart from anything else doing nothing could put them in a position of potential legal liability, and they wouldn't have risked that."

"Agreed."

"Option two: since Verkhovsky was a Russian citizen, contact the Russian authorities, who would no doubt have demanded that the *Mulvane* immediately proceed to port and then sent down a team from their consular offices."

"And they would have investigated?"

"No, they wouldn't have had the necessary expertise, and in any case Russian officials never do anything on their own initiative—it is in their character to seek orders from above. The matter would have been referred to Moscow, and the response would be for the Russians to send out a forensic team to investigate. That would have taken weeks, probably weeks just to get visas, given how out of favor the Russians are these days."

"What's the third option?"

"Britain. Since the *Mulvane* has British registration, and indeed the charter company is also British, then that would have been the obvious path to take. Essentially, dump the whole matter into the hands of the U.K. authorities and let them deal with the Russians and so forth."

"The *Mulvane* would have had to sail back to England?"

"Gibraltar, more likely. But Urquhart's summer cruise would have been over."

"Inconvenient, certainly, but hardly the end of the world."

"Given the supernova, the end of the world is at hand anyway. But I think you're failing to draw an obvious conclusion."

"What?"

"If the summer cruise were to terminate, what would the guests do?"

"Go home, I suppose."

"Exactly. They would scatter, as would the crew. All of the suspects would be gone."

I saw where she was heading.

"But by having 'accident' on the death certificate the cruise continues, and therefore all the potential suspects are still gathered together, effectively imprisoned on board and available to be investigated."

"Precisely." I had to hand it to Welles, she thought through things ahead of time. "I should also point out that the document Dr. Wu completed was technically a 'Provisional Certificate of Death on the High Seas.' Legally, it is exactly that, *provisional*, and therefore subject to amendment."

"But the matter still has to be investigated."

"Certainly, but where shall we find an investigator?"

She pantomimed looking under the plates. I was beginning to get it now.

"Ah, you mean you."

"Yes, I mean me. And you."

"Why me?"

"Two reasons. Firstly, you're the only person on board, apart from Urquhart, who knows who I really am. Secondly, you are male. Men speak differently to other men than they do to women. You have to talk to all of the men, but casually—we can't let anyone know that there are suspicions about Verkhovsky's death. And take your time: we're all going to be together for the next three months, so there's no need to rush things."

"And ask them what? 'Hey, did you pop Verkhovsky?'"

"The immediate aim is to find out where they were and what they were doing between 11:15 last night and 5:10 this morning. The secondary aim is to fill in the bigger picture: why did they get invited in the first place? I buy Urquhart's claim that he has never met any of the guests before, but there has to be a connection of some kind: he didn't just pick names out of thin air. Yours we know—he was the subject of your doctoral dissertation. Franklin Gilbert's we know: he wants to acquire Urquhart's newspaper. Tess Lysett's we know: her father is an old school chum. That leaves another eight unaccounted for, including Verkhovsky himself. We need to know the connections."

"I might have one already." I explained about the Exeter portrait, and that therefore Adelina was known to Urquhart long before this voyage, back when she was still a teenager.

Welles thought about this for a while before responding. "That tells us that the connection goes back a long way, but it still doesn't explain what it is."

"Maybe it's Adelina who's his secret daughter, not Rasputina Quantrill."

"Perhaps they both are. But leave the women to me; they won't tell you anything."

I filed away this offhand remark without comment and looked forward to the day when I could reveal some juicy nugget from one of the women that Welles had missed.

"You know, it's likely that Verkhovsky simply did fall overboard in a drunken stupor," I said. "He probably clutched at the railing as he fell, hence the wood fibers."

"Maybe, and if so no harm has been done. But watch your step: if it was a murder and the killer thinks you're investigating, then you might end up falling overboard, too."

XIX

T HE *MULVANE* SAILED FROM MARSEILLES IN THE AFTERNOON
with the sun and the supernova both blazing above in a pure azure
sky. We made passage past those somber fortified islands: Fort de
Ratonneau, Batterie du Sémaphore, and the Château d'If where Dumas's
Count of Monte Cristo learned of men's duplicity the hard way.

His lonely time in that forbidding pile made me wonder about
Verkhovsky's lonely last hours, specifically the period between
dismissing Kustaa and disappearing over the side. Verkhovsky was the
sort of man who craved an audience; for him to have released Kustaa
and deliberately sought solitude was not in character. That meant there
had to be a specific reason.

It seemed to me the most likely reason was that he was working up
courage, and the more I considered it the more I was coming around to
Renard's theory, despite Oriana's dismissal of it: a man seeing the good
life coming to an end might choose a different path. But there were other
possibilities, and I suddenly realized the most obvious of all.

I found the chief steward in the main salon.

"Milosz, was the mailbox cleared when we were in Marseilles?"

"Yes, it was done this morning before we sailed. If there's a letter you dropped in afterward, I'll make sure to have it mailed as soon as we hit Spain."

"Did you clear the mailbox yourself?"

"No, Fabia did."

Fabia was fetched. Milosz remained in the room; I would have preferred to speak to her alone but since he was her supervisor I supposed he had the right to stay.

"How many letters did you mail this morning?"

"Just two."

"Did either have the sender's name?"

"No, but one la Marchesa handed to me herself." Lady Isabella informing her friends about the dramatic happenings on board, no doubt.

"And the other?"

"I don't know who wrote it."

"Any distinguishing marks?"

"It was just an ordinary *Mulvane* envelope."

"The address?"

"I didn't look. But not France."

"How do you know?

"The postage. It was 1.65 euros: too much for France."

THERE WAS A REARRANGEMENT IN ACCOMMODATIONS SINCE there was one less passenger on board. Franklin Gilbert was offered the now-unoccupied stateroom across from Urquhart's, with either Shotter or myself to move into his vacated cabin, but Gilbert demurred, saying that two people having to shift was inefficient, and he was used to his cabin by this stage and did not want to move.

I told Shotter that he should have the stateroom because it made the most sense, given that there would be plenty of space to stow his photographic gear, but he insisted that we flip a coin instead. Rasputina Quantrill was sitting nearby and offered to fetch her lucky silver dollar for the exercise. It was duly brought and presented for our inspection, a heavy coin dated 1971 with Eisenhower's profile on the obverse, and on the reverse a depiction of an eagle alighting on the cratered surface of the then recently conquered moon, with the earth hanging conspicuously in the background.

"There were still great men about in those days," Quantrill said, "and they did great things."

I called tails but it was Eisenhower who came up.

"You get the stateroom," Quantrill said to Shotter.

"No, you do." Without waiting for a reply he called over Milosz, who had a habit of always being on hand as one supposes a good chief steward should. "Could you ask the maids to move Miss Quantrill's things into the vacant stateroom? When that's done, I'll move into her old cabin."

"Very good, sir." Milosz went off to see to it.

Rasputina regarded Shotter in appreciation. "How very gallant of you, Jack Shotter."

"Not exactly great, but it will have to do."

THE *MULVANE* TOOK ON A STRANGELY FESTIVE AIR, SURPRISING given recent events and even more surprising in the nieces who, following the demise of their benefactor, now presumably faced an uncertain future. But when I again happened upon Bébé Nikolaishvili at the piano this time she was playing not somber Rachmaninoff but what sounded like a sprightly polka. Marta Domaradzka was standing by her. She looked much less skyscraperish now that she was not required to wear exaggeratedly high-heeled shoes and without the diminutive Verkhovsky for contrast.

"That was a lively piece," I said after Bébé finished.

"Chopin. We are to make the concert for all of you, and it will be part of the program, I think."

"You play too, Marta?"

For some reason, this comment set them both laughing.

"We were students together at the Moscow Conservatory," Marta explained. "You have to already be concert-grade for admission there."

"Oh, I had no idea."

"I play the violin." She looked pointedly at the bench on which sat a violin case. "Have you ever seen an Amati?"

"I'm afraid that I don't know what an Amati is."

"You've heard of Stradivarius?"

"Yes."

"Amati is better, even if this one is Hieronymus II, not Nicolò." She opened the case, revealing the violin within. The varnish was oddly wine-colored, and to my eye the thing looked somewhat battered, but when she pulled it out, picked up her bow, and played a few brief bars of instantly recognizable Bach I was astonished, not just by the instrument—incredibly pure and incredibly piercing—but also by her obvious mastery of it.

"I'm amazed to learn that the two of you are musicians. How is it that...I mean, how come you're not playing professionally?"

Bébé held up a hand, which I took as a signal excusing my want of tact.

"It is only very top students who will have the solo career, you understand, and so only very top students who will escape Russia. Marta and me, we not very top. If we stay in conservatory, we would be destined for roles in orchestras, probably in regional cities, like Nizhny Novgorod." She crinkled her nose at the prospect.

"Or Novosibirsk," Marta added, "'Pearl of the Permafrost,'" a comment that caused them both to burst into laughter anew.

I understood now: it had been a choice between doing what they wanted but in a place they despised, or escaping to the West but at the price of Verkhovsky—and they had chosen the West.

"How long have you had the Amati?"

"About twenty minutes."

"Twenty minutes?"

"Mr. Urquhart gave me the Amati this morning."

Urquhart had mentioned that he was giving the women welcoming presents—I had not been sure at the time if this included the nieces, but apparently it did.

"And me, he gives me piano," Bébé added.

"But how will you get it ashore?"

"No, not this one. He said that after cruise I may go to the Fazioli showroom in Milan, just by La Scala, and he will buy for me any piano I choose. I will have my own Fazioli!" She sounded a few triumphant chords on the keyboard in emphasis. "But instruments is not all that Mr. Urquhart has give Marta and me."

Bébé reached into her bag and pulled out a passport, which she passed to me. It was a Russian one, red like Verkhovsky's.

"I thought you were from South Ossetia?"

"Pah, no one recognizes South Ossetia, so we all have Russian passports, which only slightly less worse. Open to new stamp."

I opened it to the new stamp and spent a few moments in examination. It was a *carte de séjour*, the French permanent residency status of the type that Verkhovsky had tried unsuccessfully to arrange for himself. It was dated today.

"I have one, too," Marta said. "Now, we will play in orchestras in Europe. We will be happy."

I was astounded: how had Urquhart arranged all this in a day?

"You remember our conversation from before?" Bébé asked.

"Yes, of course."

"The violin and the piano, they are very generous, worth many euros. But that stamp...to me and Marta, that stamp is priceless."

I RAN INTO URQUHART COMING UP AS I WAS GOING DOWN TO my cabin.

"You've made two women very happy," I said. "And I've learned what an Amati is."

"Don't be too impressed. There were several Amatis who were luthiers in Cremona, stretching across generations. Hieronymus II is considered one of the less talented."

"It was more than just the instruments, I think."

"Ah, so they told you about the visas. Well, I'm about to make another woman happy, I hope, and I think the means may be of interest to you." He was carrying a narrow aluminum case, apparently containing another welcoming gift. "Why don't you join me?"

I accompanied him to the library where the Marchesa and Adelina stood before the portrait of the latter, evidently just unveiled.

"I ran into Dr. Evans and asked him to join us," Urquhart announced. "It was he, Lady Adelina, who named your portrait *Lustration*, and I'm sure he can give it context better than I can." Urquhart turned to the Marchesa. "And now, Lady Isabella, I hope that you will permit me to offer this small token to welcome you aboard the *Mulvane*."

Urquhart laid the case on the center table. It was broader than a briefcase but thinner, and fitted with heavy recessed locks, as if meant for the transport of historical folios of great importance. I imagined some precious item of incunabula within, or a document pertaining to her ancestors perhaps, like an ancient land grant or a patent of ennoblement signed by some Holy Roman Emperor. But when he opened the case it revealed a series of sketches.

"I believe these may be familiar to you," Urquhart said. "Indeed, it is my understanding that the artist specifically drew them for you."

He laid the drawings out across the table, four in total.

"I dare say you never expected to see them again."

"How right you are, Mr. Urquhart." She looked at them in a fair imitation of a person gazing upon something not seen for a long time. "I well remember Signor Dalí drawing them for me when I was a young girl. How very kind of you to have recovered them for me."

I was on the verge of making some exclamation of recognition when a glance from the Marchesa silenced me, lightning-fast and unnoticed by the other two.

The drawings were those same swirling rhythmical Dalí renditions of Don Quixote that she had shown me in her stateroom three days previously. Not similar; they were identical.

XX

W E DINED FORMALLY FOR THE FIRST TIME THAT EVENING. For us men, it just meant a simple dinner suit but even so there was variation: mine was regulation in cut and color; Jack Shotter wore instead a white jacket and bow tie; Franklin Gilbert's cummerbund was bright tartan; Wu outshone us all in a silken suit, dark gray just short of black, and whose coat buttoned to the neck and ended in a Mandarin collar.

"Definitely inscrutable," I said to the doctor, joining the other three on deck under the awning.

"I feel like Dr. No," he replied. "I'll continue the Fu Manchu to complete the look, although I'll have to shave it off before returning to Vancouver—it would be hazardous to my patients: they might die laughing."

"At least you aren't dressed up like a Christmas tree," Gilbert said, evidently not impressed with the colorful cummerbund.

"It's probably reversible."

"It is—I checked. But I feel obliged to wear it this way for the first night at least since Urquhart went to all the trouble. Apparently, it's Gilbert clan tartan; I didn't even know there was a Gilbert clan, let alone Gilbert clan tartan."

Jamys the Manxman approached, evidently on cocktail duty this evening.

"Dry Martini for me," Gilbert said.

"Me, too," Shotter added. "Seems the drink to have in this outfit."

It ended up being Martinis all around, and so it was to be for the remainder of the voyage: every evening we four men would gather on deck early, in advance of the women to be on hand when they arrived, and start the evening the right way: with a single very strong and well-made Martini.

The women began to come up on deck. The first to arrive were Rasputina Quantrill and Tess Lysett. Rasputina wore a shimmering gold sheath that would have been right at home at an old Hollywood party at the Chateau Marmont following a premiere of the latest Fred Astaire flick. Tess was dressed in a more restrained but no less fashionable outfit, black with violet accents, something suitable for cocktails at the Savoy when Harry Craddock was serving behind the bar. They joined us and Rasputina ordered Manhattans for them both.

"I have undertaken to educate Tess in the finer things," Rasputina explained, "beginning with the art of the cocktail."

Oriana Welles followed and she would have been denied entrance to the Cato Club in what she wore tonight: a silvery silk halter-top dress that left her back and sides bare to the waist. There were long slits up the sides to further expose flesh.

"I think the pretense of you being male may now be safely dropped," I said quietly when she came by my side.

Marta and Bébé were next and once again skyscraperish, but apart from that changed completely: gone were the sullen and bored women of before, replaced with two fresh faces eager to engage with the rest of us. Strangely, their gowns were the most conservative in cut so far, more than even the Bishop of Chichester's daughter, but perhaps they were pleased to be relieved of the requirement to wear skimpy outfits.

"Your necklace is beautiful," Marta said to Tess after fresh cocktails had been ordered. I had noticed it myself, not a full necklace but more of a stylized yoke, with one side slender but solid, ending in a single diamond-studded star, and the other a shower of diamond-encrusted threads draping over the collarbones and stretching down the décolletage.

"It's my welcome-aboard gift," the blushing Tess explained. "The style is called *la Comète*, the comet—Chanel, circa 1930."

I understood the design now: the loose cascade of diamonds was meant to be the comet's tail. But it could be interpreted in a new light: the star as Betelgeuse, and the tail as the burst of matter exploding from its supernova.

"There's also a bracelet," Tess continued, holding up a forearm to display the object around her wrist, similar in design and as glittering as the necklace. "Earrings as well, but my ears aren't pierced so I couldn't wear them."

"Did you get jewelry, too?" Shotter asked Rasputina.

"No, I got a car."

"A car! What sort?"

"A Morgan, an English sports car—have you heard of them?" Shotter shook his head. "They look like nothing else. I saw one parked out front of the Hôtel de Paris when I was walking down to board the *Mulvane*, and amid all the fancy cars vying for attention it stood out: lower than everything else by a foot, top-down, fitted with fenders and running boards and tiny doors that you could easily step over to get in— very idiosyncratic: something made for fun rather than to impress. The color scheme was striking, too: dark navy blue bodywork, mirror-finish glossy, and a bright red leather interior. Strictly a two-seater; there's not even a trunk. I thought it was a vintage car that must have been restored, but it turns out that they still make them that way, by hand, the same as they've done for decades. I mentioned seeing the car to Urquhart, thinking how well it fitted with his 1930s theme and what a pity they didn't sell them in America because it would be perfect for Beverly Hills. Anyway, he told me today that he has placed an order for a Morgan identical in specification to the car I saw, and he will have it privately imported. For once my mother will be jealous of me instead of me being jealous of her."

Between the visas and the auto order, Urquhart had had a busy day.

"Did you men get anything?"

"They've received the pleasure of your company," Urquhart replied, coming up on deck from below and having overheard the question. "And what better gift could there be?" He came aft to join us.

Like me, Urquhart was dressed in a standard dinner suit. He opted for ouzo instead of a Martini, saying that he had lived too long in Greece to change his *aperitivo* now. The drink arrived and after the first sip he turned to my former cabinmate.

"I understand that you're a diver, Mr. Shotter?"

"Yep."

"As am I. There's a spectacular submarine peak near Es Vedrà called the Aguja—it means needle. Perhaps we'll take the Zodiac and go dive on it?"

"Sure, count me in."

"Very good." Urquhart turned back to the rest of us and raised a glass. "To making our first landfall." Technically, the first *scheduled* landfall—it seemed that Marseilles was already forgotten, and the death of one of his guests had not dampened our host's spirits.

The Marchesa and Adelina emerged from the deckhouse, the last of the party to arrive. The Marchesa wore a dark high-buttoned ensemble, something that made the sight of her grand-niece beside her all the more startling. Adelina was dressed in a creamy satin gown perfectly cut to accentuate her long slender curvature. It was backless apart from some ribbons that I supposed were a structural necessity to keep the rest in place. There seemed no possibility of wearing anything beneath it: the upper part was too minimal and the lower part too tight. She wore her hair up, emphasizing the long neck and undulating vale of collarbones below.

Her arrival silenced everyone but Urquhart.

"Anything but champagne for such a vision would be a travesty," he said. Jamys went off to fetch it.

The Marchesa looked pleased with the compliment to her grand-niece but Adelina immediately changed the subject.

"I see from the chart in the main salon that our destination is no longer Ibiza. Have you changed your mind, Mr. Urquhart?"

"No, just added a quick detour on the way. We shall still explore Es Vedrà as planned, but since Betelgeuse has chosen to explode I did a little investigation while we were in Marseilles. There is a small astronomical observatory on Mallorca in the town of Costitx, and I have arranged time in it for us. I thought it might be interesting to see the supernova up close."

Urquhart had been busy, organizing not just the visas and car but an observatory as well.

"So we will get to scrutinize the agent of our doom for ourselves."

"Or perhaps our salvation."

"That hardly seems likely."

"Redemption can come in strange forms."

"As in an Apocalypse?"

"Perhaps humanity is due for one."

The champagne arrived. When we all had a fresh glass in hand our host offered a toast.

"To new beginnings," he said, and we drank to it.

Verkhovsky's name was not mentioned, neither then nor at any other time during the evening. Forty-eight hours ago, he had been with us on this same deck; now it was as if he had never existed.

THE DINING TABLE WAS OVOID, A MUCH CHUMMIER SHAPE for a large dinner party than the usual rectilinear, which excludes from easy conversation those people on your side who are not immediate neighbors. Little name cards in silver holders indicated our places, and I found myself between Jack Shotter on one side and Rasputina Quantrill on the other.

"I should tell you about the seating arrangements," Urquhart said. "Usually at a formal dinner one's neighbor is of the opposite sex, but given that we are five men and seven women it won't be possible. Also, at sea it is customary to have the same seat for the entire voyage, which is fine for a transatlantic crossing but not, I think, for a three-month Mediterranean cruise. So our seating will be random: our place cards will be mixed up each evening in that bowl on the sideboard and Milosz will take them out one at a time, assigning places around the table in the order that they are drawn. Except me: I reserve for myself the right to the head of the table."

Dinner was served: Coquilles Saint-Jacques to start, cooked in the traditional half-shells and accompanied by a crisp Chablis. Conversation turned to the welcome-aboard gifts, and I realized what a good idea it was to have presented them now, serving as a natural distraction from the events of the previous two days.

"I must say that I've never sat at a table surrounded by so many beautiful women," Wu said. "Nor so wonderfully dressed. Miss Lysett, your comet becomes you particularly."

"Thank you, doctor, but it's an unforgivable extravagance on Mr. Urquhart's part." She turned with a smile toward the head of the table. "My father will chide you for spoiling me, sir."

"Will you play your new violin for us later?" Shotter asked Marta, sitting across from him.

"Tonight, no—I must get to know it first. But later in the voyage, then yes, it would be my pleasure."

"Marta and Bébé have agreed to give us a concert in the future."

"Oh really, how wonderful."

"I hope the piano is tolerable, Miss Nikolaishvili. I asked them to have it tuned before the voyage."

"Better than tolerable, it is a Bechstein. Ravel composed on a Bechstein; so did Bartók. Scriabin and Richter preferred them. Paul McCartney played one on 'Hey Jude.'"

Bébé obviously loved pianos—the subject even improved her grammar.

URQUHART WAS NOT THE ONLY ONE WHO HAD BEEN BUSY IN Marseilles. Ernesto the chef had gone to the fish market in the early morning, and we profited from his diligence that evening. The main course was simple fillets of pan-fried Saint-Pierre washed down with a flinty Sancerre. Ernesto himself appeared while it was being served, looking sweaty and harried but also pleased: he knew that his cooking was a success.

"The Saint-Pierre is Mediterranean," he explained, "and these fish were brought in at first light today. Very fresh, so a simple Meunière preparation is best. The scallops are not a Mediterranean dish—these came from Île d'Oléron, near La Rochelle on the Atlantic coast. My thinking was that there will be plenty of Mediterranean fish to come, but the *marché aux poissons* in Marseilles is likely the best chance we will have for fresh seafood from elsewhere, and so I took advantage of the opportunity."

He was commended for his foresight and left us, smiling with pleasure. Conversation reverted to the gifts.

"Will you take the *Lustration* with you back to Montreux?" Gilbert asked Adelina.

"No, the painting will be hung in my aunt's villa in Bellagio."

"I hope that it never goes into a museum," I said. "Not even the Wentworth—it's not something I'd want people standing beside taking grinning selfies."

Gilbert nodded. "That's what I was thinking. I confess my ignorance of art, but even a philistine like me can see that it's not meant for the crowd. It's too..."

"Intimate?"

"Personal?"

But none of these suggestions seemed quite the word he was looking for, so he just shrugged his shoulders and resumed eating.

"How did you know what Adelina looked like?" Rasputina asked. The question was directed at Urquhart, but it was the Marchesa who answered.

"I provided a few family photographs."

"Oh, I thought we were all strangers—I hadn't realized that you two were already acquainted."

"We were not, we just briefly corresponded immediately prior to the voyage."

It sounded plausible, but I knew that it would have taken many months to compose and complete the *Lustration*—probably months just to get the mercurial paint right. And, in any case, recent photographs did not explain the Exeter portrait.

ERNESTO'S ABILITIES OR INSPIRATION DID NOT EXTEND TO dessert.

"We have no pastry chef embarked," Urquhart explained. "It seemed to me that we should instead make purchases from ashore, allowing us to sample the local delicacies wherever we go. I suggest we eat these in the leisurely Mediterranean fashion, not at the table but afterward with coffee where people can pick and choose as they like."

This was met with murmurs of approval and we retired to the main salon. Conversation soon picked up from where it had left off.

"Uncorrupted," Gilbert said after taking his seat, having found the right word at last. "It seems to me a painting that is too unsullied for our times."

An ungenerous observer might have assumed that Gilbert was trying to get on Urquhart's good side, but I could tell that he had given the matter serious consideration and was quite sincere. There was an ensuing silence that I decided to fill.

"A lack of affectation?" I offered. "A clarity of conception and purity of purpose?"

"I can see why you're an art historian, Evans—yes, exactly."

"The idea isn't original to me: it was what drove the Pre-Raphaelites, with whose work I think there are parallels. But why don't we hear from the artist himself?"

All eyes turned to Urquhart. He put aside his coffee cup.

"You realize that the worst person to talk about a painting is the person who painted it? If the artist had command of language he would not have needed brushes and oils in the first place. All I will say is that, in my opinion, most good art is an attempt to get at truth: the reality that lies below the shifting surfaces of things. I particularly wanted to get at that truth now, in our time of reckoning, so to speak, hence the *Lustration*."

"You wanted honesty?"

"Yes. To my sense, honesty has largely disappeared from the world. I don't just mean in the obvious ways, like social media and so on. I mean in the big picture, too. There's the rise of authoritarianism abroad, for example, strutting despots whose every utterance is a lie, and in the West an alarming erosion of the sober clear-minded citizenship necessary for any democracy to function. What was once reasonably thoughtful political debate is now just the ranting of soccer hooligans. And everywhere, the pernicious new religion called political correctness, something that has come to suppress open public discourse as effectively as an Inquisition. I am a recluse for a reason: I find that the world has become an unpleasant place, run by fools."

"'A tale told by an idiot, full of sound and fury, signifying nothing'?"

"Perhaps Shakespeare had it right."

"Yet you've chosen to re-enter the world. With strangers, no less."

"With people whom I have never personally met, true, but that is not to say necessarily unknown to me."

"How did you choose us?" Rasputina asked, with American directness. "Is there a common thread?"

"Indeed there is, but instead of my simply revealing it why don't we turn it into a game to be played during the voyage: first person to guess wins."

"Wins what?"

"Ah, that too must remain a surprise, something not to be revealed before we reach Ledos."

"Ledos?"

"The Aegean island on which I have lived for many years, and where we will conclude our voyage, at least figuratively, although the *Mulvane* will return you all to the mainland at the Piraeus."

"Are there other people on the island?"

"Not normally. Apart from weekly visits from the housekeeper and her husband—old fisherfolk from a nearby island who bring me mail and supplies—I live quite alone, but they house-sit the island during the occasions that I'm away."

"So you will resume being a recluse?"

"I don't think I've stopped. Being ensconced aboard a private yacht hardly constitutes a re-entry into the world—more a case of sampling it from a safe distance. Speaking of which, shall we sample these delicious-looking treats?"

While we were talking, three platters of pastries had been laid out on the sideboard. Each came with a menu card, explaining what they were: *calissons*, almond-and-candied-melon nougats from Aix-en-Provence; *tarte tropézienne*, an orange-flavored cream-filled cake from St. Tropez; and *navettes*, cookies that are a specialty of Marseilles and shaped like a little boat that supposedly took Mary Magdalene on a voyage to that city.

I helped myself to the *navettes*. I noticed Adelina cut a large slice of the cake, but after returning to her seat she placed it on the side table by her great-aunt. The conversation resumed after people had settled back down.

"I quite agree with our host," the Marchesa said, pausing with a fork in hand to pick up on the previous topic. "I blame poor upbringing, both at home and at school, and so I have tried to see to it that my niece is at least well educated."

"Where do you go to school, Lady Adelina?"

"Just Adelina, please. The school I go to is the Institut Lavaux."

"What do you study there?"

"Economics, but in a very broad and liberal sense. It was once a finishing school. When such places died out they usually became boarding schools for secondary education, but Lavaux took a different path. It became a tertiary institution, still strictly girls only and there remains a little of the finishing school about the place—there are even deportment classes, although not called that—but academically, Lavaux models itself on the London School of Economics."

"In my day, it was enough to work on the shop floor as a grounding for business," the Marchesa added, "as I was required to do in my father's shipyard. Today, that is no longer the case. Now, it's money that matters, and one must master the art of managing it if one is to succeed in the world."

"I think that's precisely the mechanism by which the authoritarian states are outmaneuvering the democracies," Urquhart said, "by money.

They create a surplus, something made possible by the subjugation of their own populations, and then use that surplus to purchase Western assets—the Chinese are the carpetbaggers of our time. I hope, Dr. Wu, that my singling out China does not offend you?"

"On the contrary, I was born in Hong Kong and the history of my native land under Chinese rule is a sorry tale—I am only too well acquainted with the face of oppression. Indeed, I would go further: I would say that the Chinese state, although nominally Communist, is in fact fascist. Hong Kong is today's Sudetenland; Taiwan is tomorrow's Poland."

The Marchesa sighed. "In my father's day it was possible to hide in the hills with a rifle and fight back," she said. "You could see your enemy then, but now they are invisible, hidden behind the lawyer's brief and the banker's vault."

Gilbert stood and went to a shelf where a few newspapers lay in a pile, retrieving one before returning to his seat. "This morning I went ashore and found a newsstand that stocks international papers, including my own." He opened the paper, folded it to a story in the business section, and offered it to the Marchesa. "I regret to inform you, Lady Isabella, that it has just been announced that Ripelli, the great Italian tiremaker, is to be acquired by a state-owned Chinese concern."

She accepted the newspaper and briefly scanned the story before putting it aside.

"I knew the Ripellis when I was a young girl," she said. "They lived in Milan but had a villa in Tremezzo. Old man Alberto was in charge then. He was planning his grand new office tower that still stands proudly outside the Porta Nuova. I remember him and my father discussing the building while we children played at their feet—they thought of it as a fitting symbol for Italy's postwar revival, something to declare the return of Europe to peace and prosperity. I am certain that if Alberto were still alive Ripelli would never have been sold to the Chinese." She put down her coffee cup with care, obviously saddened by the news. "I will have the Mercedes reshod with Michelins as soon as we get back."

BEFORE TURNING IN THAT EVENING I WENT UP TO THE LIBRARY, remembering that Oriana and I had left the ship's log on a side table after meeting with the French authorities. It was no longer there. I checked the bookcases, thinking that one of the maids must have put the thing away when tidying up. But there was no sign of it on the shelves, either—someone had taken the ship's log.

XXI

T HE NEXT DAY WAS SPENT AT SEA ON PASSAGE TO Mallorca. Among the breakfast dishes was a plate of pancakes and a jar of maple syrup—today was July Fourth, and the pancakes were topped with a toothpick bearing the Stars and Stripes. I was standing by the starboard rail after having consumed a stack of them, looking out across the sea, when Oriana Welles joined me.

"Any progress?" she asked.

"Verkhovsky might have written a letter before he died." I explained my theory that he had dismissed Kustaa, at least in part, to write one, and recounted my conversation with Fabia. "Unfortunately, she didn't look at the address."

"Just our luck: an incurious maid."

"She said that it had to be international because the postage was 1.65 euros."

"I'll look up French mail rates: maybe there'll be a clue as to which country."

"By the way, do you have the ship's log?"

"No, I don't. Last I saw, it was on a table in the library when we were meeting with Dubois and Renard."

"It's not there anymore."

"Perhaps someone put it away on the shelves."

"No, I checked."

"Maybe Trevelyan took it."

"You don't seem too concerned."

"I'm not. There was nothing in it that we didn't already know."

"True," I admitted. "Still, we should locate it and lock it away."

"Were you able to establish where anyone was when Verkhovsky went overboard?"

"No. Frankly, I don't know how to bring it up—'Hey, what were you doing at the time of the murder?'"

I expected at least displeasure, if not an outright rebuke, but Welles surprised me.

"I've had the same problem. The only thing I got was from Tess Lysett, who said that she was woken up by the storm."

"What storm?"

"My question exactly. She claims there was a storm that first night, and a wave or some salt spray came in through her porthole—she leaves it open for the fresh air and the sound of the sea."

"Then it was probably a dream."

"That's what I thought, but she said there were still traces of moisture the next morning."

"A passing squall?"

"Again, as I suggested, and again she said no: the water had mostly dried and there were salt crystals, so it must have been seawater, not fresh."

I thought about this for a while.

"If Verkhovsky was looking at the supernova, just risen astern, he would naturally have done so from the rear of the deck, as Trevelyan suggested. But you can't go all the way back because of that built-in bench where the Marchesa sits. You would have to go on one side or the other. Where exactly were those faint scratches in the railing you found?"

"Just to the right of the bench when facing aft."

"So, port side?"

"Yes."

"Tess Lysett's cabin is the aftermost on the port side. The portholes are low to the water and Verkhovsky was fat."

"You think it was the splash of him going in?"

"I do. Does Tess know what time it was?"

"No, she just said there was a storm and so she closed the porthole and went back to sleep. It could have been Verkhovsky."

"It could. Or just spindrift. Or maybe even condensation becoming salty from running down the ship's side before dripping in. I think that it must get moist at night at sea; I saw dew on the deck that first morning."

"We're not making much progress."

"On the contrary, if it wasn't suicide then I think I know who must have done it."

"Who?"

"Urquhart."

"How?"

"He probably approached Verkhovsky from behind and simply tossed him over. Verkhovsky would have been too drunk to put up much resistance. Urquhart could have lifted him by the legs to get sufficient leverage." I bent down and imitated the maneuver. Oriana Welles had very fine calves, I noticed. "It would have been over in an instant and not have left any marks on the body, just those wood fibers under the fingernails as Verkhovsky clawed desperately at the rail, but by then it was too late."

"But why?"

"Motive? I don't know. But think how strange it is for Urquhart to have invited Verkhovsky in the first place. Why do so? Verkhovsky didn't fit in with the rest of us and would clearly have been a tiresome fellow passenger. It doesn't make sense for Urquhart to have asked him except for some hidden purpose. Perhaps Verkhovsky wronged him in the past somehow, a shady financial transaction, say, or maybe he just slighted one of Urquhart's paintings."

"That's just speculation."

"Yes, but how is it that he arranged French resident visas for the nieces in a day?"

"He has money. Money hurries up bureaucrats: a fast-track fee, say, or something less legitimate."

"Did he have copies of their passports, from when you were making guest arrangements?

"Yes."

"Then he probably began the process earlier, and that suggests he somehow knew Verkhovsky wouldn't be around anymore. In any case, it has to have been Urquhart for the simplest of reasons."

"What?"

"Because he was the only person who knew that Verkhovsky was going to be on board. None of the rest of us knew who our fellow passengers would be until the day before we set sail. Except you, of course. Did you throw Verkhovsky overboard?"

"No, but I confess I wanted to."

THE OBSERVATORY AT COSTITX IS NOT A TRUE OBSERVATORY because its primary telescopes are situated not onsite but instead atop an isolated Andalusian mountain on the mainland, higher than anywhere on Mallorca, far removed from sources of manmade light, and whose operation was via remote control in Costitx where the imagery was transmitted for processing.

However, there was a planetarium and it was there that one evening, after a little bus took us up from Palma, that the facility's head—a trim woman in her late fifties perhaps destined to astronomy by her surname, Vega—explained to us what was going on in the heavens above.

"Interstellar distances are difficult to grasp," Dr. Vega began. "A light-year is the distance covered in twelve months by something traveling at 300,000 kilometers per second. Not per *hour* but per *second*.

Think of it this way: if the Sun was the size of a golf ball Betelgeuse would be 150,000 kilometers away, about four times around the Earth."

As she talked, video imagery appeared on the planetarium's dome, illustrating the lecture.

"And although Betelgeuse is a star, not all stars are the same. Betelgeuse is a red supergiant, which is very different from a yellow dwarf, like our Sun. Again, if the Sun was the size of a golf ball then Betelgeuse would be fifty feet in diameter, many orders of magnitude bigger."

We saw them overlaid: Betelgeuse dark red and massive; the Sun just a small yellow dot at its center—something giving a good sense of what a cataclysmic event it must be when something that big collapses then explodes.

"Since the distances are so large the stars appear to us as fixed in space, except that the time of their rising and setting advances by three minutes and fifty-seven seconds every day. This is because during a day the Earth itself advances a little on its own orbit of the Sun. Multiply that nearly four minutes by the number of days in a year and you get twenty-four hours: back to where we started. Today, Betelgeuse rose at 4:41. Tomorrow, it will rise at 4:37, the next day at 4:33, and so on. On this same calendar day next year, it will again rise at 4:41, back to where it began."

During her explanation the imagery had rushed through the year to come, the rapidly incrementing date showing on the left and Betelgeuse rising ever earlier.

"The ultimate light pollution for astronomy is the Sun itself, and since right now the supernova and the Sun are rising at around the same time there would be no point in trying to use our telescopes on Earth to observe it. The only way to clearly see Betelgeuse at this time of year is to rise above the atmosphere, and so tonight we are being fed imagery from the Hubble telescope by way of NASA's Goddard Space Flight Center, and we'll get a very good view of what has become of Betelgeuse."

A star map appeared on the dome.

"This is what the sky looks like from the Hubble right now. And this is what it looks like with the constellations overlaid."

Faint bluish images appeared: a crab, a bear, a hunter. On this last, forming the point of Orion's right shoulder, Betelgeuse was highlighted.

"Now, let's focus on Betelgeuse."

The image gradually magnified, zooming closer and closer to the star, a strangely disorienting experience in the pitch dark of the planetarium, almost dizzying, as if falling into space. Soon Betelgeuse began to emerge as something more than just a point of bright light, and by the time the magnification ended it occupied most of the ceiling.

I had expected something akin to a ball of fire, and certainly symmetrical, but the image splayed across the ceiling above us was nothing like that. It seemed to me almost animate, like a single-cell creature: an amoeba under the microscope, albeit in this case an amoeba millions of miles wide. It was roundish but misshapen, and very colorful: lightning-bright white at the core and then a mixture of greens and blues and purples as it spread outward, veering to the other end of the spectrum at the cell wall: yellows and reds. Most curious of all were the many thread-like tendrils, like celestial scintilla delving tentatively into the cosmic void.

"The supernova, day three," Vega said. "The ethereal bluish glow comes from the neutron star that is now at the core of the system. When Betelgeuse collapsed and then exploded, two things occurred. Firstly, a neutron star was created from the collapse, incredibly dense. A golf ball made of the same material would weigh billions of tons—*billions*, not *millions*—and it is extremely hot: the surface temperature would be about a million degrees Celsius. It is also rotating very fast, thousands of times a minute. Secondly, all other matter not part of the neutron star has been blown into space. That's what those many filaments are: fragments of either Betelgeuse itself or any object in its path, shredded by the supernova. It will continue to expand for centuries, eventually becoming a nebula: essentially a gigantic cosmic cloud of dispersed matter, light-years in breadth. The vivid coloration comes from streams of charged particles propelled by the neutron star's magnetic field into powerful jets shooting out into space."

No art could compare to the vast and wonderous thing we were looking at now: magnificent, awful, beautiful, terrifying.

"Is that the radiation that's coming to us?"

"What we're seeing in this image are photons, the particles that are what we call light, and which of course travel at the speed of light. They have momentum but no mass. Behind them, a little slower, is the cosmic radiation. That's comprised of particles with mass as well as momentum, mostly hydrogen nuclei traveling at near light speed, highly energized. They will reach us soon and appear as auroras in the sky, like the Northern Lights, but they will be everywhere, not just the polar regions, and likely much more spectacular."

She was trying to keep it upbeat, but it was clear that Dr. Vega was as uncertain about the future as the rest of us. And so we continued to stare up in silence, struck dumb by the profound and pitiless indifference with which the universe regards humanity. Each man, a universe to himself, is to nature nothing but a single grain of sand in an immense and unmeasurable desert, something whose existence or non-existence goes unnoticed and unremarked, just a passing speck of dust. We are, that image said, an inconsequential irrelevancy to the cosmos.

XXII

T HE *MULVANE* MADE THE CROSSING FROM MALLORCA TO Ibiza via an overnight passage, coming to anchor at sunrise. As the guests emerged on deck that morning we were greeted with the sight of Es Vedrà, rising like a cathedral from the sea—the second time in twenty-four hours that nature had revealed her immensity, although this time not on a galactic scale.

Nature was not the only one revealing herself. Today was to be spent in or on the water and so after breakfast the passengers shifted into bathing gear for the first time on the voyage. Either the women had not been provided with 1930s swimming costumes or had chosen to ignore them, instead opting for their own modern and much skimpier outfits. I should describe these now, so the reader can picture them as they appeared at their most revealing that day, something that was to have relevance to upcoming events.

Rasputina was predictably glamorous, appearing on deck in a loose semi-transparent blouse whose pattern matched that of the glittering bikini beneath, designed more for lounging poolside at the Beverly Hills Hotel than actual swimming. A flamboyantly broad straw hat, gold-rimmed round sunglasses, and strappy platform-soled sandals completed the look.

Tess Lysett I would have thought a one-piece girl but she too was bikini-clad, although a bikini of sufficiently modest cut that the Right Reverend would unlikely have objected, and which was not revealed until the moment she rose and took off her shirt before entering the water, awkwardly self-conscious and probably having been talked into the swimsuit by Rasputina, who was giving her instruction in more than just cocktails. The lessons were working: by the end of the day, Tess was playing paddleball wearing nothing but the bikini, laughing along with the others and completely at ease.

Adelina appeared on deck as I was coming up from below, and so I first saw her that morning from the bottom up: simple white canvas deck shoes and a pair of blue tennis shorts, a white men's collared shirt, rolled at the sleeves, untucked and unbuttoned to reveal a one-piece swimsuit beneath, plain navy and embroidered with the insignia of the Institut Lavaux.

Oriana had opted for a one-piece as well, black, but unlike Adelina's high-necked and serviceable swimsuit hers had a deep vee in front and was cut high above the hip: a suit meant not for duty in school swim meets but for display of the female form.

But it was the nieces who were most notable for brevity. Bébé wore a mesh bikini whose top she removed with a south-of-France lack of reserve as soon as hitting the beach, fully exposing what had already been partially revealed: a tattoo executed in the Japanese manner depicting a samurai slaying a dragon. It was a large work, stretching from the left breast where the warrior, sword raised, looked down upon the beast whose long serpent-like body formed a series of switchbacks stretching down the abdomen. The whole thing was vividly colored in reds and greens and blues—highly detailed, precisely executed, and with a finish that was smooth and glossy. The design matched the contours of the body on which it was inscribed: the drape of the samurai's sleeve followed the curve of Bébé's breast and the dragon's tapering tail ended in a curl centered on the belly button.

Marta wore a micro-bikini whose top probably covered fewer square inches than her sunglasses and below that a thong, similarly minimalist.

Unlike the gyspyish Bébé, Marta was not naturally tan and her pale skin revealed blotches from new garments not entirely colorfast.

Last on deck that morning was the Marchesa, swathed head-to-toe in linen. She took her accustomed seat by the stern rail, intending to remain aboard, attended by Fabia.

BOTH BOATS WERE LOWERED. I CAME TO THE RAIL WHERE Kustaa was standing in the inflatable below, loading dive equipment. I gave him a hand by passing gear down: tanks; weights; fins; masks.

"You're diving, too?"

"No, I'll be acting as the divemaster, so I'll stay in the Zodiac."

"Why's it called a Zodiac?"

"It's the brand name. Zodiac invented rubber inflatables, although this one is technically a RHIB."

"RHIB?"

"Rigid-hull inflatable boat. Inflatable sides but aluminum bottom." He stamped briefly on the hull to demonstrate. "The stiffness lets them go faster than if the entire boat was rubber."

He installed a blue-and-white flag at the prow, but it was made of metal rather than fabric so that it would always be visible, even without a breeze.

"What's that for?"

"Signal flag Alpha, which when flown alone like this means 'I am operating divers below,' a warning to other boats to keep clear."

"I see," I said, impressed that someone I had until now thought just a steward possessed such skills. "The charter company train their crews well."

"I didn't learn diving from them," Kustaa said dismissively. He turned side-on and lifted the sleeve of his T-shirt above his left shoulder, revealing a tattoo beneath. Much smaller than Bébé's, but it too depicted some fierce creature, although in this case only the head. "A sea eagle," he explained. "The emblem of the Rannikkojääkärit—the Coastal Jaegers."

"Coastal Jaegers?"

"I did it for national service but ended up staying for six years. We have conscription in Finland: it's our way of keeping a reserve force in case Russia attacks."

"And that's where you learned diving?"

"Yes. After I left I had no skills except the water, so I ended up crewing private charters. Not a bad life: the Mediterranean is much better than the Baltic."

Now I understood why it was Kustaa who had recovered Verkhovsky's body.

"So you were already trained as a diver?"

"Diving is just a skill, and I learned many skills in the Jaegers. But we were trained for only one thing."

"What's that?"

"To kill Russians." He was smiling, apparently remembering his more murderous days with fond affection.

THE SPEEDBOAT WAS ON THE OTHER SIDE OF THE *MULVANE*, tied up at the foot of the accommodation ladder, and for the first time I was able to see something more of it than just the underside of the hull. It was a beautiful craft—an antique Italian Riva Aquarama—built of varnished mahogany polished to a mirror shine and finished with chrome fittings that glistened in the sunlight. The luxurious leather and burled-walnut interior featured an impressive array of instruments and the steering wheel looked suitable for a sports car. Aška and Džana were loading a cooler and picnic basket behind the front seats, while in the back George, the engineer's mate, was deep in the bay of one of the two big inboards. Gilbert sat nearby, looking at the exposed engine.

"Learning to be a mechanic?"

He looked up. "I've always been a car guy."

"Car?"

"Sure. Rivas were powered by American automobile engines." He pointed toward the motor. "This one's fitted with twin Chrysler 440s— big block V-8s. My first car, a '69 'Cuda, had one just like it."

It sounded like a muscle car when George fired it up, a deep bass rumble that was doubled when he started the other engine, something that must have echoed for miles along the sheer cliffs of Es Vedrà.

The diving party departed for the seamount in the Zodiac. The rest of us, including Jamys and Aška to help with umbrellas and picnic hampers, were transported in the Riva to a little sandy cove on Es Vedrà. This required multiple trips as the boat could only fit four people comfortably.

The morning was spent swimming in the crystalline water or snorkeling along the reef, and the Riva was put to work as a ski boat. This activity was always conducted in twos, with one person in the boat acting as spotter with eyes aft while the other skied, and then switching around. I was paired with Adelina. She was a natural, rising effortlessly on the tow and seeming to not so much plow through the water as skim above it, slender and graceful, something that gave me a sudden insight into the *Lustration*. I realized that the painting's swirling silvery froth was obviously sea-like, something I had missed before, and the fluid emergence of Adelina's image from the background mimicked Venus arising from the sea. I immediately thought of Botticelli's *Birth of Venus*, not just because of the similarity in theme but the Venus herself: same smooth pale skin, same quiet patrician calm, even the same long golden tresses: Adelina Pallavicini bore a remarkable resemblance to Simonetta Vespucci, Botticelli's inspiration and a celebrated Florentine beauty. I made a mental note to ask Urquhart about it later.

Things were quieter after a long picnic washed down with bottles of Prensal Blanc, the local white. The sun had moved past the meridian and the supernova soon followed, leaving much of the cove in the shadow of the steep cliffs surrounding it. Most people chose to read or nap. Oriana took a towel down to the far end of the strand where there was still a section of sunlight, apparently wanting to continue working on her tan.

I walked down to join her.

"I think I've got a second suspect," I said, safely out of earshot of the others.

"Yep." She was lying prone and had been reading but now closed her book. "The tattoo gave it away."

"You've seen it too?"

"Of course."

"Kustaa showed it to you?"

"Huh?"

"Kustaa, the Finn. He's more than just a steward. He's ex-military; hates Russians."

"He's got a tattoo?"

"It's the head of a sea eagle, the emblem of his old outfit. I think he was trained for special operations; certainly for diving. Kustaa told me frankly that he was trained to kill Russians—his exact words—and no doubt he would have the skills and strength to hoist Verkhovsky overboard before the latter even knew what was happening. Who did you mean?"

"Who do you think? Tattoo, fully uncovered and prominently displayed?"

"You mean Bébé?"

"Yes, Bébé. Here, rub some suntan lotion on my back." She handed me the tube.

It is one thing to sit with a woman wearing a swimsuit, quite another to touch. I squeezed out a small squirt of lotion and quickly applied it.

"Do it properly," she ordered. "I don't want to get burned."

I tried to be more thorough.

"But what's the tattoo got to do with it?"

"What does it depict?"

"A samurai, sword raised, about to decapitate a serpent-like dragon, very precisely rendered."

Oriana turned to look up at me, but her eyes remained invisible behind her sunglasses. "I see that you've studied it carefully."

"I'm an art historian. I'm trained to observe such things."

"Who kills dragons?"

"Apart from samurai? I don't know; some character from Tolkien?"

"You're not much of an art historian, are you? Unless of course the art happens to be draped across a woman's body."

I suddenly realized what she must mean; there had been many depictions of the same subject: Rubens; Tintoretto; Carpaccio; Uccello; even Raphael.

"St. George," I said.

"Of course. And of which country is St. George the patron saint?"

"England."

"Okay, but what other country?"

The name made it easy enough to guess. "Georgia, I assume. And so it's probably a national symbol of Bébé's country, which is why she had it done."

"Yes, exactly. And so did Marta, except hers was the Polish national symbol: a crowned eagle, wings spread."

"I didn't see a tattoo on her."

"Marta's wasn't real; it was done with a type of dye called Jagua—it looks like a normal tattoo, but fades away as the skin renews its surface layer."

"Ah, I thought her skin looked splotched—now I know why."

"No, you don't know why."

"Huh?"

"Bébé told me. She and Marta got their tattoos together, at the same place. Verkhovsky wasn't smart enough to figure out the symbolism in Bébé's, but he recognized Marta's instantly. The Russians historically despise Poles—you heard Verkhovsky's contempt when he discovered that the vodka was Polish. When Verkhovsky saw that tattoo on Marta he lost his temper and made her pay. That's what the splotches are: not fading dye but fading bruises."

I remembered Verkhovsky's grazed knuckles when he first arrived on board, the injury that Wu had later detailed as "abrasion of the metacarpophalangeal joints." Now I understood why the nieces had seemed so sullen.

"Remember what you said before," Oriana continued, "that it had to be Urquhart because he was the only one who knew Verkhovsky was going to be a passenger? But that's not true, is it? Marta and Bébé both knew. Two close friends, one of whom had just been beaten. It could have been them."

"But they were dependent on Verkhovsky."

"What if they'd gotten wind that it was all going to end? What if they found out that the French were planning to deport him? What if they came across the Comoros passport and guessed that he was going to make a run for it? What if they realized he wasn't taking them with him, and their sojourn in the West would soon be over? Verkhovsky was no longer of any value, just someone who abused them."

"Would either of them have the strength to throw him overboard without a struggle?"

"Who better than Bébé and Marta: the only two people who could get close enough without raising his suspicions? And Verkhovsky was intoxicated: he would have been slow to realize what was happening, too late to resist."

Except for that final desperate grasp at the guardrail, I could not help thinking. But Oriana was right: we had two more suspects—three, counting Kustaa.

XXIII

THE DIVING PARTY WAS ALREADY BACK WHEN WE returned on board the *Mulvane*, and I could tell right away that something had happened on the trip to the Aguja. Urquhart was nowhere to be seen, but Shotter and Kustaa were on the fo'c'sle washing down the equipment with fresh water and laying it out on deck to dry before being stowed away.

Kustaa appeared his usual purposeful self but Shotter was deep in thought, so distracted as to not notice my approach, and he jumped with surprise when I spoke up.

"How did the dive go?"

"The dive?" he said, as if having forgotten it. "Yeah, it went fine."

"Did you spear our supper?"

"No, I took a camera. Urquhart had a speargun, but he didn't use it."

"Get any shots of the seamount?"

"A few." He must have realized that even for him, never talkative to begin with, he sounded strangely curt, and so he added as an afterthought. "And some fish. Grouper and a school of what I think were Bonito. I'll show you the prints when they're developed."

I left him alone to contemplate whatever it was that had happened down there. That night, I discovered what it was.

THE EVENING'S EVENTS BEGAN WHEN I RETURNED TO MY cabin to dress for dinner. There was an envelope on the desk, printed with the ship's crest and bearing my name. Inside was a brief note written in the same hand.

Dear Evans,

I wonder if you would join me for a private discussion in the library directly after dinner this evening.

Yours,
R.A.U.

I had been half-expecting this, for what purpose would inviting me on the cruise have been if not to propose some sort of collaboration: a *catalogue raisonné* perhaps; or a retrospective exhibition; or maybe even a biography, authorized so that he could control the narrative. I was already prepared with answers to all of these potential proposals: yes to the catalog; as for a retrospective, I would undertake to champion the idea of mounting one at the Wentworth with Sir Dickie; but no to the authorized biography, although I would be willing to attempt one that was not subject to his imprimatur.

When I arrived in the library after dinner I realized at once that my assumptions were wrong. For a start, Urquhart and I were not alone: Jack Shotter sat in the corner, still deep in thought. Urquhart rose and mixed me a drink unbidden—like the Martinis before dinner, whisky and sodas had become the standard after-dinner drink for the men on board.

On the table was a silver tray bearing a small decanter etched with a geometric Art Deco design and filled with dark liquid. Beside it were matching liqueur glasses: we were apparently to be joined by at least one of the women.

It turned out to be three: the Marchesa and her grand-niece entered the compartment, followed by Oriana Welles. We men stood, and Urquhart welcomed the ladies.

"Thank you for agreeing to join us, Lady Isabella, Lady Adelina. May I offer you a glass of *amaro*?" The Marchesa inclined her head in assent, apparently speaking for them both. Urquhart went to the table and filled two glasses from the decanter—whatever was to come, he preferred that it be accompanied by plenty of alcohol.

He served the *amari* and then sat on an armchair angled to face the Marchesa.

"Madam, I have asked to speak to you and Lady Adelina tonight about a matter that you might perhaps find disagreeable, even distasteful. I therefore state from the beginning that should at any time you choose to hear no more you merely ask that the conversation end and it will immediately cease, never to be mentioned again."

In response, the Marchesa merely sipped her *digestivo*, but I could tell that, far from making her apprehensive, this little introduction had only whetted her appetite.

"I should also state that, while Mr. Shotter is necessarily familiar with what I am about to discuss, Dr. Evans is not—I kept him in the dark deliberately so that he may give his expert assessment unsullied by any prior persuasion on my part, should you choose to seek it."

I expected to see the Marchesa more concerned now, for this could only be about the Dalís that had somehow come into her possession before Urquhart made a gift of them, but she remained perfectly composed.

"Miss Welles, too, is unaware of the matter that I am about to raise, but her involvement may be necessary for what is to come." He wanted his private investigator on hand. I realized that Oriana would be blindsided as amid all the Verkhovsky fuss I had never thought to tell her about the incident with the Dalís.

Urquhart put aside his glass and leaned forward, a man getting down to business and wanting to get it right.

"After dinner two evenings ago we discussed the decline of the West and the economic means by which it is being acquired by the forces of oppression. You might recall commenting that during the Second World War your father was able to pick up a rifle and join the partisans, but these days there was no longer any clear way for an individual to fight back."

"Indeed," the Marchesa replied.

"That conversation set me thinking."

"And?"

"I believe that I have found a way to fight back."

Urquhart stood and picked up the decanter, an effective dramatic pause. He refilled the Marchesa's glass and replaced the decanter before continuing.

"We discussed the recent Chinese bid for Ripelli, famed for inventing the radial tire and having equipped many a champion race car during the postwar period—themselves often Italian. It is a company that has stood as a symbol of the remarkable economic and industrial rebirth after having overcome the then-recent challenge of the fascists and the continuing challenge of the Russians."

"Equally fascist," the Marchesa said. "And fascist still." Kustaa was not the only person aboard unfavorably disposed toward Russians.

"I propose, Lady Isabella, that we seek to defeat this takeover bid."

"How?"

"By rousing public opinion against it."

"That never works," she said dismissively. "A petition here, a public meeting there—the politicians simply ignore it."

"Very true. And that's why I'm proposing a different approach, a way to fully engage the public and boycott Ripelli should the deal proceed, something certain to derail it. As you said, today it is the money that matters: threatening the company's revenue stream is the one sure way to defeat the takeover bid."

"And exactly what is it that you propose?"

"There is something beyond tires for which Ripelli is famous, something quite different: a calendar. The Ripelli calendar is eagerly anticipated every year. It is considered to be a showcase for the finest photographers and has been shot by the greatest names of postwar photography: Helmut Newton, Richard Avedon, Karl Lagerfeld, Annie Leibovitz, and the like. Indeed, so famous is it that it's referred to as simply 'The Cal.' However, I should tell you that the calendar originated in the 1960s as a giveaway for the mechanics who fitted their tires—it was thus intended to be hung on the walls of workshops, and so the content was..."

"Mr. Urquhart, you forget that I was a welder in my father's shipyard. I am well acquainted with the subject matter of such calendars."

"Quite, and so it remains today: the photographs are of women, usually seminude or nude, although I hasten to add that there's no prurient or salacious aspect: the photos are no more obscene than a Rubens or Raphael."

"I still don't see what you're proposing."

"An anti-Ripelli calendar, madam, photographed by Mr. Shotter and with Lady Adelina as the model. The purpose to be made plain: to encourage a boycott of Ripelli should the Chinese deal proceed. This alone would garner extensive media coverage, but with a model who is a member of one of Italy's most distinguished families, heir to the Marquessate, and of course herself supremely photogenic, I think that we may safely assume publicity would not be a problem. I propose to print a quarter million copies, the cost of which I will underwrite myself, and then distribute them free of charge throughout Italy and Western Europe."

A long silence followed, eventually broken by the Marchesa.

"No, Adelina cannot become a media object," she stated flatly.

"And nor will she. There would be no interviews, no television appearances, no calendar signings, nothing like that. There'll be no need—the calendar will speak for itself, and it makes the fact of the protest all the more potent: not the product of a publicity seeker but the opposite: an obviously reserved woman compelled to speak out."

"Photographed where?"

"Entirely in Italy, shot as we visit various locations during our cruise."

"Inside, I assume?"

Urquhart cleared his throat before responding, a man who knew that he was about to lose his case.

"Mr. Shotter and I spent much time today discussing this very question. I realize that of course if you and Lady Adelina were to entertain the proposal at all, you would naturally prefer interior shoots. However, despite the obvious difficulties, Jack favors exterior shoots due to a number of technical factors: for a start, he is without studio lighting. I, too, favor exterior shoots, but for a different reason: it is to be a protest, and protests are only effective when made publicly. If it is to be done at all, then in my view it should be done properly."

"So you are basically proposing to display my grand-niece naked in public?"

"There would of course be arrangements made with the local authorities beforehand to clear the locations, many of which would already be private—villas and such—and we would engage appropriate security personnel, but there's no denying the basic fact of it: I'm afraid the answer to that question is essentially yes."

The Marchesa was about to respond when Adelina spoke for the first time.

"Outside will be fine," she said, as if the question were of no importance, like whether or not to dine alfresco. "Shall we join the others now?"

And with that simple pronouncement the matter was suddenly decided. Whatever objection the Marchesa had been about to make she swallowed, and instead with an inclination of her head toward our host indicated her assent to the proposal.

XXIV

T ESS WAS THE FIRST TO SPEAK AFTER WE REJOINED THE others in the main salon and Urquhart had finished explaining that in Italy we were to shoot an anti-Ripelli calendar.

"How marvelous," she said. "Just like Lady Godiva. Can I be an extra?"

This question was directed at Shotter, whose mouth opened but no words came out.

"Both of us," Rasputina added. "I'll really upstage my mother this time, splashed naked across the workshop walls of Europe." She swept an arm in a wide arc, indicating the vast breadth of her anticipated exposure.

"Us, too?" asked Marta. Bébé nodded enthusiastically.

"We could be a sort of Greek chorus," Tess continued, her words tumbling over each other in joy at the prospect. "We'll stand in the background, or perhaps act as attendants to Adelina. There must be precedents in art." This last was directed at me, and as it happened I had been thinking of one that same afternoon.

"Botticelli's *Birth of Venus* has two female attendants," I said. "The one on the right offers a robe and the one on the left blows Venus toward shore." Tess clapped in delight, and I foolishly continued. "And I suppose his *Primavera* would have roles for you all: the three Graces dancing on the left, Flora on the right, and Venus presiding over the whole thing in the center."

"Wonderful, you must make us a list."

"We'll need twelve of them."

"They should all be Italian, I think."

"I've always wanted to be a goddess."

"We'll have to work on our tans."

"But no tan lines!"

Urquhart and Shotter, stunned by this sudden coup, looked at each other dumbstruck, the former opening his arms in a gesture of a man unsure what to do next, the latter just shrugging his shoulders in reluctant acceptance—the Gang of Four had prevailed.

Urquhart responded for them both. "Miss Domaradzka, Miss Nikolaishvili, and Miss Quantrill—your generous offers to participate are accepted with much pleasure." He turned to Tess. "As for you, young lady, I'm afraid not."

"Why not?"

"You're too young."

"Nonsense. I'll be eighteen in a week: an adult, able to make my own decisions."

"No."

"What if I wear clothes?"

"Still no"

"But why?"

"Because your father would object."

"No, he wouldn't."

"Should we call him?"

"Yes," she responded defiantly. "And he will give his consent."

"Will he?"

"Of course. Such a thing would mean nothing to my father, continually confronted as he is with the most bizarre perversions—he sits in the House of Lords, you know."

Before turning in I went back up to the library, intending to get a new book. The room was already occupied. Welles was standing with a volume in hand that I recognized: the missing ship's log.

"You found it."

"Yes."

"Where?

"Here on the shelf. You must have overlooked it before."

"It's undamaged?"

"That's what I'm checking, to make sure nothing's been changed. It seems fine."

"But it's written in pencil; someone could have erased it."

"They use 2Hs—the lead is too hard to use without leaving an impression and I don't see that anything has been erased. Here, you check."

I did, taking my time, but she was right: I could see the indentation left by the pencil, and any attempted erasure would have been obvious. In any case, there was nothing to erase: it just contained routine position-course-speed data of the type Trevelyan described, terse descriptions of the weather and sea state, a note on the appearance of the supernova, plus the details of when Verkhovsky was found missing then later found drowned, all of which we already knew. The earlier ones were in Zabala-Extarte's distinctive upright lettering—he had been on watch 4:00-8:00 that morning—and the latter were in Trevelyan's old-fashioned longhand.

I handed it back to Oriana. I was certain that the log had not been on the shelf when I searched earlier, which meant that someone had taken and then returned it, a fact that made the lack of any alteration all the more puzzling.

XXV

T HE CONSULTATION WITH THE BISHOP OF CHICHESTER took place the following morning, with Tess and Urquhart calling him together from the satellite phone in the captain's cabin. The call was not a long one: they returned to the main salon ten minutes after having gone up to make it—perhaps the Right Reverend Lysett had long ago learned that to oppose his headstrong daughter was to invite calamity. Tess emerged triumphant, although her victory was not total: there had been no broaching of the possibility of her appearing *sans vêtements*, and so by default she was to remain clothed, but Tess had gotten the core of what she wanted: the opportunity to stand shoulder-to-shoulder on the photographic ramparts with her fellow comrades fighting against those who would sell out to despots and thugs.

Meanwhile, the sun deck—the *Mulvane*'s uppermost deck, running above the bridge, captain's accommodation, and the library, and whose sole fitting was the funnel—was set aside for sunbathing and declared off-limits to all males on board, passengers and crew, so that the process could be done leaving no tan lines.

The passage to Carthage was made in three days. We docked in a marina at Gammarth, a modern facility on the northeastern side of Tunis, and about the last contemporary thing we saw there; in sprawling Tunis it felt as if we had been plunged back in time, not just by the ruins of ancient Carthage but by Tunis itself, little changed since French colonial days—an old North African city quietly brooding under the baking sun, moving to its own drowsy heat-soaked rhythms and laughing at the endless running about of Westerners, racing hither and thither in search of something—success, satisfaction, happiness?—but, as the rushing never abates, apparently never finding it.

Urquhart arranged for a guide to accompany us to the ruins. I dislike guided tours—the guides are usually obsequious or pedagogic, two qualities equally unattractive—preferring instead to proceed at my own pace and in my own company, with some Baedeker ancient or modern in hand to expound the sights privately and quietly, but Urquhart's choice turned out to be a good one.

We found him waiting for us under the whitewashed horseshoe-arched arcades of Le musée national de Carthage, a small and elderly man, his face bearing the gray stubble of a close-cut beard, and dapperly dressed in a threadbare gray suit with worn tan brogues—a vivid contrast to the shorts-and-sneakers-clad tourists milling about. As indeed were we: the men in trousers and collared shirts; the women wearing dresses and skirts, none with bare shoulders, and in a nod to local sensibilities two of them, the Marchesa and Tess Lysett, wore headscarves—perhaps Tess was used to heeding religious mores from having to attend her father's services.

"Welcome to Tunis," our guide said as he shuffled forward. "My name is Firas Hamouda, and I have the honor of occupying a chair in history at the Ez-Zitouna University."

"Professor Hamouda, I do hope we're not late," Urquhart said, coming forward to shake his hand.

"Not at all. I find it a great pleasure to sit here in the shade and take in this view."

It was a fine view indeed, for we were high on a hill, the Byrsa, and below us the ruins of Carthage tumbled down to the sea. The Gulf of

Tunis swept in a broad blue arc across the water and in the distance rose the mountainous spine of the long peninsula that ends at Cap Bon.

"Shall we enter the museum?"

He led us inside, going to an area where a model of ancient Carthage was encased in a vitrine.

"I think it is easier to get a sense of what the ruins represent by first seeing what they were before the city's destruction," Hamouda said. "There have been many Carthages: Punic Carthage; Roman Carthage; the Carthage of the Vandals; the Byzantines; the Islamic conquest; the French colonial occupation; and perhaps we are now in another era: that of the post-Arab Spring. Each of these Carthages was brought about by war or revolution—one is tempted to conclude that such a sequence is a monument to the indefatigable resiliency of man, but perhaps it is also evidence of his innate destructiveness."

He led us to the vitrine.

"I shall discuss only the first: Punic Carthage. This model shows how the city appeared in the Third Century B.C., before the Punic wars, and you can see right away what an impressive metropolis it must have been, as magnificent as Rome under the Flavians or Antonines, but four centuries earlier."

He was right: before us was a great mass of classical temples, broad basilicas, columned peristyles, and grand plazas.

"This was the forum—the central administrative area—situated on the hill where we now stand, and with the harbor below. Carthage was founded three thousand years ago by the Phoenicians, perhaps by Virgil's Queen Dido herself. The Phoenicians, centering on Tyre, were a trading people, and that is what generated the wealth required for the construction of such a city. You need only see the harbor to appreciate the importance of this trade, actually two harbors: the mercantile harbor to begin with and then at its terminus the naval harbor with the armed triremes that protected that trade. Imagine the feat of engineering it would have been to have built these harbors in an age before powered machinery."

The Gulf of Tunis is a natural shelter, but the precisely geometrical harbors were obviously manmade: the first perfectly rectilinear, with two long parallel moles and wharf after wharf projecting inward from them, and then ending in a second harbor that was an exact circle and whose central hub looked like a large round temple but, given the harbor's role, was likely a naval arsenal.

"Now let us return outside and match in our imaginations what we have seen here with the ruins of what it was to become."

Professor Hamouda led us across the plaza and under the shade of some scraggly pines. Nearby stood a few columns, last survivors of the city, for most of it was just the bases of walls or steps or cisterns: masonry too low to have been further knocked down.

"Picture it as it once was," he said. "Palaces and temples, statuary and columns, monumental marble sparkling under the Mediterranean sun. People busy in the forum, clad in fine silks from faraway places and bejeweled with gold and gemstones. Below in the harbor the white sails and steady oars of triremes passing to and fro, bringing forth the bounty of the ancient world. Carthage dominated the western Mediterranean and could not imagine, had hardly even heard of, the obscure tribe in Latium that was then struggling with Sabines and Etrurians for its very survival. But the Romans did survive, and thrived, and decided that it should be they who ruled the world: thus, the Punic Wars.

"There were three of these wars. In the first, Rome took Sicily from Carthage—Sicily was the bread basket of the western Mediterranean, and its capture assured the food supply. In the second, Hannibal famously marched his army across the Alps, war elephants and all, and brought Rome to its knees. But the Carthaginian leaders, feeling the war already won, refused to invest further resources. Rome soon rebuilt her armies, crushed Carthage, and ensured its continued weakness by imposing harsh indemnities, much as the Allies did to Germany after the First World War. Like Germany, Carthage nevertheless recovered and was soon again a threat. At the elder Cato's continual urging war was again resumed, and this time the Romans utterly annihilated Carthage, burning it in a conflagration that lasted seventeen days, and after which they salted the soil to render it barren."

He swept his arm over the scene before us.

"Here is the place from which, while still a child, Hannibal set forth with his father to conquer Spain, and it is here that he returned thirty-five years later, exhausted by a lifetime of war, in a futile attempt to save Carthage. Here it is where the elder Scipio came to receive the surrender of the city, and where the younger Scipio was to come fifty years later and raze it to the ground. And here it was where the younger Cato, refusing with republican pride to submit to a triumphant Caesar, cast himself upon his sword."

Technically, that was in neighboring Utica, but the point was clear: we were gazing over land upon which much history had been made.

"And so, after all that effort expended, all that treasure spent, and all that blood spilled, what was the end result? The answer: that which we see before us: a bunch of broken old rocks."

"But a new city, too," Gilbert said, nodding toward Tunis, sprawling over the other side of the Byrsa. "Life continues."

"Your optimism does you credit at a time when the heavens above seem about to destroy us."

"We Americans are optimistic by nature; I'm a prisoner of my upbringing."

"As indeed am I, an accepting fatalism being the heritage of the East."

They were smiling, men who enjoyed a little verbal joust now and again.

"Let us return inside the little museum and look at the exhibits. Please feel free to wander as you like. For anyone who chooses to remain with me, I will briefly discuss a few items that I find particularly engaging before leaving you to explore on your own."

As we walked back across the plaza Tess fell in by his side.

"Tell us about your university," she said, offering a supporting arm, which he gratefully accepted.

"It is quite small and very old."

"I go to Oxford, which is quite big and very old."

"How old?"

"It was established about 1100, I think."

"Ez-Zitouna was founded in the year 120 A.H., which in your calendar is the year 737." I could sense Tess's surprise at this, for Oxford commonly understands itself to be the world's second-oldest university, after Bologna. "Of course, it was not then called a university but a madrasa—sometimes it is still known by that term."

"What's it like?"

"The building in which I work has a pretty little shaded courtyard, paved, and at the center of which is a well. It is surrounded by colonnades, what in Western religious architecture would be called a cloister."

"Sounds like an Oxford college quad," Tess said. "What's your favorite part?"

"The library, mademoiselle—Ez-Zitouna's is notable for the breadth and richness of its collections. Such books of such age! Full of many wonders and much nonsense, but always a pleasure to ponder. I confess that I even like their smell."

XXVI

W E LUNCHED AT A ROOFTOP CAFE GIVING BROAD VIEWS over the old city, the Medina. The food remained Mediterranean but here was infused with the flavors of North Africa: sesame seed oil; dates in abundance; couscous strewn with almonds and pomegranate seeds; and above all harissa, dense and hot, blowing across everything like a Sirocco from the Sahara.

After the meal only the Marchesa returned to the *Mulvane*. Urquhart, Gilbert, and Wu accepted Hamouda's invitation to see the library. I was tempted to join them, but I was not going to visit Tunis without spending time in the Bardo. I could tell that Tess, too, would have liked to see the library but, perhaps not wanting to put the professor in the awkward position of having brought a woman into a madrasa, instead chose to join me. The remainder of the party decided to tour the Medina, Shotter with a camera ready, but the women were more interested in the souks.

After ensuring that her great-aunt was comfortably in the car going back to the yacht, Adelina elected to join Tess and me.

The Bardo is the national museum of Tunisia and notable for its collection of Roman mosaics, recovered from many ancient sites around the country. It is housed in a Fifteenth-Century Hafsid palace, once the residence of the ruling bey, ornately decorated and brilliantly tiled, a suitable location for the works within. The three of us soon separated, enthralled—at least in my case—by the treasures before us.

I came to a strange mosaic, difficult to interpret. It depicted Venus, unclad but for a cape that was thrust back behind her shoulders. In her right hand she held out a red rose, as if inviting the viewer to come pluck it. Stranger still were the two centaurs flanking her: they were both female—centauresses, I suppose—something that I had never seen in an artwork before. They were heavily made up, like the Venus figure, with kohl around the eyes. They held a garland above her—probably myrtle, the traditional wreath of Venus—plus a crown. There was a Latin inscription, but instead of clarifying it only served to further obscure: "Polystefanus rationis est Archeus": Polystefanus (Greek? many-crowned) is the reason Archeus (Greek again? inner spirit or driving force).

"What is it?" I was suddenly asked; Tess had come beside me unnoticed.

"Good question. I was wondering that myself."

"Tell me when it's okay to read the label."

I looked in surprise from the mosaic to Tess. It was true that I made it a habit to not read the object label—tombstones, curators colloquially call them—until having first studied the artwork and drawn my own conclusions.

"How did you know?"

But she ignored the question and went to the label anyway. After reading it she returned to my side.

"Want to know?"

"Yes"

"They're not sure either. Perhaps it was celebrating a chariot race, where Polystefanus and Archeus were the names of two of the horses in a quadriga. Mares, presumably, given their personifications. They won, hence the crowning, but it's all a bit of a guess, really: why is it Venus who's being crowned? Date also uncertain, but Late Empire, Third to Fifth Century A.D. It came from a house in Ellès, which is a site in the interior, not far from where Scipio defeated Hannibal at Zama."

"Thank you."

"Are you adding it to the list?"

"What list?"

Tess rolled her eyes. At least, unlike Bébé, she was not snapping her fingers at me.

"The list for the photo shoots. It's Roman, therefore Italian, and so it counts, notwithstanding having been located in Tunisia. We could shoot it at an old Carthaginian site in Sicily."

"That's not a bad idea."

"We'll need a pair of racehorses. I'll ride one."

I made no comment on this, since the centauresses were as naked as the Venus.

"I'll find Adelina and show her," Tess said, and off she went.

After Adelina was found and fetched and duly shown the mosaic, the three of us quit the museum and headed to Sidi Bou Saïd, a small Santorini-like village of blue-and-white houses perched high above the sea, not far from where we had started the day on the Byrsa. The town is something of a bohemian retreat, and so while sitting on the terrace of a little cafe and looking out over the water below we ordered, without guilt, glasses of pastis to accompany the many plates of meze— it had been just fig and pomegranate juice with lunch.

Betelgeuse had already set and the sun was lowering in the west, illuminating the view in front of us and reducing the harsh dry heat of day to an enveloping warmth at dusk. Adelina had seemed distracted since leaving the Bardo, all but silent.

I wondered what had irritated her: surely not Tess, indefatigably good-natured; maybe the mosaic, a reminder of having agreed to pose for a calendar about which she was having second thoughts; or perhaps her reticence, now and during the cruise, was due to something that had been weighing on her, and what could that be but Verkhovsky's death?

Tess turned to me.

"How did you know this place existed?" she asked.

"There was an event in the history of modernism called Die Tunisreise: the Tunis trip. Three young artists—Paul Klee, August

Macke, and Louis Moilliet—came to Sidi Bou Saïd in the spring of 1914 and stayed through the summer. When they and the canvases they painted here returned to Europe it supposedly had a deep influence on the direction of art, especially German Expressionism."

"What happened to them?"

"The artists? Klee became famous, a contemporary of Picasso, and his paintings are scattered throughout the museums of the world. Moilliet I'm not sure. Macke was killed later in the same year, 1914— one of the early casualties on the Western Front. Of the three, I think of his work as the best."

Adelina had remained silent during this exchange.

"What did you think of the Bardo?" I asked her.

She considered the question for a while before answering, as if it might be a trap. "I'm glad that I went but not for the reasons you might assume. It wasn't the exhibits, it was the place itself."

"Yes, a very beautiful palace."

But she waved aside my remark and put down her glass, the better to focus on what she had to say.

"More than just beautiful, I thought. For a start, it was not large. Most palaces are enormous, trying to overawe with their size, but the Bardo is on a sensible human scale. Grandeur was not the aim. It wasn't built to impress anyone; it was built to be a place in which to live well. Such attention to detail—the work of people who took the trouble to do things properly. I would take the modest Bardo over pompous Versailles any day. And the decoration: tilework that was floral or geometric, arabesques that seem to endlessly flow. Abstract beauty, not the stuff of a painting which—please excuse me for saying this, Evans—might fascinate for a few minutes or perhaps even a few hours but which I find soon becomes unengaging."

"Even the portrait of you?"

"Especially the portrait of me. No, that came out ungenerously, and it's not what I mean at all. The *Lustration* is a great work—even I can see that—but I just don't want to have to face it every day. I want something calm, something non-specific, something into which the mind can seem to sink and then move along in its own wandering way without being confined by the work itself."

I was tempted to ask her what she thought about the other portrait, the one hanging in Exeter College.

"There are precedents," I said. "Calligraphy for example, in which one takes pleasure despite ignorance of the meaning. It's the characters themselves that matter, not what they say. Or perhaps even Abstraction as a whole."

But this did not satisfy her.

"I'm putting myself badly," she said with a smile. "I need another drink."

I called over the waiter for a second round. I could see that Adelina was using this pause to compose her thoughts, and when the drinks had been delivered she took up her theme.

"At the risk of sounding insane, here is what happened at the Bardo: the palace spoke to me. This is what it said: 'What have you achieved beyond my bey? You can travel from continent to continent in mere hours, you might say—but you do so jampacked like rows of galley slaves into a metal tube breathing unnatural air and seeing nothing on the way. I say the life of the bey who dwelt here was better. He would have taken an unhurried voyage to his destination, up on deck breathing the clean salty air and enjoying the sunshine, able to get about at will without worrying about other passengers in the way or the drinks cart blocking the aisle or the wretched seatbelt sign ordering you not to move—something illuminated not for safety but at the behest of the airline's liability lawyers. You call that the miracle of modern air travel; I call it a dungeon in the sky. Whose way is more civilized? But, you say, I can instantly communicate with someone on the other side of the world—and I say all that means is that you can never escape the grip of others, tied to them by your telecommunications tethers, imprisoned not physically but electronically, whereas my bey can sit at leisure and compose a letter clearly and thoughtfully, a physical thing with presence and persistence, unlike your words on the ether, lasting but an instant and then sprinkled into the wind. Whose way is more civilized? But we are free, I hear you declare—and I say that is just a word and nothing more. No one is free, because each of us is dependent on the whole for everything: our food, our drink, our shelter, our existence. The forms change; the fact remains. And so logically it comes down to a simple matter: the only question is how to live well with the resources that one has been allotted by fate. Look at me!—my bey has bested you, I believe.'"

This was an astonishing speech to come from the lips of someone who had barely spoken on the voyage until now: Rousseau, Buddha, and the American Transcendentalists all rolled into one. And all the more astonishing because I had felt the same thing myself earlier in the day atop the Byrsa, but I said nothing about that now—it would have sounded false, even condescending. Instead, I wondered if a Rousseauian-Buddhist-American Transcendentalist would feel any scruple in tossing a Russian oligarch over the side. They might even see it as a moral obligation, something implicit in the social contract.

"If that's what the palace said to you, then I agree: the building itself was the best art in the Bardo." I raised the glass. "Here's to being intimately addressed by inanimate objects."

The women laughed, raised their glasses with mine, and we drank to it.

XXVII

O UR NEXT DESTINATION, PORTO EMPEDOCLE, WAS NAMED for the philosopher Empedocles, native of nearby Agrigento, a city on the south coast of Sicily over which the Romans and Carthaginians had frequently fought and so a suitable location for a photo shoot based on the Bardo's mosaic.

It was Empedocles who first conceived the four ancient elements: earth, air, fire, and water. Conveniently for our photo shoot, he was in addition to being a philosopher said to have had a passion for horse racing.

Porto Empedocle is two hundred miles from Tunis, a passage with one full day spent at sea. It was during the afternoon of that day, with most of the women on the sun deck and the Marchesa taking a nap, that Wu found Oriana Welles and me in the main salon. He invited us to join him in his cabin.

I was envious when I entered Wu's accommodations, the owner's day cabin, almost as opulent as the nearby owner's stateroom occupied by the Marchesa but decorated in a more reserved and masculine style and, unlike the stateroom, it only had regular portholes instead of wide windows. Wu immediately got down to business.

"You recall that during the examination of Verkhovsky's body I took a blood sample?"

"Yes."

"In Marseilles, I made arrangements to have that sample tested by a medical laboratory. Tunis was the first chance I've had to get the results."

"And?"

"There are three items of note. To begin with, Verkhovsky was suffering from high cholesterol. He might have believed that red meat made him virile, but in fact it was killing him. At a minimum, he should have been taking a statin and of course he needed to lose weight—this last not just for the cholesterol: he was grossly obese and there would have been any number of insalubrious or morbid conditions that weight loss would have ameliorated."

Although the patient was dead the doctor still resented the causes of his ill health, a physician by nature as well as vocation.

"Which brings me to the second item. It was obvious that Verkhovsky's blood alcohol level would be high, as indeed it was. In Europe, this is measured as milligrams per deciliter, and Verkhovsky's was eighty, which is the equivalent in our terms of 0.08 percent blood alcohol content—high enough to be considered legally intoxicated, although not excessively drunk. But I must tell you that alcohol was not the only intoxicant in Verkhovsky's system. There was another: cocaine. I had already observed from the medical examination that he must have once been a habitual user. It is now apparent that he still was."

"So that night Verkhovsky was both high and drunk?"

"Indeed."

"A dangerous combination."

"As it proved to be."

But I had meant dangerous not for Verkhovsky but for whoever had tossed him over the side that night—there had been the chance that Verkhovsky, high on cocaine, would grab a hold of his attacker and that they would tumble overboard together.

"And the third item?" Oriana asked.

"I believe that Verkhovsky may have been epileptic."

"You can tell that from a blood sample?"

"Directly, no. Indirectly, yes, by medication: Verkhovsky's blood had an elevated level of potassium bromide. Potassium bromide is a sedative—it is the source of the term *bromide* when used in the general sense, meaning something intended to soothe or placate. Its medical use is in the treatment of epilepsy. Potassium bromide was once widely prescribed in the U.S. and Canada but ceased to be some years ago, except for dogs—in fact, a routine blood examination at home today would not have picked up its presence because it is no longer tested for."

"Dogs?"

"Yes, dogs can suffer from epilepsy, too. In Europe, potassium bromide is still prescribed for humans, especially in the treatment of myoclonic seizures. I checked the pharmacopeia. They are marketed as "Dibro-Be mono," 850 milligrams, and come as white tablets in pop-foil strips. The labeling is usually in German since that's where they're manufactured. Did you come across such a thing when going through Mr. Verkhovsky's effects?"

"No," I said. "We saw no medications at all."

"None? No potassium bromide is strange enough, since we know it was in his bloodstream, but no medications of any kind for someone of Verkhovsky's age and physical condition would be most unusual."

"You're saying they may have been stolen?"

"That's a possibility. Or maybe one of his nieces held his medications for him."

"I asked," Oriana said. "They say no."

"Perhaps they were tucked away somewhere in a manner that led to them being overlooked?" It made me think of the cocaine in the talcum powder tin, something that I had indeed missed—Verkhovsky was good at hiding things.

"We'll never know now. All his stuff went ashore with the body."

"Maybe the French came across some medications when they inventoried his effects," Oriana said. "I'll contact Renard to see if they discovered anything."

It was not until we had left the cabin that I broached the other possibility with Oriana.

"Wu said that potassium bromide is a sedative. It could have been used to make Verkhovsky easier to handle."

"That's what I was thinking. You realize what this means?"

"What?"

"Until now, we've assumed that whoever did it would have had to physically overpower Verkhovsky, which in practical terms eliminated the women, unless the nieces were working together."

"But not now—anyone could have done it."

"Almost anyone. The Marchesa wouldn't have been able to, even if he was unconscious."

"True," I agreed. I left unspoken the thought that Adelina could have done it for her.

XXVIII

The site selected for the first of the photo shoots was the deceptively named Valle dei Templi, Valley of the Temples—not a valley but the opposite, a ridge, located a few miles outside Agrigento and along which a series of temples had been built in the Fifth Century B.C. Only one of these remained substantially intact, the Temple of Concord, but when scouting the site—something Shotter and I did after the *Mulvane* docked at Porto Empedocle—he identified the Temple of Juno as his preferred backdrop.

"Stark," he explained in his characteristically succinct manner. "No trees, just columns."

It was true: there was nothing but towering golden stone against a background of clear blue sky. At least here the columns were still standing, albeit in graceful decay, as opposed to unfortunate Carthage where everything that could tumble down already had. Many retained entablature linking them with their neighbors, and the stone had an appealing honeyed hue that reminded me of a Cotswolds village.

We returned to the *Mulvane* at the same time as Urquhart and Oriana came back from Agrigento, where they had met with the local authorities to make arrangements. The four of us sat on the deck under the awning and compared notes while drinking gin and tonics to wash away the dust.

"Everything you've heard about Sicilians is true," Urquhart began. "Even I, living in Greece and not unacquainted with the sticky fingers of petty officialdom, was taken aback."

"Palms here are not just greased," Oriana added. "They get a complete lube job." She held out her own palm, counting off on her fingers.

"Use of the facility from 8:00 A.M. to 10:00 A.M., when it opens to the general public: two thousand euros." She went to a second finger. "Although it will be just us in the park, for some reason the place must be fully staffed: another thousand." Third finger. " 'Ah, but I forget, how clumsy of me, it will of course be overtime, and therefore at one-and-a-half normal rates.' " She struck her palm against her forehead, apparently imitating the gesture that had accompanied this remark. "Another five hundred euros." Fourth finger. "And then, of course, there is the 'consideration' for the police—that's exactly what he called it: *la considerazione per la polizia*—another five hundred euros." Lastly came the thumb. "Then, on top of all that, he tried to add twenty percent VAT—on a bribe!"

Urquhart took up the tale. "That's where Oriana bamboozled the fellow. She said, 'Oh, we had hoped to pay you in cash, but if there's any tax involved then of course there'll need to be an audit trail—and I had so wanted to avoid unnecessary paperwork.' At the mention of the word *audit* all talk of VAT ceased."

"At least he helped with the horses. There's a local racehorse owner he knows, a Signor Aldo, whom he called while we were in the office. Strange to say, the horses will come gratis: he, Signor Aldo, will bring them himself, so I guess the price is that he gets to be on the set for the photo shoot. I hope you don't mind?" This last was directed at Shotter.

"Not at all," he said. "I just hope that after all this I don't forget to put film in the camera.'

WE HAD A SPARE DAY BEFORE THE EXORBITANTLY PROCURED shoot in the Valle dei Templi, and the next morning the *Mulvane*'s passengers split into three parties. Most people opted for the beach. A second party, Urquhart and Gilbert, decided to climb Etna. I sensed that they would prefer to do this alone—a chance to get down to brass tacks on the *Daily Courier* deal—and so I declined the invitation to join them. Besides, I had another duty to perform: add to the list of artworks that would be the basis for the photo shoots.

Despite Tess's delight when she came up with the idea, the production of new art based on Old Masters is far from original: there are numerous contemporary examples—paintings, photographs, even movies—that use the same source of inspiration, and so I hoped to add a little interest by seeking out some items that were less obvious than the Botticellis. The Ellès mosaic was a good start, and I already had in mind another work, a de Chirico at the Met that depicts Ariadne wakening to discover that she has been abandoned. I even knew where to shoot that one: in EUR, Mussolini's Rome, where the bleak travertine arches of the monumental totalitarian buildings uncannily match those in the picture—perhaps Il Duce's architect had had the de Chirico in mind when designing them. Certainly the location, an excessive fascist fantasy, would be as surreal as the painting.

I had an idea that I might find something to add to the list in Castelbuono, directly across the island from Porto Empedocle. I had never been there—never before to Sicily—but I knew the town had an old fortification, Ventimiglia Castle, which housed a museum with an eclectic mixture of art, including holdings of a local artist, Paolo Cicero, active during the interwar years and so appropriate for our voyage.

Shotter, wanting like me to leave the two older men to themselves, elected to come along. Adelina decided to join us—going to the beach would necessarily involve time in the sun, and since in conservative Sicily going topless was not an option it would result in tan lines that would be distractions in the calendar shots.

The three of us bundled into the car straight after breakfast, our early route across the mountain roads doubly illuminated now that Betelgeuse was rising noticeably before the sun, and the angular separation between the two served to remove shadows rather than emphasize them.

Castelbuono was not disappointing—the Cappella Palatina alone, exuberantly Rococo, was worth the trip—but as we stood in the gallery with the Ciceros I could see that the paintings left my companions underwhelmed.

Me, too. Most of them were small and indifferently executed, but one seemed to be a candidate. It depicted a woman, naked, on the floor of what was perhaps a cave or grotto. The pose was unusual, legs slightly curled where she lay but torso raised, held aloft by a right arm held out behind her, a posture that carried a suggestion of expectation or longing, and which reminded me of Wyeth's *Christina's World* that hangs in the Modern (the pose in that work due to the subject's affliction, polio). But unlike that painting, here the sitter faced the viewer and it was her gaze, calm and composed, that gave the painting its subtle power, an effect aided by a swathe of golden light visible through the otherwise overgrown entrance behind her.

Adelina joined me.

"This one's better than the others," she said.

"I think so, too."

"Tell me about the artist."

"Local, a native of Castelbuono. Probably best known not for his paintings as for being associated with Aleister Crowley."

"Who's Aleister Crowley?"

"An Englishman." I had looked him up in an encyclopedia the previous day, and so had the biographical details at hand. "Wealthy and eccentric. Cambridge educated. Supposedly a sorcerer and certainly a seducer. Accomplished mountaineer. Morphine addict. Grand master-level chess champion. Sometime spy. He invented a religion called Thelema, dedicated to occult practices, and after the First World War he opened an abbey in Cefalù, not far from here—that's where Cicero became involved. Mussolini shut the place down when he came to power, and Crowley was deported. I think he moved to Tunis."

"What happened to the abbey?"

"Abandoned. The walls were originally covered with Crowley's murals—he was an artist, on top of everything else—but the fascists had them whitewashed as being degenerate and obscene." There is nothing totalitarian states despise more than degeneracy and obscenity, despite themselves being degenerate and obscene.

"I think there was an attempt to restore them, but it didn't work out."

"Can we go there?"

"I don't know. We can give it a try."

THE "ABBEY" TURNED OUT TO BE JUST A LARGE HOUSE LYING abandoned amid grounds gone wild, a place we would never have found had the car's navigation system not known it. We made our way to the building itself, with crumbling stucco walls and a red-tile roof much of which had collapsed. A tin sign warned in two languages that trespassing was forbidden, but we pushed our way past into the house and were obviously not the first to do so. The interior showed signs of temporary occupation, mostly graffiti, but very specific graffiti: there were Thelemic symbols and sayings everywhere.

In one room there was a portrait of Crowley himself, recognizable by the big bald head and strangely pointed ears, and further identified by the caption ΘΕΛΕΜΑ—*Thelema* in the Greek alphabet—and 666, the number of the Beast—"Beast" having been Crowley's preferred form of address. He gazed out wickedly, a high priest always ready for some not-too-pleasant initiation. The opposite wall contained an opening to the outside, probably originally a doorway but the brickwork had crumbled away leaving it jagged and overgrown. I found a section of true fresco, that is, images painted while the plaster was still wet: some of Crowley's original work had survived the fascist whitewashing. It was hard to tell what they represented: a jumble of abstract figures, like a Matisse, but here there was no hint of Provençal pleasure in sun and sea but instead a ritual of some kind.

"This part is original," I said. "Probably preserved because the roof above this section of wall is still intact."

"It's like the grotto in the Cicero," Adelina said, and suddenly we both realized what she was suggesting: an impromptu photo shoot.

"Look at the light." A shaft of sunlight lit a spot on the floor, a natural place for Adelina to replicate the pose in the painting.

"And there," Shotter added, pointing to the wall where a second shaft of light, from Betelgeuse, lit the Beast figure on the wall behind, serendipitously providing what would be a naturally dramatic scene: beauty gazed upon by malevolence.

"We'll have to be quick," he warned, but Adelina was already unbuttoning.

Shotter removed his camera from the little case he habitually carried over his shoulder and began making settings.

"Evans, would you mind keeping watch? Warn us if someone comes."

I left the house and went twenty yards down toward the road, close enough to scramble back quickly. The abbey was located on a hill a little out of town and there was a rocky prominence providing a ready-made lookout point, on which I stood. Down below I could see the castle and cathedral of Cefalù, and beyond them the ageless Mediterranean, sparkling with light, unchanged after a hundred religions had come and gone along its shores.

I was thinking that there must have been many people before me who had stood on this same spot and gazed over this same view when Shotter and Adelina suddenly appeared through the undergrowth.

"What's wrong?"

"Nothing," Shotter said. "We just had to be fast to take advantage of that light. I got it, I think." His face was alive, obviously sensing that despite the lack of preparation the shoot had been a success, or perhaps this was just a natural reaction to Adelina naked. "Although with film you can never be sure until you get the actual prints."

We agreed not to tell the others until he had developed the roll to see how it turned out.[*]

---

[*] It turned out very well, despite being unplanned and shot with the simple camera and consumer-grade film that was all Shotter had with him at the time. The photograph selected from that session, with somebody's Basquiat-like graffito rendition of Crowley's big bald head on the wall behind Adelina's left shoulder, lurking treachorously and spotlighted by Betelgeuse, became one of the most celebrated of the calendar's photographs, eclipsed in renown, I think, only by the Venuses. That it was a rapid on-the-fly session was somehow conveyed in the final result, capturing a sense of the shoot's trespassing urgency—an effect enhanced by the rough grain that Shotter brought out in the developing, so coarse that it seemed as if the grit of the place had got into the film stock.

XXIX

I NOW THINK OF SICILY AS A FULCRUM, THE POINT AT which personalities were prized loose from the blur of unfamiliarity, emerging as distinct characters, generally richer and deeper—although perhaps, as with some paintings, I am reading too much into them: an occupational hazard for an art historian.

It was also the time from which the Verkhovsky story, piece by painstaking piece, started coming together.

Despite the impromptu photo shoot at her own suggestion, I found Adelina's emergence the least surprising. That enigmatic power had always been there, a latent sphinxlike potency that had marked her as exceptional from the moment I laid eyes on the Exeter portrait. She held it mostly in check, by nature undemonstrative, but it was never far from the surface.

Most interesting to me professionally was Shotter. I had never before seen an artist at work—really at work, which is not paintbrush in hand or eye to the viewfinder. In good art, those are just endpoints in a process that takes place mostly in the mind, and I could see it happening in the distracted intensity with which Shotter focused on Adelina: he was totally fixated by the subject matter, completely consumed with the artistic project on which he was engaged, always considering and absorbing.

I wondered if she felt it, but someone who looks like Adelina is used to being scrutinized, and she let attention slough away with patrician indifference.

Gilbert, too—there had been something of the supplicant about him in the beginning, as he had admitted: he was essentially submitting to a three-month interview to see if he was fit to acquire Urquhart's paper. But now there was a harder edge to him, the mien of a man who has had success or soon expects it—I wondered if the issue of the *Daily Courier*'s future had been settled atop Etna.

A fourth transformation is more difficult to characterize. I still do not understand exactly what that transformation was, and it took a horse for me to see it.

Signor Aldo arrived onsite at precisely eight o'clock on the morning of the Valley of the Temples photo shoot. He brought not just the racehorses, accommodated in a float towed by one of the three vehicles in his entourage, but also by five large gentlemen: his driver and four supplementary thugs. It was apparent from the deference of the park staff that Signor Aldo was the local Mafioso. It was also clear from his pristine suit, polished shoes, black shirt, white tie, and matching carnation, that he expected to be included in the shoot.

Gilbert and I headed him off and the nieces, accustomed to handling the type, came and made soothing small talk—an awkward scene was averted.

Meanwhile, the horses were unloaded and saddled: two fine specimens, matching bays and obviously genuine Thoroughbreds, but unsettled and skittish—I feared they would never be held steady enough for the shoot, especially as their riders were required to hold aloft a long garland above Adelina. Rasputina and Tess had been designated for the roles of Centauresses because they were both experienced riders: Rasputina's mother, in addition to the Beverly Hills mansion, owned a ranch in Montana, and Tess, raised as a proper English miss, had been taught jumping from an early age.

Three locals had been enlisted for the shoot: a florist to prepare the garland, plus a hairdresser and makeup artist for Adelina. When the latter two released her we were ready to begin. Rasputina and Tess approached the horses, who immediately tried to back away. Rasputina looked nervous but Tess simply grabbed the bridle, gently but firmly brought the horse's head down to hers, gave it a little nuzzle and a few words of encouragement, and then mounted like a butterfly alighting upon a rhinoceros. The horse, so lately restive, remained perfectly immobile while Tess settled herself in the saddle. She then took it for a little test drive, cantering to the park entrance and back. Tess, apparently satisfied with the result, gave its neck a quick pat of approval and then trotted over to her position beside Adelina. Rasputina's horse, apparently abashed by the good behavior of its companion, immediately became equally biddable, and neither animal caused the least difficulty during the long shoot.

As I say, I am not sure what the metamorphosis I claim to have seen was, other than the obvious observation that it was a demonstration of unsuspected competence. I remember the look on Tess's face when she first mounted the horse: her lips twisted in an unconscious little moue— part uncertainty, part determination—and the unhurried grasp of her left hand gathering the reins, long fingers twisting about them in slow time, the way a mermaid might pluck algal tresses from the briny depths.

No doubt the outfit helped: riding pinks, but both Rasputina and Tess had contributed to the spirit of the shoot by unbuttoning their shirts to the navel, and had obviously dispensed with underwear.

I realized that twice now I had too easily dismissed Tess Lysett.

I NEED NOT DWELL ON THE OUTCOME OF THE VALLEY OF THE Temples photo shoot: all the world is familiar with the result. The black lace headscarf that Adelina added ad hoc to her costume, or lack of costume, is properly called a chapel veil, a leftover from Spain's long occupation of Sicily, during which women wore a mantilla when in church, and was an item that she had picked up from a street stall in Agrigento. The cape, coincidentally continuing the ecclesiastic theme, was a cardinal's *ferraiolo*, chosen because the only place a suitable cape could be located was in a clerical supply store. It all worked: Adelina's shadowed and expressionless stare was visible through the veil, as if challenging the viewer to understand the meaning of this strange scene, the red of the rose matching that of the cape and the jackets of the two centauresses flanking her. Behind them, the golden columns of the temple rose against a pure sweep of blue sky. Shotter filmed from low down—he was on his knees for much of the shoot, sometimes completely lying down in the dirt, and the effect was to emphasize the verticality of the scene: Adelina's long slender form, the Thoroughbreds' legs, the soaring columns of the temple behind them.

I envied him, not writing about art but making it.

WE RETURNED TO THE *MULVANE* MID-MORNING, FAMISHED— there had been no time to eat beforehand. Ernesto had laid out a sort of Italian brunch: fresh pastries and sweet rolls for those still in a breakfast mood; wine, prosciutto, and insalata Caprese for those ready to move on to lunch. I went below to wash up, thinking that I would have both meals, one directly after the other, when I ran into Wu coming the other way, carrying his medical bag and with a stethoscope around his neck.

He looked up in surprise.

"Oh, you're back already," he said.

Neither Urquhart nor Wu had joined us at the shoot that morning. From the look on Wu's face, having just emerged from Urquhart's cabin, it was suddenly clear why we had a doctor embarked.

"Everything okay?" I asked.

"No, it is not! What fool would climb Etna with such a condition?— now the price must be paid." He was angry but checked himself from further compromising patient confidentiality. "Please excuse this outburst, Evans. I hope that you will ignore it."

"Certainly, think nothing of it." The doctor went on his way.

"Did you know that Urquhart has some sort of medical condition?" I asked after having recounted the conversation with Wu.

"Yes, of course," Oriana replied. "That's why we brought along a cardiac specialist." We were standing right aft, out of earshot of the others. The Marchesa was taking an afternoon nap, and so her usual bench by the back rail was unoccupied.

"But this changes things."

"How?"

"A man knowing that he is dying has a different perspective."

"You mean, might be more willing to murder odious oligarchs?"

"Yes, among other things."

"Urquhart's not dying, at least not any more than the rest of us. He suffers from a heart arrhythmia. It's not life-threatening, although mountain climbing is obviously not recommended—no wonder Wu was annoyed."

"Still, there has to be a reason why Urquhart, cultured and intelligent, would have invited Verkhovsky, crude and obnoxious. It certainly wasn't for the pleasure of his company."

"So you're back to your original idea—Urquhart tossed Verkhovsky overboard?"

"It's the only theory that explains why Verkhovsky was invited." If Oriana remained unconvinced on that score, she was openly skeptical about the next thing I had to tell her. "There's something else: I think my cabin has been searched."

"What makes you say that?"

"My hairbrush was moved."

"Your hairbrush?"

"I put it in exactly the same place every time after using it. It had been moved."

"Who puts their hairbrush in *exactly* the same place?"

"I do."

"I think I see now why you're unmarried."

"Nevertheless, the fact remains that someone moved it."

"Probably just the roll of the ship. Or maybe one of the maids bumped it when cleaning."

"It wasn't bumped; it was on another shelf. And why would the maids be cleaning inside a bathroom cabinet?"

"Evans, you're starting to sound a little paranoid. Think about it: what would anyone be searching for? And even if there was something worth searching for, would they really be looking for it in your bathroom?"

I had to admit that she had a point and decided not to pursue the matter. Oriana pulled from her pocket a sheaf of folder paper, which she offered to me.

"What is it?"

"Printout of an email from Renard, in response to my request for the inventory of Verkhovsky's personal effects."

There were two sections. The first was the inventory of items unloaded from the *Mulvane*. The second, longer, listed his personal effects located in French territory—the French authorities had been to the house in Villefranche-sur-Mer and itemized what they found there. I quickly scanned this second list. Notable for its absence was the Lamborghini—I wondered what had become of it. One item stood out: *Reçu de la Galerie Tremblay, Cannes. Reçu* means receipt. Tremblay is a well-known art dealer located on la Croisette and specializing in modern art. The listing did not specify whether Verkhovsky had been a buyer or a seller.

I reverted to the first section, reading it more carefully this time.

"No medications, as we thought."

"Exactly."

"So where did the potassium bromide in Verkhovsky's bloodstream come from?"

"Not Urquhart. He has no history of epilepsy."

"But someone had to have given it to him. And why would that have been but to sedate him, making it easier to toss him overboard?"

"Agreed," Oriana replied. "I would say that if we locate the potassium bromide, then we've found Verkhovsky's killer."

XXX

T HE *MULVANE* COULD HAVE MADE THE PASSAGE FROM
Porto Empedocle to Monaco in two days, but we were in no hurry.
After the fuss with the photo shoot in Agrigento, there was a general
feeling that we would rather be on our own for a while. It was further
understood, among some of us, that a period away from the demands of
land would be best for Urquhart right now. Besides, it would not do to
return to Monaco before Tess turned eighteen.

So it was that the yacht sailed slowly westward along the southern
shore of Sicily before turning north and gently threading the Aegadian
Islands into the Tyrrhenian Sea. We barely made way, which delighted
the laconic Tom Simmons, since it put no strain on his engines, and also
the women as they could sunbathe unbuffeted by ship-generated breeze.
We were sometimes joined by dolphins who took to diving in and out of
our bow wave but, perhaps finding the ship's slow progress too little of
a challenge, the pod would peel off and look for better sport elsewhere.

We sometimes stopped completely, and the accommodation ladder
was lowered for people to swim. Even when stationary, the *Mulvane*
never rolled much, and it was Tom Simmons who explained this to me.
When she had been refurbished, the yacht was fitted with something not
part of the original equipment: a modern active stabilization system. This

comprised a series of waterjets in the hull below the waterline controlled by a central unit that detected roll and automatically activated the jets to counter it, so that even while dead in the water or lying at anchor the yacht's movement was always minimized. It worked well: no one ever suffered mal de mer aboard the *Mulvane*.

In the evenings, the awning would be removed and we had dinner under the stars. The moon cooperated—it was full on the evening we sailed from Porto Empedocle—and since Betelgeuse was setting earlier than the sun it had the night sky to itself.

Ernesto, perhaps sensing that we had had a surfeit of seafood, added variety to the menu: pasta with Sicilian sausage or ragu Bolognese, and from a barbeque set up on deck grilled veal chops over polenta or sliced steak Florentine.

The days passed leisurely; the men unwound; the women got ever browner.

We made landfall at Capo Comino on the Sardinian coast and continued north, paralleling the Costa Smeralda. This area is a well-known watering hole for the wealthy, but we felt no desire to mix with them. However, we did employ the Riva for occasional reconnaissance missions.

Shotter and I were returning from one of these—we had poked into La Celvia, a traditional haunt of *il bel mondo*—but by the time we got back the *Mulvane* had rounded Isola di li Nibani and was now heading northwest for the Strait of Bonifacio, so we ended up approaching the yacht from her seaward quarter rather than directly from land.

It was mid-afternoon. The sun was still high but the supernova was beginning to set below the mountains of Sardinia, and the women on the sun deck, five of them, had stood to watch. They were facing west, either with their backs toward us or at most side-on. None of them was wearing a swimsuit.

My hand was moving to the button for the Riva's horn, but Shotter was already opening his camera. I guessed it was fine, since the lowering supernova rendered them mostly in shadow from our side, and indeed the resulting shot was deemed suitable for the calendar's back cover. It was a compelling photograph, the postures varied—one girl on tiptoes with hand raised to shield her eyes; another with knee bent and a book still in hand, a third caught precisely in profile, apparently looking north and with the supernova rendering her in perfect silhouette; the fourth momentarily contemplating something on deck while casually brushing a strand of hair behind an ear; the last with a hand clapped to her straw hat, the only thing she wore besides sunglasses.

Its very informality made it, the casual lack of artifice or pose resulting from unconsciousness of the camera: just a group of women enjoying sun and sea, an ageless Mediterranean theme. And then, all of a sudden, I realized that I had another artwork for the photo shoot list.

If there is a single painting that more than any other ushered in the era of modern art, it would be Picasso's *Les Demoiselles d'Avignon*. It depicts five women, all nude, and it was the sight of those five on the *Mulvane*'s sun deck that forcefully brought it to mind. Moreover, the dominant color in that work is an ochre-tinged pink. In the Strait of Bonifacio that we were soon to sail through there is a beach—la Spiaggia Rosa, the pink beach—where the sand is the same hue as the painting, an obvious place to shoot it.

As soon as we returned on board I went straight to my cabin and for the first time used the handset marked *Bridge*.

FOUR OF US STOOD BY THE NAVIGATION TABLE, EXAMINING the chart. I pointed to the island of Budelli, located at the eastern end of the strait.

"That's where it is," I said.

Trevelyan looked put out.

"You'll have to do it quickly," he said. "Bonifacio can be a difficult passage and I don't want to transit it in the dark."

"Exactly where on the island is the beach?" Shotter asked.

"Here." I showed him the little bay.

"On the eastern side?"

"Yes."

Shotter turned to the captain. "This afternoon wouldn't work anyway: the sun would be behind the scene. To get the light right it needs to be shot in the morning."

Trevelyan looked even more put out. "I suppose that we can delay the transit, although I'll have to crack on afterward to meet our dock time in Monaco."

"There's another complication." I turned to the fourth member of our party, Oriana, who until now had remained silent. "The beach is part of the Maddalena Archipelago National Park. Access to it is controlled: you're only allowed to go with a guide. I'd arrange one myself, but I don't have a phone."

Trevelyan had been merely irritated by the proposed change in plan, but the implication that Oriana would have to suddenly make the arrangements left her visibly annoyed.

"Why are we doing this anyway?" she complained. "Picasso was Spanish, not Italian."

"The theme is part of the common Mediterranean heritage—the sweet life, sweet but savage, too."

Oriana was unimpressed with this explanation but she agreed to contact the park authorities, and a guide was subsequently organized for the next day. It was not until after she had done so that I explained there were five figures in *Les Demoiselles*: the fifth had to be either her or Tess.

THE PHOTO SHOOT TOOK PLACE EARLY THE NEXT MORNING, with the sun still low and illuminating the east-facing beach to best advantage. Only Shotter and the women went ashore—the minimum number necessary. They met their guide and were taken to the beach where they were given the rare privilege of going onto the sand for the shoot but with a strange proviso: they were not allowed to wear any suntan lotion since the chemicals might affect the microbial algae that give the sand its distinctive color.

Tess was the fifth figure, the one in Picasso's painting who sits with her back to the viewer and is thus the most modestly posed, although it

was not clear that this would be sufficient to avoid censure from the
Bishop of Chichester.

XXXI

F OR THE EVENING OF TESS LYSETT'S BIRTHDAY celebration we were again accommodated in the Hôtel de Paris on place du Casino. This temporary absence from the yacht served two purposes. Firstly, tonight was an occasion for the women to dress up, and so the arrangement would avoid the possibility of anyone's coiffure being disturbed by the breeze or having a gown grazed when going ashore—indeed, we were beginning the evening at the hotel bar followed by dinner in their grand restaurant, so there would be no need to even leave the establishment. Secondly, it gave the crew of the *Mulvane* a break: we were back in what was, despite the London registration, the yacht's operational home port, and so they could reconnect with their normal lives for a couple of days.

We men gathered on the terrace of the Bar Américain fifteen minutes before the women—the location had changed but not our routine. However, tonight we all wore white tie and decided to vary the drink for the occasion, ordering instead of Martinis the house specialty, la Condamine cocktails. By the appointed hour everyone other than Tess had arrived.

A little later, just as the lowering light had taken on the soft shade of early evening, Tess emerged onto the terrace. Describing the parts—a strapless gown of brocaded silk, embroidered in silver thread with little stars splayed across a deep navy background, cut corset-like above the waist but then puffing out below; hair up in an understated but elegant arrangement; neck and wrist adorned with the antique *la Comète* jewelry—does not do justice to the whole. She was, to use an old-fashioned but appropriate term, radiant.

We burst into spontaneous applause.

I AWOKE LATE THE NEXT MORNING, NOT HAVING RETURNED from the casino until 2:00 A.M. Among those still reducing the champagne stocks when I left was Oriana, but by the time I arrived hurriedly shaved and showered in the lobby she was already there, clear-eyed and not a hair out of place—like any good member of the Cato Club, she knew how to hold her liquor.

"The car is here," she said, her voice betraying almost no brittle edge of annoyance at my late arrival. "The concierge has the keys."

I shelved my planned suggestion that we first have a reviving cup of coffee.

THE CAR WAS A FERRARI, ONE OF THOSE OLD CALIFORNIAS that were among the last of the naturally aspirated models, and the cheapest the agency had available. The delivery agent, who might have been expected to explain the car's operation, had been released by Oriana when I failed to show up precisely on time—I felt like I was back at Harrow and in trouble for being a minute late to assembly. At least the top was already down. I finally figured out how to start the thing—no key; instead, you put your foot on the brake pedal and then press a bright red button on the steering wheel. It burst loudly into life, the engine's thundering rasp unsuppressed by turbochargers, something in which I would have delighted on any morning other than this one.

Oriana dealt with the navigation system, entering the address for our destination: Verkhovsky's villa in Villefranche-sur-Mer.

It was only ten kilometers to Villa Astenia but for some reason the car's perverse navigation system chose to take us via the Moyenne Corniche, notwithstanding that the villa lay on the water, directly off the Basse Corniche, and so it took nearly an hour—this was just not my morning.

After calling on the intercom, the front gate opened remotely and we drove on through the garden to the house, a large Belle Époque mansion painted white and with the sea sparkling beyond—Kirill Verkhovsky had lived well. The broker came out the front door as we pulled up, and her look of annoyance at being made to wait immediately melted into one of expectation at the sight of the car—the Ferrari had achieved the purpose for which we had rented it: to make the woman assume we were wealthy enough to afford a place like the Villa Astenia and therefore incline her to answer our nosy questions.

The broker was an Englishwoman, probably the one the *immobilière* routinely dispatched for property viewings by anglophones. She was a little vague but recognized a hangover when she saw one.

"Would you like some coffee?"

"No," Oriana said.

"Yes," I countered.

The broker suppressed a sigh: this was going to be a difficult viewing.

"Why don't we start in the kitchen?" she suggested, trying to sound upbeat. "I'll put on the espresso machine while we look it over. I'm sure you'll love it—all topline appliances."

This last comment was directed at Oriana, and I imagined that the woman must not have had much experience in the real-estate business, to have so completely misread a prospective buyer as to have imagined that Oriana cooked. There was a reason that she was a member of the Cato Club: it was to be fed.

We entered the villa and the music that I had thought must have been coming from elsewhere was suddenly much louder.

"Can we turn that off?" I asked.

The broker raced to a remote control and killed the noise.

"Sorry," she said. "Most people like it."

"I'm sure the sound system is just fine."

"No, I mean the music itself."

"Huh?"

"You don't know the history of the property?"

"No," Oriana quickly interjected, in case I blew this invitation to have our questions answered without even being asked. "I hope you'll tell us all about it."

"With pleasure." She cast an uncertain glance in my direction. "Maybe we should do it while the coffee's brewing."

It seemed that the Villa Astenia had been a retreat for a famous rock band in the 'Seventies; they had even recorded an album in the basement. Oriana listened patiently while I drank repeated espressos, and gradually the story was brought up to the last resident.

"A Russian oligarch," the broker admitted, her voice dropping to a whisper as if discussing an unsavory topic. "And his houseguests."

It was not hard to guess whom she must mean by houseguests.

"What happened to him?"

"He died. Drowned at sea, so they claim."

"So they claim?"

"Suffice to say that there had been some unpleasant gentleman of East European persuasion inquiring after him lately."

"Russians?"

"KGB," she replied with a nod. "Or whatever they call it now."

"FSB," I said, my first and last contribution to the conversation.

"How long had he owned the villa?"

"Owned? No, he never owned it; just rented it."

"Rented?"

"Yes. He had originally hoped to buy it, but I understand that there were complications regarding his status in France, and so he was renting until these were resolved. He died before it happened. He was only here for six months."

"And before?"

"Varenna," she replied. "On Lake Como. He had a villa there, too, but he didn't like it. He said that the locals resented his success and the Côte d'Azur was the only place where a man like him could be properly appreciated."

Varenna: a town I knew to be right across the water from Bellagio, home of the Marchesa della Brianza.

THE NEXT STOP WAS THE GALERIE TREMBLAY IN CANNES. I made sure to park on la Croisette directly in front but it turned out that we had no need of the car to gain the cooperation of the manager: as soon as I revealed that I was the curator for contemporary art at the Wentworth Collection I was persona grata.

"I would like to know what you can tell me about the artworks of a man for whom I believe you are the dealer, the late Kirill Verkhovsky."

"Ah yes, most unfortunate. The *policiers* were here last week, asking the same thing."

"You were handling a consignment on his behalf?"

"Yes, may I show you?

Verkhovsky might have been disagreeable as an individual, but his taste in fine art was first-rate. Or maybe he was advised, and the paintings were purchased as a means of diversifying his portfolio. There were only four of them, all oils—a mysterious Jean Charlot landscape that I might have considered acquiring in my professional capacity, and three good futurist works. Most spectacular of these was a Gino Severini, a large brilliantly colored canvas that accomplished the difficult task of reconciling cubism with neo-classicism—another painting that I longed to possess; a Carlo Carrà, *Le Figlie di Loth*, the daughters of Lot being a recurring theme in his work—I had seen an alternative version in the

Vatican Museums; and lastly a delicate and shadowy Natalia Goncharova self-portrait, deceptively understated.

Futurism is an offshoot of modern art that arose under the intellectual aegis of Filippo Marinetti, who summed up his artistic program with a memorable aphorism: "An automobile in motion is more beautiful than the *Victory of Samothrace*"— he might have appreciated the vehicle parked outside. By mid-century the movement had petered out, but it was being newly appreciated in current art criticism— Verkhovsky's advisor, if he had one, had chosen with a keen eye to potential capital appreciation.

I looked again at the Carrà and realized that I had found another work for the photo shoot list.

"There were also four drawings," the manager said. "A set of Don Quixotes by Salvador Dalí."

With this unexpected bombshell we suddenly had a connection, or at least the beginnings of one, between Verkhovsky and Urquhart. I tried to disguise my surprise and continued the conversation as evenly as I could.

"Dalís, you say? What became of them?"

"They were sold."

"To whom?"

"I regret that of course I am not permitted to reveal the purchaser's identity, but I would be happy to forward your contact details, should you wish to make an inquiry."

"How long had Verkhovsky owned them?"

"For several years, if I remember correctly. The paintings were somewhat more recently acquired, purchased from time to time as circumstances dictated."

I took "as circumstances dictated" to be a euphemism for "as he secreted money out of Russia." More lately, Verkhovsky had been converting the paintings back into cash, now legitimized, before fleeing on his Comoros passport—art as a method of money laundering is an activity with a long history and a promising future.

"Were the drawings authenticated?"

"Oh, yes: they even came with a letter of provenance from the original owner, for whom I believe Dalí drew them when she was a young girl. As I say, I would be happy to forward your contact details, should you wish." Left unsaid was that he would be extracting a fee as the go-between.

"No, that won't be necessary," I told him. "But if you could please send copies of the documentation for the Charlot and the Severini to the Wentworth I would be grateful. Prints, too, if you have them." I gave him my card, which he accepted with the sincere smile and warm handshake of an art dealer sensing an institutional purchase in the offing. He turned to Oriana.

"And Madame Evans, it has been a very great pleasure." This remark was accompanied by a small bow. Oriana blushed slightly, but she did nothing to correct him.

I HAD PERKED UP BY THE TIME WE LEFT THE GALERIE Tremblay—indeed, I was famished. On the way back from Cannes we decided to take a detour up to Saint-Paul-de-Vence, one of those little *villages perchés* that cling to the peaks rising steeply from the coastal plain. It boasts a famous establishment, La Colombe d'Or, where Chagall, Matisse, and Picasso had once paid for their meals with paintings. We were able to nab a table in the courtyard for a late afternoon lunch.

It was not until we were settled in and had ordered that I explained about the incident with the Dalís.

"You mean that the Marchesa had them in her possession before Urquhart gave them to her?"

"Yes, briefly. Soon after she came aboard."

"How could that be?"

"I presume that she simply came across them, probably guessed that they were intended for her and so decided to include them with the other drawings that she'd already arranged for me to evaluate. Urquhart wasn't yet on board and so there was little risk of them being noticed missing before she returned them."

"You think?"

"What other explanation is there? Things were disorganized that first day, same as when any ship is about to put to sea. In fact, I found the *Lustration* uncovered, even though Urquhart had wanted it concealed until the painting was presented to Adelina. Perhaps the Dalís were lying out in the library, too."

"So the Marchesa just takes these drawings, includes them with her own, and then returns them before Urquhart is any the wiser. But what for?"

"A free consultation, provided without any awareness that they were to be a gift, and therefore without prior prejudice."

"What do you make of the fact that Verkhovsky once lived on Lake Como?"

"The Marchesa might have known him before the cruise."

"I imagine it unlikely that Verkhovsky would have been admitted into her social circle," Oriana said, "but I think she would at least have known *of* him."

"You're right. Lake Como is mostly old money; the Italians there would probably have shunned him. Maybe that's what made him move to France—what's the use of conspicuous consumption if people just ignore you? At least on the Riviera there are other *nouveaux riches* you can show off to."

Oriana sighed in frustration. "We've learned a lot today, but it all seems to lead nowhere."

"We know the Russians were paying him visits."

"Probably why he didn't take medications, given their fondness for poisoning nationals abroad. But I think the whole Dalí/Como thing is a red herring."

"Why?"

"Because the one thing we know for sure is that it wasn't the Marchesa. Verkhovsky could have been drugged into a stupor for all it matters. It still would have been physically impossible for her to toss him overboard. Like I said before: she's simply too frail."

"You're right," I admitted, before asking the question that until now I had avoided. "But what if her grand-niece helped?"

I HAD PLANNED ON TURNING IN EARLY THAT EVENING TO complete the recovery from the night before but found myself unable to sleep and so went for a walk around Monaco instead. I circumnavigated the entire principality—not a great feat, as it is smaller than New York's Central Park, but nevertheless sufficient to have hopefully induced slumber. I was strolling up from Larvotto back toward the hotel when I recognized one of the people coming out of a noisy nightclub: Milosz, the *Mulvane*'s chief steward. He had a laughing girl on his right arm and was making a show of checking the time on his left. It was dark and he did not notice me among the throng on the sidewalk, but as I passed behind him and glanced at the watch I realized that I recognized it. That same distinctive timepiece had been on Verkhovsky's wrist at the Casino de Monte Carlo two weeks before.

XXXII

F OR THE SECOND TIME, THE *MULVANE* SET SAIL FROM
Monaco. The event was accompanied by less excitement now and
I wondered if it was because the other passengers, like me, were
reflecting on all that had happened since we first left the principality.

We made passage across the border and along the coast, anchoring
off Ventimiglia for a day, San Remo for another, Imperia for a third. In
each place colorful pastel houses spilled down steep slopes to the water,
providing a picturesque background for us on board, and no doubt an
equally beguiling sight for those on land, for proximity to shore caused
no interruption to the tanning routine on the sun deck. So it was that the
Italian Riviera became our backdrop for swimming and sunbathing by
day, drinking and dining by night.

The transition from French to Italian Riviera was also marked in the
galley, where Ernesto acknowledged our passage across the border by
switching from sauces of Niçoise olives and fat caper berries to the staple
of Liguria, pesto.

After dinner, people would mostly talk or read. Bébé sometimes
played the piano, but never the pieces intended for the proposed concert,
which she and Marta practiced in private. Bridge became popular, with
Gilbert and Adelina forming a pair against Wu and the Marchesa—by

the frequent exclamations coming from their table it was evident that these were hotly contested affairs. Occasionally, we played some of the board games with which the *Mulvane* was equipped, and one evening the men, including Welles, had a poker night that lasted into the early hours. Marta and I played chess continually: a board was set aside for our use on which we would make moves at leisure, any time of day or night, recording it in the accompanying notebook and leaving one of the spare queens on top, the color signaling whose turn was next. But mostly I liked to sit back with a scotch and soda after dinner, or go out on deck and lean on the rail, taking in the night air while looking at the lights ashore and the stars above. One evening I found Oriana already out there. Since we were alone I took the opportunity to quietly tell her what I had witnessed outside the nightclub in Monaco.

"You think Milosz stole Verkhovsky's watch from his corpse?"

"No, Verkhovsky wasn't wearing it that day. I only saw his watch once, in the casino the previous night—he probably just wore it of an evening, an item of jewelry rather than a means of keeping time."

"How can you be sure it was the same watch?"

"It was very distinctive, with a transparent dial so that you can see the movement underneath. It's the sort of watch that costs as much as a car, not something a ship's steward would possess. Besides, we didn't find it among Verkhovsky's personal effects."

"Maybe he didn't bring it on board."

"No, I checked Renard's inventory: the watch wasn't listed there either."

"So Milosz sneaks into Verkhovsky's cabin, takes the watch but gets caught and, fearing exposure, tosses Verkhovsky overboard?"

"Yes, something like that."

"How did he get caught?"

"Maybe Verkhovsky came below to get something—we know that he had to have done so at least once, for the cocaine."

Oriana nodded in reluctant acceptance. "Just what we needed: another suspect. Does it occur to you that instead of being narrowed down the list just keeps getting longer: Urquhart; Marta and/or Bébé; the

Marchesa with Adelina's assistance; Kustaa the Finn; and now Milosz the chief steward?"

"You're forgetting someone."

"Who?"

"Whoever gave him the potassium bromide."

XXXIII

WHEN ORIANA AND I RETURNED INSIDE TO THE MAIN salon we found Captain Trevelyan with the other passengers. There had been a conversation about our next port of call, Genoa. A layover to provision and fuel there had already been planned but Simmons had detected a vibration in the starboard shaft and suspected that the propeller might have become entangled in a fishing net or hit some hard piece of flotsam. After we were secured alongside he wanted to send Young George, as he called his cousin, diving beneath the hull to inspect it. If whatever was found there required dockyard repair then Genoa—one of Europe's leading ports—was a place with the facilities to do it. In any case, it would be more than the planned stop and go, potentially several days.

"Actually, that would suit me," Shotter said. "I could go up to Milan and collect my gear from the studio." He had not come professionally equipped to shoot the anti-Ripelli calendar, he explained, and this would give him a chance to correct the situation.

"And it would also suit myself and Adelina," the Marchesa announced. "We would like to invite you all to come up to the villa in Bellagio."

"Ten guests? Such an imposition."

"Not at all. When I was young we had house parties that were larger, and I believe it's time that the old place was brought alive again."

And so it was decided.

MUCH PLANNING WENT INTO THE PROPOSED PROGRAM DURING our passage, made even slower by Simmons' caution with the starboard shaft, which he locked to prevent further damage and so acted as a drag. On arrival in Genoa, Urquhart would initially remain on board to review the results of the underwater inspection but would come up to Bellagio in time for a *festa* planned for the next day. A Jeep was booked for Shotter, something with enough room for all his gear. The Marchesa's Mercedes would be waiting for her and Adelina to whisk them up to the villa so that they had an opportunity to prepare. It was perhaps to give them more time for this that Urquhart suggested a competition for the rest of us, part road trip, part provisioning expedition, part auto rally.

"There is a rental company that specializes in vintage Alfa Romeo Spiders," Urquhart explained, "those little two-seat sports cars manufactured last century and made famous in *The Graduate*. Four of them will be delivered to us in Genoa. The idea is to break into four teams of two people each and have a race to Bellagio. But there's a catch: each team must detour to a different village, one that's known for a particular product that is highly prized, and they must bring some of this prized product with them for consumption at the *festa*."

"Which villages are they?"

Urquhart consulted a sheet of paper.

"The first is Polesine Zibello, a little town on the Po north of Parma. Like Parma, it's known for its ham, but in this case one of special quality called Culatello di Zibello, aged hanging in dark cellars and famed for its flavor.

"The second is Bagolino, at the foothills of the Alps north of Brescia. It is known for Bagòss, a cheese produced only in that village, solely from the milk of a particular breed of cow called Bruna, and aged for at least a year.

"The third village is Barolo in Piedmont, and I need not tell you what is produced there: whichever team gets that one will be expected to return with a case from a good vineyard.

"The last is not a village but a Carthusian monastery: the Certosa di Pavia—the Charterhouse of Pavia—a little south of Milan, where they produce a prized herbal liqueur based on an ancient recipe: Gratiarum Carthusia, roughly, 'Grace of the Charterhouse.' Presumably some sort of Chartreuse. The team that gets the monastery will be expected to acquire a bottle or two, but the monks are a silent order and so some sign language might be required."

"How will the teams be decided?"

"Let me respond with a question of my own: who can drive a manual transmission?"

Fortunately, there were four of us familiar with stick shifts: myself; Welles; Marta; and Franklin Gilbert, who had raced dirt track carts as a kid and obviously fancied his chances in the rally. Rasputina and Wu had only ever driven automatics; Tess and Bébé could not drive at all.

We used a blind draw of the table setting tags in Milosz's bowl to decide the teams, and then a second draw of the place names inscribed on folded scraps of paper for the destinations. The results were as follows:

Welles (driver)/Wu (navigator)—Certosa di Pavia (Chartreuse)
Marta (driver)/Tess (navigator)—Bagolino (cheese)
Gilbert (driver)/Bébé (navigator)—Polesine Zibello (ham)
Evans (driver)/Rasputina (navigator)—Barolo (wine)

It was a race, but speed was restricted. The little Alfas, although nimble, were never fast, and there was a further limitation: *autostrade* were forbidden; it was to be secondary roads only. The fact that we would be going different distances was resolved simply: time taken would be divided by the distance required for the journey, as determined by a navigation app—whoever had the highest average speed would win.

Shotter volunteered to supplement the provisioning by bringing dessert, which he would acquire from a venerable Milanese *pasticceria* in the Quadrilatero d'Oro, near where he lived. The Marchesa undertook to provide silver cups for the winners—the race was on.

WHEN THE *MULVANE* CAME ALONGSIDE IN GENOA, SIX vehicles were waiting on the wharf: Shotter's Jeep; four shining little Alfas parked in a neat row, all in different colors and accompanied by an agent to see to the paperwork; and lastly the Marchesa's Mercedes, which was being buffed by the waiting chauffeur and whose glossy black tires revealed that it had indeed been recently reshod.

Allocation of the Alfas was done in the same way as the determination of the teams, by blind draw, and the key that Rasputina pulled from the bowl for us was to the sweet little slate-green 1750 Veloce that I had hoped we might get—the day was starting well.

Soon we were on the old Roman Via Aurelia, hugging the coast and heading westward. The top was down and we both wore hats: Rasputina that same broad-brimmed affair she had appeared in on the first day at sea, and me the panama. Progress was initially swift because, although not an *autostrada*, the Via Aurelia is multilane in the environs of Genoa, but as we left the city behind it reverted to a single lane and we slowed to the pace of the heavy coastal traffic. Rasputina no longer had to hold a hand on her head to stop the hat blowing off, and the wind noise was sufficiently reduced to make conversation possible.

She turned and said, "Sorry you got me instead of Oriana."

"Why should I be sorry?"

"Everyone knows you two are an item."

"What are you talking about?"

"Evans, it's not like anyone doesn't notice that the pair of you take every opportunity to be alone together."

I suddenly realized how our collaboration on the investigation could appear to others.

"I was enlisted to assist with the formalities following Verkhovsky's death because I speak French," I explained. "Although I speak French so badly that the people in Marseilles preferred to conduct the interview in English. Nevertheless, I was involved, and so there you go."

"That was weeks ago."

"There's been a continuing correspondence with the authorities—inventories of personal effects and the like."

"Requiring you to rent a Ferrari and whisk Oriana to a restaurant in Saint-Paul-de-Vence for lunch?"

I thought it best to change the subject.

"Did you ever speak to Verkhovsky before he was lost overboard? Anything more than an introduction, I mean."

"No, I avoided him."

"Any general impression?"

"Yes, he reminded me of my mother's agent."

"Did he seem depressed to you?"

"As in suicidal? No, not the type: too conceited to contemplate killing himself—again, like my mother's agent." She paused for a moment before continuing. "When he was discovered missing, my first thought was that he'd probably been thrown overboard."

"I must admit that the same idea occurred to me."

"Did you have a suspect in mind?"

"No."

"That's okay—I know who would have done it."

"What?"

"If Verkhovsky had been thrown overboard, then I know who would have done it. I have the evidence. Mystery solved." She waved a hand airily, showing how simple it was.

"But who? And what evidence?"

Rasputina raised her chin and looked out the window in a manner that on her mother would have been called insouciant.

"Whether or not I reveal that, Evans, will depend entirely on the lunch venue. You set a pretty high bar with Oriana—I hope you choose wisely."

She refused to say anything more on the subject until I had provided her with a satisfactory meal, instead burying herself in her cell phone to research Barolo wineries—our phones had been returned to us for the rally since the Alfas, never reliable even when new, were now around fifty years old.

We turned inland at Varazze and began the long climb on winding roads from Liguria into Piedmont. I took it slowly, not wanting to overheat the engine, and meanwhile we debated the virtues of the various wineries Rasputina looked up. A few were traditionalists, making their wine the old-fashioned way, crushing in cement vats and aging in huge *botti grandi* barrels that were taller than a man, casks that had been used for generations. Others adopted the international style, favoring aging in toasted French oak *barriques*. We decided that neither was quite right for the Marchesa: she did not reject modern methods—as her management of the shipyard had demonstrated—but wanted them to be adapted in ways that respected local traditions. We found a suitable candidate and Rasputina called ahead to make an appointment.

"Should I make a reservation for lunch, too?" she coyly suggested.

"No."

WE WERE MET AT THE ESTATE BY THE WINEMAKER WHO AFTER introducing himself took us through the facility. If we were to have had any chance of winning we should have just bought our wine and left, but it was not that sort of place and so instead we enjoyed a pleasant hour touring the cellars in the company of a man who knew his business and was proud to show it off. In the tasting room, we tried two single-vineyard Barolos and, unable to choose between them, bought a case of each. These had to be repacked into flat three-bottle boxes to fit into the trunk.

We had to briefly stop at the entrance when leaving, waiting for the automated gate to open. Since we were facing uphill and with a load in the trunk I gave the Alfa extra revs when the time came to release the clutch and move on.

"I'm amazed at how you manage that," Rasputina said.

"Drive a stick?"

"Yes."

"You'll have to do it yourself soon."

"What do you mean?"

"Your welcome-aboard present—I doubt that a Morgan would come with anything other than a manual transmission."

Rasputina's eyes opened wide—the idea that her new car might not be an automatic had never occurred to her.

"I don't know how to drive a stick."

I pulled over and shut down the engine.

"You might as well begin now."

"Now?"

"The more you do it the easier it becomes."

"We haven't got time. We'll lose the race."

"We lost the race when we agreed to the cellar tour. Come on, don't be a scaredy-cat."

I got out and went around to the passenger side. Rasputina reluctantly eased herself across the gearshift into the driver's seat. There were a few stalls to begin with, but she quickly got the hang of it. The little rural roads were all but empty, a good place to learn a stick, and we were soon scooting across the bucolic Barolo countryside.

We passed on the way signs identifying crus whose names are famed in the world of wine: Annunziata, Bussia, Falletto, and the Ginestra from which both our Barolos had originated. These gave me an idea for lunch. At the center of most Italian villages is a little piazza with a modest trattoria where you can get a good meal, fast and cheap. That is what I had been planning, but those passing signs gave me another idea: a picnic in a vineyard.

We parked in Barolo. There was an *alimentari* that would do, and I asked Rasputina to pick up a bottle from the nearby *enoteca* while I assembled the picnic.

"Don't forget a corkscrew."

When I returned to the car loaded down with bread, cheese, and salumi I found that Rasputina had equipped us with more than just a corkscrew: she had purchased an entire picnic basket.

The road race having long since been lost, we ate our lunch in leisurely fashion: on a blanket spread beneath a chestnut tree at the edge of what is the most famous of all Barolo crus, Cannubi, located just north of town and by happy coincidence the source of the wine that Rasputina had selected.

I lay down on the blanket after the meal, intending to doze before we hit the road again.

"Did that lunch qualify?"

"Yes," she said, "much better than any fancy restaurant."

"So are you going to tell me who might have murdered Kirill Verkhovsky now?"

"Yes, I am." She lay down like me, on her back, but 180 degrees in the opposite direction and with the crown of her head brushing against my right shoulder. Only our heads were together—a literal meeting of the minds. It was a strange arrangement, suggesting a subconscious reluctance to get too close, yet nevertheless intimate, given that we would have been nose to nose if not both facing up. "It would have been that deckhand from the Isle of Man."

"Jamys?"

"Yes."

"How do you know?"

"He said he was going to do it."

"He told you?"

"Not me, but I overheard him. Maybe I should start from the beginning."

"Please go ahead."

"Do the staff leave you little bottles of mineral water at night in your cabin, the same as they do for us women?"

"Yes."

"I woke up in the middle of that first night, the night Verkhovsky went overboard. I'd already drunk all my water—he was right about the bresaola, it was too salty. Anyway, I didn't want to unnecessarily disturb the staff so instead of ringing for someone I got up and put on a robe to go upstairs and get another bottle from the pantry, you know the one that's in that little space forward of the dining room and available to us twenty-four hours a day?"

"Yes, I know it."

"When I went up, the lights were still on in the main salon, and so I went forward along the deck instead."

"What time was this?"

"I don't know; I never checked."

"Was it dark?"

"Yes."

"So it was before 5:00 A.M., otherwise you would have noticed the supernova.

"Agreed."

"Was Verkhovsky still inside?"

"Yes, and still at the bar."

"Alone?"

"I think so, but I didn't look carefully; I just wanted to get by unseen."

"What happened next?"

"I continued forward and then into the deckhouse by the door on the port side. I went to the pantry and had gotten a new bottle of water when I was suddenly trapped."

"By Verkhovsky?"

"No, by Jamys and Aška. They went to the compartment next door, the place where they keep all the silverware and tablecloths and stuff— a storeroom, I suppose."

"And?"

"Well, I needn't tell you the details, which I'm sure you can guess— it seems that Jamys and Aška are romantically involved, but presumably there's not much privacy in the crew quarters."

"None at all: I saw them for myself when we did the medical examination."

"Anyway, to begin with, they were talking. Most of it I couldn't make out, but something must have annoyed Jamys and he raised his voice. I heard him very distinctly say, 'If that Russian pig tries it again I'm going to toss him overboard.' Aška shushed him, and that was it."

"Then what?"

"There was no way for me to get by them, and I wasn't going to go the other way, which would have meant encountering Verkhovsky. So I waited, and when eventually they left I did, too, and returned to my cabin."

"You didn't think to bring this up before?"

"Of course I did. But when Dr. Wu made a finding of death by accident there was no point: why get two nice people into trouble for no reason?"

"Yes, I see."

"I assumed they just returned to their bunks and had nothing to do with Verkhovsky's death. But if you're now suggesting that it might not have been an accident after all, then I suppose Jamys has to be the prime suspect."

XXXIV

RASPUTINA AND I WERE NOT THE LAST TO ARRIVE AT THE Villa Pallavicini. Marta and Tess came in an hour after us, Tess having suffered a reciprocal error when navigating from the cheese acquisition at Bagolino, sending their Alfa east instead of west and so they had ended up at Lake Garda instead of Lake Como.

Marta made a fair show of appreciating the opportunity to see two lakes in one day; Tess just looked abashed.

Urquhart arrived later, too, but in dramatic fashion: he came by helicopter. The aircraft set down on the open lawn of the formal parterre in front of the villa. The rest of us, alerted by the noise, went out to watch. After it left and conversation was again possible, Urquhart briefed us on the result of the underwater inspection. The *Mulvane*'s vibrating shaft had been caused by a sharp gash in the leading edge of a propeller blade, probably from having struck something floating just beneath the surface, not uncommon in the densely trafficked Mediterranean but repairable by divers and not requiring dry-docking, which would have held us up for days.

We moved from the parterre to the sprawling English garden in the back, which was to be both the scene of tomorrow morning's photo shoot and the setting for tomorrow evening's feast. Adelina and her great-aunt went over the arrangements.

The party eventually broke up with people wandering the grounds or returning to the villa, and I had an opportunity to talk to Oriana alone. I briefed her on what Rasputina had told me, ending with the observation that now at last we had a real suspect, Jamys.

"Perhaps," she said, less impressed than I had expected.

"Perhaps? He said he was going to do it."

"A murderer who goes about declaring his intentions? Seems very convenient."

"He wasn't declaring his intentions; he didn't know Rasputina was next door."

"True."

"I think it's an important discovery," I said, "one that *I* learned from a *female* passenger."

"Oh, really, Evans—you're such a child. If I'd known you needed coddling I would have brought along some bonbons."

I was about to protest when Oriana held up a finger, silencing me. And then I felt it, too—there was someone else nearby. We were standing beside a privet hedge, and the obvious place for anyone to be close but invisible would be on the other side. I stepped lightly down to the end of the row and turned the corner. There was nobody there, but in that dense foliage anyone could have overheard us and then slipped away unseen.

The *Primavera* photo shoot, based on the Botticelli of the same name, took place in a grove in the villa's garden the next morning.

Adelina had suggested the location, and presumably the house party was planned in part to facilitate the shoot. The participants were prepared with appropriate costumes. Adelina wore a high-waisted medieval-style dress whose silken folds were not quite opaque but which was for Venus, usually depicted nude, a relatively chaste outfit. She stood, as in the painting, beneath an arch—in this case, a rose trellis—and mimicked the same cryptic posture: head tilted questioningly at the viewer and right hand raised in a gesture that could have been anything from an admonition to a benediction.

The three Graces, dancing in a circle to the left, made no attempt at modesty: their gossamer-thin robes were as transparent as in the Botticelli. Bébé was posed as the middle figure, the one with her back to the viewer, so that her tattoo would not be a distraction. Marta and Rasputina completed the dancing threesome.

On the far right of the painting is a nymph, fleeing from Zephyrus blowing through the trees. That made six female figures, and Oriana had been prevailed upon to pose as the nymph, something to which she reluctantly agreed. She wore two robes, one on top of the other, but as a fig leaf it was a failure: no member of the Cato Club gazing upon her now could have maintained the pretense that she was male.

But it was the figure between Venus and the nymph who, both in the photograph and the painting, stole the show. She was the goddess Flora, and Tess—standing willowy, winsome, and rapturous—did look every inch otherworldly. She had been designated for the role because in the painting Flora, modeled on Botticelli's beloved Simonetta Vespucci, is the only figure fully clad. The preparation of her outfit was entrusted to not a fashion designer but a florist-couturier in Belgravia who had a history of making fabulous dresses woven through with fresh flowers. He did not disappoint: the gown that had been flown into Milan that morning and delivered to Bellagio by refrigerated courier was a showpiece, shot through with an abundance of flora but dominated by cream- and lilac-colored roses. Her hair was strewn with cornflowers and forget-me-nots, her arms and neck with irises, pansies, hyacinths, and more—she was a walking garden.

Featuring six figures and so necessarily a broad scene, the shot famously became the fold-out centerpiece of the calendar. The oversized version, commissioned soon after the calendar's original print run had been exhausted, became a seemingly ubiquitous poster: a permanent spring adorning countless walls around the world.

Everyone could sense that the photo session had gone well and the resulting high spirits flowed over into the feast in the garden that began that afternoon and continued until late into the night. The women retained their makeup and costumes from the *Primavera* shoot, helping the festive air. We sat at a single long table on the lawn, changing places frequently, and the food was served family style; there was no formality to the proceeding.

Gilbert and Bébé, narrow rally winners over Oriana and Wu, were crowned with laurel wreaths in a victors' ceremony beneath the trellis, and the Marchesa presented them with two silver trophies that had been engraved in the village that morning.

Music was provided by an antiquated gramophone brought out onto a patio; when one of the girls felt like dancing she would put on a vinyl record. These were mostly old Italian pop or jazz recordings, and my overriding memory from that night is the scent of jasmine in the air, the laughter of the girls dancing like crazed maenads, and Paolo Conte endlessly singing the praises of *gelato al limon*.

FOR THE RETURN TO GENOA NEXT MORNING THE DRIVERS retained their same Alfas, with whose individual idiosyncrasies they were by now familiar, but the navigators were swapped, again via a blind draw.

I drew Tess Lysett.

"Sorry," she said, apparently remembering the unintended detour to Lake Garda. "We'll probably end up on Mars."

But there was no race now and the freeway restriction was lifted, so it would be just a simple jaunt in the slow lane of the Autostrada Serravalle straight through to Genoa. Since on the way we would pass by the Certosa di Pavia I suggested a stop there, and Tess agreed.

"Maybe we'll ask them for directions," she said.

"They're a silent order."

"They can point."

IT WAS WHILE WAITING FOR TESS TO FINISH PACKING THAT I wandered into one of the villa's sitting rooms and was surprised to find there the four Dalís already framed and hung—the Marchesa must have made it a priority to do so before the party.

Salvador Dalí has something of an equivocal reputation in the art world, a little bit too much of a successful self-promoter to be taken entirely seriously—a ridiculous view, as if the true artist must live in noble poverty or bohemian squalor to be considered genuine—and looking again at those drawings with their swift and certain pencil strokes it was clear to me that, self-promoter or not, Dalí was entirely the real thing: a consummate draftsman of economy and skill.

I took a frame from the wall to admire a drawing more closely and received a surprise: the blue silk wallpaper behind it was of a deeper shade, matching the outline of the frame. Something had already hung there for what must have been many years, exactly the same size, preventing the wallpaper behind it from fading. Given the precise match, whatever it was must have been in the same frame. I checked the other three and it was true for all of them: they had been hanging here long before the Dalís were returned.

It seemed that the only explanation, however unlikely, was that four different items must have already been here, perhaps some of those same drawings the Marchesa had shown me that first day on board, and they had been so close in size to the Dalís that the new drawings fit straight into them without any need to resize the frames or recut the matting.

<h1 style="text-align:center">XXXV</h1>

T HE CERTOSA DI PAVIA DID NOT OPEN TILL MID-AFTERNOON, so Tess and I stopped for lunch beforehand in Milan. Tess had never been to the city. I gave her an impromptu tour: climbing to the roof of the Duomo; viewing the Da Vinci codex at the Ambrosiana; visiting the Brera.

I am aware that most people do not share my interest in art and restricted this last to a walkthrough, sufficient to get a sense of the place and stopping for any length of time at only four works, all *quattrocento* or *cinquecento* portraits.[*]

We stood before the last of these, the Sofonisba Anguissola self-portrait. The artist stared back at us across half a millennium, bright-eyed, intelligent, and with that suggestion of a smile of the habitually good-humored—she was a little like Tess herself.

"Why these portraits in particular?" my companion asked.

"They're all secular for a start," I said. "I hope you won't be offended if I tell you that I have little feeling for religious art."

"Why should I be offended?"

---

[*] *Ritratto virile* – Francesco Torbido, known as Il Moro; *Autoritratto in veste di abate dell'Accademia della valle di Blenio* - Giovan Paolo Lomazzo; *Ritratto di uomo* - Filippo Mazzola; *Autoritratto* - Sofonisba Anguissola

"A bishop's daughter?"

"Pah! The Church of England—does that even count as a religion anymore?"

"What do you mean?"

"I mean that I'm probably no more religious than you are." She tapped me lightly across the knuckles with her Brera floorplan, a mild admonishment delivered with a smile. "You mustn't be presumptuous. Now, if we're done, perhaps you'll take me to lunch."

She put her arm through mine and we left, crossing the adjoining botanical garden to the Hotel Bulgari. The Bulgari is one of Milan's fashionable gathering spots and if I was alone I would no doubt have been told there were no tables available, but in the company of the unselfconsciously chic Tess a prime spot was soon found in the garden restaurant where, like the expensive automobiles parked out front, she would be best put on display.

"I like those four paintings because they depict people full of vim and vigor," I said after we had settled back with welcoming glasses of prosecco. "They show men and women eager to take on the business of living and doing it to the full. Much of the art in the Brera, being sponsored by the church, I find quite grim—sometimes technically excellent and occasionally even innovative, but it has nothing to do with life, or at least life as I understand it. That's why I prefer those lusty portraits of men and women engaged in the here and now; it was people like them who created the Renaissance."

"An art historian who prefers Il Moro to Michaelangelo?—you are a heretic."

"I hope you don't feel cheated."

"On the contrary, I'd have felt cheated if you'd shown me something other than works you genuinely liked. Dishonesty, in all its forms, is the one true sin."

"You sound like Oscar Wilde—he said that there was no sin except stupidity."

"I think he was onto something."

"How did a bishop's daughter acquire such an uncanonical concept of sin?"

"I'm amazed that the canon survives any education at all. It certainly didn't with me."

"What was your father's reaction to that?"

"Nothing at all; it's not like we sit around the dinner table discussing the true nature of the Trinity. Strange to say, I don't think he's all that religious either. Certainly, his sermons rarely delve into dogma; mostly he just urges people to be decent to one another."

"Well, here's to that." We drank to it and ordered.

IN ITALIAN HISTORY, THERE ARE TWO FIGURES KNOWN AS Il Moro, the Moor. Unlike the standard anglophone connotation, in which "the Moor" means Othello, neither of the Italian Il Moros was genuinely Moorish—both earned the cognomen only because of their dark coloration. One of them, the painter, we had encountered that morning in the Brera, where Il Moro's portrait of an anonymous man, painted circa 1520, was one of the pictures I had shown Tess. That afternoon, in the Certosa di Pavia, we stood before the tomb of the other, Ludovico Sforza, Duke of Milan, who in that age of complete men stood out as the most complete of all, with the many contradictions that involves: he usurped power quite illegally, but was legitimized by those otherwise irreconcilable enemies, the Pope and the Holy Roman Emperor; he saved Italy from the French when all around him were capitulating, although it was he who had invited them in the first place; he found time between wars to be a generous patron of the arts—it was he who commissioned Da Vinci's *Last Supper*—and at a time when the marriage of a ruler was arranged for purely strategic reasons and without any expectation of emotional attachment, he had wedded the beautiful and vivacious Beatrice d'Este, twenty years his junior, and the pair fell madly in love, the most romantic couple of the era. Beatrice herself became as powerful a force as her husband in the struggle with the French while simultaneously making the court at Milan the most cultured and admired in Europe—all this despite dying before her twenty-second birthday. Il Moro never smiled again.

The pair were reunited forever, carved in marble relief on the lid of their tomb before which we now stood. Tess looked up from her guidebook.

"Did you know that by the time she was my age Beatrice had already recruited Da Vinci to her court, conducted a sensitive diplomatic mission to Venice, and born a son who was to become another Duke of Milan? She takes my breath away."

"Then her sister might exhaust you."

"Her sister?"

"Isabella, the more famous of the two."

Tess was too familiar with ecclesiastical etiquette to take out her phone while still inside a church, but as soon as we were back in the cloister she looked up Isabella d'Este.

"I'm astounded," she said at last, putting away the phone. "Isabella ruled Mantua while her husband was held captive, went to war to defend it, was an implacable enemy of one pope and the trusted confidante of another, and the list of artists whom she patronized reads like a who's who of the Renaissance. You're right: she exhausts me."

"It was a different time. In that age people had energy and vitality—the need to not just be, but also do."

"I think I see now why you showed me those portraits."

"There was an art historian, Kenneth Clark, who claimed that energy is the essential ingredient to any civilization. He said that a society could have all the outward amenities of civilization—'fine sensibilities and good conversation and all that'—and yet still be dead."

"What would he have made of our society today?"

"I imagine his optimism would have been tested."

"Do you know the name Bonacolsi?"

"No."

"You might know him as Antico."

"Yes, the sculptor."

"He was one of the artists who Isabella patronized. He produced bronzes for her. This is one of them."

She again pulled out her phone and was soon showing me a photograph of a small bronze depicting a woman sitting bare-breasted on a tree stump, her robe having fallen from her shoulders and lying in gilded folds in her lap. Her hair was held back by a fillet, also gilded. The rest of the sculpture was plain bronze, the unburnished patina almost black with age. The title was *Seated Nymph*.

"According to the article, that's probably Isabella herself," Tess said.

"More likely the sculpture was a copy of a Roman original. That's why they nicknamed him Antico—he did copies of antiques."

"But he could have made the face that of Isabella."

"He could."

"She looks like Isabella does in her portraits."

"Are you suggesting we use this bronze as the basis for one of the photo shoots?"

"I am. What do you think?"

"I like the idea."

"We'll have to find a tree stump somewhere. And I'll have to get my hair done with a golden fillet."

"*Your* hair?"

"Yes, of course. I am full of vim and vigor, and must express myself—it is not sufficient to be, I must also do, as surely you of all people will understand."

I suddenly realized that I had been hopelessly outmaneuvered—once again, I had underestimated Tess Lysett. It occurred to me that if I ever needed to send someone on a sensitive diplomatic mission, she would make an excellent candidate.

TESS AND I RETURNED TO GENOA, THE LAST TO ARRIVE AFTER the long lunch and abbey stopover. The *Mulvane* set sail soon after we were back on board.

That evening I found a present left on my desk. Tess had made a point of stopping by the bookstore on the way out of the Ambrosiana, and now I found out why: the slender box contained a facsimile from the *Chiose Ambrosiane*, a famous illuminated manuscript of the *Divine Comedy*, confiscated by Napoleon in 1796 and returned twenty years later, after Waterloo. I had admired the manuscript during our visit that morning although said nothing about it, but Tess missed little. The reproduction, taken from the richly illustrated opening page, was intended to be used as a bookmark. The accompanying note read, "Thank you for playing Virgil to my Dante today—Milan would not have been half as nice otherwise, although it seems unfair that you may call me Tess but I'm not allowed to call you Hugo. I can't go on addressing you as Evans; what am I to call you?"

XXXVI

THE COMPARTMENT BENEATH THE STAIRS LEADING FROM the passenger accommodations up to the main deck was used as a housekeeping closet, storage for the fresh bedclothes and bath towels the maids needed when servicing the staterooms.

Until now, Shotter had developed film in his cabin, an awkward operation, but when he returned on board with a truckload of gear it was decided to convert the closet into a darkroom. It was already fitted with shelving so Shotter had space to lay out his developing trays, held secure against the ship's roll with sticky putty. There was no porthole that could let in light from outside and Young George installed rubber weather stripping on the doorframe to ensure that none would seep in from the passageway. He also fabricated a *No Entry* sign to be hung from the door handle when the compartment was in use. The clear bulb was replaced with a red one.

To make room for the displaced linens we passengers were each to empty a large drawer in our own compartments to be set aside for the staff's use. I was emerging from the cabin after clearing mine when I ran into Shotter, arms full, moving gear into the new darkroom.

"Need a hand?"

"Sure," he said. "Grab some of that stuff on the deck by my bunk."

I went to his cabin and found the floor littered with photographic equipment: tripods; trays; plastic bottles of chemicals. I was grabbing two of these last, one for each arm with fingers hooked through the handles, when a label caught my eye. It was on the bottle in my right hand. It read *Potassium Bromide*.

"What's up?"

Shotter had returned and was puzzled as to why I was standing dumbstruck in the middle of his cabin.

"I was just wondering what all these chemicals are for."

"Developing and printing," he said. "I'm going to develop all the film myself. I always do; I don't trust the quality control in professional labs. Developing has to be done right: you only get one chance, and I'd rather do it as soon as possible after exposure in case something happens to the film. Prints are less important, but I'm guessing that our fellow passengers will want to see them—I do as well—and so I brought along an enlarger and all the rest."

"What are these used for?"

I held up the two bottles.

"That one is Rodinal," he said, pointing to the one in my left hand. "It's a black-and-white developer. I don't know if I'll use it yet—it emphasizes grain, which can be effective but also a distraction—I brought it along just in case."

"And this one?" I held up the potassium bromide.

"I sometimes add that to the fixer."

"What for?"

"I didn't know you were so interested in photography."

"I'm an art historian. I like to hear about technique from an expert."

He nodded, accepting the assertion at face value.

"In black-and-white photography, the chemical in the film that reacts with light is silver halide. The last process in film development is bathing in a fixer to remove any unexposed silver halide, ensuring that the image won't change—that it's been 'fixed.' "

"And the potassium bromide?"

"It's what's called an anti-fogging agent: it improves differentiation between exposed and unexposed crystals of silver halide, which makes the fixer more effective and so reduces the chances of the image blurring over time."

I did not immediately respond, having a vague memory that guilty people supposedly tend to babble, but Shotter said nothing more and eventually it was I who broke the brittle silence.

"Thanks for the explanation. I'll leave these in the darkroom."

THE *MULVANE* WAS JUST UNDER THE MAXIMUM LENGTH allowed to berth in the little harbor of Portofino. Even though she could fit it was a complex operation in close confines and made more difficult by a brisk afternoon breeze that had blown up during the passage from Genoa—even the Rapallo ferry paused to give her maneuvering room. I could see the tension on Trevelyan's and Zabala-Extarte's faces as they went from bridge wing to bridge wing, assessing the yacht's drift as they slowly turned her for docking. Finally, we were secured fore-and-aft with the stern by the stone pier and the bow tethered to a mooring buoy.

Having gone through the trouble of docking, we decided to stay for an extended period. Portofino is a picturesque town with steep hillsides of pine groves and bougainvillea-shrouded villas surrounding a harbor busy with boutiques and cafes. To the south lie the Cinque Terre, within easy reach. The *Mulvane* was the biggest boat in the marina and perhaps the prettiest, too—tourists and townspeople flocked down to the port to admire her.

The photo shoot after Carlo Carrà's *Le Figlie di Loth* took place in a villa perched on the promontory that forms the southern arm of Portofino harbor. The villa operated as a vacation rental for the wealthy but was currently unoccupied and the agents were grateful for the unexpected business, however brief. It was a spectacular location and also a spectacular house, including a tower with arcades mimicking those of the painting, plus the seascape beyond similarly matching the picture.

Lot had two daughters and so Marta was enlisted to join the shoot. The Carrà has a wistful and solemn air, a nod to neo-classicism, and Shotter captured that sense of pensive melancholy perfectly. The two women playing the daughters did, too. For the emotionally elusive Adelina, this would have come naturally; to Marta less so, but she was a pliable model, able to readily translate the requirements of the shoot into a suitable pose and expression.

We dined that evening on the terrace of the Hotel Splendido, the grande dame of Portofino. After Rasputina's mistaken assumption, I made no attempt to get Oriana alone while in company that night. It was not until the next morning, when she and I were playing tennis at the hotel's lone court, that I was at last able to tell her what I had discovered. The conversation took place across the net after our first set, by which time it was clear that no one else was joining us.

"Now we know where the potassium bromide came from," Oriana said. She was merely glowing, but I was already in a full sweat. "Do you buy the explanation that it's used for film developing?"

"I do," I panted. "We should confirm it, of course, but Shotter sounded convincing."

"You two were roommates that first night when Verkhovsky went overboard. Was he in the cabin?"

"I went to bed before he did. I heard him come in, I think."

"You think?"

"I didn't open my eyes."

"So you heard someone, presumably Shotter, come in?"

"Yes."

"What time?"

"I don't know. I told you, I didn't open my eyes."

"Did you hear him go out again later?"

"No, but I'm a heavy sleeper and there's a lot of ambient noise—the sea rushing by outside, the hum of the ventilators, the creaking of the ship—so it's possible he could have gone out again without me being aware."

"What would be the motivation for Shotter to do away with Verkhovsky?"

"Perhaps he didn't want to share a cabin."

"Given that the bottle was among Shotter's photographic chemicals, who would know that it also had a pharmaceutical application?"

There was a long pause as we both studied the net, lost in thought. Our heads came up and our eyes met.

"Wu," we said simultaneously.

"But why would Wu risk stealing a sedative?" I asked. "He's presumably already got a supply of his own."

"They would be prescription drugs and therefore accountable. But if instead he uses Shotter's potassium bromide then it can't blow back on him—he'll never be required to explain anything missing."

"But it was Wu who told us about the potassium bromide to begin with—we would never have known if not for him."

"Which insulates him from suspicion. He assumed that an autopsy would be done and traces of the drug found. The fact that he found it first makes him appear above suspicion."

"But what would he have had against Verkhovsky?"

"Who knows? Maybe they had an argument that night."

"That's the issue with all our suspects, no real motive."

"Marta and Bébé?"

"Okay, they have a real motive."

"You said Kustaa hates Russians."

"That's weak."

"Milosz might have been caught stealing his watch, and Jamys threatened to do it."

"They're more plausible."

"Well, I'm sorry to tell you, Evans, that we have another suspect to add to the list, and this one has an excellent motive."

"Who?"

"When we returned to Monaco I asked my colleagues at Saunders Walker to see if they could find out anything about Verkhovsky. I told them to focus on his finances since we've got no idea what became of the money. It turns out that he parked a large portion of his fortune in a single investment: the *Daily Courier* newspaper, so much so that he hit a regulatory reporting limit, which is how they found out about it. My colleagues assume that he did it to try to gain leverage in obtaining U.K. citizenship or at least permanent residency—oligarchs have tried this tactic in the past, with success. And it fits: we know that he was desperate for a way to avoid going back to Russia."

"So he was a part-owner of our host's newspaper, which means that it must have been Urquhart after all. I knew that it had to be Urquhart because it's the only explanation for why he invited Verkhovsky."

"No, Verkhovsky was already on the guest list before he acquired the shares."

"Then who?"

"The buyer, of course."

I realized how reasonable this sounded. Any potential purchaser of the newspaper would naturally be concerned if a questionable Russian oligarch suddenly acquired a large chunk of stock. How convenient it would be if that questionable Russian oligarch were to disappear.

"Franklin Gilbert," I said. "We have another suspect."

XXXVII

Time passed at a leisurely pace in Portofino. One day, I found myself at a loose end. Marta and Bébé were shopping ashore; Rasputina, Tess, and Wu were hiking the Sentiero Azzurro—the Riva dropped them at Riomaggiore and would pick them back up again at Monterosso. Shotter was teaching Oriana photography; I wondered if this was a way for her to surreptitiously question him. Gilbert and Urquhart were huddled in the library, talking terms of the proposed takeover, and the Marchesa was engaged in correspondence in her stateroom, a woman who would have written her letters by hand with or without the electronics prohibition. I found Adelina on deck under the awning, reading.

"There's an old Benedictine abbey, San Fruttuoso, on the other side of the peninsula and which is accessible only by sea. Want to go take a look?"

She closed her book. "Should I pack a picnic?"

"I believe there's a little beachside restaurant where you can have anything you want, as long as it's spaghetti *ai frutti di mare*."

"That's just what I feel like. Give me five minutes."

It was closer to fifteen. When Adelina reappeared it was in a sailor's shirt, capri pants, deck shoes, and a rough straw hat with a sturdy lanyard securing it under the chin. No makeup, just a pair of Ray-Bans and the scent of sunscreen.

Since the Riva was away we took the Zodiac. When we cleared the harbor I opened up the throttle and we went skidding across the water. The sea was calm but even so the inflatable bucked and jigged, sufficient to make us have to hold on tightly. Adelina laughed with delight at the joyride.

The abbey came into view, and as I slowed to enter the long cove leading to it I realized that we were lucky the speedboat had been away: had we taken the Riva we would have been required to secure to a mooring and catch the dockmaster's boat ashore, but with the Zodiac I could just run it straight up onto the pebbly strand.

We toured the abbey, still in use, and which was the final resting place of many a dead Doria, the Genoese clan that had given the abbey their protection and the most famous of whom, Andrea Doria, had built the tower that still bears his name, intended to protect the monks from Barbary pirates. Soon we were at a table overlooking the water, drinking Pigato, the local white, and with two steaming plates of spaghetti in front of us.

Adelina looked out over the sparkling bay. "As monasteries go, this is hard to beat. Do you ever wish you could just abandon the world and live in peace in someplace like this?"

"Not if it meant being a monk."

"What about without the religion?"

"Like Urquhart?"

"I was imagining a Doria prince dropping by and just deciding to never leave."

"Again, no. What about you?"

"Maybe. I don't think the isolation would bother me."

"Does that mean you're contemplating not returning to school?"

"I'm done with school; I submitted my thesis this past spring."

"For an undergraduate degree?"

"I did an extra year, an honors year, during which one must deliver a dissertation. I graduated in June."

"What was the title?"

"Cross-border Capital Investment with Authoritarian Regimes: Free Trade or Faustian Compact?" She laughed out loud. "Tell me that doesn't send you to sleep."

"You've got nothing on mine: *Revelation in the Catoptrographic Art of Rothesay Ambrose Urquhart.*"

"Catoptrographic?"

I explained how I had come to coin the word. If ever Adelina was going to tell me about the Exeter portrait this would have been the time, but she said nothing.

"What comes next?" I asked her.

"I haven't decided yet. A doctorate perhaps: why do an honors year if not to proceed to a doctorate? Or perhaps a role in some economics think tank. But I'm in no hurry to make up my mind."

"Meanwhile, you're still fighting for the cause."

"How's that?"

"The anti-Ripelli calendar."

"Oh, I see. Well, that's true as far as it goes, but you mustn't underestimate the vanity of us women. We're not immune to the compliment of being admired."

I was able to pay the compliment of admiring her after lunch when we went swimming. Adelina had on underneath her clothes not the Lavaux-logoed one-piece she had worn in Ibiza but a skimpy bikini, something that garnered the entire attention of the beachgoers as she made her way gingerly over the shingle and into the sea. There is an underwater statue of Christ offshore, so we swam out and dived down to look at it, then returned to the beach and lay on towels to dry. We were both supine, eyes closed against the twin threats of the sun and the supernova.

"In your aunt's villa, there's a room where the Dalí drawings have been hung."

"Yes, the blue room."

"But the frames were there before. Do you know what was in them?"

"Sure, the Dalís."

"But Urquhart just gave them to her. Back to her, I mean."

"Yes, but before Nonna sold the Dalís she had them reproduced, and the reproductions were put in the frames that held the originals. She wanted it to look like it did before, even though they were just copies."

"Were the copies made by a professional artist?"

"I'm not sure. Maybe they were only prints, just fancy photographs. There's a French term for it that I can't remember."

"*Giclée*?"

"Yes, that's it."

Giclée is a process of fine art reproduction using very precise inkjets and careful color matching, but in the end it is still a print: no brushwork or, in the case of a drawing, no impression left by the pencil, such as I had seen in the Dalís the Marchesa had shown me in her stateroom that first day.

THAT EVENING WHEN I RETURNED TO MY CABIN AFTER DINNER, I found that it was already occupied. Rasputina was sitting in an armchair in the corner. She was holding a small pistol, and it was pointed at me.

"Bang," she said.

"It's considered bad manners to point guns at people, Rasputina, even if they're unloaded."

"Who says it's unloaded?" But then she released the magazine which fell from the grip into her lap, empty. "Although I really should shoot you. You had me all to yourself the other day and didn't make a single pass—I've never been so insulted."

"If I'd known you'd be waving a gun at me I'd have been a regular Don Juan."

I stepped all the way inside and closed the door. It occurred to me that I should start locking it.

"Are you and Oriana still in contact with the French authorities?" she asked.

"Yes."

"Well, you can add this gun to the inventory."

"You found it in Verkhovsky's stateroom?"

"Yes. I didn't want to bring it up in front of the others—some people get nervous around guns."

"Where was it?"

"Under the bed."

"We looked under the bed."

"I don't mean under the mattress, I mean under the actual bed. You know how it's built into the deck, and has a pair of drawers fitted beneath where the mattress lies?"

"Yes."

"So, when we had to clear out a drawer for the maids I just shoved everything of mine into the one next to it. But some of my stuff was too high and ended up being pushed down behind the drawer when I next opened it. I had to pull the drawer all the way out and poke around to find my clothes—that's when I discovered this." She pulled back the slide which then remained in the rearward position, leaving the breech open, and passed it to me.

"How come you're so familiar with firearms?"

"Consequence of a movie-star mother. You wouldn't believe some of the nut cases that try to stalk her. She made me learn how to use a gun when I was still a teenager. The magazine was full when I found it; here are the rounds."

Since she was not carrying an evening purse Rasputina had secured these in the only way possible. She slid a hand under the deep vee of her gown to the underwear beneath, which was doing duty as an impromptu bandolier. Her hand reemerged with several shiny brass-clad shells.

"Jacketed," she said, passing them to me. They were warm and smelled pretty good, too.

"Jacketed?"

"There's a hard metal casing over the soft lead of the bullet."

"Is that significant?"

"It means that whoever Verkhovsky intended to shoot, he expected them to be wearing body armor."

XXXVIII

THE AURORAS BEGAN ON THE FIRST NIGHT AFTER WE sailed from Portofino. They were green to start with, mysterious flares sweeping in great waves across the night sky, initially faint but visible to us, out at sea and away from all man-made light.

Over the coming weeks they were to increase in intensity and vary in form: often as near static curtains hanging in the sky; or sharp javelin-like thrusts; or arcing like a rainbow; or slowly undulating serpents of light; sometimes they seemed to fill the whole sky. The colors varied, too: red, blue, yellow, and pink, although green remained the dominant hue. It was astonishing to witness, a wild spectacle with all the heavens for a stage, but in the back of the mind one could not help thinking that if this immense cosmic shower is doing that to the atmosphere, then what is it doing to life on earth?

Betelgeuse, or its supernova remnant, was rising ever earlier, which felt like an extended dawn, effectively lengthening the days even though we were well past the summer solstice and heading toward the autumnal equinox—the days should have been getting shorter. This, coupled with the auroras, meant there was never true darkness anymore, even away from artificial light.

We proceeded south, making stops on the way. Livorno is the seaward gateway to Pisa and Florence, so we docked there for day trips to those destinations. I went to neither, instead joining Ernesto and Milosz on a provisioning expedition centering on Bolgheri, a wine-growing region south of Livorno, to restock the *Mulvane*'s depleted cellar. Bolgheri is home to a famed Super Tuscan, Masseto. The vineyard is normally closed to visitors but Urquhart had arranged access to the winery and some of their reserve stock, the publicly available production having been sold out years in advance. It was while Ernesto was loading a case of this that I took Milosz aside and frankly told him what I had witnessed outside the nightclub in Monaco.

"I knew I shouldn't have taken that watch," he admitted. "I don't know what came over me."

"How did you notice it in the first place?"

"I found it when I was searching for his passport."

"Why were you searching for his passport?"

"The first officer told me to."

"Zabala-Extarte? Why?"

"For communication to the authorities."

I remembered it myself, the initial document presented to Dubois and Renard that night in Marseilles—before getting down to any business, bureaucrats are always concerned with first establishing identity.

"So you took the watch after we recovered Verkhovsky's body?"

The question puzzled him. "Well, of course. What else..." It slowly dawned on Milosz what I was getting at. "Dr. Evans, you can't believe that I—" He was unable to finish the sentence, ever worse implications occurring to him.

"Don't concern yourself, Milosz."

He looked mightily relieved at this apparent reprieve.

"I should return the watch."

"To whom?"

"Next of kin."

"His estate is being handled by the French authorities. Best to just keep the thing and say nothing—certainly Verkhovsky has no further need of it."

Milosz wanted to reassure me that he was not a dishonest man, despite having just admitted to theft, but I was saved from the need to hush him by the return of Ernesto.

IT WAS NOT UNTIL WE WERE ANCHORED OFF ELBA, ABOUT TO pass from the Ligurian into the Tyrrhenian Sea, that I had an opportunity to report the conversation to Oriana, ending with the observation that for once we had managed to reduce the list of suspects instead of expanding it.

"But it doesn't clear him," she objected, less impressed than I had expected. "Milosz could have just made up the story when you asked him. Perhaps he'd already prepared one just in case."

"We can corroborate it with Zabala-Extarte."

"No doubt that part will check out. It doesn't mean that Milosz couldn't have taken the watch earlier."

"True, but it didn't sound that way: he was genuinely shocked when he realized that he could be seen as a murder suspect—literally speechless. Besides, who would flaunt the watch of a man he has just murdered?"

"Don't underestimate human depravity," she warned. "Some people are fundamentally evil, and Milosz might be one of them."

XXXIX

Our period in Ostia, the port of Rome, was the longest of our stops in any single place. One reason was the numerous attractions of a city so steeped in history; another was the many photo shoots we did in or around there, five in total.

The Basilica di Sant'Andrea delle Fratte denied our request to shoot with their *Angelo con la Soprascritta*—the angel with the superscription, a Bernini sculpture I had added to the list—so we shot instead with Giulio Catari's copy of the same work on the Ponte Sant'Angelo, situated in a public space and requiring no one's permission. We photographed early in the morning before the tourists with their cameras and immigrants with their trinkets had arrived. The rising sun bathed the dome of Saint Peter's, acting as backdrop, in a luminous golden glow.

Another public shoot did require permission as it took place at the Trevi Fountain, policed to prevent people from doing exactly what we intended: recreating the famous scene from Fellini's *La Dolce Vita* where Anita Ekberg takes an impromptu dip. This was the one scene before which Adelina balked, despite being, like that on the Ponte Sant'Angelo, shot clothed.

"I don't think I can pull it off," she confided to me on board the *Mulvane* the day before the shoot. "It needs a sort of careless sensuality that I just can't get right."

"We don't have to do it."

"I think that we should, but with Rasputina instead of me."

Rasputina agreed to the proposed substitution and proved equal to the task, mimicking Ekberg's combination of casual disregard and sybaritic indulgence perfectly. When the shoot concluded the crowd of people watching from behind the police barriers applauded the performance.

We reverted to referential obscurity with a shoot based on Bartolomeo Veneto's cryptic *Portrait of Lucretia Borgia*, that much maligned or maybe justly vilified daughter of Pope Alexander VI; highly educated certainly; adultress probably; poisoner perhaps. We shot it in the Villa Borghese gardens. If the Ekberg session had been ideal for Rasputina, then the Borgia shoot was perfect for Adelina: she was a vision of enigmatic detachment, holding out a posy in what might have been an offering, long golden hair tumbling down below her shoulders, one breast bared as in the portrait, as if to declare that as the daughter of a pope she was beyond all opprobrium, and bewildering the viewer with that penetrating return gaze.

But the best of the sessions in the city of Rome was shot in EUR, the stark and somber fascist dream town five miles south of the Colosseum. The acronym derives from Esposizione Universale Roma, Mussolini's site for the proposed 1942 World's Fair. By the time 1942 came there was no question of a world's fair: Italian troops were being routed across North Africa and Mussolini was soon to fall from power.

We shot the *Ariadne* scene by the Palazzo della Civiltà Italiana, a desolate travertine block that eerily matches the bleak arched building in de Chirico's picture, painted twenty years before the palace was built. Shotter photographed the scene in black and white, and he must have opted for the Rodinal when developing the film: there was a misty graininess, veil-like, echoing Adelina-as-Ariadne's sole garment, a gauzy robe—something that emphasized her vulnerable solitude as she awakens to find herself abandoned in the dismal and dystopian cityscape.

The last of the photo shoots was set not in Rome but twenty miles south in the Giardino di Ninfa, the site of a Nymphaeum during the classical period, and it was indeed the sort of place—dense, lush, and shadowed—where you could imagine turning a corner and suddenly happening upon a distracted nymph.

This was where we were to shoot Tess in the role of Antico's *Seated Nymph*. It had been preceded by a second telephone call to the Bishop of Chichester, but the results were no different than the first—perhaps Tess's father had learned that most difficult of parental lessons: when to realize that your child is a child no longer, and step aside or get run over.

We split into three groups: one to take the path to the left, another the path to the right, and the third—the Marchesa, Adelina, Gilbert, and Urquhart—who would enjoy espressos in the garden cafe while the other two scouted locations.

I went to the right with Wu and the nieces. Bébé and Wu were debating the relative merits of different pizza styles. Bébé lauded Roman pizza alla pala, whose combination of dense fluffy interior dough and crisp exterior crust she declared unsurpassable. Wu warned her to wait until we had been to Naples before drawing hasty conclusions. I took the opportunity to talk quietly with Marta.

"We went through Verkhovsky's things before handing them over to the French, including his passport. It had only lately been issued, and so there was no way to tell if he had traveled recently. Were you aware of any journeys he made?"

"We never traveled anywhere outside the Riviera. Verkhovsky went on a trip once, but he was only gone a single night."

"Do you know where?"

"He didn't tell us; he refused to discuss it. But it didn't matter: I saw the luggage tag."

"What did it say?"

"L.A.: he'd gone to Los Angeles."

"Just overnight?"

"He came back the next day"

"Are you sure?"

"Very sure: we were disappointed, having hoped he would stay away longer."

A sudden and unexplained trip to Los Angeles that Verkhovsky refused to discuss—I hoped that we would not be adding Rasputina Quantrill to the list of suspects.

We found a suitable location for the shoot: a length of the Ninfa River, really just a stream, flowing gently on the right and a soft bank of lush foliage on the left. There was a picturesque Poussin-like ruin whose collapsed wall would serve as the seat.

The others were summoned and the site agreed. Shotter began setting up his equipment as Rasputina and the nieces fussed over Tess like bridesmaids before a wedding. The Marchesa had settled into a shaded bower by the lake on the other side with Adelina and Urquhart in attendance, so Gilbert, Wu, and I went to join them, intending to leave Tess to her big moment unobserved, but then she called me back.

"Aren't you going to check the pose?"

"The pose?"

"To make sure it's the same as the Antico, of course."

It sounded plausible, but there was the hint of a smile accompanying this explanation. When the time came I dutifully checked the pose, but it was not until much later that I got to see how the shoot turned out.

Despite all that verdant color Shotter again chose to photograph in black-and-white, but it was a good choice. Although predominantly black-and-white he nevertheless contrived to make the robes and fillet appear gold-colored—gilded, as in the Antico. The technique, I learned, was to take each photograph four times in rapid succession, the last in color. On each of the three black-and-white shots he used a different chromatic filter: firstly yellow, which made the clouds seem to pop from the sky, then green, adding attractive contrast to the surrounding foliage, and lastly blue, which had the effect of making Tess's skin, still fair despite her tan, appear very dark, emulating the patina of the Antico. The color shot was for the robes, and the final photograph was a seamless combination of all four.

But for all the photographic tricks it was Tess who made the shot work, transformed from her normal happy and vivacious self into a subdued, contemplative, and dreamy presence—just how a nymph might look when left to herself in the peaceful solitude of her native habitat.

I cannot say that I underestimated Tess this time. Having done so thrice already I was prepared for the shoot to turn out to be a good one, but even then I was taken aback when I saw the final result: she seemed to me to be a riparian vision of Pre-Raphaelite perfection, an entire art movement's agenda summed up in a single simple picture. Of all the photographs in the calendar, if allowed to keep just one that is the shot I would choose.

XL

W E SET SAIL FROM OSTIA, EXHAUSTED WITH ROME. Ernesto, bursting with local produce and ideas, extended the experience by providing for dinner that first night back at sea a feast of Roman staples delivered in imperial-sized proportions: carciofi, concia di zucchine, and bruschetta as *antipasti*, bucatini all'Amatriciana and tonnarelli cacio e pepe as the *primi piatti*, and for *secondi* typically heavy Roman stews: coda alla vaccinara and trippa alla Romana.

Most people opted for the ox-tail but four years at Harrow had hardened me to unappetizing foodstuffs, and I wolfed the tripe down happily.

After dinner, we moved to the main salon, too sated to do anything but sit.

"A fitting end to Rome," Urquhart said after a while. "Lucullus would have been proud of that meal."

"Thank goodness there were no larks' tongues. One more thing and I would have burst."

"Do the Romans really eat that way every night? The only fat people I saw were tourists."

"I think they must argue the calories off."

"That's for sure," said Gilbert. "What does *mortacci tua* mean?"

Adelina was not one to laugh easily but she did now, a loud and uninhibited ringing sound that would have displeased her deportment teacher at Lavaux. Even the Marchesa smiled.

"May I ask where you heard it?"

"In traffic, which in Rome must be the worst in the world. Mainly from people on those little scooters or in small cars hailing each other in passing."

"I suppose that you might call it a hail," Adelina said. "It means something along the lines of 'I do not hold your ancestors in high regard,' although expressed more earthily."

"Oh, I see."

The little silence that followed was broken by Urquhart.

"So what was the general impression of Rome?" The question was intended for all of us but directed toward the Marchesa for her response first.

"It's no good asking me," she protested. "We Milanese have a saying: *la cosa più bella di Roma é er treno per tornà a Milano*: the best thing about Rome is the train back to Milan."

"Perhaps we should hear from those who were seeing it for the first time," Urquhart suggested. "Miss Quantrill, what did you think?"

"The thing that most impressed me was Saint Peter's. I've never seen anything so magnificently and densely ornate. And so large! No wonder it took centuries to complete: there's not a square inch that isn't carved or painted or decorated in some way."

"Overdone?"

"To an American of the Twenty-First Century, I think so. But that's an unfair criticism: Michaelangelo and Bernini built the thing to please the angels, not Angelinos."

"What about you, Bébé?"

"I was most surprised by EUR. I did not know before that it was a place, that it exist, and it seem to come from other world. Not pleasant but I cannot help looking myself. It is like Stalinist building—it captures the eye and turns the stomach."

"Very well put, if I may say so. Tess?"

"For me, the highlight was the Forum, and I have no reservations about it although no doubt many a wicked thing occurred in or around there: gladiatorial combats and brutal executions and the like, not to mention the murder of Caesar. But it seemed to me a place of quiet and classical beauty, whatever its history may have been. I think I was fortunate because I went there first thing in the morning when it was still cool and before the tourist crowds arrived—I almost had the place to myself."

"And now perhaps we should have the view of an art historian—Evans?"

"Art-wise it's a treasure trove, obviously: the overcrowded attic of Western culture. But listening to Tess and Bébé and Rasputina just now, there's something that I've never realized before: architecturally, Rome contains buildings that are the pinnacle of three distinct eras. Pinnacle might be the wrong word; what I mean is that they are supreme architectural expressions of the spirit of the age."

"The zeitgeist?"

"Exactly, and they embody it better than buildings anywhere else. The Forum and so on, for example, best capture the ruling spirit of antiquity."

"But surely that honor should belong to the Parthenon in Athens," Urquhart objected.

"Yes, I put it badly. I should say they best capture the ruling spirit of *late* antiquity, when democracy had been displaced by dictators, and philosophy had been displaced by bread and circuses. Architecturally, beauty was replaced by size, but the Romans did introduce the arch, which in turn led to the vault—something all but unknown to the Greeks, and which allowed for the construction of those monumental structures on a previously unknown scale: the great baths; Trajan's Forum; Agrippa's Pantheon; the Colosseum; the triumphal arches themselves. These capture the spirit of late antiquity perfectly, I think. Similarly Saint Peter's: the ultimate expression of Baroque. And as for EUR, I think we may count that as the chief architectural example of fascism, more even than Speer. I don't think any other city can boast of having the top zeitgeist-capturing architecture of three ages. Even two is a stretch: Paris's Grand Siècle and Belle Époque, say, although surely Versailles is the supreme instance of the former; or London's Age of Reason, expressed chiefly by Wren and made possible by the Great Fire, and of which I suppose St. Paul's is the prime example, plus the Imperial Age: Buckingham Palace, the Houses of Parliament, and all the rest. Or New York: the pre-war exuberance of Art Deco, as exemplified by the Chrysler and Empire State buildings, and those pristine post-war skyscrapers like the United Nations and the Pan Am building that proclaimed the Internationalist Age. But none of these cities has three eras, at least not so unquestionably at the architectural apogee of each as in Rome."

"So architecture can embody the prevailing zeitgeist?"

"The best buildings always do, I think."

"Then what of today?"

"Today?"

"Yes," Urquhart said. "I put this to all of you: what building of today best expresses the spirit of our own age? What is our Parthenon, our Saint Peter's, our Pan Am?"

There was a long silence that followed this challenge as people considered the question.

"The new World Trade Center?" Rasputina responded, but the offer was made in the hesitant tone of someone unconvinced of their answer, even before receiving a response.

"An undistinguished and insipid replacement," Urquhart declared, "embodying none of the optimistic grandeur of the original." Rasputina nodded in agreement.

"The Sydney Opera House?"

"Too old—it belongs to the swinging 'Sixties."

"The launch towers at Cape Canaveral?"

"Ditto."

"That building in Dubai, the world's tallest, I think?"

"If we're willing to assert hubris as being the ruling spirit of our age, then perhaps that would do."

"Those Frank Gehry buildings in Bilbao and Los Angeles?"

"Aimless curvature as an emblem of an era?"

"Well, you've obviously got something in mind, so why not just tell us?"

"Ah, but you're mistaken," Urquhart replied. "I have nothing in mind because I think there's nothing to offer. There is no great building that embodies the spirit of our age because there is no spirit—we live in empty times. Or perhaps it is in minor buildings, in the many private houses of quiet excellence, that one finds the only appealing architecture of our era, and that too is emblematic of our times: character and intellect have retired, withdrawn from the public arena, leaving a void that is inevitably filled by the fatuous and wearisome—hence, among many other ills, the second-rate public architecture of our age. There is no building that embodies the zeitgeist of our era because there is no zeitgeist to embody."

"This is why you became a recluse?"

"It is. To me, the current cultural and social milieu is banal and enervating, oppressive to the spirit, and I found that I could no longer paint there. Fortunately, I had the means to do something about it, and so I bought an island in the Cyclades and retired to a place where I need never see the world again."

"Until now?"

"Until now—although, as I've mentioned, it's questionable whether a luxury yacht counts as a return to the world."

"For what purpose?" I asked him blankly.

Urquhart spent a few moments in deliberation before responding.

"To know one's purpose, now there's a challenge. This is a question that has been struggled with since the pre-Socratic Greeks. Heraclitus said that all things change—*panta rhei*—and so to achieve any purpose would be an illusion, since it is destined to soon dissolve back into the endless flow. Parmenides was even worse: nothing really changes, except superficially, and so any attempt at any purpose is a waste of time in the first place. Perhaps let us settle for Hypatia of Alexandria's happier formulation: she said that life is a gradual unfoldment, and that the further we travel the more truth we find."

THERE WAS A GRADUAL UNFOLDMENT WAITING FOR ME WHEN I returned to my cabin that night in the form of a note from Oriana slipped under the door, but it brought us no closer to the truth.

"The French postal service has just a single rate of 1.65€ for a standard-sized letter under twenty grams going to any international destination," she had written. "Same for anywhere, whether Italy or East Timor—isn't that just like the French?"

A little harsh to criticize the French postal service for mail rates inconvenient to our investigation, but I understood her frustration: we did not seem to be making progress, and the voyage was more than half over.

XLI

ALTHOUGH THE GREATEST ROMAN ARCHITECTURE CAN be found in Rome itself, not so the paintings. There is little extant Roman painting anywhere, but an exception is Pompeii, a sleepy provincial city that would have been forgotten by history had Vesuvius not buried it, and inadvertently preserved it, in the year 79 A.D. Here, excavated from beneath the lava, have been recovered hundreds of paintings, especially in the form of frescoes—the ancient Romans liked nothing better than to decorate their walls.

The most stunning of these murals are located in the Villa dei Misteri, the house of the mysteries. On the walls of the villa's *triclinium*—the dining hall, in which the Roman aristocrats feasted in splendor, unaware that Vesuvius was about to consume them—is a series of twelve panels depicting in lapis lazuli blue and cinnabar red a Dionysian mystery: the secret initiation of a young woman into the cult of that strange part-Roman, part-Greek, part-Oriental god of ecstasy and insanity, Dionysus.

One of the panels depicts a ceremonial flagellation: the initiate, naked, genuflects before a winged goddess, equally naked, who with whip raised is about to flog her, and as our party stood gazing at the frescoes this is the scene that we settled on for the anti-Ripelli calendar.

Shotter's initial thought was to do the session in the room with the original in the background, but the authorities in Pompeii would not agree to the arrangement and so we were forced to think of something else. This turned out to be fortunate.

We spent the rest of our time in the Gulf of Naples touring the region and the chaotic city after which it is named. Wu and Bébé resolved their pizza disagreements, and I was able to see some fresh art for the first time, having never before been to Naples.

Adelina used some of her time to get a new hairdo.

It was a startling change when she returned on board, her previously long hair, which she had typically worn up, was now shortened to a bob above the shoulder, reminiscent of a flapper's cut and therefore appropriate for the interwar-years theme. More stunning was the color: not her natural soft Botticelli shade but instead a bright platinum blond that seemed to shine like a beacon.

It was hard to say what lay behind this sudden transformation: an assertion of individuality perhaps, no doubt long suppressed by her background of old money and private schools; or it could be that with all the heat and humidity her long hair had become too burdensome; maybe it was just an effort to add variety to the calendar shoots. Whatever the reason, it had the effect of changing someone who was already an object of attention into a person whose presence dominated a room. When the time came, it would also help make the Dionysian mystery photographs all the more striking.

The *Mulvane* moved on from the Gulf of Naples to Capri, and it was there that we found the location for the shoot.

An island is a suitable place to withdraw from the world—as Urquhart's retreat to Ledos demonstrated—and Capri has a long history as a refuge, going back at least as far as the emperor Tiberius, who spent much of his unhappy reign there. But perhaps the most extreme example on the island is Casa Malaparte, a spectacular 1930s villa designed on strictly modernist lines and located at the tip of a remote promontory where it sits perched on an isolated cliff a hundred feet above the water, accessible only by sea or a very long hike.

We accessed it by sea, coming to anchor in the lee of the shore.

The house is built in the form of a long block running along the length of the promontory. The roof is a flat fenceless patio accessed by a broad pyramidal staircase like that of a Mayan temple, and ascending it invoked, for me at least, something of the sense of ominous dread that a thousand years ago a victim destined for sacrifice might have felt—not so much a stairway to heaven as a scaffold to heaven.

The calendar shoot was not Casa Malaparte's first foray into the visual arts: much of Godard's *Contempt* was filmed there.

The shoot took place on the roof. In this session, Shotter's technical expertise with film and artistic expertise as a photographer were both highlighted—the final result had a fashion shoot feel, albeit a highly fetishistic form of fashion. Bébé took the role of the flagellating goddess, and now her samurai/St.-George-and-the-dragon tattoo was not an impediment but an asset that Shotter made use of with judicious skill: unmissable but not overtly emphasized, serving to quietly assert her status as a threatening oddity. She stood in thigh-high patent leather boots with the whip raised and one heel planted on the only item of furniture on that otherwise stark expanse: a travertine cube that normally served as a side table. Her shock of jet-black gypsy hair was a superb contrast to the smooth flow of Adelina's bright blond bob. And how vulnerable the latter appeared: shot from the side on her hands and knees, head looking up in what might have been an appeal for clemency (or a secret knowingness; you could never tell with Adelina) and naked apart from white stilettos and a pearl necklace, her ribs visible: an underfed although unusually long-limbed waif. The filming went on for two hours during the transition from late afternoon until after sunset, and when with the onset of dusk the auroras began to appear Shotter was able to capture their mysterious flights across the heavens as a spectacular backdrop while still keeping the composition clear, without the loss of color saturation that usually accompanies the onset of darkness—the technical achievement I alluded to above.

Afterward, I had an opportunity to take Oriana aside.

"About a month before the voyage began, Verkhovsky made a quick trip to the U.S.," I told her. "He left in the morning and was back the next day."

"How do you know?"

I related the conversation with Marta.

"And she's sure it was the U.S.?"

"The luggage tag was still attached to his bag and she saw it: L.A."

"L—A—what?"

"What do you mean?"

"Those luggage tags use three-letter codes, not two. Did she tell you what the third letter was?"

"No. Does it matter?"

"It does. There are no direct flights between Nice and Los Angeles—I know because we had to arrange for Rasputina to change planes in Paris."

"Okay, so there was a stop."

"Which means the whole thing takes a long time. Fifteen hours each way, so thirty hours at a minimum. There and back in twenty-four is not possible."

"Maybe he left very early in the morning, and got back late the next day."

"No, the eastbound transatlantic flights are red-eyes only. It couldn't have been L.A."

"Perhaps he took a private plane—he was an oligarch, after all."

"But then there would have been no need for luggage tags; luggage tags mean commercial. It couldn't have been L.A. he went to."

"Then where? And why?"

"Where, I don't know. As to why, all we can say is that whatever he was up to, he didn't want the nieces along as witnesses."

XLII

Having covered Naples and Capri, we completed the triumvirate of Campania with the Amalfi coast. The *Mulvane* spent most of this period anchored off Positano, and it was there that for the first time we saw the rise of Betelgeuse by night—the relentless inching forward of four minutes a day meant that by staying up late enough it would now be possible to witness the supernova's ascent into the evening sky.

We made an occasion of it, pairing the observation with the advent of a full moon. The awning was removed and we dined on deck bathed in silvery lunar light with the auroras swirling away overhead. Eventually the supernova arose in the eastern sky like an accusing finger, small but intensely bright, auroras or not. We watched in awed silence.

There is a French term *l'appel du vide*—literally, the call of the void—which is used to describe that unnerving sense when standing at the edge of a cliff of vaguely imagining hurling oneself off it. I have found this term useful in describing some art—it is rare, but occasionally certain works, the *Lustration* among them, invoke this sense of wanting to metaphorically fall forward and somehow plunge headlong right into them. But I have never felt it before as I did that evening while watching the supernova ascend into the aurora-strewn sky. Oblivion, but beautiful oblivion: a siren singing of self-surrender to the infinite cosmos.

THE LONG-ANTICIPATED RECITAL TOOK PLACE IN A CALM SEA off the Aeolian Islands north of Sicily, just before the entrance to the Strait of Messina, a fitting location as Bébé and Marta had styled themselves as Scylla and Charybdis respectively. These roles suited them: Bébé's wild mass of black hair and unrestrained play was suggestive of a dangerous shoal, and Marta's rapid bowing on her Amati, so fast as to be sometimes a blur, had the sense of a whirlpool about it.

The recital was preceded by a photo shoot.

Shotter suggested it, perhaps to ensure that—as with Rasputina at the Trevi Fountain and Tess in the Giardino di Ninfa— Bébé and Marta would have a shoot to themselves. Or maybe he did it to take advantage of the backdrop: the island of Stromboli, a monumental cone thrust up from the sea and which is an active volcano, topped by fiery jets and with glowing hot lava flows visible on the slopes. We stopped offshore but did not anchor—the water was too deep, something already suggested by the steepness of the island. Instead, Trevelyan set the autopilot to keep the *Mulvane* in precisely the same spot and pointing the same way.

The shoot took place at night to capture those glowing background lava flows, and the concert began soon after. It opened with a Chopin polonaise, presumably chosen by Bébé as a salute to Marta's Polish roots. Marta returned the compliment with that most well-known of Gypsy-based pieces, "Brahms's Hungarian Dance No. 5." From then on the pair played as a duo: Kreisler's difficult "Praeludium and Allegro"; Bartók's "Violin and Piano Sonata No. 2" as the centerpiece; and finishing with a work they could not have known was one that I have always admired for its ethereal beauty, Debussy's "Violin Sonata in G Minor," written in 1917 at the height of the First World War and the last piece he ever composed.

This was over an hour straight of music with no break, a strain for any performers, but they responded to our enthusiastic applause at the concert's conclusion with an encore very unlike the earlier pieces: Miles Davis's "Right Off," with Bébé somehow having effectively transcribed John McLaughlin's spontaneous guitar shuffle into a piece for the piano. Marta played the Miles Davis part, effortlessly converting from the clean purity of earlier into a heavier and harsher bowing with extended and deliberate scrapes that successfully emulated Davis's trumpet technique. The concert was more than a success: it was a demonstration of professional virtuosity from two highly talented musicians.

THE *MULVANE* REMAINED IN STATION OFF STROMBOLI THE next day, giving us a chance to enjoy a beach ashore that had a striking feature: it was jet black. This was a result of volcanic activity creating a supply of basalt that, eroding over time, became sand. Rasputina, Tess, Marta, and Bébé played in it like ten-year-olds, ending up smeared and streaked, something washed away with the next dip in the water.

Adelina had the idea to use the beach for the *Birth of Venus* photo shoot.

It would be a long way from the Botticelli: for a start, there were no other figures in the shoot. In the painting, Venus emerges naked from the water but Adelina had a gown that she wanted to wear—it turned out that when the Marchesa's Mercedes had whisked them up to Bellagio it had dropped her grand-niece at a famous designer's atelier in Milan on the way. Adelina was a favored customer, one that the company's creatives no doubt valued because anything would look good on her. She had explained the circumstances, and they designed a one-off gown: ocean-blue chiffon gradually grading in undulating waves to turquoise green, cascading down her body and held in place by a single thin strap: suitable attire for a goddess emerging from the sea.

The setting chosen for the shoot was an outcrop of rounded black boulders by the end of the beach where the waves broke up in spume and spray. The gown was soon wet and wind-whipped, but this just added to the drama.

That day, Shotter captured Adelina's otherworldliness on film as brilliantly as Urquhart had in paint (twice). But his masterstroke was to erase the background entirely and replace it with the same image of the supernova that we had seen in Costitx. What a stunning apparition she is in that shoot, long arms reaching out as if to encompass space itself, and fingers like the searching tentacles of some extraordinary celestial sea creature. More remarkable, Adelina seems still to be tall and slender notwithstanding that in the final picture Shotter cropped her legs and feet emerging from the bottom of the gown.

It is this photograph that was famously used for the calendar's front cover.[*]

I suppose that by now it has reached the status of an image so iconic as to be more-or-less instantly recognizable, even by those who have never heard of the anti-Ripelli calendar. Any picture selected for the cover would necessarily need to be one with the subject clothed, but even without this restriction that shot would have been the right choice for the circumstances at the time: not a conventional Venus emerging from the earthly sea but an astral Venus arising from the cosmic void; a space-mermaid cast forth from the celestial tumult, thrust into unlikely being by the reckless and relentless supernova.

THAT EVENING, I JOINED ORIANA BY THE RAIL.

"L—C—A," she said without greeting.

"What?"

"It's the three-letter airport code that I think Marta must have seen, and mistaken for L.A."

"Where is it?"

"Larnaca"

"I've never heard of Larnaca."

"It's the main airport in Cyprus, a place whose banks are particularly noted for being used by money launderers, and known to be favored by Russians. My guess is that the suitcase went out empty and came back full, getting cash on hand as part of the preparation for making a run for

---

[*] And the cover of this book [Ed.]

it with the Comoros passport. No doubt those bundles of banknotes we found in his safe were some of it."

"And the rest?"

"A deposit box perhaps, or maybe they'd find it if they dug up the backyard in the Villa Astenia."

"What next?"

"I'll let my colleagues at Saunders Walker know. They'll put out inquiries but I don't expect to get anything back—the financial secrecy laws in Cyprus are why the oligarchs bank there in the first place."

There seemed nothing more to say and so I stood in silence for a while, leaning on the rail and looking across the water at Stromboli, the spiderweb of lava flows a vibrant contrasting orange to the background auroras.

"It's interesting how they're able to keep the ship in precisely the same position and pointing in the same direction," I said.

"Sure."

"Makes you realize how capable the automatic pilot is."

She turned her gaze from Stromboli to me.

"I was wondering if you were going to think of it."

"You already have?"

"Of course. Opportunity-wise, Zabala-Extarte is the best suspect we have. Since he was on watch he's the only other person on board who we know was awake at the time. When Betelgeuse exploded he would surely have noticed it, even though the *Mulvane* was heading in the other direction. It would naturally have made him look aft, and he would have seen there the stumbling and drunken Verkhovsky, perhaps already by the rear rail, gazing at the sky. Zabala engages the autopilot and then quickly goes back, approaches Verkhovsky from behind, and tosses him into the sea."

"But why?"

"That's the problem: no motive."

"No facts, either."

"No facts?"

"No hard facts. All we have is a bit of scraped wood that you removed from underneath Verkhovsky's fingernails. Everything else is just supposition—like supposing that anyone else besides Zabala was awake—or at best some strained hypothesis—Kustaa being motivated by his military training, for example, or Gilbert wanting to eliminate a shareholder."

Oriana considered this for a while before responding.

"You have one hard fact," she said.

"What's that?"

"Somebody moved your hairbrush."

XLIII

WE TRANSITED THE STRAIT OF MESSINA ON THE FIRST day of September, something which brought home how quickly the summer that had once seemed to stretch far into the future was suddenly slipping away. There was less than a month left of the cruise.

After long periods in Italian ports, the *Mulvane* resumed a regular seagoing routine, weighing anchor early in the morning and then underway until dropping anchor again at our next destination. The remainder of the day would be spent swimming, or perhaps on a trip into town. Occasionally, we would dine ashore but more often on board, likely the best restaurant in town and certainly the one with the finest view.

We crossed Italy from toe to heel, passed Brindisi—where Caesar had once embarked an army in pursuit of Pompey and Octavian had once embarked an army in pursuit of Antony—and then made passage up the Adriatic, crossing from one side to the other: Dubrovnik; Pescara; Rovinj; Ravenna.

My fellow passengers were all distinct characters by now, as if under the ripening Mediterranean sun their inner reality had been expressed externally, the way a grape maturing on the vine comes to express its terroir. Adelina became ever more beguiling, ever more remote. Tess exuded joy at whatever new thing appeared on the horizon, at merely being alive. Wu's Fu Manchu was fully grown and would have impressed Salvador Dalí—the doctor was a constant observer, quietly assessing us all, as if aiming for perfect inscrutability. Gilbert was the focused entrepreneur, concentrating his entire will on getting the *Daily Courier* deal done.

He got his wish.

Agreement on the sale was announced one evening before dinner. We were anchored off Sveti Stefan in the little country of Montenegro. Urquhart and Gilbert had spent the afternoon ashore. There is a small island whose Fifteenth-Century buildings had been converted into a resort. Unsuspected by us, the lawyers and investment bankers had flown in ahead of time, and the final negotiations were concluded in the island's former chapel. The documents were signed on what had once been the altar. "The deal was consecrated," Gilbert quipped.

He was visibly excited; Urquhart simply looked relieved—I think the negotiations had exhausted him, and he was just glad they were over. I could not help wondering how much the sudden death of a significant shareholder had helped close the deal.

Although Gilbert genuinely wanted Urquhart's newspaper, it turned out that what he most coveted was not the publication itself but the associated distribution network. Franklin Gilbert had a big idea: he was going to create a new newspaper, a global newspaper, but one that would be unlike anything today. For a start, it would be printed not on newsprint but as a glossy magazine.

"Advances in printing have made this practicable," Gilbert explained. "Once a factory was required; now it can be achieved with something not much bigger than a breadbox." The idea was to sprinkle these small and cheap point-of-production facilities through the supply chain, lessening not only the cost but also the time to delivery—as a bonus the carbon footprint would be reduced, as most of the daily delivery mileage would be accomplished by binary data transmitted over the airwaves rather than trucks hauling loads from a central facility.

The differences would be in content, too. There would be no sports, no weather, no lifestyle section, and "absolutely nothing to do with so-called celebrities you've never heard of and who've never done anything worth celebrating," as Gilbert put it. The publication would be restricted to genuine news, doing just one thing but hopefully doing it well, and distributed daily throughout initially the U.S. and the U.K., but eventually anywhere English was spoken, even if not as a first language. The format would sometimes be in conventional articles, but also from time to time in long-form essays and papers, designed to give the broader context or in-depth analysis, or in the style of briefing papers such as the president might receive, summarizing the situation, bullet-pointing the essential core elements, and giving a list of options in dealing with it. There would be emphasis on accuracy and detail, Gilbert insisted, two qualities that had gone missing from modern reporting: hard numbers instead of vague characterizations; specific assessments rather than broad-based statements. And lastly, there would be a point of view.

"Even-handedness in current reporting has come to mean just passing on the press releases from the various sides without critique or comment," Gilbert said. "The only 'equality' is giving equal weight to whatever they say, whether nonsense or not, and it's a disservice to the reader and the societies the newspaper is meant to serve." Gilbert's glossy new paper, although remaining politically aloof, would be unapologetically discriminating in its reporting of various claims and assertions. "Rather than 'All the news that's fit to print,'" Gilbert said, "the motto of my new paper might be 'All the news that's fit to print and no lie not shown for what it is.'"

The publication was also to be heavily illustrated, not just with photography but also with diagrams and charts to make clear the matter at hand.

Advertising, too, would be different. Only whole-page ads would be accepted, with no copy other than the company name. Thus it had to be the design that drew the reader, and Gilbert hoped this would compel the agencies to come up with creative artwork to get the message across, in the process changing the ads from intellectually dishonest and visually off-putting to something more engaging and attractive.

There would be no online version of the publication. If you wanted the paper you would have to be a subscriber.

"It'll be claimed that in buying the *Daily Courier* I'm making a bet on newspapers," Gilbert said. "But what I'm really doing is making a bet on paper itself, and I believe it's a good bet. Think of everything that paper as a medium has already overcome: the advent of telephones, then radio, then moving pictures, then talkies, then television, and now the internet and social media—I think there's an appetite for something more than unedited gibberish, and that's where my new paper will come in. It won't suit everyone, but for those with a desire for informed reporting it will be a godsend."

"What is it to be called?"

"The *Global Courier*, a combination of the names of the primary paper I currently publish and the one that I've just bought. But I'm open to suggestions."

"*Verba Sequentur*," Oriana suddenly offered. "It's the second half of a quotation from Cato the Elder: *Rem tene, verba sequentur*—grasp the subject, the words will follow. It seems to me that's what your new publication will be: the words that would naturally follow from a genuine grasp of the subject."

Gilbert stood momentarily nonplussed.

"Well done," he said at last, "that's perfect."

THE LAST STOP ON THE ADRIATIC WAS VENICE, AND THE most extravagant. It was here that we would do the final calendar shoot, based on Titian's *Venus of Urbino*.

The painting is a large one, four feet high by six feet wide. It depicts a young woman, nude, reclining in pampered indulgence on a plush lounge. In the room behind her, two maids search through a chest for something with which to clothe this beauty. The subject is traditionally identified as Venus, although more likely it is a portrait of the famous Venetian courtesan Zaffetta. The painting occupies an important place in art history and would have done so even if the artist had not been the great Titian, as it was the first Old Master to depict eroticism openly, without any pretense of a classical allusion—even today when coming upon it in the Uffizi one is surprised to be confronted with a female figure so open to the pleasures of the flesh.

The painting is set inside a Venetian palazzo and so Urquhart rented one—Ca' Zenato—located on the Grand Canal. Since to use the setting he had been required to take the whole palazzo, fully furnished and staffed, it became a second home, more convenient than the *Mulvane* which, after a careful passage across the treacherous lagoon, had taken a berth in docking facilities located at the distant western end of Dorsoduro.

During the cruise I had received a number of letters. Some of the correspondence was with Sir Dickie regarding my finds at the Galerie Tremblay; mostly they were return letters from friends delighted to have received a note in letterheaded longhand, expressing envy at my good fortune to be cruising the Mediterranean aboard a luxury yacht, and laughing at the ink stains—I had not used a nib and ink since Harrow, where penmanship was still considered a skill that any gentleman should master.

The routine aboard the *Mulvane* was for a crewmember to distribute incoming mail to individual cabins, leaving it on the passengers' desks. In the palazzo, the staff were not familiar with who was who, and so they left the entire mail delivery on the long table in the *portego*, the entrance gallery located on the first floor. I was sorting through this for my mail when I noticed a manila envelope, bigger than the others, addressed to Oriana.

Another thing taught at Harrow is that not only does a gentleman never read another person's correspondence, he does not even inspect it. But there was no way to miss the sender's name printed in bold type at the top left corner: LIFE SCIENCES EXPRESS: BIOMEDICAL LAB SERVICES.

I put it aside and continued looking through the mail. A second envelope caught my eye. This one was addressed to Verkhovsky, and after returning to my room I had no Harrovian compunctions about opening it.

The stamp was Greek and the sender was "Minotaur Luxury Services—Premium Concierge & Immobilier—Athens." I quote it here in full.

Dear Mr. Verkhovsky,

Thank you for your recent letter, to which I now have the honor of responding.

We have several superb properties available that I believe you will find more than adequate to your requirements, both from the points of view of luxury and refinement, and also privacy and security.

I can assure you that we are accustomed to handling matters of this type with the level of discretion that a personage of your illustrious position would naturally expect. We are also entirely delighted to deal strictly in cash.

As per your instructions, I will personally be at the Piraeus to meet you on the arrival of your yacht. I have arranged a suite for you at the Grande Bretagne—under our company's name—and it would be my pleasure to again accompany you when you are ready to tour the properties.

I remain at your service,
Stylianos Athanasiou

Now I knew to whom that last letter Verkhovsky wrote had been addressed. *Illustrious*—he would have loved that.

The palazzo supplied each suite with a tablet whose primary purpose was as a directory, but there was internet access and I used mine to look up Minotaur Luxury Services. Predictably, it was a firm specializing in services for the wealthy: private jets; crewed yachts; staffed villas; chauffeured limousines; personal security. The website had impressive graphics but no street address. I tried looking up Stylianos Athanasiou:

there was nothing on him specifically, but I did discover that the surname is Cypriot rather than Greek.

"It all makes sense," I said to Oriana after I had shown her the letter. "When he received the invitation to the cruise Verkhovsky was already planning to go on the run. It must have seemed like the ideal opportunity to engineer his disappearance, but the only place he knew for sure we would be going was the last one, the Piraeus, hence deciding to hide out in Greece. But that suited him: it's conveniently close to Cyprus, and his bankers there probably gave him Athanasiou's contact details."

Oriana nodded in agreement. "Plus the letter rather than email," she said. "Verkhovsky was smart enough to know that if the Russians were monitoring him then they would also be monitoring his electronic communications."

"Is it that easy?"

"Easier."

She would know.

"There's no mention of the nieces," I noted.

"Yes, he was dumping them. And dumping them in a foreign country, too."

"Enough of a motive for murder?"

"People have killed for less."

XLIV

THE *VENUS OF URBINO* PHOTOGRAPH IS THE LAST IN THE calendar, December's, and it was best saved for the end because of its startling frankness. Before the shoot, Adelina had her hair dyed dark brown and curled to match Titian's Venus, a vivid contrast to the preceding blond bob—this simple modification changed her look completely. And in the previous shoots she had worn at least some clothing, even if only pearls and shoes, and her poses had been, while always stylish and often challenging, never frankly sensual. Here she was totally naked, and although not explicitly provocative neither was there any attempt at modesty, just like the painting on which it was based. She had the demeanor of a languorous courtesan caught in quiet repose, entirely at ease.

The setting, an ornate salon running the full width of the facade on the palazzo's *piano nobile*, added to the sense of indulgent opulence: high frescoed ceiling; embossed leather wallpaper in burnished bronze-gold; the chaise upon which Adelina lay upholstered in embroidered silk; San Giorgio visible in the background through the big arched windows, lying across the lagoon in Palladian splendor. By those windows Marta and Bébé were posed as the maids, having found black-and-white outfits, perhaps borrowed from Ca' Zenato's staff, to fit their roles.

I noted earlier that Sicily, where the first photo shoot took place, was a fulcrum, the point at which individual characters began to be prized loose from the indistinct blur of new faces. Now it seems to me that Venice, where the last photo shoot took place, is where it all started to fracture.

It began almost as soon as the shoot ended.

We were soon to quit the palazzo and return on board the *Mulvane*. Since the palace possessed museum-quality art that was normally inaccessible, I was going from room to room photographing them and attempting attributions. The staff, surfeited with great art as Venetians are, were quite indifferent and could identify none of them—"*Forse Robusti?*" one of the housekeepers offered in response to my question about a particular work, as if having a Tintoretto in the house would be routine.

I was on the *secondo*, puzzling over a small portrait. This floor, like the *piano nobile* below it, had a colonnaded loggia giving onto the canal, and suddenly I heard voices raised in argument coming from it.

One was easily identifiable, Gibert's, booming with annoyance.

"It has to be at the sale price," he said. "anything else is patently unfair."

"On the contrary," came Urquhart's quieter but no less angry voice, "it is anything but market price that would be unfair."

"His money was dirty and you know it."

"That has yet to be determined."

"I'll be damned if I'll pay market for it. I'd rather sue to have the sale vacated."

"As is your right. But know that—"

By that point I had returned to the stairs and was quietly making my way back down them, so I heard nothing more. But I had heard enough: the dirty money comment could only refer to Verkhovsky, and no doubt the discussion had been about the disposition of his holding following his demise.

Not all was going smoothly with the *Daily Courier* deal.

Marta pulled me aside that afternoon after the shoot. Something had disturbed her, leaving her pale despite the tan.

"You asked me before if Verkhovsky had taken any trips."

"Yes."

"I told you about his trip to L.A. But I remembered today that there was another trip, one that I forgot because it wasn't by plane; it was by car."

"Where to?"

"I don't know. We didn't go with him."

"Too far for you both to have squeezed into the Lamborghini then."

"He didn't take his own car. A car came for him."

"Car service?"

"No, a car belonging to the people he went with."

"Who were they?"

"Verkhovsky didn't introduce us. When he came back, he said they were business associates. He didn't talk about it much."

"How long was he away?"

"He came back the next day. But there are two things I must tell you."

"Yes?"

"The first is that he didn't take a bag. Not even hand luggage."

"He didn't expect to be away overnight?"

"He didn't expect to be away at all. They just arrived unannounced at the villa and ten minutes later they were gone, taking him with them."

"What's the second thing?"

"There were three men."

"Okay."

"One of them was down on the *fondamenta* today. I think he's keeping watch on the palazzo."

"Are you sure?"

Marta spent a moment considering this question before replying.

"No, I am not: how can you be sure of recognizing a person you've only seen briefly once before, and that months ago? But all during the photo shoot Bébé and I were standing at the window by the chest, and so I got a good look."

"Did Bébé recognize him, too?"

"Bébé refuses to discuss it. She is angry with me for coming to you; she says Verkhovsky is in the past, and we should forget him."

"I see."

"I think he is the same man, although I can't guarantee it. But I am certain that he is of the same type."

"Same type?"

"He was a thug."

XLV

A THIRD EVENT SIGNALING WHAT I THINK OF AS A fracturing was far more spectacular, almost Biblical. The *Mulvane* had sailed from Venice and we were heading down the Adriatic. We had escaped the crowds but not the sweltering heat: the air was humid and had that ozone-rich smell of an impending thunderstorm. Threatening anvil-heads were gathering to the north, although the sky above us remained clear. The surface of the water was covered in a layer of salt haze, sufficiently lowering sea-level visibility for the *Mulvane* to blow her fog horn, something that sounded like the plaintive wail of a mournful beast, and which set the tone for what came next.

We were on deck for cocktails. It was already getting dark but the auroras were vivid enough that we had not turned on the outside lanterns. The effect was eerie: a ship moving slowly on a mist-shrouded sea with waves of astral light washing across the shadowed faces of my fellow passengers, emphasizing angles and planes, something more suitable for Halloween than the Mediterranean summer.

Some strands of Marta's hair suddenly rose, well clear of her head, almost horizontal.

"What's happening?" Shotter asked. He was looking not at Marta but down at his arm. And then I felt it too, a strange prickling of the skin.

"Look!" Bébé exclaimed. She was staring up at the ship's mast. We followed her gaze and saw there something indeed fit for Halloween: an ethereal blueish glow, flickering at the peak of the mast and from the tips of the yardarm, and sometimes sweeping along the crosstrees in waves of neon-like luminescence. The ship was enveloped in an aurora of its own.

Trevelyan emerged from the deckhouse.

"St. Elmo's fire," he explained. "Static electricity discharging from the atmosphere; we'll probably get a lightning storm later."

"Is it dangerous?"

"Not at all, but it is unusual. Probably that shower of particles from the supernova helped kick it off—anyway, enjoy the show while it lasts." He disappeared back toward the bridge.

We remained fixed in place, staring at the mast, struck dumb by the sight above us.

The Marchesa was the first to break the silence, speaking to no one in particular, slow and deep-voiced, like a Sibyl delivering a prophecy.

"A portent of evil."

"Not at all, madam," Wu assured her, "merely a scientific phenomenon." His remark was meant to reassure, but it had the opposite effect.

"If you really think that, doctor, then I'm afraid that you are fooling yourself."

"As a physician, I'm naturally obliged to be a man of science."

"Nonsense! Your science is just a fig leaf for your ignorance. The truth has better things to do than reveal itself to men."

Wu was too much of a gentleman to take up the argument, even after having been told that he was talking nonsense, but I could see that he was offended. The outburst was so uncharacteristic that I could not help wondering if there was more behind it than just an unnerving meteorological event: something about Wu that the Marchesa knew, or perhaps the other way around.

The usual bridge game, in which Wu and the Marchesa would have partnered, did not take place that evening.

Oriana seemed unperturbed when I told her about the conversation with Marta.

"It doesn't worry you that the Russians might be watching us?" I asked.

"Not at all. Don't be concerned: they're no threat to us—in fact, it's to be expected."

"Expected?"

"Think of it from their point of view. One of their nationals who they want back in Moscow has been dragging his feet. He's clearly reluctant to return and possesses the means to do something about it. Suddenly he gets an invitation to a long cruise from someone they've never heard of, and the next thing you know he's reported drowned. Questionable enough already, but on top of it all there's no post-mortem and the identification is made by the French based on documents provided by the people on this mysterious yacht, even the death certificate itself. To them, it must have smelled like a setup."

I had to admit that when she put it that way I could see how they might be suspicious.

"They think Verkhovsky faked his death?"

"It's an obvious line of investigation. All they need do is catch a glimpse of him to confirm it, but of course that's not possible."

"What would have happened if they did?"

"Then they would no longer have been unthreatening."

The *Mulvane*'s first stop in Greece was the island of Corfu, at the entrance to the Ionian Sea. We avoided the resort areas and instead explored places mentioned in or related to Homer: the deserted bays beyond Palaiokastritsa where Odysseus supposedly encountered the ship-burning princess Nausicaa; the traditional village of Nymfes, untouched by time and whose waterfall-fed rockpools could have served as an alternative location for Tess's *Seated Nymph* photo shoot; the Achilleion, a palace named for the least admirable of all Homeric heroes; and the island of Pontikonisi, where Poseidon reputedly turned Odysseus' ship into stone.

The cruise was ending as it had begun, pursuing the *Odyssey*—the original and our own.

We anchored off Pontikonisi early in the morning and this was to be the site of another, much different, fracturing. A prominent feature of the island is a twisting white staircase, stark against the surrounding green and which from a distance resembles the tail of a mouse, hence the literal meaning of the name: Mouse Island. The staircase leads up to a chapel, the Church of Pantokrator, part of a Byzantine monastery dating from the Twelfth Century.

I came on deck at daybreak. Betelgeuse was already high in the sky and the auroras were being replaced by Homer's rosy-fingered dawn. I thought I would have the sunrise to myself but then Urquhart joined me. He suggested that we go ashore and see the church before breakfast.

We took the Riva which he piloted himself, maybe just wanting the pleasure of a fast run or perhaps because it meant that the speedboat would necessarily remain at Pontikonisi, and so no one could use it to join us.

We secured to the jetty and began climbing the stairs.

"Are you pleased to be back in Greece?" I asked.

"I am pleased to be back on an island. I'm happy that my island is in Greece, of course—who could object to the Cyclades? But in truth it could have been at the edge of the Outer Hebrides or in the middle of the Sulu Sea—what mattered to me was not the location but the isolation."

"To be left alone?"

"To not hear the constant clamoring of the cows all mooing for the milking shed." He smiled, a rare event. "I am speaking figuratively, of course. Real cows I don't mind at all."

"Tess mentioned that you and her father were in the same Divinity class at Oxford."

"I read Greats but took Divinity on the side because in those days I was dedicated to truth. But to reach truth one must first cast aside deceptions, and the most obvious of deceptions is religion. My aim was to study Divinity to better debunk it. I was young and optimistic then, foolishly believing that people could be better if only they would choose to see. Another lie, of course—the last thing people want to see is the truth; in fact, they will go to great lengths to avoid doing so. Perhaps rightly: the truth would only crush them."

"I take it that you don't expect Gilbert's new paper to succeed?"

"If anyone can make it work, he will. Gilbert, unlike me, remains a son of the Enlightenment, along with a useful dose of practical American pragmatism—a latter-day Jefferson with a tincture of Thomas Edison thrown in."

We reached the top of the stairs. Urquhart was breathless from the short climb, and I wondered how he had managed Etna. There was a modest paved court giving onto the church, surrounded by cypress trees.

"And so here we are."

It was not much of a church: simple whitewashed stucco walls, a small porch, a little mission-style campanile to the side, and an octagonal lantern in the middle of a red-tiled roof.

I walked over and tried the front door. There was no lock, just a simple latch.

We went inside. The interior was gloomy and bare apart from the altar, decorated with icons depicting the usual somber long-faced saints against a background of brilliant gold leaf. We stood before them for a while in silence, eventually broken by Urquhart.

"And so it turns out there was not much of a difference between the monks and myself. We both chose isolation on uninhabited islands, and we both amused ourselves with shiny little pictures."

"But these icons are just more deceptions," I said. "The *Lustration* is the truth."

"Is it?"

"If that's not truth, then I'm in the wrong business."

We left the chapel and it was a relief to be outside again. The sun had risen, and the first golden rays were sweeping across the water and skimming the tops of the cypresses.

"I've seen the Exeter portrait," I said.

"I wondered if you had."

"So not all the passengers were unknown to you."

"On the contrary, I had never met any of them before this voyage. However, I had *seen* Adelina before, many years ago."

"Where?"

"In Venice. She was standing on a dock by the Grand Canal. There was a group, all dressed in the same school uniform, but she stood apart from the others, literally and metaphorically. Apartness is the quality she best embodies, don't you think?"

"You took a photograph?"

"No, I did a sketch but it was quite rudimentary, made in the few minutes before a launch came and whisked them away. It was a starting point, I suppose, but when it came time for the painting it was mostly from memory. Memory and imagination, I should say."

"How did you learn who she was?"

"It was the hotel's private jetty, and they told me the name of the school—Headington. When the time came it was a simple matter to identify her from the yearbooks."

"But how did you know what she looked like now?"

"I didn't. The *Lustration* was as I dreamed Adelina might appear now. That's one reason it's so swirly: I couldn't be precise because I didn't know what she looked like after all these years—the Marchesa's photographs came later, requested only as an excuse to account for the painting. I generally dislike photographs: they limit memory rather than aid it—after a while one ceases to recall the real thing and remembers the recorded image instead."

"You have a remarkably detailed memory."

"I certainly did in that case, but it's not surprising. I'd never seen anyone so self-contained and that glimpse of her was emblazoned on my mind. How childish she made my visions of a better world at the same age seem, and how correspondingly ridiculous the resulting disappointment."

"So, hope?"

"No, acceptance."

"I don't believe you." The flatness of my response startled him. "As I said, I've seen the painting."

For the second time in the same day he smiled. He put his hand on my shoulder

"You shall have access to whatever documents you may wish. I will catalog all of my paintings and their dispositions as best I can remember. Many of them I still possess; you will see when we get to Ledos. You may choose any two: one for Sir Dickie and one for yourself." He raised a hand to halt my response. "Now, we should head back for breakfast, no?"

XLVI

I N THOSE LANGUID LAST WEEKS THE PASSENGERS WITHDREW more and more into themselves, both as a whole—we avoided the tourist sights and no longer dined ashore—and also individually. Part of this was climatic: the heat was relentless and a breeze seemed never to blow. It was too hot to do anything but swim, and the *Mulvane* spent many hours anchored in isolated coves where we cooled ourselves in the sea. Part of it was Hellenic, the result of being in an ancient land where things proceeded at a more measured pace, as if the weight of so much history slowed everything down—Greece suggested a retreat into simpler ways. This was reflected at dinner: we no longer dined formally, and even flamboyant Ernesto settled for typical Greek peasant food: plates of taramasalata and tzatziki with flatbread and oil to begin; simple grilled lamb or fish to follow; dainty honeyed cakes or slices of baklava for dessert.

Another incident in what I characterize as the fracturing came as an intrusion from the outside world, warning of our impending reentry into it. The sun deck had remained the preserve of the women and they were all deeply tanned now, even fair Tess. The routine was to spend the middle of the day at anchor in some deserted cove where they would alternate between sunbathing and swimming, but one day we discovered that we were no longer alone. The alert was raised in the form of a cry from the sun deck. I was aft at the time and looked forward to see Trevelyan emerge onto a bridge wing and look up at the deck above him.

"Everything alright up there?"

Adelina appeared at the rail with a T-shirt thrown on.

"It's a drone," she said. "Someone's spying on us, I think."

I looked up and spotted it, about the size of a serving tray, the whirr of the tiny rotors faintly audible, buzzing back and forward like an oversized insect above the *Mulvane*.

Trevelyan disappeared back inside the bridge, soon reemerging on the wing, this time with Kustaa. Kustaa was carrying a shotgun.

By now everyone had been alerted and come out on deck. The women, hastily clad, lined the railing on the sun deck, watching the drone that was watching them.

Kustaa raised the shotgun, spent a moment matching his aim to the movement of the drone, and fired. The drone burst apart in what was a spectacular spray of debris for such a small device. The pieces fell or floated down to the sea.

The thunderous report of the shotgun made everything seem quiet afterward. The operator must have been hiding somewhere in the scrub ashore. Kustaa aimed the shotgun in that direction and the silence was soon broken by the sound of a car starting up and then rapidly beating it along some unseen road.

Trevelyan gave a quick instruction to Kustaa who then discharged the second barrel, but with the shotgun raised to ensure that it would just be for noise—a warning not to return. He and the captain were both smiling: apparently, this was an old game. Trevelyan looked up at the women.

"Paparazzi," he explained. "They often haunt the coast, looking for luxury yachts like ours and hoping to catch celebrities. I think we've seen the last of that one." Trevelyan was in good humor, slapping the grinning Kustaa on the shoulder, but he underestimated the effect that this incident was to have on the women. The sunbathing never resumed—a predictable reaction—but beyond that, it seemed to snap something in their collective consciousness, as if until now the voyage had been in a state of precarious equilibrium whose delicate balance, suddenly upset, could never be restored.

Strange to say, I felt this psychological shift myself. Until now I had enjoyed the cruise, despite the murder or perhaps even because of it—indeed, I found that I had a liking for investigating a juicy crime. But the drone incident was like being woken up from a delirious dream only to be confronted with dull reality. Even if you could fall back asleep, you knew that the dream was gone forever.

The outward evidence of this change of mood was subtle but it was there.

The Marchesa continued to preside over the after deck from her accustomed perch at the stern, but in the afternoons when it was hottest and most of us were in the water she retired to the cool of her stateroom. Gilbert pored over business documents and did not appreciate interruptions: here he was with the polite veneer removed, the man his subordinates would be familiar with, tough and unforgiving, and I could not help thinking how fortunate I was to have the affable Sir Dickie as a boss. Marta and I continued our chess matches but the intervals between moves became longer. The card games had resumed until one evening the Marchesa hissed at Wu for having played a trump badly. Shotter photographed the shore and occasionally us. The faces were the same but the expectant energy behind them was gone—maybe just the natural lassitude that accompanies the end of a vacation, or perhaps the realization that our private paradise was soon to be abandoned.

With no further photo shoots to engage them, the women turned to drama. Urquhart mentioned that there were the ruins of a small amphitheater on Ledos—although never inhabited the island had been used for the staging of plays, convenient for an audience arriving from the circle of surrounding islands for which Ledos was a geographical hub, and the isolation suiting the semi-sacred nature of drama in the classical period. Ruin or not, a play could still be staged there for the tiny audience aboard the *Mulvane*.

They selected Sophocles' *Elektra*, probably because the primary characters are mostly female, or perhaps because there was a translation in the ship's library. The sun deck became a rehearsal stage.

Meanwhile, the Homeric journey continued. We visited Othonoi, Homer's Ogygia, where Odysseus had long lingered with Calypso; and Ithaca, Odysseus' homeland, where Penelope had woven delayingly; and the passage between the Peloponnesus and Cythera where Odysseus had endured endless storms, although not a breath of wind blew when we were there.

The day came when the *Mulvane* rounded Cape Maleas and entered the Aegean Sea. There was less than a week of the cruise remaining. We sailed on, past Milos and Sikinos and Ios and a dozen other islands, scattered like sparkling jewels on the Homeric wine-dark velvet of the sea.

We reached Ledos at last, and the *Mulvane* set her anchor for the final time.

I went up to the sun deck for a better view and gazed over the island, scorched and barren but mysterious, too. There were the ruins of a small temple visible in the cove but no other sign of civilization, present or past. Despite the fact of the Greek temple the scene made me think of neither Homer nor Sophocles but instead William Shakespeare—specifically, *The Tempest*. Urquhart, still a cipher to me after three months, would of course play the enigmatic sorcerer-king Prospero, and I supposed that Adelina would be the enchanting Miranda. Tess was a natural for the nymphlike spirit Ariel.

I wondered who would take on the role of monstrous and deformed Caliban.

XLVII

W E WENT ASHORE TO LEDOS, GATHERING IN A GROUP on the little stone jetty as the Riva went back and forth picking up and delivering passengers. When we were all across Urquhart led us on a tour along a semblance of a path circumnavigating the island. This could have been a challenge for the Marchesa but she managed to make her way without undue delay, parasol in one hand and walking stick in the other, and of all of us I was surprised that it was she who showed the most open and undisguised delight in the place, a look of pleasure without reservation.

"Ledos in just forty acres," Urquhart explained as we walked along. "There are no streams or springs, which is why the Greek government was willing to lease it. To them, it was just a small arid island with no potential for development, but it suits me."

"What do you do for fresh water?"

"I had an underground cistern dug to collect rainwater, but I don't use it much. I am looked after by an old couple, Hermes and Eleni, who live on Thera, over there." He pointed to an island visible on the horizon to the southwest. "Hermes was a fisherman, but now he uses his boat to ferry supplies to me, including Eleni's home cooking. He brings bottled water, too."

We came to the northern side of the island. There was an inlet whose rocky shore had been eroded into a series of elaborate arches and bridges, quite complex. Waves are rarely large in the Mediterranean, but even the small ones rolling in now caused water to spray up through fissures and blowholes.

"There are grottoes down there," Urquhart explained. "One of them is large and colorful; I call it the Emerald Grotto. In the smaller ones there's not much airspace, and so when a wave comes in the pressure makes the water burst up like that. When the wind is from the north it can be quite spectacular."

"Can we swim there?" Bébé asked.

"Certainly."

"How marvelous," Tess said, and it was clear that the women would soon be returning.

We continued around to the next cove and came to the amphitheater. It was smaller than I had expected, just ten rows or so sunk into the natural amphitheater of a gully facing the sea. The stage was a single large slab of rock.

"I guess there'll be no scenery for our play," Rasputina said.

"It's the sea that's the scenery."

"And the auroras."

"What better for a Greek tragedy?"

We crossed the last promontory and the temple came back into view, completing the circumnavigation.

"No one knows to whom the temple was dedicated, so when I had it restored I was able to name it for whichever god or goddess I chose."

"Who did you pick?"

"Thelxinoë, a muse, although not one of the famous nine."

"What was she the muse of?"

"Enchantment."

Another echo of *The Tempest*.

"Is there more?"

"This is it."

"But where do you live?"

"In the temple."

We walked over. I saw that what from the *Mulvane* had seemed a ruin was partially rebuilt but in a manner sympathetic with the original. The additions, mostly new columns or missing sections of existing columns, matched the color of the original and were similarly weathered. There was an entablature but no relief work in the frieze or pediments. The only attempt at ornamentation was a simple dentil design for the cornice.

We entered the temple. There were outer and inner colonnades, the former Ionic, the latter Doric. The only genuinely enclosed space, one with walls, was what had originally been the cella, where once a statue of the god would have dwelt. Now it was Urquhart's bedroom—perhaps he considered this no real change in function. It was occupied by a simple peasant cot, a rickety wardrobe, a nightstand, and a lantern.

But it was obvious that Urquhart lived his life out in the unwalled area, where on the seaward side several easels stood, without canvases, and a large sturdy cabinet by the cella wall was filled with tubes of oil paints, jars of brushes, palettes and thinner and cloths, the essential equipment of a working artist—plus something less usual: a thick glass jar filled with mercury.

On the other side was the kitchen, just a trestle table on which stood a small spirit stove with a coffeepot on the burner and a storage box that sealed tightly to be insect-proof. Standing by the table was what at first I thought was an old-fashioned refrigerator, but it turned out to be a genuine icebox. The top section was occupied by a single big block, surprisingly large since Urquhart had been absent for three months— perhaps Hermes had brought over a new one in preparation for the owner's return.

An armchair by the front stoa was the sole concession to comfort. There was a desk stacked with paperwork, and I wondered if among that pile were my own importunate and unanswered letters. In any case, it was clear that ascetic hermit he might be—for how could his life on Ledos be described any other way?—but he was a hermit who maintained a hefty correspondence with the outside world. Beside the desk was a bookcase brimming with volumes, but even so I wondered how long it would take before he had read them all.

"Hermes brings me new books," Urquhart said, as if reading my mind. "He doesn't speak English—even the characters of our alphabet are alien to him—and so he has little idea what he's buying: he just grabs whatever catches his eye. You might say that my reading is highly eclectic, but that's not necessarily a bad thing."

The Marchesa stood smiling at the surroundings.

"There are few places on earth where I feel truly comfortable," she said. "This is one of them. How very right this feels."

"May I get you a chair?"

"Thank you."

Urquhart fetched one of the rattan cane chairs by an easel, cushioned, apparently the seat he used when working on a picture.

"Is there electricity?" Rasputina asked, less entranced than the Marchesa.

"No, I find that I have no need of it. There's a pump for the cistern over there." He pointed to a wellhead emerging from the rocks, beside which stood one of those big old-fashioned handpumps that one thinks of from Wild West movies. "And Hermes brings a big block of ice every few months for the icebox. I also have a kerosene stove and kerosene lanterns."

"What are those buildings?"

There was a triplet of ancillary structures, all simple stone sheds, on the landward side, about fifty yards away.

Urquhart indicated the larger one on the left. "That's where I store my canvases. You're welcome to have a look if you wish; it's unlocked." He pointed to the middle one. "That's where I store my fishing gear and diving equipment—if Eleni's cooking runs out I catch my dinner." He pointed at the last and smallest structure, on the right. "That's the head. It also uses a hand pump, although seawater rather than fresh. The operation is obvious once you see it." He looked at us all looking back at him and smiled. "Now you know why we will remain accommodated aboard the *Mulvane*."

"I think it's wonderful," Tess said. "All of it, especially that cove of grottoes. Can we go swimming there now?"

"Certainly. Did you bring swimming costumes?"

"Swimming costumes? Pfft!" And off she went, followed by the others, even Oriana and Adelina.

"Coffee, Lady Isabella?"

"Thank you."

Urquhart checked the storage box. "I can offer you melomakarona—Greek honey biscuits—or some fresh grapes that Hermes and his wife must have left."

"The melomakarona, please."

Urquhart put on the coffee. We could hear distant cries and squeals from the grottoes. Gilbert looked through the bookshelves. Wu studied the temple while Shotter photographed it. I walked over to the shed on the left, the larger one.

There were dozens of canvases inside—whatever else could be said about Urquhart's choice to live on Ledos, it had been a productive one. But as I examined them one by one in that cramped space with just the little light that oozed through the doorway, even in those unfavorable conditions I could tell that there was more to these works than mere quantity. "I paint from memory," he had told me, "memory and imagination," and while staring in wonderment at painting after painting it suddenly became clear why he had needed to be alone: that crowded imagination required room for release, and Ledos was where he had found it.

Here was a new way of looking at the world, I realized, but something difficult to characterize: a cleanliness of concept, an artlessness if one may speak of art that is artless, a putting aside of form to get at the underlying substance. The Pre-Raphaelite sympathy that I had felt in the Exeter portrait was evident, and to it had been added a rich Surrealistic sheen, something that I should already have noted in the *Lustration*, but which was now forcefully and undeniably before me—they were dreamscapes, but executed without conceit; dreamscapes whose sole purpose was to be the landing pad for Urquhart's voluminous flights of imagination.

I will not attempt to catalog what I found in that stone shed (something I have since done elsewhere and with more academic rigor than would be appropriate for this journal). I will only state that I suddenly understood two things with absolute certainty. The first was that I had been exceedingly fortunate all those years ago to have happened upon the Exeter portrait and chosen Urquhart as my dissertation subject, for I had unwittingly specialized in a genius.

The second thing I now knew was why my hairbrush had been moved.

XLVIII

I ROSE EARLY IN THE MORNING, SOMETHING RARE IN GRAY
England, but here I found myself eager to greet the new day. I came
on deck to discover that Urquhart had beaten me to it. Perhaps after his
long isolation on Ledos his biological clock had synchronized with the
movements of the sun, and I wondered if Betelgeuse blowing up had
affected it.

He was staring at the sky with disapproval, although it was a fine
day.

"Do you feel the change?" he asked.

"What change?"

"The air."

As a matter of fact I did. "It seems fresher, less humid."

"Indeed. And see those high clouds?"

"Yes."

"It means that a meltemi is coming."

"A meltemi?"

"A north wind, very strong."

"It feels calm."

"By this afternoon it'll be blowing hard. It will last several hours at
least." I understood his concern now: this evening the women were to

perform *Elektra*. "But there is a silver lining, literally silver: the atherina will be running."

"Atherina?"

"Smelt. Whitebait, I suppose you'd call them. Come, let's go catch breakfast."

We took the Zodiac and pulled it up onto the pebble beach. Urquhart fetched a fishing net from the middle shed and we waded into the water off the western point of the cove. We separated and deployed the net. Twenty minutes later, breakfast had been secured.

By the time we returned on board, most passengers had risen. Rasputina did not look impressed when we explained that the silvery mass of little fish in the bucket was to be breakfast.

"But how do you fillet something so small?" she asked.

"Fillet them? No, we'll eat them whole."

And so we did, even Rasputina. Ernesto was an old hand with whitebait and quickly had them coated in flour and frying in a pan. With a squeeze of lemon and a sprinkling of oregano, they made a fine start to the day.

THAT MORNING, WHILE IT WAS STILL CALM, THE TWO PAINTINGS I had selected were brought aboard the *Mulvane* and safely stowed away. By mid-afternoon, the meltemi was blowing hard, something that pleased the women because it turned the cove with the grottoes into an impromptu waterpark. This time they brought their swimming costumes and so we men were allowed to join them. The sea had risen with more than just the surface chop that a breeze usually brings to the Mediterranean. There were real waves, several feet high and packing a punch—entry and exit from the water had to be timed carefully to avoid getting swept onto the rocks. The blowholes were spectacular now, sending forth streaming geysers with each incoming wave. The Emerald Grotto was a vibrantly green cave whose colorful light patterns swirled with the churning sea. I found myself in there with Tess, and we talked while bobbing in the water with the roar of the sea outside, a strange place to have a conversation, but it was there that she told me about herself, more than the superficial facts with which I was familiar.

She had enjoyed a happy childhood and loved her parents dearly but was nevertheless eager for escape and the opportunity to plunge into a new life. Religion, which had necessarily clung to her father, had left her in her early teens while still at boarding school, and Tess had been grateful for the intellectual freedom that she found there and again at Oxford. I had already recognized that she possessed an inner strength of will one would not necessarily expect from the carefree exterior, and that day I felt it as forcefully as I had the power of the Urquhart paintings the day before—an intelligent and boundless energy eager to express itself and which would take no prisoners while doing so.

Until then, I would have thought Tess constitutionally incapable of killing Kirill Verkhovsky, but now I realized I had again underestimated her—were the circumstances sufficiently compelling, Tess was more than capable of doing whatever was necessary.

ELEKTRA WAS STAGED AMID A HOWLING TUMULT AND A raging sea. The auroras were especially vivid in the meltemi-cleared atmosphere, their illumination welcome because the lanterns flickered uncertainly, despite being enclosed. As a backdrop, it could not have been more dramatic. Spray from the waves crashing behind the stage was sometimes swept across the scene, and the players were soon soaked through.

The actors might have been dampened but not their spirits: the performance was a lively one. Since the wind was behind them their words were not immediately swept away. This plus the fact that the amphitheater was so small allowed the audience to follow the action on stage, although it meant that we became damp, too.

Elektra is a simple tale: the return of the exiled Orestes and the incitement by his sister Elektra to murder their mother, Clytaemnestra, and her usurping consort, Aegisthus—revenge for having themselves murdered Agamemnon on his return from the Trojan Wars a generation before.

It has seven roles but there were only six women to play them. There is also a chorus, a significant part of any Greek tragedy before Euripides. They resolved the numbers problem by, firstly, having Oriana play both the Paedagogus and Aegisthus, who never appear on stage at the same time, and, secondly, writing the non-speaking role of Plyades out of the performance entirely. Orestes was played by Bébé, suitably fierce, and Marta made a superbly haughty Clytaemnestra. Adelina took the role of the Chorus, above the fray in the play as in life. Tess played Chrysothemis, urging her sister to rationality over rage. But it was Rasputina who stole the show: she was a natural on stage, seeming to totally inhabit the vengeful character of the eponymous heroine, and she projected with gusto, the only person no one ever had difficulty hearing. It made me wonder why she had never sought to follow in her mother's footsteps.

At the play's completion, we returned to the temple and received a surprise. There were no longer any lights bobbing out in the bay. It seemed that the *Mulvane* had disappeared.

XLIX

U RQUHART HAD COME ASHORE EQUIPPED WITH A HAND-held two-way radio, urged on him by the captain wary of the weather, but had left it in the temple during the play to stay dry. He raised the *Mulvane*. Trevelyan reported that the yacht had dragged her anchor, forcing him to weigh in order to ride out the night in open water. In any case, the sea was now too high to transfer passengers by boat, and so we had no choice but to wait until the calm of dawn to return on board.

A cold supper of Greek *mezedes* had been brought ashore when we landed, and while the women changed into dry clothes—mostly shirts raided from Urquhart's closet—we men laid it out: spicy spreads with pita; feta in oil; marinated beets; octopus salad; fragrant meatballs in a tomato sauce; half a dozen other dishes. This was washed down with retsina and plenty of prosecco to celebrate the performance. The meal was also to be a farewell: it was the penultimate dinner of the cruise, and tomorrow evening we would be too busy preparing for disembarkation for a late night.

The feast was consumed, the wine drunk, and the players toasted. At last we sat back, coffee or *raki* or both in hand, sated and silent. The Marchesa dozed in the armchair. The bed had been pulled out and four of the women lounged upon it. Oriana occupied one cane chair, Adelina another. Wu sat on an upturned crate. Gilbert sat on the floor with his back to the cella wall and Shotter lay supine, a folded dishtowel under his hands linked behind his head serving as a pillow. I sat on a step using a column for a backrest, and Urquhart did likewise.

The wind whistled through the temple, eerily high-pitched, and the crashing of the waves provided a continuous background bass. I checked the illuminated dial of my vintage watch: it was five hours to first light. But then first light suddenly came: the supernova rose and the Temple of Thelxinoë became enchanted, flooded with a maze of silvery light and, where columns intervened, lurking shadow.

Conversation picked up and naturally fell to the play.

"In the end, was Elektra a heroine or a villain?"

"Heroine."

"Neither heroine nor villain. In a Greek tragedy, they're always a bit of both."

"Heroine, but a flawed heroine—she did not master her emotions but was instead mastered by them."

"I vote for villain. She was a murderess, so how could she be anything else?

"But it was Orestes who did the actual killing."

"He was just his sister's tool: Elektra was the real murderer."

"Must murder be a crime? After all, the victims were themselves the murderers of Elektra and Orestes' father. They had it coming, I'd say."

"Murder is murder, all the same. It's always a crime."

"Always?"

"Okay, there may be exceptional circumstances where it's justified."

"What about non-exceptional circumstances?" It was Oriana who posed this strange question. "Is it still always a crime?"

"What do you mean?"

"Suppose a murder were to be committed offhand, without much of a motive. Must it still be a crime?"

"Yes, of course."

"All the more so, surely?"

Urquhart, who had been silent through this exchange, had his eyes pinned on Oriana. "I take it that you are of a different opinion?"

"I am."

"Would you care to offer an example?"

"Are you sure that you want me to?"

"I think it's inevitable, now that you've come this far."

"I could always step back from the brink."

"As Chrysothemis urged Elektra, but she was destined to fail."

"And you forget that I'm a lawyer."

"So?"

"Words have implications in law."

"Perhaps you could speak hypothetically?"

"Hypothetically?"

"Yes, as something posited for the sake of argument rather than stated as outright fact. That should assuage your forensic concerns, I think."

"So I am to proceed?"

"I believe it's our fate that you should do so."

Everyone was fully awake now.

"Very well. Let us suppose, hypothetically, that Kirill Verkhovsky did not *fall* overboard. Let us instead suppose that Verkhovsky was *thrown* overboard."

A long silence followed this statement, eventually broken by Wu.

"I made the medical examination of the body. There was absolutely no evidence of foul play."

"You missed two things, although I hasten to add through no fault of your own." Wu did not look pleased at having his professionalism impugned. "The first of these was that there were wood fibers from the *Mulvane*'s stern rail under Verkhovsky's fingernails."

"I specifically checked under the fingernails," Wu said, tight-lipped. "It is a routine procedure in an examination of this kind. I am certain that there was nothing there."

"And nor was there. I had already removed the material, before your examination took place—theoretically speaking, of course."

"But why?"

"What would your conclusions have been if you had found those wood fibers?"

"The cause of death would have been unchanged: asphyxia by drowning. However, I would have left the manner of death open, to be determined by a coroner's court."

"And what would have happened next?"

"Presumably the French authorities would have instigated an investigation."

"But the French would have done nothing since the incident occurred in international waters, where there is no legal jurisdiction. Plus the victim was neither a French citizen nor a permanent resident, and the ship does not have French registration. Even if foul play was suspected, they had no authority to investigate. Nor, as they made clear, did they wish to."

"But something would have had to be done."

"Certainly. Captain Trevelyan and the charter company would have conferred. The *Mulvane* has British registration and so they would have contacted the British authorities. Since the British port of Gibraltar was conveniently close that's no doubt where the *Mulvane* would have been directed. What would have occurred once we got there?"

"An autopsy?"

"Yes, performed in that small colony by a local not very used to forensic medical examination. Plus a criminal investigation, conducted by police officers similarly inexperienced. The passengers and crew would have been interviewed and statements taken, but the authorities would have found no evidence on which to hold any suspects. It would have been the end of the cruise, of course—no one would have wished to continue with a murderer aboard. The passengers would have dispersed back to their homes. The crew would have been reassigned to duties elsewhere. And almost certainly whoever—theoretically—threw Verkhovsky overboard would have gotten away with it."

"But what's the alternative?"

"Remove the wood fibers so that the finding is death by accident, permitting the cruise to continue unhindered and therefore ensuring that all the suspects remained on board, allowing for a slow, considered, and methodical investigation to be conducted."

"By whom?"

"By me. At this point, I should explain that I am more than just Mr. Urquhart's assistant. I'm a lawyer and licensed investigator at the London agency of Saunders Walker Investigations."

"You're saying that you knew there was going to be a death?"

"Not at all. My agency was engaged by Urquhart long before the *Mulvane* put to sea. We were tasked with tracking down the people on the guest list and making arrangements for them to join the cruise, as I did with each of you. But it so happened that when Verkhovsky was lost overboard I was on hand to investigate, and so I doctored the evidence to ensure that I would be able to do so—theoretically."

"But why would anyone want to murder Verkhovsky?"

"Why would anyone not want to? He was an odious individual and clearly didn't fit in with the rest of us. Indeed, it was a puzzle that he'd been invited in the first place, and it was this conundrum that led my colleague to conclude that if he had been tossed overboard then it must have been our host who did it, since it was he who invited Verkhovsky in the first place."

"Your colleague?"

"I enlisted Dr. Evans to assist in the investigation."

"Ah," I heard Rasputina softly exclaim.

The only face to show no surprise was Adelina's. Maybe this was due to her natural composure, but I could not help thinking that I now knew who had been on the other side of the hedge that day in the villa's garden. Oriana continued.

"Evans got involved because he spoke French—or so we believed—although in the end the authorities chose to speak English rather than endure Evans' French. I also thought that he was in a better position than me to subtly question the male passengers—another mistake, as Evans lacks all subtlety."

"But couldn't he have been the murderer?"

"No," Oriana answered, "he snores."

"What?"

"You snore."

"I do not."

"Actually, you're right—normally you don't, but you did that first night. Our cabins share a common bulkhead. My bunk is on the other side, directly opposite yours, and I imagine that our heads are just inches apart. I can assure you, Evans, that on the first night you snored. That's why I enlisted you: of all the passengers you were the only one I knew couldn't have done it—you were too busy keeping me awake."

"So you thought it was me?" Urquhart asked.

"Still do," I replied. "Why else invite Verkhovsky?"

"That's the central question," Oriana continued. "Motive. And indeed when we came to motive we discovered that there were surprisingly many people on board who might have had one. Let's start with the crew. Kustaa is a Finn, and historically Finns, like most peoples unfortunate enough to share a border with Russia, have good reason to dislike Russians. But Kustaa was more than that: he was trained as a special forces soldier whose mission was specifically to counter any Russian incursion. So devoted was he to the cause that he had the emblem of his unit tattooed on his shoulder. One can imagine him that night serving the drunken Verkhovsky, an especially loathsome member of a nation to which he was already ill-disposed, and deciding to be rid of him then and there. He had the physical strength and the operational training to have tossed Verkhovsky overboard without any fuss. And remember that he was the last person to see Verkhovsky alive; we only have his word for it that Verkhovsky dismissed him earlier. Maybe he remained with Verkhovsky through the night; perhaps it was Verkhovsky's insistence that he do so that led to an argument. And, lastly, there is the fact that it was he who volunteered to dive into the sea when we found Verkhovsky, something justified by his background, certainly, but also how convenient if wanting to ensure that someone he had tossed overboard was in fact dead before recovering the body."

"It sounds very circumstantial. Kustaa must have come across Russians before without killing them."

"Although unlikely one as obnoxious."

"Good point."

"Then let me give you another," Oriana continued. "Milosz. I'm sorry to say that our chief steward is a thief. He stole a watch belonging to Verkhovsky, a very expensive and distinctive one. When the crew was given shore leave in Monaco Milosz wore it to a nightclub, no doubt to impress the girl he was with. Probably he thought he was safe because Verkhovsky never wore the watch aboard the *Mulvane*. But Evans had encountered Verkhovsky in the casino the night before we sailed, and he had been wearing the watch then. When Evans saw Milosz coming out of the nightclub wearing the same watch he recognized it. He later confronted Milosz, who admitted to the crime but claimed that he had taken the watch from Verkhovsky's cabin after the latter's death. We only have Milosz's word for this. He could just as well have stolen it that first night, sneaking into the cabin while Verkhovsky was engaged with the vodka bottle upstairs. Maybe Verkhovsky came below and caught him."

"Verkhovsky seemed pretty well ensconced in the bar that night."

"And no doubt had every intention of remaining there, but he needed a little pick-me-up to continue his drinking bout."

"A pick-me-up?"

"Cocaine. Kirill Verkhovsky was a cocaine user, a habitual one, according to Dr. Wu's medical examination. Sure enough, we found a stash hidden in his cabin. The lab results revealed that there was cocaine in his bloodstream, so we know he ingested some that night. That's probably why he dismissed Kustaa from behind the bar: to slip down and bring some back to enjoy with the vodka. Maybe he stumbled upon Milosz stealing his watch. We can picture Milosz seeing his career come to an end and probably facing jail time, too—sufficient motive to take advantage of Verkhovsky's intoxication and toss him overboard."

"Milosz sounds more likely than Kustaa."

"But there's a third crewmember, Jamys, with an even better motive. Jamys and Aška are romantically involved, but there's no privacy in their crews' quarters. They apparently arranged to meet late that first night in the storage area forward of the pantry. What they didn't know was that Rasputina was next door getting water. The only other way out for her was back through the main salon, but that's where Verkhovsky was encamped at the bar and so Rasputina was stuck. They were talking but Rasputina couldn't distinguish what was said, except once, when Jamys raised his voice. Rasputina heard him say, very distinctly, 'If that Russian pig tries it again I'm going to toss him overboard.' Verkhovsky had already shown himself to be ill-mannered with the staff. Perhaps there had been an incident with Aška. In any case, Jamys is a suspect, and not just with a motive but an outright statement of intention."

Many eyes went inquiringly to Rasputina. "That's how it happened," she confirmed, "but I should emphasize that Jamys's words were said in anger—the sort of thing that any young man in love might say. I don't think we should put much weight on it."

"Still, it presumably makes him the prime suspect."

"Not quite," Oriana said. "We haven't gotten to the passengers yet."

"Us?"

"Yes."

"But who? And why?"

"I will tell you. But first, we should understand the circumstances of the victim. We know that Verkhovsky was a Russian oligarch, never an attractive type to begin with but in this case I think we can agree a particularly unpleasant example. He made his money in the usual way that oligarchs do, not by vision and hard work—Verkhovsky wouldn't have known a gas rig if one fell on him—but by a combination of corruption and carpetbagging. The Russian government wanted him and his wealth back home. He had never obtained permanent residency in France—the French authorities frankly refused him; in fact, they were going to deport him. His Russian passport, issued for only a year, would soon expire. He was faced with becoming a stateless citizen on the run from the Russian FSB and unable to find refuge—and even if he had, we know how fond the Russians are of poisoning their countrymen abroad. He took no medications, probably for that reason, and had nothing confidential on his phone, a safeguard against hacking. So afraid was he that Verkhovsky had a handgun with ammunition designed to pierce body armor of the type that an FSB agent might wear. And with good reason: it seems that the Russians think Verkhovsky may have faked his death, and in Venice they had a man keeping watch on the palazzo to see if he was still alive. In any case, Verkhovsky was desperate. He acquired a passport from the Comoros Islands, an obscure Indian Ocean archipelago, as his means of escape. He was looking to cash in his assets to take the money with him. Among those assets were the Salvador Dalí drawings that had once belonged to the Marchesa, and so let us begin there, with the mystery surrounding the Marchesa's Salvador Dalís."

"What mystery?"

"Of how the Marchesa came into possession of them prior to Urquhart's return of them."

"I'm not sure I follow."

"That's because you are not aware that the Marchesa showed the drawings to Evans before Urquhart made a gift of them. How could that be? Let's review the history of the sketches: Dalí visits the Pallavicini villa in Bellagio when the Marchesa is still a child. He draws a series of sketches of Don Quixote to amuse her—perhaps she was reading Cervantes at the time. The drawings remain in the family until circumstances require that they be sold. The Marchesa wants to keep the fact of the sale quiet, and so works discreetly through a private dealer rather than sell them openly at auction. Imagine her horror when the dealer completes the sale and the buyer turns out to be Verkhovsky, who has taken up residence in Varenna, right across the lake from Bellagio."

"An embarrassment perhaps, but hardly a motive for murder."

"But what if the Dalís she sold were forgeries? What if the Marchesa retained the original Dalís, had copies made, and sold those instead, using her acquaintance with the artist as proof of provenance, attested to in a letter certifying them as genuine? Now, years later, Verkhovsky is in trouble and trying to convert the Dalís to cash. But he likewise does not want to go through a public auction because that would alert the Russians that he's going to make a run for it. So he goes through a private dealer—Galerie Tremblay in Cannes—and it was from them that Urquhart acquired the Dalís to make a gift of them to the Marchesa. But they must have been forgeries because that's the only way to explain how the Marchesa possessed the originals before Urquhart gave them to her."

"They couldn't have been forgeries," I objected. "Galerie Tremblay is a serious dealer, not one to rely solely on a letter of provenance as sufficient authentication for an unsigned and uncatalogued work. They would have had an analysis done, confirming that the wood fibers in the paper were consistent with the stock Dalí used, and of the correct age. The lead in the pencil would likely have been checked, too: it can be dated. They must have been genuine."

"You think so? Let's examine the evidence supporting that claim. One, the letter of provenance, signed by the Marchesa. Two, the type and age of the paper. Three, the dating of the lead in the pencil."

"And technique; Dalí was an especially skilled draftsman with a highly characteristic style. Those are the elements that Tremblay would have used to authenticate."

"So we'll add a fourth item, technique. Now, let's go through them one by one. Firstly, the letter. If the Dalís were forgeries, then we can safely disregard a letter of provenance from the forger, correct?"

"Yes."

"And as for technique, however skilled a draftsman Dalí may have been, there surely exist artists of sufficient ability that if they put their minds to it could have emulated Dalí's style. They were only copying— not creating an original."

"I suppose that's true. But it still leaves the paper and the lead pencil. There's no judgment involved; it's hard science."

"Quite so." Oriana turned her gaze onto the Marchesa. "When Dalí gave you the drawings, Lady Isabella, he gave you the pad and pencils with which he drew them, too, didn't he?"

The Marchesa sighed before speaking. "Yes," she said, "and when the time came to make the copies, those were what were used."

It occurred to me that Oriana would have made an excellent prosecuting attorney. The Marchesa continued, unflustered.

"But I'm afraid that you have the sequence of events quite wrong. They *were* the originals that I sold, and the reproductions—as I thought of them, not forgeries but merely copies—were only commissioned to occupy the frames of the originals, left hanging in the same place as before so that my friends would not remark on their absence, which of course would have revealed that I was in somewhat straitened circumstances. There was no question of counterfeit, and naturally it made sense to use paper from the same pad, already correctly sized, and the same pencils to ensure the same effect.

"But then that lout turned up in Varenna. He took on locals for staff, and it was one of them who alerted me to the fact that he had acquired my Dalís. Until then I had been perfectly content with the sale: they had fetched a good price and maintaining the villa was more important to me than a few drawings, but when I learned that Verkhovsky had bought them I became quite vexed. You'll be unsurprised to learn that his staff disliked him, and it was easy to convince one of them to substitute the reproductions for the originals. The silly oaf couldn't tell the difference anyway."

Gilbert interrupted.

"Oriana, all that you've said is no doubt true, but there's something critical you've missed."

"What?"

"The Marchesa couldn't have tossed Verkhovsky overboard. It doesn't matter how drunk he was; he could have been comatose. She physically couldn't have managed it."

"True, unless someone helped her." Oriana's gaze fell upon Adelina. "Someone like her grand-niece."

Adelina returned Oriana's gaze unblinkingly.

"I could have dealt with Verkhovsky whether or not he was alerted to danger," Adelina said evenly. "And if he was a threat to my great-aunt I would have been entirely willing to throw him overboard. But the fact is that at five o'clock that morning I was in my bed and sound asleep."

"I'm sure you were; we're only speaking hypothetically. Which brings us to another suspect—theoretical, of course."

"Who?"

"Franklin Gilbert. I've mentioned that Verkhovsky was soon to be stateless and desperate for refuge. When the French refused him, he set his sights on that same country that many of his compatriots had chosen in the past: England. And he was sufficiently cunning to understand that were he to acquire a significant equity holding in a major British newspaper his chances of being granted residency would be proportionally higher. He began buying shares in the *Daily Courier*, the paper that Gilbert wanted to acquire. But having a disreputable Russian as a major shareholder, one with potentially enough votes to swing a seat on the board, would have been an anathema to Gilbert, a serious media mogul with lofty ambitions for his new purchase. Buying out Verkhovsky would have been expensive; how much easier to just toss him overboard, instantly resolving the issue at zero cost."

Gilbert did not enjoy being identified as a murder suspect, but he responded evenly enough.

"It did disturb me that Verkhovsky had acquired such a large block that it hit the disclosure limits, although not for the reasons you suppose. I was wary not of his potential presence on the board but of his representing a rival bid. We soon realized that Verkhovsky himself wouldn't have sufficient resources to acquire the paper outright and supposed that he was just fronting for a competing group who preferred to remain anonymous for now—a Trojan horse, in other words. Normally, people vying for control of a publicly-listed company are careful to avoid hitting regulatory reporting thresholds until the last minute, and so that had puzzled us, but now I see why he did it: he wanted the British authorities to become aware of his holding and look more favorably on his application for residency or whatever."

"And you could have physically accomplished the deed?"

"You mean toss him overboard? Yes, I think so—even had Verkhovsky not been drunk. I didn't, but I have no way to prove it. As far as I know I don't snore, at least not loud enough to be heard in an adjoining cabin."

"There's no need to prove anything, Gilbert—we're only speaking theoretically. And in any case, we have a better suspect among the passengers than you. Two of them, in fact, and surely the most obvious of all: Marta and Bébé. Verkhovsky had been their means of escape from lives too narrow for them, but then they must have discovered that it would all soon be over. Perhaps the Comoros passport gave it away, or the mysterious trip with a suitcase of money. Maybe they read his mail and learned that the Russians were summoning him to return, or that the French were deporting him. In any case, it suddenly became clear that his usefulness was coming to an end. And who but Marta and Bébé could have gotten their hands on Verkhovsky without him becoming alerted before it was too late?"

"Hardly a reason to toss him overboard."

"But there's more: Verkhovsky may have been a means of escape from oppression, but he was himself oppressive. And he had recently become more oppressive still, violently so. We are all aware of Bébé's spectacular tattoo, but Marta got one at the same time. Hers was not a permanent one but drawn with a dye that fades. When they decided to do it they agreed that the tattoos would be representations of their nationalities: Bébé's samurai killing a dragon is an allusion to St. George, patron saint of her native Georgia. Verkhovsky didn't make that connection, but there was no doubting Marta's tattoo: the Polish eagle, crowned and wings spread, a symbol of the centuries-long struggle against Russian aggression. Verkhovsky recognized that one well enough, and it enraged him. To cut a long and predictably ugly story short, he beat Marta for having gotten it. The bruises were still visible that first day on the beach in Ibiza. Sufficient motive?"

"More than sufficient," Urquhart declared, and there were murmurs of agreement all around.

"The pig," Bébé said. "I wish I kill him." The words were said quietly, but there was no doubt that she meant them.

"At this stage," Oriana continued, "I think we need to briefly step out of the hypothetical and into the factual. Specifically, I will elaborate on what was in Verkhovsky's bloodstream. Alcohol is a given, since he had been drinking steadily from the moment he came on board, pausing only to eat dinner. His blood alcohol content was 0.08 percent, legally drunk, although not excessively high—Verkhovsky was used to pacing himself."

"But doesn't blood alcohol go down over time? And since Verkhovsky's body was recovered hours after he drowned, mustn't it have been much higher before?"

Oriana looked to Wu and he, apparently having forgiven her, took up the explanation.

"No, when a person dies there are no longer any metabolic processes to break down the alcohol, and so the levels remain as they were. But there are other post-mortem artifacts that the medical examiner must be cautious of. The first of these is that a body can create alcohol, artificially increasing the reading. This happens particularly if there is a high glucose level in the bloodstream: bacteria or yeast or even fungi can convert that glucose, which is just a simple sugar, into alcohol—there are numerous documented cases. Secondly, if there has been contamination of the blood sample then the chances of this occurring are elevated, a consequence of more exposure to the organic elements that perform the process. In Verkhovsky's case, I judged that any such effect would have been immaterial: there were no wounds that would have allowed significant exposure, and of course the body itself was effectively brined. So, the blood alcohol content was an accurate characterization of the subject's state immediately before decease."

Oriana took up the explanation. "The second substance in Verkhovsky's bloodstream I have already mentioned: cocaine. Cocaine is a stimulant. It would have further impaired judgment already made poor by the alcohol, but it would also have made him more difficult to deal with once he understood the danger.

"But there was a third substance, one that was only caught by Dr. Wu's diligence and the fact that the blood sample was tested in Europe, where this third substance is still prescribed. That substance is potassium bromide. It is used in the treatment of certain forms of epilepsy. It is also a bromide in the general sense of that term, a sedative, something to keep people calm, hence its use for epilepsy.

"We found no trace of potassium bromide among Verkhovsky's effects, nor did he have any known medical history of epilepsy. Therefore, we conclude that it was administered by someone else, presumably to make him easier to handle later on."

"What you're saying is that Verkhovsky's murder could not have been a spur-of-the-moment act; it was premeditated—carefully planned, in fact."

Oriana did not respond, leaving the implication to stand for itself.

"You say it's a prescription medicine?"

"Yes."

"Then that points to only one person."

Wu suddenly had all eyes upon him.

"But it was I who ordered the tests that discovered it," he protested.

"And what better way to divert suspicion?"

Wu was about to protest further, but Shotter spoke up first.

"Actually, I've got some potassium bromide. Not pills; in fluid form. It's used in developing black-and-white photography." He looked at me. "But you already know that, right?"

"I do."

"I suppose anyone could have taken some, if they knew it was there."

"Yep."

"But who would know, except the person I was sharing a cabin with that first night?"

"Sounds reasonable."

"Lucky you snore, I guess."

"Which just leaves you."

"So it does."

Gilbert spoke up. "Oriana, it sounds like what you're telling us is that we're all suspects, apart from Tess and Rasputina."

"Theoretically, they are, too. No one can say for certain that Tess was asleep in her cabin that night, and Rasputina has already admitted being up in the early hours to fetch some water and seeing Verkhovsky. Speaking hypothetically, any of the passengers could have done it, and many had a genuine motive for doing so."

"You didn't mention the first officer as a suspect," I said, "but he's the one person that we know for sure was awake when Verkhovsky went overboard. We also know that the automatic pilot would have been capable of handling the ship while he left the bridge."

"He has an alibi, Evans—in fact, it was you who discovered it."

"What?"

"The missing log. I should explain that in Marseilles the ship's log was among the documents brought into the meeting with the French. It was left in the library. Afterward, it went missing. Eventually, the log was found on one of the bookshelves, presumably having been put away by a maid tidying up, although Evans insisted that he had searched those same shelves before and it wasn't there. At the time I thought he must have overlooked it, especially since nothing had been erased or amended, but in the end he was right: the log had been taken away by someone and then returned.

"After checking with the staff, all of whom said they had not placed the log on the shelves, I decided to quietly take the matter to Trevelyan, since it was his document. He leafed through it and saw at once that there had been an alteration: not an erasure or amendment, which is what Evans and I had been looking for, but instead an addition."

"What?"

"Four words: 'Appearance of the supernova,' added to the same line as the hourly position entry for 5:00 A.M. Evans, you might recall that Trevelyan had seemed distracted when we consulted with him that night before reaching Marseilles, as well he might after the events of the day. But it wasn't just a passenger lost overboard that was bothering him; it was also the absence of an entry for the advent of the supernova, something that the officer on watch cannot have failed to see, but had not noted in the ship's log. It wasn't until you pointed out how capable the autopilot is that I realized its relevance, but not because it allowed the first officer to leave the bridge and murder Verkhovsky. Very simply, he had turned it on and gone to sleep. He would have made the position entries later, after he woke up, copying straight from the GPS record, but he could make no entry for the supernova because he didn't know what time it happened. Later, when the Notice to Mariners came in specifying the supernova having occurred shortly after five, Zabala-Extarte decided to add it to the log so that the fact of him sleeping on watch would not become apparent. That's why the log went missing: he took it to add that entry. But what he didn't know was that it was too late: the captain had already noted the absence of an entry for the supernova, and when I showed him the log with it now added there could be no doubt what had happened. This voyage will likely be Zabala-Extarte's last with the charter company; it will certainly be his last with Trevelyan."

"So where does that leave us?" Gilbert asked.

"Back at the beginning."

"The beginning?"

"Yes, back to the fundamental fact that my colleague Evans latched onto from the very start and would never let go of: it was Urquhart who invited Verkhovsky in the first place."

L

I F Urquhart objected to again being the focus of
Oriana's hypothetical allegations, he showed no sign of it.

"So you're saying that this had something to do with Verkhovsky's stake in the *Daily Courier* after all?" Gilbert asked, unconvinced. "Urquhart invites him on the cruise to toss him overboard?"

"No. The guest list was drafted before Verkhovsky acquired his equity holding."

"Then why?"

"Exactly: why? Urquhart's explanation to the agency was that with the world potentially coming to an end it made sense to splurge now, and so he'd decided on an extended summer cruise aboard a luxury motor yacht. Money, perhaps about to be worthless anyway, was no object. He wanted to surround himself with people whom he had never met and who would thus be of interest, not the same old crowd with whose faces one is familiar and whose stories one has heard before.

"But it wasn't that simple, was it? For example, although he'd never met you, Gilbert, there was still an obvious connection: you were already engaged in an exploratory offer for the paper. Evans, too: he is an art historian whose doctoral subject had been Urquhart. Tess is the daughter of an old school chum. As for Shotter and Wu, a photographer would be useful aboard a cruise where electronics were banned, and a doctor was probably a necessity given the length of the cruise, his own poor health, and the advanced age of one of the guests."

"And what about the Marchesa? What's his connection with her?"

"The connection is not with Lady Isabella but her grand-niece. Urquhart first painted Adelina many years ago after seeing her on a Venice pier during a school outing. The landing was part of Urquhart's hotel, and they told him which school it was—Headington. Later, when he wanted to invite Adelina on the cruise, it was a straightforward matter to identify her from the yearbooks."

"I remember it," Adelina said. "We were going to the Accademia that day. I don't recall anyone with an easel."

"I made a sketch on a pad," Urquhart admitted. "The oil painting came later, based on that sketch."

"So the *Lustration* is not the first?"

"I think of it as a revisit—generally a bad idea artistically, but sometimes a revision can outshine the original."

"Is the first painting here?"

"No, I donated it to my alma mater, Exeter College. When Evans was there it was hanging in the Rector's residence. I'm sure if you're ever up at Oxford they'd show it to you."

"What's the connection with me?" Rasputina asked.

"That's very straightforward," Urquhart said. "I am a great fan of your mother. You were both invited but she had film commitments; she suggested that in any case you might find the cruise more fun without her along. I must add that after seeing you on stage tonight I am now a great fan of yours, too."

"So that still leaves us with the basic conundrum: why would Urquhart have invited Verkhovsky, if not to kill him?"

"He did," Oriana stated flatly.

"He did?"

"He did."

A long silence followed. I was so used by now to playing the plodding Watson to Oriana's brilliant Holmes that I was surprised to be proved right.

"Why?"

"For the simplest of reasons. What everyone has missed the significance of, myself included for a time, was that Urquhart did not invite just Verkhovsky. He invited Verkhovsky *plus his two nieces*."

"Marta and Bébé?"

"In the initial guest list, there was only Verkhovsky's name. When my agency did the investigation the fact of Marta and Bébé naturally emerged. I subsequently briefed Urquhart. His response was that he supposed there was no choice but to invite them, too."

"Are you saying it wasn't Verkhovsky that Urquhart wanted to invite, but Marta and Bébé?"

"Not Bébé in particular. But Marta, yes, most assuredly."

"Why?"

"As I said, for the simplest of reasons. Marta is Urquhart's daughter."

The silence that followed this revelation was eventually broken by Marta.

"But my father is—"

"A very fine man," Urquhart interrupted, "and certainly your true father. However, not your biological one."

"But how..."

"I think I can answer that," I said. "Marta's mother was your model, wasn't she?"

"So you recognized it?"

"I think you meant me to."

The portrait of the woman who must have been Marta's mother had been among those in the storage shed, and I now suspected that Urquhart's offer to take one for myself and a second for Sir Dickie had been motivated, at least in part, by a desire for me to go through them carefully and recognize the painting for what it was. Even then I had almost missed it: I had recognized instead that the magnificent portrait of Marta's mother must have been of the same woman who was the subject of the Wentworth's Catoptrographics; it wasn't until later that I realized she was familiar for a second reason: the resemblance with

Marta's pale skin and patrician face, and above all the distinctively sharp angle of the jaw.

Urquhart turned to face Marta directly. "I met your mother in Paris, in a cafe. We fell into conversation; she agreed to model for me. We began an affair, but destined to be short-lived: your mother was only visiting on a tourist visa, and she soon returned home. I heard nothing more from her until a letter arrived six months ago. She had already known your father before visiting Paris, and they were married shortly after her return to Grodno. She had not yet realized that she was pregnant and believed she was just out of sorts from all the travel. In any case, she never told you or your father the truth. She would have kept it from me, too, but then you became involved with Verkhovsky. Your mother is a very proud woman, but you came first, and the situation was beyond her. In short, she asked me to intervene. I agreed to do so, and the rest I think you know."

I realized that the second portrait of Adelina had been something of a genuine *Lustration* after all: a masterpiece atoning for a murder. Gilbert turned to Oriana. "But since you presumably knew nothing of this letter, how could you have guessed that Marta was Urquhart's daughter?"

"As soon as it occurred to me that Urquhart might have engineered the Verkhovsky invitation so that Marta and Bébé were included, a family relationship was an obvious line of investigation. I decided on DNA tests. Since I would be getting them done for the nieces I decided to do the other passengers, too, in case there was another connection that I was missing."

"But how could you get DNA samples?"

"From our hair," I said.

Oriana smiled. "Well done, Evans—you figured out why your hairbrush was moved. Yes, the DNA was extracted from hair samples. I enlisted one of the maids—I won't reveal who—to collect hairs from passengers' hairbrushes or combs, carefully bagging and labeling them so they wouldn't get mixed up. I sent them to a lab when we returned to Monaco. The results came back while we were in Venice."

Gilbert turned to Urquhart. "So you chucked him overboard?"

Urquhart nodded wordlessly, but Oriana laughed.

"Oriana," Urquhart warned.

"No, it was you who told me to proceed, and I'm not stopping now."

"What's going on?" Gilbert demanded.

"Urquhart didn't do it," Oriana explained. "He's lying."

"But you just said that he did."

"No. The question asked was *Why would Urquhart have invited Verkhovsky, if not to kill him?* My answer was *He did*. And this is true: he did invite Verkhovsky on the cruise to ensure that he never had anything more to do with Marta, and Urquhart was prepared to kill him if necessary. Indeed, I believe that he was planning to do so, but then something happened."

"What?"

"Someone else beat him to it."

LI

THE SKY WAS GROWING LIGHTER IN THE EAST. THE meltemi had died down and the sea, although still disturbed, was now calmer. We had been talking all night but the silence following Oriana's declaration that Urquhart had not murdered Verkhovsky because someone else murdered him first seemed to have left us all speechless, too worn out by the long night of revelations to ask the obvious question: if not him, then who?

It was Urquhart who eventually spoke, so quiet that he was hard to hear.

"That was why the first stop was originally planned to be Ibiza—the dive trip to the Aguja was where I...it had been intended for the purpose. I would have proposed to Verkhovsky that we dive together, all mano a mano in front of the other passengers, and Verkhovsky—'virile man'—would of course have accepted, even though he didn't have a clue. There were only two sets of dive equipment, so we were guaranteed to be alone down there. He would have just done whatever I told him to. How easy a mishap would have been to engineer and then explain—novice diver, swift current, treacherous waters—and even if the Spanish authorities suspected something how difficult it would be to prove.

"When it became clear that morning that Verkhovsky had fallen overboard, and then later when we found him drowned, it felt like a miracle, a divine reprieve."

"Did you know then that he'd been thrown overboard?"

"No. Until tonight I was like the rest of us: I thought it was an accident."

"The rest of us, except one."

"But you must have now realized who that one is, to have been willing to take the blame yourself."

"Was it your daughter?"

But instead of replying, Urquhart looked at Oriana. "Why don't you finish now?"

"Very well," Oriana stood, addressing us like a professor delivering a lecture. "The solution—the *hypothetical* solution—depends on three essential elements: salt, water, and light. One instance of salt we've already encountered: the potassium bromide. We have two theoretical sources: prescription medicine from Wu or photographic developing solution from Shotter. I have no definitive proof, but I'm quite sure that the potassium bromide came from neither of these two sources."

"Then where?"

"Ask yourself: when on that first night did the subject of salt come up?"

This question was met by silence as people reviewed the evening. It was Adelina who eventually responded, one of her rare contributions tonight.

"During supper—the bresaola."

"Exactly. And what happened?"

"Verkhovsky complained that it was too salty, although it didn't stop him from eating most of it."

"And who ate the rest?"

"Rasputina. And Evans, too, I think."

"Yes, Rasputina, who later that night was made so thirsty from all the salt that she had to go to the pantry for a second bottle of water. And Evans, who doesn't snore but was so knocked out by the bromide that he did snore, abundantly so. I think we can confidently assert that the potassium bromide was administered in that manner."

"Who put it in there?"

"Who served it?"

"Aška!"

"You're saying that Aška murdered Verkhovsky?"

"Not at all. I only say that she administered the potassium bromide. Recall the conversation between Jamys and Aška that Rasputina overheard. Verkhovsky had obviously done something to annoy her, something beyond his standard rudeness with staff. Perhaps he made an advance—the 'virile man' act again. In any case, when he demanded meat she doubtless saw an opportunity and went to the galley to fetch some. Before returning, she laced it with potassium bromide. The purpose would not have been to make it easier to throw him overboard later—Aška could not have known that he would stay up beyond everyone else and conveniently place himself by the stern rail at five o'clock in the morning—she was just using it for its basic purpose: as a bromide, that is, something to keep his attentions from her."

"Hah!," Bébé exclaimed. She and Marta smiled at each other before Bébé continued. "Aška need not bother," she explained, snapping the air with her fingers as she had done at me, her way of emphasizing what she was saying, I now understood. "'Virile man' not so virile. 'Virile man' big joke: that is why he have us around, to make the pretending, yes?"

Marta put the matter more plainly. "We were for show only."

"Nevertheless, Aška could not have known that. The virile man act was no act to her; it was a threat."

"Where would she have gotten potassium bromide?"

"Who knows? Perhaps she has a relative with epilepsy; maybe she has an epileptic dog. More likely she obtained it illegally. I imagine that an attractive young woman like Aška doing service on luxury yachts where the clients would often be less than charming—Russian oligarchs like Verkhovsky, or oil-rich Arabs who still think of women as chattel— would find a bromide useful. And she had learned to administer it effectively, a way to blunt unwanted attention without causing a scene, something that might have cost her her job. She probably always packs the stuff with her when beginning a new cruise."

"So the potassium bromide is a red herring?"

"No, the fact remains that Verkhovsky ingested it, and so it would have dulled him, making him less able to defend against what was to come. But before getting to that there is another instance of salt and water to consider. Sometime during the night, Tess was awoken by a storm. It was powerful enough to have whipped up the sea so that some of the seawater, or at least spray from the sea, came in through the porthole, forcing her to get up and close it. The thing is, no storm was forecast, the ship's log recorded no foul weather, and no one else experienced it. Nevertheless, the evidence was undeniable: there were still traces of moisture the next morning, but much of it had evaporated, leaving behind salt crystals. There can be no question that it was indeed seawater."

"A freak wave?"

"That's possible. Or a sudden rise in the wind, as can happen at sea as we've just experienced, and was just as quickly gone. And Tess's cabin is right aft; her porthole is the last on that side. Any sudden increase in wind or sea from the port quarter might have gone unremarked on the bridge, where the crew face the other way. However, there has been another possibility suggested."

"What?"

"That the water resulted from the splash from when Verkhovsky went into the sea."

"Oh, how awful."

"Do you remember what time it was, Tess?"

"I didn't check my watch."

"Did you see anything while you were at the porthole?"

"No. There isn't much to see. The porthole is located above a cabinet and it's too far to stretch across and peer down into the water. I did look up at the sky to see if there was a storm, but it just seemed all gray to me."

Oriana continued. "There was a second incident involving water. That morning, the morning after Verkhovsky disappeared, there was dew on the deck. We were not yet used to seagoing life, but let me ask you now: has anyone noticed dew on any other morning?"

"Yes, when we were in Venice."

"When the *Mulvane* was docked?"

"Yes."

"And therefore when the ship was stationary. Dew forms in still air, typically the calm air of the early morning. But on a ship at sea it is never calm. Even on the rare occasions when there is no wind the vessel itself causes a breeze by the fact of its passage. So let me ask, did anyone notice dew at any other time while the ship was underway?" After a long pause, during which no one responded, Oriana continued. "No, because it didn't happen. Dew on a moving ship is not something likely to occur in the middle of the Mediterranean summer. Yet it happened that morning on the *Mulvane*."

"Meaning that we must have stopped?"

"Meaning only that it is an odd phenomenon, worth taking note of."

"You said that light was a factor, too?"

"Yes, and it's the most important of all, the key to what went on that night. The light I refer to is of course the new light, one never seen before: the supernova. Betelgeuse exploded just as it was rising, suddenly becoming a brilliant point of light in the sky at five o'clock that morning. It performed two functions that were crucial to what came next. The first is that it enticed Verkhovsky from the bar out onto the deck. The *Mulvane* was steaming southwest, toward Ibiza, and Betelgeuse rose in the northeast—in other words, directly astern. This drew Verkhovsky aft. Who knows what he was seeing, or thought he was seeing in a mind addled by vodka and cocaine? But whatever it was, that vision lured him to the stern rail, perhaps in wonderment, perhaps in terror. But the critical point is that he went to the stern rail. There, stupefied by all that he had ingested—knowingly and otherwise—he was, to put it bluntly, a sitting duck."

"You said the supernova performed two functions?'

"Yes, and the second is quite straightforward: it awoke the killer."

"Who?"

"The only person that it could have awoken. All of us occupy cabins with portholes, too small to admit enough light to wake someone up, unless it was shining straight in. But we know that's not possible because Betelgeuse arose astern and all the portholes are along the sides, so no direct light could have come in.

"Then...?"

"All of us, that is, except one. The owner's stateroom is fitted with not portholes but windows, large ones, two of which face directly aft. Plus it is heavily mirrored, no doubt to ensure that it is always light-filled, but which in this case would have served to further help awaken the occupant, someone who, perhaps with age, had found herself to be a light sleeper in any case."

"You mean Lady Isabella?" Gilbert interrupted. "Are you mad, Oriana? We've already agreed that there is no way she could have physically done it, even if Verkhovsky was a sitting duck.'"

"Unless she had help."

"Adelina again?"

"No, not a person but a thing. A fitting. Specifically, a firehose. I don't know if any of you took up the invitation to see the *Mulvane* when she led the Dunkirk celebrations at Dover last May, but if so you cannot have failed to miss the fact of her firehoses, tremendously powerful, and which on that occasion were directed to shoot great spumes of water into the air, but which could equally well serve, when directed onto the back of a man standing by a rail, to forcefully shove him overboard."

"But Lady Isabella would be as incapable of handling a firehose as of throwing Verkhovsky overboard herself."

"She would not have had to. The nozzles are mounted on swiveling brackets, you see, the same that were used when she was at Dover, and so all the Marchesa needed to do was point one of them and open the spigot. Not a great physical hardship, and of course the Marchesa well knows how to operate such an arrangement, having been a worker at a shipyard when she was a young woman."

"But it sounds incredible."

"Incredible perhaps, but it is the only explanation that fits the facts. One: the gushing stream of saltwater—fire mains on ships use seawater—that came into Tess's cabin, enough to make her believe that it was a storm, and something that happened at the same time as Verkhovsky went overboard.

"We don't know that it was the same time."

"Yes, we do. Tess saw a *gray* sky, not a *black* sky, not a *blue* sky. With Trevelyan's assistance, I checked the astronomical details. Nautical twilight, when the sky first begins to show a glimmer of something other than total darkness, began that morning at 4:41 A.M.; Betelgeuse rose at 5:01; civil twilight, when color comes into the sky, began at 5:27. Therefore, Tess awoke between 4:41 and 5:27, the same period during which Verkhovsky went overboard.

"The second fact that this theory explains is the dew. Why was there dew on the deck of a vessel making way in the middle of summer? The answer is that there was no dew; the deck was still wet from the firehose. And then there's a third item, the bruising on Verkhovsky's back. In the medical examination, Dr. Wu characterized it as a dorsal contusion consistent with having hit the sea back first. Even at the time, I could see that he was not entirely satisfied—the deck of the *Mulvane* is not so high above the waterline that a fall would cause much bruising—but in the absence of defensive wounds, and also of the wood fibers that I had removed, the doctor drew the obvious conclusion: some people bruise easily and Verkhovsky was a poor physical specimen; it must have been from the impact with the water. And indeed the bruising *was* caused by impact with water, but not the sea: it was where that powerful stream from the firehose blasted into Verkhovsky's back and cast him over the side."

Gilbert raised no further objections, nor did anyone else. The ensuing silence was eventually broken by the Marchesa.

"You are quite wrong," she declared. "The supernova did not wake me; I was already awake." She eased herself in the armchair, as if feeling the weight of the accusation as a physical discomfort.

"As you have correctly guessed, my dear, with the advance of years I find myself often waking early, one of the many indignities of growing old. I had been intending to read when suddenly that mysterious light came pouring in through the stern windows.

"I put aside my book and looked aft. I understood at once that Betelgeuse must have exploded at last. What a wonderful and mysterious thing it was! Suddenly, I was delighted instead of annoyed to be awake early: I would be the first to witness this marvelous new object in the heavens. I put on a robe and left the stateroom.

"When I had first gazed aft through the rear windows there had been no sign of Verkhovsky, but by the time I came out onto the deck there he was. In your account you imagine him gazing up in wonder. Ha! That was not at all the case. He was by the stern rail, yes, but he was there because he was vomiting—no doubt because of those many foul substances that he had ingested, although perhaps it was just the result of a stomach too weak for the sea. But he had not made it there in time: he had been sick on the deck and upon my seat by the stern rail. The disgusting creature!

"There is a traditional sea shanty, in English, that I was taught when I was a child and learning that language: 'What Shall We Do with a Drunken Sailor?'—do you know it?" The Marchesa continued without waiting for a response.

"That's what immediately came into my mind. The answer to the question in the song's title is delivered in a succeeding verse: *Put him in the scuppers with a hosepipe on him*, and that's what I decided to do. At the same time it would wash down the deck, something that needed to be done before it had soaked into the timbers and dried to a hard crust.

"As you say, Oriana, I know how to operate the firehose of a seagoing ship, something that all dockyard welders are trained to do, given the hazards of their profession. I soon had the nozzle pointing aft along the deck, or so I believed, and then turned it on, as far as it would go. There was a pause as the hose fattened with the coming stream of water, and then: gush!—out it came. The jet of water blasted into Verkhovsky's back with great force: he was shuddering as if being pummeled from behind and gripped the guardrail to hold on. Then, suddenly, he simply vanished.

"I was taken aback and did not quite believe what I had seen. Indeed, I wondered if he was playing a trick on me. I turned off the firehose. I had not brought my cane with me, and so with the wet deck I had to grip the rail while slowly making my way aft. When I got there...nothing. He was gone. I wondered if the whole thing had been a nightmare."

"You didn't alert anyone. The bridge?"

"No, I can't say that the idea even occurred to me. What I did was return to the firehose and once again turn it on, this time ensuring that all that disgusting filth was washed away, as if to wash away with it all remembrance of what had just occurred."

"What next?"

"What next? I went back to bed and slept peacefully."

No one spoke for a long time. The Marchesa closed her eyes, perhaps again sleeping peacefully after having gotten the admission of murdering Verkhovsky off her chest. It was Urquhart, back in his role as host, who broke the silence.

"And so we have reached the conclusion—hypothetically speaking, of course."

Gilbert picked up on the cue at once. "Yes, a superb theoretical construct, Oriana. How well you seem to account for all the facts."

"Although now that I think on it," Tess said, "I believe that when I looked out of the porthole that night the sky may have been rather more black than gray."

"I was in the navy," Shotter added, "and I seem to remember dew at sea, even when underway."

"In any case," I said, "we know from our investigation that Verkhovsky was at the end of his tether, being pursued by the Russians and deported by the French, destined to lead a life on the run hiding out in whatever unpleasant corners of the world he could get into with a Comoros passport. That was of course the real reason he was drinking so much that night: to work up the courage to kill himself."

"Yes, there is little doubt that it was suicide," Wu said. "I merely made the finding of accidental death as a kindness to whatever relatives he may have had."

Oriana smiled. "Well, I did my best to keep us all entertained with a story until the *Mulvane*'s return. And I do believe there's a boat coming for us now."

We followed her gaze, turning toward the water and seeing there that the *Mulvane* had returned, hove-to in the bay, and the Riva was speeding across the water straight for us.

We were soon to leave Prospero's enchanted isle. It occurred to me that Oriana had made good on her unlikely claim that it was possible a murder committed for no very good reason might nevertheless be overlooked. It also occurred to me that there had been a Caliban among us all along.

LII

T HE *MULVANE* SLOWED AS WE ROUNDED CAPE SOUNION, located at the southern tip of the Attic peninsula. There, atop the sheer cliffs and stark against a deep blue sky, stands the Temple of Poseidon, the great stone edifice that for three thousand years has marked the last sight of land for ships leaving Athens and the first thing seen on their return.

We stood along the starboard rail gazing at it as we sailed by—all except the Marchesa, who had not emerged from her stateroom since retreating into it following our return aboard the *Mulvane* twenty-four hours previously.

The atmosphere on board had been subdued on the passage from Ledos. Most people went straight to bed after returning to the yacht following what had been a sleepless night, and even the alluring sights of the Cyclades as we threaded through those ancient islands could not lighten the mood. When we gathered for the farewell dinner that last evening, no amount of good cheer could change what had happened, although everyone made an effort.

The next morning I dressed in my own clothes for the first time in three months and moved forward a hundred years in time, returning to the Twenty-First Century. They felt strangely alien to me now.

Our phones were returned and I used mine—still working despite the supernova—to send a short note to Sir Dickie informing him that he was now the owner of an original Urquhart, as was I, and to expect both me and the paintings to soon show up at Portman Square.

The passengers gradually came up from their preparations below and gathered in the main salon as the yacht made the last leg of the voyage down the Saronic Gulf—again excepting the Marchesa. The women were startlingly different in their modern clothing—Rasputina especially, in jeans and sneakers, such a change from her glamorous 1930's Hollywood persona—although Adelina looked as calm and composed as ever, remote and unchanging in whatever she wore. Addresses were exchanged; farewells were made.

We came alongside at the Piraeus. Athens' seaport was a busy, boisterous, chaotic, and malodorous bedlam—and it put a smile on my face. I found that I was happy to be re-entering the real world again— sharp-elbowed and jangling the nerves, but how alive the place seemed.

If the purpose of a vacation is to recharge the batteries for life, then the *Mulvane*'s cruise had done a good job.

Cars had been ordered to take us wherever we needed to go. For Adelina and the Marchesa it was not far: they were returning to Italy by sea, and their ferry was docked just across the harbor. Marta and Bébé were heading by train to France via Milan, and the latter could barely contain her pleasure at the prospect of soon sampling the pianos in the Fazioli showroom. Shotter was bound for the same city but traveling by air. Wu would like to have spent some time exploring Athens, but his locum was anxious to move on and so he was flying back to Vancouver right away. Tess was heading straight out, too, needing to prepare for the upcoming Michaelmas term. Gilbert was taking his company jet to Teterboro and offered a ride to anyone who wanted one, but nobody else was going to New York.

Oriana joined me by the rail as I was looking down at the dock, watching our luggage being landed.

"Maybe we'll be on the same flight back," she said.

"No, I'm staying on for a few days. No art historian could land in the Piraeus and not spend at least a little time in Athens."

"I hope your Sir Dickie won't mind."

"With a new Urquhart? I could go to Antarctica for all he cares."

"And so, what do you think of your doctoral subject, now that you've spent summer with him in the flesh?"

"As much of a mystery to me as before."

"Wasted time?"

"Not at all. I've had three months with the *Lustration* for a start."

"What next?"

"London. The Wentworth. I'm going to attempt a biography and an accompanying *catalogue raisonné*. He doesn't want it, but he's agreed to cooperate to the extent of giving me full access to his papers. What about you?"

"London, too, and back to Saunders Walker, although I might consider starting my own agency."

"Given how you cracked the Verkhovsky case I have no doubt it would be a success—you're a natural."

"My partner wasn't completely useless."

"No, not completely."

"Let's catch up for a drink at the Cato Club when you're back."

"I look forward to it."

WHEN WE HAD ALL SAFELY DISEMBARKED AND WERE STANDING on the dock, the *Mulvane* began to perform her final duty: heading back to sea to return the mysterious magus to his magical isle. Urquhart gave us a final wave as she pulled away and then disappeared inside. I never saw him again.

There was an extra car left on the dock after the others had gone, a black Mercedes of the type that is standard for chauffeur-driven services in Europe. I walked over.

"Mr. Athanasiou?"

"Mr. Verkhovsky?"

"No, I'm afraid that Verkhovsky died on the voyage."

I had expected an unctuous type, but except for the black suit and tie Athanasiou could have passed for a plumber. He shook his head in discontent at the news that his client was dead and took out a pack of cigarettes. He tapped some out, offered them to me, and then took one for himself.

"Murdered?"

"The official finding was an accident. He fell overboard and drowned."

"Probably pushed," Athanasiou said, in the manner of a man long used to dealing with the Verkhovskys of this world, and I could not help liking him.

"Yes," I agreed, "I suspect that you're right."

"Bad for business."

"Does it happen often?"

"From time to time. Usually, they just disappear back into Russia; occasionally they disappear entirely." He smoked in silence for a moment, perhaps ruminating on the ill effects of capricious international relations on his trade. "You need a ride to the airport?"

"No, I'm staying on for a few days."

"Got accommodation?"

"Not yet."

"I can do you an excellent deal on a suite at the Grande Bretagne."

THUS ENDED THE SUPERNOVA CRUISE THAT SUMMER, AND therefore so too must this chronicle of it.

I realize that some readers will wish to know what became of the *Mulvane*'s passengers and generally how things turned out. I cannot claim to be sure in every case, but I have appended an epilogue with an accounting of what subsequently happened, as far as I am aware, after we went our separate ways that day in the Piraeus, several years ago now.

A summing up is customary at this stage of a narrative, but I find that I have no summation to give. In many ways, the events of that long cruise are still reverberating through our lives—certainly through mine—and so definitive conclusions cannot yet be drawn. What I will say is this: I have never before been, and never expect to again be, in the company of such a brilliant group of people. They are distinguished in my mind not by their prosperity or pulchritude, although certainly some were wealthy and the women becoming. Nor even are they distinguished by their intellectual heft, although there was no shortage of that either— not always book-learning or college degrees but genuine intelligence, by which I mean the ability and will to think clearly, no matter the subject, and by that measure they were undoubtedly the smartest group of people I have ever encountered.

But to my sense what most distinguishes them is courage: the courage to fight vigorously against pretentious art; against mindless conformity; against enervating dogma; against willful stupidity; against political tyranny; against brutalism and barbarism in all its forms, even if it drives a Lamborghini and possesses a fat bank account. And so I have arrived at the conviction—one that I hope is conveyed in the Urquhart biography—that courage is the essential element for civilization to thrive: the courage to resist, no matter the circumstances. Sometimes that means taking on the world, as Gilbert has done; sometimes it means withdrawing from it completely and living like an anchorite, as did Urquhart. And occasionally it might require direct action, whether via means of a photo calendar or perhaps even a firehose.

Epilogue

I WILL PRESENT THIS EXEUNT OF THE ACTORS IN THE SAME form as they were introduced, that is, via a guest list, a little extended, and in more or less the same order as the original.

Mr. Rothesay Ambrose Urquhart — Died by his own hand on the island of Ledos two months after the completion of the *Mulvane*'s Mediterranean cruise.

Art can be a cruel undertaking. As a profession it practically guarantees poverty, although this was not a concern in Urquhart's case. But it also means that recognition, should it ever come, will be mostly posthumous—it is almost an axiom of art that to enjoy fame one must first expire. So it was with Urquhart: he was all but unknown when I happened upon the Exeter portrait. Today, while not a household name, he is certainly known throughout the professional art world and his best paintings fetch seven-figure sums at the auctions.

But art is most cruel to the best artists. They glimpse the sublime and on rare occasions even capture it, but the sublime can be a difficult burden to bear and the cost is sometimes insanity (Goya, Degas, Pollock) or death (Van Gogh, Rothko, Urquhart).

I realize that I will never experience it first-hand—it is why I am an art historian and not an artist—but even had I the ability to glimpse the sublime I wonder if I would want to.

The suicide had obviously been planned long before we put to sea, and presumably ill health was a factor. Much that had seemed strange was suddenly explained, like the expenditures, extravagant even for a wealthy man, or the willingness on that last night to take the rap for murdering Verkhovsky. And the overriding purpose of the *Mulvane*'s summer cruise had finally been made clear: Urquhart was tying up loose ends.

Lady Isabella Daniella Luciana Pallavicini-Giustiniani — The Marchesa died peacefully in her sleep a year ago, and the savvy reader will already have realized that this journal would never have been published were she still alive.

Her funeral was one of two occasions since disembarkation from the *Mulvane* that all the surviving passengers have gathered together.

Lady Adelina Chiara Pallavicini-Giustiniani — Adelina inherited the Marquessate on the death of her great-aunt: she is now the Marchesa della Brianza and mistress of the villa in Bellagio.

Adelina established the Fondazione Pallavicini, an institute headquartered in Bellinzona, Switzerland, that acts as an economics think tank and whose principal aim is the aligning of economic policy with foreign policy. Specifically, she has advocated for restrictions on financial relations with authoritarian regimes. This has had some success, most notably in encouraging the European Union and the United States to better coordinate their China trade policies. Also, it was her foundation that provided the first draft of the agreement preventing China from playing Airbus and Boeing against each other, something that had threatened E.U./U.S. cooperation.

The *Lustration* remains in Adelina's possession, hanging above the mantle in the main salon of the Villa Pallavicini—she has apparently found a way to live with her portrait every day.

Mr. Kirill Verkhovsky — Kirill Verkhovsky's unclaimed body was buried in a pauper's grave at Fos-Berre, a gritty industrial area northwest of Marseilles.

The oil and gas concessions that had been the source of his wealth were seized by the Russian government. They also laid claim to his assets in France, but the French were having none of that. The estate was liquidated and the funds were used to cover the administrative costs and pay for his burial. The remainder was taken by the French government under the legal principle of escheatment: any assets not legitimately claimed go to the state.

The bond was returned in full, with French bureaucratic efficiency, six months after his death.

The four paintings at the Galerie Tremblay ended up in various collections; the Gino Severini was acquired by the Wentworth.

The bank accounts that must have existed were never identified: Verkhovsky had covered his financial tracks well, no doubt to hide the money from the Russians. They probably made some Cypriot bankers rich. His holding in the *Daily Courier*, about which I had overheard Urquhart and Gilbert arguing, was acquired by the latter for undisclosed terms.

Verkhovsky's name is remembered today, if at all, only by the Lamborghini whose absence from the inventory had been noted at the time—it turned out that he had not owned the vehicle but leased it, and when leaving it dockside that day the *Mulvane* sailed it had been for the lessor to repossess it, one of the liquidations he was making before fleeing on his Comoros passport. Today, when residents of the Riviera see it loudly whizzing by they exclaim, "There goes Verkhovsky's ugly Lamborghini!"

Ms. Malgorzata (Marta) Domaradzka — Marta inherited much of the Urquhart estate and is now a wealthy woman. She continues to perform concerts and make recordings, always playing her Amati. She lives in the Sixth Arrondissement in Paris and vacations on the island of Ledos in Greece, which is hers for the next seventy years or so.

Ms. Babilina (Bébé) Nikolaishvili — Bébé acquired her Fazioli piano from the showroom in Milan shortly after the voyage ended. It eventually accompanied her to Paris where she now lives with Marta, and they usually perform together (as the "Scylla & Charybdis duo"). Their first recording consisted of the same works in the same order as the concert on the *Mulvane*, and their transcription and rendition of Miles Davis's "Right Off" became what counts as a hit in the world of classical music.

Mr. Franklin Gilbert — Gilbert was mistaken in his estimate of the demand for his new newspaper. He said he would call it a success if it hit 50,000 subscriptions globally; it currently has more than that in the New York metropolitan area alone. The *Verba Sequentur* has been a resounding success. It has even become something of a worldwide publication of record: research libraries maintain copies of it bound by month and year.

Has it made a difference? That is hard to say. What is civilization but a thousand small things, no single item signifying much in itself, but collectively they form the framework that makes life something other than mere existence. If the newspaper's impact is judged by the number of imitators then it has had a profound influence, but these also-rans are just empty gestures, attempts to not be left behind made by the people who publish what Gilbert is trying to counter in the first place. The essential quality of the *Verba Sequentur* is not the thing itself but the spirit that drives it, dedicated to clear-eyed, intelligent, sober, and rational understanding. This is not consistent with a blind dedication to profit that puts return on equity above all else, and which inevitably ends up catering to the lowest common denominator.

Ms. Rasputina Quantrill — Playing Elektra must have sparked an acting interest in Rasputina that had lain dormant under the shadow of her famous mother. She, Rasputina, has now starred in two movies: *Shallow Rider* and *Take Me With You My Darling, Take Me With You.* The latter is not the romantic comedy that the title might suggest but instead an account of the breakdown and death of Rolling Stones' guitarist Brian Jones. Rasputina plays the part of Anita Pallenberg. The movie was an "Official Selection In Competition" at the Cannes Film Festival, which means that it was short-listed for the Palme d'Or.

Rasputina is now referred to by her own name, not as the daughter of Amelia Quantrill.

Driving a Morgan sports car has become a status symbol in Beverly Hills.

Dr. Hugo Evans — I had returned to the Wentworth and already begun the Urquhart biography when the news of his death came through. Per Urquhart's wishes, there was no ceremony or funeral. The remains were cremated and the ashes were cast into the Aegean.

Several weeks after Urquhart's death, I received an envelope from the estate's lawyers. There was a letter signed by the solicitor, and inside a second envelope bearing the *Mulvane*'s crest, still sealed. The handwriting was familiar to me, and I did not need the covering note to tell me that it was from Urquhart. I quote it here in full.

Evans,

The end of the world is coming, perhaps not for everyone, but most certainly for me. If you are reading this, then that end has already come.

I will leave the details to the lawyers; my purpose here is to explain the fundamental facts. There is a trust fund to which will go the balance of my estate after various other bequests have been satisfied—I expect that it will amount to a substantial sum. The purpose of that trust is to endow an art museum, and you are to be offered the directorship. Should you choose to accept then it is you alone who will decide how it is to be run, not my rantings from the grave.

The paintings that you saw on Ledos will naturally form the core of the initial collection, but if it were to become a museum dedicated to me then it would be a failure. I have strived to make my art personal and true, two qualities that I find almost completely absent from contemporary art, which is mostly derivative and trite, unfit for thinking minds. So, if you will permit me, I ask that you consider making the ultimate goal of the new museum to collect art that is personal and true.

As for the location, I explored the possibility of acquiring my old digs in either Paris or New York. The SoHo site was available, and so I bought the entire thing: a substantial cast-iron building on Mercer, big enough to accommodate not just the gallery but also a residence for its director.

As to the name: choose anything you like, as long as it contains no reference to me.

R.A.U.

The Thelxinoë Museum of Contemporary Art opened a year later. I am, with Sir Dickie's blessing and encouragement, its founding director.

Mr. Jack Shotter — Jack continues to operate his studio in Milan, and since the publication of the calendar he has been in high demand. We communicate irregularly but in the way that real friends do, able to pick up a conversation from six months ago as if we had last discussed it six minutes ago. His work brings him my way from time to time, or mine his, and we always catch up.

He is a frequent house guest at the Villa Pallavicini.

Dr. Wu Hoi-on — Wu continues his practice in Victoria, British Columbia, and is highly active in support of human rights in Hong Kong. He has been the recipient of what might be considered the ultimate accolade for that work: censure from the Central Committee of the Chinese Communist Party.

He is also a member of the governing board of Adelina's foundation.

Ms. Oriana Welles — Oriana opened her own investigative agency in the spring of the year following the *Mulvane*'s cruise. "Welles' of Mayfair," as the English refer to it, had a moment of fame when the agency was credited with recovering tens of millions in jewelry stolen during a violent Paris carjacking.

Shortly after Urquhart's death, she received a letter from him. Folded inside the notepaper was a Roman coin—an aureus, solid gold— minted during the reign of Marcus Aurelius but bearing the image of his empress, Faustina. The accompanying note, as with my own, I reproduce here with Oriana's kind permission.

Oriana,

I never properly thanked you for your help this summer, something performed at a level far beyond the call of duty.

Early in the cruise, the question was asked if there was a common thread as to why I had invited such a strange mixture of passengers, none of whom I had ever met. I promised a prize to whoever unraveled the mystery. You certainly won that competition, and so I now forward your well-earned award. I tried to locate an aureus dating from the Punic wars—something that might have been handled by Cato Censor himself—but was unsuccessful. However, a coin bearing Faustina's image—as wise and capable a ruler as her famous philosopher-warrior husband—feels more appropriate anyway.

R.A.U.

The letter had been sent by ordinary mail even though the coin, according to the valuation required by the insurers, is worth tens of thousands of dollars.

Oriana keeps in frequent contact. She insists that I am still her investigative colleague and expects me to make myself available should a case involving art come her way.

Sir Richard Gibbons, KBE — When I came into possession of Urquhart's papers I was surprised to find a profuse correspondence with Sir Dickie. It had begun professionally when Sir Dickie was first contemplating the purchase of the Catoptrographics. He had written to Urquhart via the Sykes Gallery—now at last I knew who had preceded me there when I had urged them to forward my own letter. He had asked only that Urquhart confirm he was indeed the artist, part of Sir Dickie's due diligence before spending the Wentworth's money. But the correspondence had gradually morphed into an epistolary friendship— probably the only kind of friendship that the reclusive Urquhart could tolerate: friendship at a distance.

It had been a condition of this continuing correspondence that Sir Dickie share nothing, even the fact of it, with anyone, and he certainly never gave me so much as a hint. I thus discovered why Sir Dickie had been so accommodating with my long absence from the Wentworth: he had known about the invitation long before I did.

Planet Earth — Survived, obviously. The large-scale electronics catastrophe that had been forecast never materialized, although there were sporadic failures attributed to the supernova, including satellites knocked out and blackouts at the height of the cosmic storm—something of which we had remained blissfully unaware in our silicon-free cocoon at sea.

But perhaps it is still too early to draw conclusions regarding humanity's fate—scientists have reported signs of a sharp global uptick in genetic mutation following that rain of cosmic radiation. But on the whole Betelgeuse's supernova seems to have made people more aware of just how vulnerable our little blue planet is, and has hopefully encouraged them to take better care of it in the future.

Ripelli Tire Company — Ripelli is now majority-owned by the Italian government, the proposed Chinese takeover having been torpedoed by the designation of the company as a national strategic asset.

How much of this was due to the calendar I cannot say, but I like to think that the deal would not have been killed without it.

Ms. Tess Lysett — I have left for last Tess. At Oxford, she read English Literature, achieved a First, and after coming down was quickly snapped up by a large publishing house. There, following a period of learning the ropes as an assistant, she was made an editor at an imprint that specializes in quality fiction. She only makes around five acquisitions a year—about the same as I make for the Thelxinoë. Five does not sound like many, but to my mind they are worth five thousand generic titles.

Tess and I were married last May at Chichester Cathedral—I confess that I was not totally frank with all that passed between us in the Emerald Grotto.

The ceremony was conducted by her father.

The wedding was the second occasion that all of the *Mulvane*'s surviving passengers have gathered together. Since the bishop was the celebrant it was Gilbert who gave away the bride. Adelina, Rasputina, Marta, Bébé, and Oriana formed a formidable quintet of bridesmaids. Shotter was the best man and Wu was the groomsman.

The old cathedral was packed that day. My parents came over, as did much of my class at Williams College. A large contingent of Somerville and Exeter alumni attended, as well as many of my year at Harrow and Tess's at Wycombe Abbey. The entire professional staff of the Wentworth came. There were among the guests some minor royals with whom Tess had been at school—this, coupled with a marchesa and a movie star in the bridal party, made the press presence predictable.

Since her father was a peer a contingent from the House of Lords had shown up, too—Tess was right: they were a seedy-looking bunch.

The one misstep on the wedding day was when the bishop, despite my request that he skip my middle name, loudly asked, "Do you, Hugo Aethelwine Evans..."